ON THE EDGE OF
ETERNITY

BOOK 2

THE VAMPIRE NAVY SEAL SERIES

S.B. ALEXANDER

Cover designed by Hang Le
Cover copyright © 2021 by S.B. Alexander

On the Edge of Eternity
Book two: The Vampire Navy SEAL Series

First Edition: December 2013

E-book ISBN-13: 978-0-9887762-2-7
Print ISBN-13: 978-1-954888-15-9
Large Print ISBN-13: 978-1-954888-16-6

I always believed a little piece of heaven would have my name on it when I died. I wasn't so sure anymore. I was only sixteen on the day I became a vampire, and I hadn't imagined my life as one of the undead. I didn't want that life, but destiny had pulled me to the edge, where one step, one word, and one person had erased my humanity, changing my life forever.

It had been two weeks since I made the change. I sat on the chaise lounge in my dad's suite on the Navy SEAL compound, staring out the window. I'd dubbed it a penthouse, though it was far from being the Ritz Carlton. My father, Steven Mason, was the commander of a vampire SEAL team within the Navy known as the Jupiter Sentinels, so he had the largest living quarters on the military base.

Yep, not only was I the daughter of the most powerful of all vampires, but my dear old dad was in charge of some badass secret military vampire unit. *Go figure.* While my human life had hardly been heavenly, the window to my new world was in question, but it was too early to tell whether it would be better or worse.

From where I sat, I had a picture-perfect view of the prison building, where the SEALs kept vampire convicts behind bars. Given their super-human strength, my curiosity beckoned me to visit the creepy place and see how they kept them locked up. My father had said it was off-limits. In fact, my brother Sam, who was also a vampire, and I weren't allowed out of the open-plan apartment because of some vampire law about newborns and their bloodlust, which my father had yet to explain. The legal side of it was a mystery, but I understood the bloodlust. My throat burned with the need for the sticky red liquid almost all the time.

For the fourteenth straight day, I had nothing to do. My routine was the same. I drank my fill of Dad's blood, which he had stored in stainless containers, slept, and brooded. While the world outside of *my* prison was alive, I was dying inside. My thoughts were my enemy. I pined to see Ben, my friend who was my last link to the human world. I was uncertain what he thought of me as a vampire—he hadn't wanted me to change. He believed in mortality, the human race. The last time I saw him was the day Sam woke up as a vampire and attacked him, sinking his fangs into his best friend.

I sighed for the umpteenth time. I had an inkling that talking to Ben would have to wait a bit longer, especially since Sam's action had rattled my father. Hell, it scared the bejesus out of me too. I wanted to do exactly what Sam had done.

"Jo?" The familiar voice was low and soft.

I tore away from gazing out at the dreary day. It had been raining nonstop for over a week. I'd always thought April was the month for rain and May was the month for flowers, but Mother Nature was a little late.

"Everything okay?" My father strode over and sat down next to me, kicking out his feet on the chaise lounge.

It was the first time in two weeks that Dad had spent more than an hour in the apartment. He'd said he wanted more time with Sam and me to discuss topics he felt were important as we began our new life as vampires, but the events surrounding our change and the new prisoners on-site had meant a ton of paperwork to complete and countless phone calls to make, thanks to both military and vampire protocols.

I nodded. "Why are you asking? You mean you're not reading my mind today?"

My father's mind-reading abilities usually only worked when he touched someone, but for whatever reason, he could read mine without physical contact. He'd probably read my thoughts as he walked into the room, which would only have reinforced his decision to keep me away from humans, especially Ben.

He put his arm around me. "Sweetie. I don't do it all the time."

I wanted to believe him, but I was on edge whenever he walked into the room—we had relationship issues even beyond the mind reading to work out. We were still getting to know each other as father and daughter.

"You know they aren't getting out." He nodded toward the prison. "That building is heavily guarded."

The past two weeks had been tense for a whole host of reasons, including worrying that my Uncle Patrick would escape. My father tried to assure me I didn't have anything to worry about, but he'd seemed nervous the past few days. Not only was his brother responsible for trying to kill Sam and me, but also my dad's ex-best friend, Edmund

Rain, was now his outright enemy and in charge of the Plutariums, a rogue team of vampire ex-SEALs. Edmund was locked up, too, though I imagined them in separate cells—Patrick was human, though he had threatened he wouldn't be for much longer.

"Patrick and Edmund aren't going anywhere," he whispered.

I glared at him. "You're doing it again, Dad!"

"I'm sorry."

I relaxed against his chest. His heart beat slowly, thudding in my ear. "Dad?"

"Hmm?" he muttered.

"You mentioned something the other day about my organs not being completely developed yet as a vampire. What did you mean?"

He kissed my hair. "You have so much to learn. And I want to be there when you experience everything."

His tone intimated that he might not be around to see me do much. Dad and his team were concerned about the Plutariums. After all, his ex-best friend was trying to build an army of vampires to overthrow the government and to get back at Dad for personal reasons.

"You'll learn about our species in more depth once you're in school, but like humans, we have evolved over many centuries." He took a breath.

"There was a time in our existence that we were creatures of the dark. All those myths that humans believe to be true of vampires were actually real.

"Now, we can go out in the sun. Our hearts do beat. Our organs do function. Sure, we're not human in the sense that we don't age, and our diets are different, but we still breathe. Our heart rate is very slow, much slower than a human athlete in great shape. As vampires, we have even better endurance and strength, which means we can run faster and longer than any human. So, when I say your organs haven't yet developed, I mean your heart muscle and other organs are still adjusting to the change. Over time, they will become stronger. Your heart rate will be hard to detect. If a human were to check your pulse, they would be hard-pressed to find one. You can only hear mine because of your acute hearing."

I placed my right hand over my heart. It definitely beat faster than my father's. I glanced up at him, searching every inch of his fairly young features. "You never told me and Sam how old you are."

"I'm not sure you're ready to hear my story or know how old I am," he replied.

"You said there's a lot to learn. And I want to learn more about you."

He wasn't getting away that easily. I had signed

up for a life of eternity, and if I was going to build a relationship with my father, I wasn't waiting any longer to start on either the road to a life of bliss or one of hell. Regardless, I needed to know who I was traveling with.

"You're right, sweetie," he said. "I was twenty-two when I became a vampire. That was over a hundred years—"

A low whistle filled the air. I sat up to see my twin brother, Sam, sauntering toward us. His inky-black hair grazed his bare shoulders, and his forest-green eyes had a sparkle to them.

A smile ghosted across my face. It had been a while since his eyes sparkled.

As he approached in jeans that hung low on his hips, dimples dented his cheeks. "Pops, how come you don't have gray hair? Shouldn't you be walking with a cane?" He snorted.

My father ignored his comment. "Do you want to hear the story or not? I'm not repeating myself."

Dad and Sam had a volatile relationship. My brother still doubted that Steven Mason was our father, but Dad had promised he would provide written proof. He was waiting for our birth certificates to be delivered from the vampire government. According to Dad, the vampire government wasn't any better than the human one.

The one thing that had me perplexed was why

Sam called him "Pops" if he didn't believe he was our father. When I'd asked, Sam had said that it slipped out the first day they met and just stuck, but that didn't make sense. When I probed him even more, he just said he didn't want to talk about it.

Sam sat on the floor with his bare back against the windowed wall, his long legs extended. His normal attire since turning vamp was jeans and no shirt. He said it was too hot to wear any clothes.

I adjusted slightly in my seat while Dad shifted his arms encircling my waist.

He released a sigh. "It was the early nineteen-hundreds. My father—your grandfather—was a vampire, an immensely powerful one. Far more than me. He wanted me to change, to become immortal for the sole purpose of continuing our family heritage. I valued my humanity, so I decided against immortality. But fate or destiny has a funny way of changing your life." He paused.

He was correct about fate. It sure did have a way of disrupting things.

"I was a rising baseball star in 1905. We didn't wear batting helmets back then. Anyway, I was at bat, and the pitcher threw a fastball that hit me just above my left earlobe. It knocked me out completely. I was rushed to the hospital. My brain was swelling, and I had internal bleeding. A week later,

I woke up as a vampire. My mother told me afterward that she had to beg my father to turn me." My father's bottom jaw dug into my scalp as he swallowed.

I glanced at Sam, whose mouth hung open. Sam loved baseball and had even played for the high school team before he lost his humanity. He and Dad had something in common. I hoped that would bring them closer together. Sam's eyes suddenly lost their brilliant green color. As vampires, our eye color shifted when our emotions changed, which meant that Sam might have had a connection with Dad.

I'd felt mine shift when my father's heartbeat sped. My skin prickled with his power, which floated in the air like a thousand bolts of lightning peppering the room. I still wasn't used to the electrical charge—or magic—vampires emitted.

The three of us sat there, not saying a word.

Dad's voice finally broke the silence. "My mother was extremely happy, and my father, well... he got his wish of me carrying on the family heritage. Now, here I am, over a hundred years later."

"So, you were twenty-two in 1905?" Sam asked.

My father nodded.

"Whoa!" Sam shook his head, rolling his eyes

around. "That means you were born in 1883! No freaking way. You're old as crap, Pops."

I was just as shocked. While he looked young, there were signs that made him seem older. The area around his eyes had a smattering of creases. Nothing too deep or pronounced, but the lines were still there. His forehead also had a few worry lines. But aside from his physical appearance, it was his mannerisms that really gave away his age, with his prim-and-proper nature and how he was a stickler for manners.

"Are all the Sentinels your age?" Sam asked.

Great question. I'd been wondering how old they were. They all looked around our age, including the drop-dead-gorgeous Webb London, Dad's second-in-command.

"Well, let me put it this way. All the Sentinels turned vampire between the ages of seventeen and nineteen. It's a requirement for the vampire SEAL program. We like them young so that we can mold them into good soldiers."

"Didn't you tell me that Webb was twenty?" I asked.

"I might have, but he was nineteen when he turned. I recruited him a year or so later."

"What does it matter, Jo?" Sam asked. "They all look as young as we do."

"Not Dr. Vieira," I replied.

"You're right, sweetie," Dad said. "Dr. Vieira turned in his twenties. But... he is a doctor and not a Sentinel."

"Pops? Did you start the vampire SEAL program?" Sam asked.

Dad's cell phone rang. "I did, with the help of a few people with the human military." He slipped out from behind me. "I'll explain it to you someday." He dug his phone out of his pocket.

I sat there thinking about age. There were only a few ways natural-born vampires could die and growing old wasn't one of them. As I'd learned recently, I could die if someone beheaded me, burned me to death, or drove a cobalt blade through my heart. None of those options sounded like a party.

"Go," Dad said into his phone, walking toward the kitchen. Halfway there, he stopped mid-stride. "They can't be. They're not expected for a few more days. I thought I had time to explain it to them. *Merda!*" His tone dropped to a low growl.

Uh-oh—my father sounded irritated. I didn't recognize the last word, but I imagined it was a curse. I opened my mouth to speak.

"Sam? Jo?" Dad said.

We jerked our heads in his direction.

"Why don't both of you come and sit at the bar? I need to talk to you about a few things."

I didn't like the sound of that. Sam and I glanced at each other, and he shrugged as if he could read my mind. We made our way to the bar and pulled out two high-backed chairs. Dad stood on the other side of the counter, biting the inside of his cheek, confirming my suspicions. He did that whenever he was irritated or worried about something.

Sam slid onto the stool with ease, given his six-foot height. I had to step up on the bottom rail to climb onto mine.

"First, I know I haven't spent time with you like I wanted to. As you know, I've been busy with all the government bureaucracy. I wanted to discuss school and other things, but it seems I won't have time today either." He let out a sigh. "There are a few reasons, which I've mentioned, why you've been confined to this apartment. The critical reason is your bloodlust phase. As the two of you have experienced, the bloodlust period is difficult. You *cannot* be around humans while trying to get your hunger under control."

I thought of Ben as he mentioned humans. I could still smell his burned-sugar scent, which seemed to be glued to my brain. My mouth watered at the thought.

Dad quirked an eyebrow my way. "Problem, Jo?"

I shook my head vigorously. I had to remind myself that Dad and my brain didn't mesh well. His mind-reading talent was trouble with a capital T.

"To continue," he said, "our world has laws and a process that governs who can make the change. It's not like you decide one day you want to be a vampire and then you are."

"I didn't decide anything," Sam said bitterly. "And you didn't give Jo much of a choice, either, did you?"

Dad stared at the counter. It seemed my brother had hit a nerve.

"I'm sorry about that, son," Dad said, lifting his gaze to Sam. "I truly am."

"Dad, are you trying to tell us something?" I asked before the two of them got into it.

Dad blinked. "Yes. I thought I had more time to explain a few of our laws, but..." He placed both hands on the counter. "I don't know what's going to happen or what they have in mind, but I want you to listen and obey."

I had no idea what he was saying. My heart picked up an extra beat, and I started tapping my foot on the bottom chair rail.

"You're not making any sense," Sam said. "Why are you so nervous?"

Dad closed his eyes and pinched the bridge of

his nose with his thumb and forefinger. "Like humans, our laws are in place to protect our society, our people." He opened his eyes. "If we didn't, vampires would run rampant around the globe, doing whatever they wanted. There are some laws you'll learn soon enough, but I was hoping to at least have the opportunity to explain the Eternal Protection Law. It governs the rules and regulations involved when natural-born vampire children decide to become full-fledged vampires." He glanced at Sam then at me.

My nerves were doing some kind of tap dance in my stomach. I'd seen my father extremely pissed once before, but he didn't look as mad as irritated, as if whatever he was about to explain was out of his control.

"The Council of Eternal Affairs mandates the laws within our world," he said.

A choked laugh hung in the back of my throat. As I deciphered Dad's words, Sam snorted.

"What the fuck are you trying to tell us?"

"Son, I've warned you about your language. I don't want any swearing under my roof," he said, glowering.

The room became quiet as a church. They both stared at each other again. Black threaded through Sam's green eyes, and silver dominated Dad's emerald orbs. I had yet to get used to their ego-trip staring contests. They were so much alike in many ways, yet so different in others. Their relationship reminded me of pouring oil in water. It just never mixed well. I prayed every day that they would work out their differences. I guess I shouldn't have expected miracles, since we'd only been together as a family for fourteen days.

"Dad? Council of Eternal Affairs. Remember?" I asked, trying to prevent an argument.

He broke eye contact with Sam. "Because I didn't get prior written consent from the council for both of you to become vampires, we have to explain and justify what happened."

I didn't like his reference to "we."

"So? That should be easy, right?" Sam asked.

"Well... yes and no." Dad raked his hands through his jet-black hair. "The Eternal Protection Law is a law that the vampire government is extremely strict about. There's a lot of paperwork followed by a hearing, then a board of vampires analyzes each case. If all goes well and they approve someone to become a full-fledged vampire, then you're admitted to Grayson Manor to make the change. Afterward, there are restrictions and steps you must follow during the bloodlust period before they will allow you around humans."

A knock sounded at the door. As always, Sam grabbed my hand, stood, and planted his body in front of mine. I adored his protectiveness, but his smothering love was getting a little out of hand. We were in a secure facility and in Dad's apartment, no less.

I glanced at Dad, who was looking at his watch with his eyebrows drawn together.

Before I could ask him if everything was okay, he strode to the door then opened it.

I peered around Sam to find Webb standing in the doorway. I had to keep my mind from wandering—Dad would surely have had a cow if he read my thoughts about Webb. But every time I saw that gorgeous vampire, I couldn't control the racing of my heart. My body had a mind of its own. I gave myself a stern lecture to keep my thoughts G-rated.

He looked handsome as ever, with his wavy brown hair tied in a low ponytail. His SEAL uniform fitted his body to perfection, especially the black T-shirt that stretched across his toned chest. But what always had my belly fluttering were his cobalt-blue eyes. He looked past Dad, searching the room. When he found me, he slanted his head and gave me a captivating smile that caused instant goose bumps.

Sam growled as though staking his territory.

"What're you doing?" I asked in a tone only Sam could hear.

"Nothing," he replied.

"Bull crap. You don't have to protect me from Webb."

"Oh, yes I do. There's fire between you two," he shot back.

I laughed then pushed him. "What's that supposed to mean?" I was beginning to think that maybe it wasn't my father I had to worry about.

"Enter, Lieutenant London," Dad commanded.

Webb followed Dad's order. "Sir, they're here. We should go."

"Why are they here two days early?" Dad asked.

"The council has a pressing matter with Lord James that suddenly came up."

My father's eyes widened as both he and Webb walked over to the bar.

"Christ. I can't even take one day off without something happening." Dad looked at Webb. "What's going on?"

"Sir, I'm not sure. Regardless, we must take care of this matter with the twins today, if at all possible."

My gaze volleyed back and forth between Webb and Dad. "Lord James" didn't sound like military personnel.

As Webb placed his hands on the bar, Sam stood, blocking me from Webb.

"Son, stand down. Webb isn't going to hurt your sister."

"See, I told you." I pushed Sam out of my way.

My brother's relationship with Webb—well, it was nonexistent. A couple of times during the past two weeks, Webb had visited Dad for his signature on military papers. Each time was the same. If Sam was in the room, he would hover around me, watching every move Webb made. When I asked Sam why he kept trying to protect me, his answer was always, "There's something about him. I can't put my finger on it. Until I figure it out, I don't want him near you."

If I ever went out on a date, I would be in serious trouble—no, scratch that. My date would be in serious trouble. Between Dad and Sam, any future boyfriend didn't stand a chance. Nevertheless, that would probably be a very long time in the future. Most boys never liked me as a human. As a vampire, it would snow in hell for anyone to like me.

"I barely scratched the surface of the Eternal Protection Law when you knocked. I guess we'll see what they have to say."

"What's so urgent?" Sam leaned back against the chair.

"The Council of Eternal Affairs is on the

premises," Webb said. "They're here to meet with your father and both of you."

"Why are they here now?" I glanced at Dad.

"When I filled out the paperwork last week," Dad said, "they set a date for the hearing, which was six months out. When I explained the situation and that you'd already become vampires without their written consent, they moved us to the top of the list."

I bit my lip. "And why do you seem worried?"

"Because we didn't follow protocol, and I'm not sure what they're going to do." Dad ran his hand through his hair.

I didn't get it. "We're already vampires, Dad. Why would any of this matter now?"

"Well... they can rule to have both of you sent to Grayson Manor for the duration of your bloodlust quarantine."

I raised an eyebrow.

"In simple terms, it's our vampire hospital," Webb said. "All new vampires spend six weeks there, between the change and getting through the bloodlust period. As you know from your time in the apartment here, it's critical in the first few weeks."

Sam blurted out, "I'm not going down there and meeting with them. And I'm not going to any vampire hospital. This wasn't my choice."

My father's eyes silvered again as he glared at Sam.

"You will meet with the Council." Dad's tone hadn't left any room for arguing.

My brother had issues with authority and especially the law.

"And if I don't?" Sam argued.

I cringed. *Here we go again.* Anger dripped from Dad, spilling into the air.

"Then I'm afraid they'll take you into custody," Webb offered.

"You're going with me, Sam." I punched his arm. "We're family. I know this wasn't your choice, and I'm sorry. But you're not leaving this place without me."

"We didn't do anything wrong." Sam's voice dropped an octave.

"You're right, son. You didn't."

"But you didn't follow the law by changing us into vampires now, did you?" Sam taunted.

Dad reached over the counter.

"Sir." Webb lightly touched Dad's arm before he made contact with Sam.

"Stop it, Sam. We've been through this." My tone was soft, trying to calm him. "Why are you so worried about us going to Grayson Manor?" I asked Dad.

He was leaning against the counter, eyes liquid silver and a snarl etched on his face.

"You're safe as long as you're on this base," Webb responded as he guarded the raging vampire.

"The Plutariums are locked up," Sam countered.

"There are more Plutariums than those we captured. They could use both of you as leverage to get their leader out of prison. The council doesn't care about our problems. They follow the law and our traditions with no exceptions." Webb held out an arm, still keeping Dad at a distance.

"Grayson Manor or any place outside this base is not safe for you," Dad added, his vampire eyes slowly changing from silver back to green, indicating that his anger was dissipating.

"Look, Sam, let's just listen to what they have to say," I told him. "I lost you once. I'm not going to lose you again."

I had no idea of the full details of the Eternal Protection Law or what the restrictions were for new vampires. I loved my brother, but his resistance to authority and his anger often clouded his vision. Regardless, we were in it together, and I would do anything to make sure we stayed together.

2

A chill skittered up my arms as I entered the war room. Nothing had changed since the last time, except the seats were empty. I hugged myself, trying to relieve a shiver as memories flashed back to that day when Webb had dropped the bomb in front of an audience of vamps and described what I'd had to do to save Sam: become a vampire. Several emotions washed over me, and I clenched my fists.

"What's wrong?" Sam asked as he stood next to me, our arms brushing. Waves of heat radiated from him. He had reluctantly donned a T-shirt for the event, which had wet spots peppered on the front and under his arms.

"I should be asking you that. Your skin is on fire." I placed my hand on his like a nurse.

"Yeah. I'm a guy. We give off heat."

"Huh? You're a vamp, and vamps have cool skin," I countered.

He shrugged. "We don't really know much about what vamps are like though, do we? Besides, something is *definitely* wrong with you—I can smell fear all around."

He was right. I was scared stiff. That room didn't hold great memories, and I had some apprehension about the meeting with the council.

I let out a sigh. "I learned about Uncle Patrick and what he was doing to you while sitting in that seat." I pointed to the back row against the wall.

"Don't call him uncle. He doesn't deserve the title. I don't care if he's family or not." Sam tapped down my hand. "This place looks like a movie theater."

"I don't think they show movies in here. Unless they're the kind that shows criminals." As the last word rolled from my lips, Patrick's face flashed before me. I blinked a few times before glancing at Webb, who was gathering chairs and placing them behind the conference table below us.

"Jo? Sam? I need you to take a seat in the front row down here." He waved his hand.

My father had made a detour to take care of

something in his office, or so he'd said. I had a sneaking suspicion that he wanted to cool down before meeting with the Council of Eternal Affairs. When we reached the front row, he walked in from a side entrance that led to the command center for the facility.

He sat next to me, a nervous energy jumping off him. A glance his way confirmed my suspicions. A muscle ticked in his jaw, and that plus the beaded sweat on his forehead gave me reason to wonder whether there was something he hadn't told us.

Dad leaned over to address both of us. "I need you to listen, answer the questions if you're asked, and behave." He finished, turned, and leaned back in his chair.

The word "behave" sent a shiver down my spine. He really didn't know Sam, although he was getting a good dose of my brother's anger issues. I, on the other hand, usually obeyed, which bothered Sam. Over the years, he had been trying to get me to stand up for myself. It wasn't until that dreadful night when I fought for my life against my foster dad that I started to come out of my shell.

The side door opened, and Tripp, a Sentinel who reported directly to Webb, walked in. He wore a black cargo uniform, which offset his sandy-blond hair and bronze eyes. I'd first met him in Principal Jackson's office at Durfee. He'd always seemed the businesslike Sentinel, doing his job and obeying orders.

Following Tripp were two men and one woman. The two men were dressed in Armani suits, as though they had just stepped off of Wall Street. While the two men fit the banker profile, the woman was nowhere close. Instead, she wore a simple green dress, belted at the waist. Her long blond hair spilled down her back, while her thick brown lashes fanned out, framing tawny eyes that said confidence and compassion. She carried a stiff black leather bag and placed it on top of the table before she removed a small laptop.

Tripp stood behind her, ever the gentleman, waiting to guide her into the chair before taking his post at the door. Once she was seated, the two men sat as well.

While the woman readied her laptop, the men pulled folders and pens from their black briefcases then placed them on the table in front of them.

Once Tripp and Webb were in position, guarding the side doors, the man on my right stood and bowed. His mustard-and-black-striped tie brushed the table.

"My name is Gregory Hollings. I am lead

counsel on this matter. My colleagues, solicitor Maddox Tinsley, solicitor Matthew Atherton, and I are pleased to meet you." He glanced between Sam and me. "During the next hour, you will address this panel with manners and politeness. You will not speak out of turn. If we ask you a question, you will rise and answer it. As long as you cooperate, we'll get through this quickly."

The vampire world had too many manners.

Sam fidgeted in his seat. He seemed focused on the beautiful Maddox Tinsley. After a second or two, he looked at Webb.

At some point, I needed to ferret out what Sam's hang-up was with Webb.

"Is that understood?" Hollings asked.

Jerking my head to the front, I met three pairs of eyes staring at me. Each of them wore a deadpan expression. I nodded.

"A verbal response is required, Ms. Mason," Hollings commanded.

"Yes," I said. Then I stood and curtsied.

Why did I just do that? Did I just curtsy? Embarrassment washed over me, and heat stung my cheeks. I glanced away as each solicitor flashed me a vampire smile.

"Yes, sir." Dad rose from his seat then sat back down, all in one sweeping motion.

Sam pulled me down as he stood. "Yeah," he said with a grunt before sitting.

Hollings glowered at Sam. "I warned you about manners. You will address this panel with a 'yes' or 'no.' I don't want to hear any tired or slurred speech either. Is that understood?"

Complete silence filled the room as a mist of power whirled around—someone in the room gave off the strongest magic I had yet to experience. Forget the thousand bolts of lightning pricking my skin—the room had a total ionic charge. If someone had lit a match, the place would have exploded. I wondered if it was the anger resonating from Dad or the man speaking behind the table. I guess it didn't matter. I just prayed Sam wasn't about to pull one of his rebellious stunts. My father was powerful, but I didn't have a clue about the solicitors' abilities. And powers aside, if they were in charge of the law, then Sam was just as screwed in the vamp world as he would have been in the human one.

I froze, waiting for Sam to respond and bracing for a rebellion.

My brother rose, bowed as Hollings had before, and cleared his throat. "Yes, sir," he said with a nod, his tone dripped with more scorn than politeness.

I held my breath, hoping they didn't detect his cockiness.

"Much better," Hollings replied.

Sam took his seat. Letting out the air in my lungs, I restrained myself from kicking him. We weren't getting off to a smashing start with those folks.

"Very well. Let's proceed. We're here today to discuss your new status and what that means to you for the next few weeks." Hollings cleared his throat. "Steven, have you had a chance to explain any of our laws to the twins?"

"Not really," Dad replied.

Maddox typed furiously, keys clicking with each stroke. I guessed she was the stenographer, there to take notes.

"Before we get started, I have a few questions for you, Steven," Hollings stated. "I read through your paperwork, and I have some concerns about the twins remaining here on base during the bloodlust quarantine."

"Gregory," Dad piped in.

Hollings held up his hand. "Let me finish. If Sam and Jo remain here under your care, I'm concerned about the humans on this base, for starters. At Grayson Manor, there *are* no humans. There is no temptation. I don't need any more problems in addition to the ones we have already.

"I'm also concerned about your enemies being locked up on this base. We both know what their intentions are to devise a serum that, if successful, could wreak havoc on our world, not to mention the human one. Now, I am not here to condone or pass judgment on why you did what you did to save your children. I know how much you've struggled with this over the years. Yet who's to say that your brother doesn't still desire access to the twins' DNA for his mad scheme?"

"We're vampires already," I blurted out. "Why would they need us now?"

"Not now, Jo," Dad whispered. "Gregory? If I may?" Dad looked to Hollings for permission.

The solicitor nodded.

Dad stood. "First, I understand your concern about the humans on base. I can assure you that my children will not come into contact with any human while quarantined here. They've been confined to my apartment for the last two weeks, and I will continue to ensure that no problems arise between them and any humans. The vampire section of this base is heavily guarded, and only a few humans roam these halls, as you know."

He rubbed the back of his neck. "Second, I don't see how Patrick would have any need for their DNA. He's locked up, for one thing, and for another, we both know that all indications suggest that he needs *my* blood to further his experiments. Without it, he won't be successful.

"Therefore, I ask the council to consider leaving my children here with me so I can guard them. If they move to Grayson Manor, they're more at risk from Edmund's people, who are still out there." After his plea, Dad sat.

Hollings rubbed his jaw.

I didn't want to leave the base. If I had to be quarantined somewhere, at least I already knew the people there. To have to walk into a foreign place for probably the hundredth time in my life, well... I'd been in and out of enough foster homes and institutions over the years, and I'd hated each one of them. Besides, spending time in a vampire hospital didn't sound like a joy ride. I wasn't sure I wanted to be around my dad, either, but at least he was the devil I knew.

"Where is your stored blood, by the way, Steven?" Hollings asked.

"I have a supply in the fridge in my apartment, and the rest is locked up," Dad replied.

The man in the middle, Atherton, leaned into Hollings and whispered. Hollings nodded in reply.

"Jo and Sam," Atherton addressed us. His auburn hair was tied back in a low ponytail, which seemed to be a uniform style among most male vamps. His bright-green tie offset his deep-set gray eyes. "What do you know about the Eternal Protection Law?" he asked.

Sam and I exchanged glances.

"Okay," he said. "Maybe now's the time to go over it, so you know why we are here."

We were getting somewhere. Everything seemed confusing, and if we were going to be taken to Grayson Manor, it would be good to understand why. I wouldn't necessarily have agreed, but I was living in a new world, and knowing the law might help.

Maddox continued to type.

"Our Eternal Protection Law was enacted to keep natural-born vampires from turning into monsters. There was a time when our world was in chaos, and vampires sought revenge for personal gain and killed to live. We had to find a way to calm the masses for many reasons, including protecting humans. This law is the stepping-stone between mortality and immortality. It's a set of regulations to help us control who becomes a vampire. Since we enacted this law, it has served us for the better."

As he talked, I thought about that day I changed. The pain, the struggle, and the trauma were still vividly burned into my brain.

"The law is straightforward in its direction but complex in its delivery," Atherton continued.

"From the age of sixteen, any natural-born vampire has the option to stay human or become a fully-fledged vampire. If the latter is chosen and the family agrees, then the patriarch of the family must petition the Council of Eternal Affairs. It's important to note that this decision has to be agreed to by both father and child. Without agreement from both parties, the case is null and void. Once the petition is accepted, a hearing takes place in front of the magistrate. At this juncture, the court determines through a series of questions whether or not the child is ready to become a full-fledged vampire. I will not go into detail here since your case is past this point."

He stopped and took a sip of water from one of the bottles Tripp had placed on the table. "There is one exception to this law," Atherton added. "It states that if, for any reason, a situation dictates life or death, then leniency will be given in the application process. Any questions so far?"

"You said the agreement is between father and child. Why not the mother?" Sam asked.

"Because to become a vampire, you have to drink your father's blood, not your mother's."

"I didn't drink my father's blood. I drank my sister's."

"Ah. You understand *why*, I hope," Atherton replied.

"Yeah, I do. I know it's because of the amount of blood I lost and because of our DNA since we're twins. I heard the story. So your Eternal Protection Law doesn't apply to us, then. Plus, we're already vampires. Why are you wasting our time?" Sam asked.

Is he trying to get thrown in jail?

Sam regarded Webb with annoyance in his eyes.

I scanned each solicitor. It seemed their tongues were tied, or maybe they were trying to bite back their anger. Even Maddox had stopped typing.

"Sam, this law *does* apply to you. Just because you're already a vampire does not preclude you from the law." Hollings's voice dripped with authority.

Sam was going to get us thrown in jail or sent to Grayson Manor.

Dad sent him an I-will-kill-you look.

"Steven." Hollings's tone eased, giving way to calm the state of play. "On behalf of the council, Grayson Manor is the best place for—"

I jumped up. "No! You are not sending us there!"

Anger coiled through me, and my vision blacked out for a second, a sign my eyes were shifting into their vampire guise. My body changed in strange ways with my emotions, especially when I was angry or scared. I hadn't yet learned how to control my physical changes, but I blamed everything on the vampire puberty my body was experiencing. Still, when my eyes changed colors, it wasn't long before my fangs descended. That was the part that wigged me out—to think I had a weapon within me that could kill a human in a nanosecond nauseated me. I didn't move, well aware of the glares burning holes in my skin.

"Jo, sit down. He's not finished yet," Dad growled.

I turned toward him. "I'm tired of any authority dictating our lives. I'm not going."

Dad's eyes widened.

Then I jerked my head in the opposite direction and inclined my head at Sam. His eyebrows shot up as his eyes grew wide too. Maybe something was wrong with me. The only visible physical changes I knew I showed were my eyes changing from silver to black and possessing canines of which any wolf would be jealous.

The last person to stare at me in horror had been Dr. Case, the ER doctor who had taken care of me the night I had been rushed into the hospital. He freaked when he saw my eyes changing colors. But Dr. Case was human, and the people in the room with me were vampires and shouldn't have been shocked at something so trivial.

I raised my hand to my face. If they were trying to give a teenage girl a complex, it was working. I touched every part but didn't feel anything out of the ordinary. I breathed a sigh of relief. At least I could rule out any shape-shifting abilities.

I glanced at the panel of judges.

"Steven, were you aware your daughter's eyes changed to violet?" Maddox asked gently.

My eyes changed from silver to black, not violet, and I figured it was some kind of joke. When I woke up as a vampire, the vampire gods had decided to highlight my hair with permanent streaks of purple, which I thought was pretty random. Now this vamp was telling me my eyes were purple too.

"No, ma'am, I wasn't. This is new to me. Her eyes had been shifting from their usual color to black, like most vampires," Dad answered with a hint of trepidation.

"You know there are currently only two other vampires who have different eye colors when their emotions shift? You're one, and the other is your enemy, Edmund Rain," Atherton said.

"We're getting off topic," Hollings stated. "This discussion is not urgent to this meeting right now."

"You know what that means, Gregory," Maddox stated, sidestepping his protest.

"I do. Nonetheless, our law and why we're here are more important right now. I'm sure Steven will watch her and report back to us," Hollings countered.

"So why are my eyes—"

"Not now, Jo," Dad whispered.

"What do you mean, not now? This is my life, and I want to know what's going on." I didn't bother to keep my voice low.

"It's nothing to worry about," Dad said. "Let's get through this, then we can talk. I promise I'll explain everything later. You'll be fine. Your eyes are... there may be a reason for it, but nothing earth-shattering."

The color might not have been that worrying—after all, it didn't hurt me—but on the other hand, Dad's pause pushed an alarm button inside me, particularly because the solicitors had added their two cents.

I huffed, dropping down in my seat. A split second of darkness returned my eyes to their normal color as I began tapping my foot.

"Good. Now, Jo, would you let me finish?" Hollings asked, but there was no mistaking the bite behind his words. "As I was saying, Grayson Manor is the best place for any new vampire. It has all the best doctors, state-of-the-art equipment, and security." He glanced at Dad on the last word. "I don't feel that Jo and Sam are safe here. Not with the Plutariums only a building away."

Sam fidgeted again. His restraint seemed to be waning.

"But the council...will give you some latitude, Steven." Hollings paused and took a sip of water. "We'll allow the twins to remain in your care. However, the protocol will not be any different than that for any other new vampire during this bloodlust stage and the process immediately following it. Is that understood?"

"Yes, sir," Dad said, letting out a sigh.

"Matthew, please explain the restrictions and what is involved from here."

"Sure." Atherton reached into a folder and glanced at a sheet of paper before lifting his gaze. "First, you'll remain on this base for the next four weeks. During this time, you will not leave these grounds, and you will not have any contact with humans whatsoever."

I considered how we would stay away from them when they worked on base.

Dad leaned in. "We'll discuss that later."

"In addition, both of you will donate a vial of blood once per week for the next three months. Dr. Vieira will be responsible for taking the samples." Atherton placed the papers back into the folder.

So far, so good, though remaining on base for another four weeks didn't excite me. That meant no contact with Ben or even Darcy from school.

"Finally, at the end of four weeks, before entering St. Anne's Academy, you'll have a microchip embedded under your skin at your lower back, which will house all your personal information. This is standard procedure for all new vampires.

"Any violation or noncompliance with these requirements will result in ramifications, not only for you but for your father as well. We can't have your father in a position where he's not available to the human government. It will make them extremely nervous, which in turn will not sit kindly with Lord James." Atherton paused and looked at each of us, including Webb and Tripp, in turn. "Is that understood?"

Wait. Rewind. Chip embedded in my body? For what? No. Not understood at all. Are they crazy?

Sam and I looked at each other. He had his eyebrows raised, his eyes wide, and his mouth agape. His expression matched my thoughts exactly.

I hope my dad read this: *No way am I getting chipped. Do they think we're animals?* Those vamps were drinking some type of crazy juice.

"Why a chip?" Sam asked in a calm voice.

My head whipped around. If I hadn't known better, I would have said some angel invaded his body. My brother would usually have had them in a headlock, beating all three of them, instead of being so calm, cool, and collected.

Webb cleared his throat. Sam shot him a glowering look again, and then the electrical charge returned, peppering the air.

"Great question, son," Hollings said. "It's our way of policing the vampire population. If we didn't have laws in place, wars would break out. The result could be catastrophic. So we track our people with a unique computerized chip, which will identify you within our government and in our computer system. The vampires who don't have it are considered rogues and are dealt with accordingly."

My right foot tapped furiously on the carpet beneath my feet for two reasons. One, I was still agitated that I had to be regarded as an animal, and two, my throat burned like a raging inferno. I needed to feed. I was restricted to drinking Dad's blood until Dr. Vieira gave us the all clear sign, although the thought of the flavored blood I knew was chilling in every refrigerator on-site for the other vampires had me licking my lips, especially for the Creamsicle one I'd tried once before. I absently raised my hand to my mouth, brushing my fingers over my bottom lip, and one of my canines drew blood. The smell hit me as if a tornado had blown through the room.

Dad must've sensed it. "Gregory, can we speed this up?"

I pulled my finger away and surveyed the damage. A small dot of blood coagulated on the tip, and I stuck my finger in my mouth.

Dad grabbed my wrist and pulled my hand away like a parent would with a toddler picking her nose.

I inhaled deeply, trying to lessen the hunger pangs through distraction. I took in the flowery perfume I assumed Maddox was wearing. It helped to ease my hunger for the moment.

"Just a few final details," Atherton said. "The bloodlust period is a crucial time for all new vampires. Even after your quarantine period, humans will test your willpower. A human's scent and their blood are quite hard to resist. Therefore, I caution you when you do finally step out and mingle among them. The penalties can be severe if you harm a human. You should also know that it is also forbidden, as a new vampire, to drink from another vampire. However, we extend some latitude on this one for newborn vampires. We leave it to the elders to deem what is an emergency situation, in the event you don't have access to your father's blood. Any questions on what you've learned here today."

"Why can't we drink from other vampires?" Sam asked. "We drink our father's blood."

"For one, it is essential during your growth stage to consume your father's blood," Atherton replied. "His blood has the proper nutrients you need during the early stages. And second, until you can control your bloodlust, we don't want you draining the blood from another vampire. The result would leave them brain dead. They hardly ever recover. So, do you see why it's important to stick with the regulations?"

Sam and I both nodded.

I mentally added "brain dead" to the list of ways vampires could get hurt.

"What about the blood in the juice boxes?" I asked.

"The blood we buy from our approved blood vendors is not healthy for you right now, especially with some of the ingredients they add to it," Atherton explained.

I guessed I would have to wait to taste Creamsicle-flavored blood again.

"Anything else?" Atherton asked.

The chip still bothered me for some reason. I

stood. "I'm not having a chip stuck in me like I'm some cat or dog."

Dad grabbed my arm. "Sit, young lady."

"They can't do this." I sneered.

I wanted to strangle each of the solicitors. Well, not the pretty blonde. She was only there to take notes.

"Enough." Dad's tone hardened even more. He stood, blocking my view of the solicitors. He lowered his gaze, and his tone softened. "We'll talk about this later. Please, for me, for Sam."

I glanced at Sam, who nodded then raised his hand to his heart and tapped twice. It was a code we had developed as kids, which indicated we loved each other, and we would get through anything.

All the adrenaline rushed out of me, my body deflating from the built-up pressure. My fangs were in full view, and my throat burned, aching for blood. No matter how hard I tried to retract them, they weren't going back in until I fed.

I sat before Dad took his seat, narrowing my eyes at the solicitors when Sam grabbed my hand. His hand was as hot as a fireplace poker. The heat of it burned my palm. I stared at our hands then looked at him. He looked fine. No sweat beads were visible. I tried to pull my hand away, but he only squeezed tighter. After a minute, the sensation dulled, thanks to my vampire genetics.

"Your objection is noted, Jo," Atherton said.

Hollings rose. "Before we conclude this meeting, I need a verbal response that all of you understand the guidelines set forth. Then, Steven, I need your signature on the documents before we leave. Sentinels, are you in agreement to help the twins follow these regulations?"

"Yes, sir," Tripp and Webb responded in unison.

"Steven?"

"Yes, sir."

"Sam Mason?" Hollings looked at my brother.

"Yes," Sam replied.

My brother was being awfully accommodating, and I vaguely wondered whether his hot body temperature was burning his brain.

"Jo Mason?" Hollings asked.

The room went silent.

Giving blood once per week didn't bother me. Not drinking from humans didn't either. I got that part. The part I had a hard time agreeing to was the microchip. All eyes were on me, waiting for me to agree to what they were proposing, to follow their rules, but my tongue didn't move.

I glanced at my dad. He cocked one eyebrow as if daring me to disagree. Then I looked at Sam, and he tapped his chest twice again. My heart sank. He was the one person I couldn't disappoint.

I let out a sigh. "Yes," I said in a dissonant tone, tears clouding my vision as I kept staring at my brother.

As soon as the word rolled off my tongue, I had the feeling that I'd just signed up for something I wouldn't be able to commit to.

3

———

Once the meeting was adjourned, I ran to the apartment. My gums had been hurting ever since my fangs descended. Once inside, I pulled open the refrigerator door, grabbed a stainless-steel container of blood, flipped the top, and sucked it dry within seconds. In that moment, I was glad there wasn't a human anywhere in sight. Otherwise, that human would have been dead.

I shuddered, slid down against the cabinet, and plopped my butt on the floor. I dropped my head, resting it on my knees.

"You okay, sis?" Sam asked as he pulled open the refrigerator.

"Yeah," I muttered, not raising my head. I didn't think vamps could get headaches, but I apparently had several misconceptions about the species. My head pounded as if my brain was trying to jump out of it.

Sam sat next to me. "We'll get through this," he said, handing me another container of elixir.

I slid him a sideways glance. "What's with the nice-boy attitude? Does it have something to do with your body temperature?"

"Stop with the body-temp thing already."

"I think something's wrong with you."

"I told you, I'm a guy. We're hot-blooded."

I laughed. "That's what you want all the girls to believe, isn't it?"

Silence hung between us as we sipped our dinner.

"Well? Why were you Mr. Nice Guy in that hearing?"

He shrugged. "When the meeting started, I wanted to kill Hollings then Pops. We shouldn't have been there. Then *bam!* Webb's voice was in my head, telling me to calm down and choose my battles, or something like that."

"Wow. I wondered why you were shooting daggers at him. I thought you were going to jump out of your chair and kill him."

"When his voice popped into my head, yeah, I wanted... I don't know." Sam let out an exasperated sigh. "It's weird. I'm not sure I can go through an eternity like this."

I agreed with him. It seemed we had a great deal to learn. I hadn't been prepared to face the future as a human, let alone as a vampire. But at least as a human, I'd already had sixteen years of experience and had learned many human things to get me through life. "I think I would rather have Webb's voice in my head than Dad reading my mind."

As soon as the words spilled forth, I cringed. I wasn't sure how Sam was going to react to that.

"Webb? Do you like him?" Sam asked, his tone serious but calm.

I stared at nothing. I'd thought Webb was drop-dead gorgeous from the moment I met him. If his presence made my insides do somersaults, his voice in my head would certainly send me over the edge. I wasn't ready to admit that out loud, though, at least not to my brother. *Tread lightly*, my subconscious screamed. "No. Why?" I asked, lying through my fanged teeth.

"Bull. There's—"

"I know, fire or something. You said it earlier. No clue what that means, though." I looked at him expectantly, waiting for him to explain.

I contemplated how he would react if he found out I might have feelings for Webb—or worse, for

Sam's best friend, Ben. I shook my head. My attraction to Webb had been instant. With Ben, it hadn't been. I'd never looked at him as anything more than just a friend until we spent time together when Sam was missing. We'd made a connection, albeit a weak one, that I wanted to explore.

The apartment door slammed, jolting me back to reality.

"Jo? Sam?" my father called.

Great, the raging vampire was back.

Dad stormed into the kitchen, stepping over our legs and dodging the containers of blood as he made a beeline for the sink. He lifted the faucet handle and washed his hands. As he wiped them with a dishtowel, he turned and leaned against the counter.

"What do you two have to say for yourselves?" he asked, folding the towel then laying it on the counter.

Oh, I had a lot to say. The question was whether he wanted to hear it.

"What do you want us to say?" Sam asked.

"I would like to hear why both of you decided to display poor manners," he replied.

"Would that change anything?" Sam asked.

Dropping his gaze, Dad gnawed the inside of his cheek.

Sam shook his head. "Yeah, I didn't think so."

"By the way, I'm not staying in this place for another four weeks. I'm not getting a doggie chip in my butt. And I want to see Ben," I blurted out. Apparently, my brain wasn't connected to my mouth.

"Hmm," was all my father said.

After a silent second that seemed like hours, Dad pushed off the counter, navigated around us again, and opened the refrigerator. Sticking in his hand, he withdrew a bottle of water. I had yet to see him sip on blood.

"Jo, I see you're going to give me a problem." He twisted off the cap on the bottle, his eyes flashing silver—his mood was changing.

Not good. "Come on, Dad. By the time I get out of here, I'll be an old lady. And what about our friends?" I tried to stay calm as he continued to glower at me.

"You don't have human friends... anymore."

I choked. That statement sent anger rolling through me like a fast-moving storm. Sure, I probably shouldn't have been a brat about my demands, but he'd changed the game.

"What?" I ground my teeth as my fangs punctured the skin below my lips.

"You can't be friends with any humans."

"Who says?" I snapped, my blood beginning to boil.

"I do. You'll obey my orders. I'm your elder and your father."

"Well, that's still to be determined," Sam added. "You haven't proven it yet."

Now there's the brother I know.

Dad growled. "I told you, the vampire government is slow. And don't both of you start mouthing off. I won't have it. We're all under a lot of pressure, and with both governments breathing down my neck, I don't need you two getting into trouble."

During the past couple of weeks, I'd learned that when vampires got angry, frustrated, or irritated, they growled.

"I don't care about your damn government!" I yelled. "I want a life. One outside these four walls. You should've left me in foster care."

My fangs dug deeper into me. I imagined my skin might even heal around them in the next few minutes if I couldn't stop biting myself.

I closed my eyes, willing my canines to retreat. I inhaled deeply and opened my mouth, and my fangs popped back in, making a sucking sound.

Rubbing my lips, I checked on my brother. He had his eyebrows drawn together, his green eyes shifting into black dots as he stared at me.

I flicked my head at Dad "What? You agree with him?" I asked Sam.

"We're not going anywhere near foster care. Ever. Again. I don't care how tough this new life is. Don't bring it up anymore," Sam spat.

"Don't tell me what to do," I countered, returning the stare. A split second of darkness ensued, the sign of my eyes shifting too. Fury burned through me. They had ganged up on me.

"Enough, both of you," my father said.

My hands began to shake as I tore my gaze from Sam.

"Jo, calm down." My father's voice suddenly switched to a softer tone.

"No. I'm sick of all this." My body slowly rumbled inside as I clenched my fists. "I hate this life. My body changes in weird ways. My throat burns all the time. My hormones seem to be from some other planet. You keep us locked up in this place. I can't see my friends. Now, we're under some stupid law you say I have to obey like a good little puppy. I didn't ask for any of this. I hate you!"

Both Dad and Sam stilled.

I would've run into my bedroom and slammed the door like a child having a temper tantrum, except at that moment, the kitchen started to spin.

Breaking the long silence, Dad said, "First, I know how hard it can be when all you can think about is blood, especially when your throat burns. I can't do anything about that. Time is the healer for controlling bloodlust. As for being quarantined, it's the law. You heard the solicitors. You can't come into contact with humans for another four weeks. I'm sorry."

"Sorry? Screw your laws. What do you expect we're going to do between now and our release date?" I wagged a finger at Sam then myself. "What about school?"

"Young lady, you will obey your elders and the law. I am not going to jail because of your teenage petulance. The solicitors were very lenient. I was expecting something more severe. In fact, I was sure they were going to send you to Grayson Manor."

I sat still, trying to quell my rage, but the dizzy feeling was getting worse. "Dad. I don't care. I'm sick of people telling us what to do."

My father stalked toward me, dropping the bottle of water on the floor. He grabbed my arms and pulled me to a standing position. His eyes were still silver, and his lips formed a thin line as if sewn together.

I jerked away from him. "Don't touch me!"

Sure. "Brat" was the only word to explain my outrage. Or maybe "lunatic." Still, I'd sat on the sidelines in foster care. No more.

Sam jumped up and stood between my dad and me.

"Pops, back off," Sam said calmly.

"Sam! Let me handle this." My father flicked my brother aside.

The fire inside me rose at an alarming rate, like a beast rising out of the depths of an abyss. I wouldn't have been surprised if a burning creature slithered out of me at any moment.

My body shook, my knees wobbled, and the room around me blurred. At first, I thought it was my eyes shifting, but I knew they already had. A lone glass on the counter suddenly lurched violently. My pulse raced, and my heart thudded in my ears. The empty metal containers clanged together as they rolled around on the floor.

Dad grabbed my shoulders. "Calm down, Jo." He shook me several times. "Jo, look at me." Panic laced his voice as he framed my face with his hands.

I heard him, but his face barely registered as the room spun like an out-of-control merry-go-round. Then a loud thud sounded, followed by glass shattering. I closed my eyes and willed the dizziness to go away.

"Sis?" Sam's voice pierced the air. "Stop it! You're scaring me."

I inhaled deeply and blinked a few times. I

glanced around, and everything around me had stilled. The whirling motion subsided. I blinked a few more times then took in a deep breath and blew it out.

"Hey, you okay?" Sam asked.

"What happened?" I asked between breaths. "Was there an explosion or something?"

Dad lifted me and carried me to the couch. Good thing—I was on the verge of passing out. "Wait here," he said. Then he left the room.

Sam sat next to me. "What happened?"

"Why do you keep asking me that?"

Dad returned, handing me a glass of the sticky red stuff. "Here, drink this."

I pushed it away. I was well sated and didn't need any blood. In fact, it didn't smell as scrumptious as it usually did.

"Do you remember what just happened, Jo?" Dad sat down on the glass coffee table, feeling my neck and face as if he thought I was sick.

"I'm fine. The room started moving then spinning, and I heard glass shattering. We don't have earthquakes in New England, do we?"

"It wasn't an earthquake." Dad sounded exasperated.

"*You* were the earthquake," Sam said. "You looked like the devil, only with purple eyes. They were glowing. It was like you were hypnotized or something else had taken over your body."

My dad gnawed his cheek, staring at me with a bewildered expression on his face.

"Dad?" I asked.

"I didn't want to believe it earlier when your eyes changed to violet. It's been many, many years since I've seen anyone with violet eyes and the powers you just displayed."

"What are you talking about?" I knitted my eyebrows together.

"Remember about two weeks ago, I told you I wasn't able to read anyone's mind without touching them, with the exception of my father?" He paused, raking both his hands through his hair.

I nodded, afraid to speak.

"My father was the only other vampire in our world who could move objects with his mind. You shouldn't be able to do that at such a young vampire age. Heck, not at all. In fact, your powers shouldn't even develop for at least another year," he said with a slow blink.

"Did his eyes shift to violet?" I rubbed my temples.

"Yes. That's why the solicitors paused for a moment when they saw your eye color."

I glanced at my brother. His eyes were wide.

"So, what you're saying is that I will still be the outcast at my new school because I now have powers like the girl in the movie *Carrie*?" I covered my face with my hands. I was just glad I wouldn't be running into my high school nemesis, Blake Turner. He'd found enough reason to pick on me when I was human.

"Jo, listen to me. I'm at a loss... for an explanation." Dad sounded defeated.

"That's it?" I dropped my hands. "You're my elder, as you put it, and you have nothing else to say?" I cursed my existence. *Maybe I should stay locked in the apartment forever.* "And, by the way, did some vampire god decide that he would make a fashion statement with my purple streaks and now purple eye color?"

Dad's lips twitched into a smile. "You need to get some rest. We all do. Right now, whatever you do, try not to get upset or angry. I can't have you displaying your powers without knowing how to control them. It's too dangerous for you and those around you."

I wanted to tell him not to make me angry, then, but something in his words made the hackles on the back of my neck rise. I was beginning to think the universe had a death wish for me. Either that, or God was punishing me for giving up my humanity. "Huh?" I asked.

"You'll be fine as long as you don't get too worked up. Until I figure all this out, tone down the anger." Dad palmed the air as if bouncing a basketball.

Sam rose from the couch. "I'm going to my room. I'm beat. All the Eternal Affairs' rules and watching Jo creep out has me wiped. I'll see you later, sis." He tapped his chest twice.

After a moment of hesitation, I returned the gesture.

My father rose as well. "I need to take care of a few things in my office downstairs. Call if you need anything. I don't want either of you leaving this apartment. Is that clear?"

"Yeah," Sam shouted as he disappeared down the hall.

"Yes," I said.

"I mean it, Jo. You can't leave this apartment," he said again.

"Dad, I get it. Okay? Besides, where am I going to go? This place is like Fort Knox. It's not like I'll be jumping the fence."

He scowled at me. "Come on. I'll help you to bed. Powers like that will drain all the energy out of you."

He carried me to my room then eased me down onto my bed.

"You need rest. My father always slept for

hours after using his powers. I won't be long. Call my cell if you need me." He turned to leave.

"Dad?"

"Mmm."

"What happens if we don't get the chip put in us?"

"The vampire government would consider you a rogue, which means that you would be illegal. I have a chip, if that makes any difference at all. Now get some rest. We'll talk later." He closed the door behind him.

My initial reaction was still *no flippin' way*. Being moved around by the human government for sixteen years had been enough. I didn't want to be tied to any government again, even the vampire one. I wanted to run away and became a rogue vampire—that sounded appealing. No elders, no government, and no one telling me what to do.

I snuggled into a pillow, my mind racing as I thought back through the day. It helped that I was in my room. I loved the sanctity, the sense of peace and calm that the space gave me, a luxury I never had in foster care. I loved that I didn't have to share the room with anyone. I loved that I'd gotten to choose the soft-blue paint that adorned the walls, the queen-sized brass bed, and even the silver curtains.

My favorite piece of furniture in the room was

the chaise lounge that I sat on to read or daydream, depending on my mood. If I did daydream, it was as I stared at the different beach photos that Dad had given me from his military travels from around the world or the patched quilt that hung over my bed with my full birth name, Josephine Juno Mason, embroidered across the top. According to Dad, my mother had made one for each of us when she found out she was having twins. Dad had said he would explain how he and my mother had chosen our names, but he hadn't yet.

I reached over and plucked the remote control from the nightstand then pressed a button, and the drapes slowly closed, blocking out the daylight.

I curled into the fetal position and closed my eyes. Drawing what little strength I had left, I tried to make sense of my new so-called powers, trying to determine whether I could really make objects move with my mind or if my new powers were directly related to my new eye color. The entire day left several questions lingering. One, in particular, grabbed me by the throat, whether my father was serious about me not having human friends. I wanted to see Darcy and Ben again. As I thought about it all, sleep tugged at me, and I drifted off.

4

Jolting upright, I pulled strands of hair from my sweaty face and combed my fingers through the knotted ends. Then I wiped the moisture from my forehead with the back of my hand, smoothing my bangs in the process. Lately, it seemed I always woke up covered in sweat, but maybe it was normal for vampires to experience night sweats. Maybe it had something to do with my organs still transforming. Whatever it was, it was annoying.

I rose from bed, adjusted my shirt, then walked to the window. I inched back the curtain, unlocked the window, and pushed it up. Relief settled over me as the cool air soothed my sweaty face.

I glanced over my shoulder, and the clock on

the nightstand read midnight. I'd had six hours of sleep already and was raring to go, but no one else was awake. The only sounds in the apartment were from the refrigerator humming through the wall behind my bed, the clock in the family room ticking, and the soft breeze blowing outside. The spring air seeped in, tickling my nostrils. I longed to step outside, to absorb the scents of the night. *If I sneak out for a few minutes, my father will never know, especially at this time.*

I dialed in my vampire hearing, trying to pinpoint Dad or Sam. It was hard at times to hear my father's heartbeat, but Sam's was easy to discern because our hearts still beat faster and louder than my dad's. I strained my ears but couldn't hear anything over the other noises. I slipped on my sneakers and ventured out of my room.

Sam's bedroom door was ajar. I tiptoed over to it and peeked in. His room was shrouded in darkness, but that didn't matter. My enhanced vision allowed me to see in the dark as if I wore those SEAL night-vision goggles. It was pretty cool.

Scanning the room, I came up empty. Sam wasn't there. A sudden pang of paranoia hit me. Dad had told us to stay in the apartment, but that was hours ago. I glanced at Dad's closed door. I didn't even attempt to check his room, having no doubt that it was locked with a deadbolt. Ever since Sam had taken a gun out of his room and held Webb at gunpoint, Dad's room was off-limits to us. Plus, he had told me early on it wasn't good to wake a sleeping vampire. I had no idea what would happen, but I didn't want to find out.

Fear tightened the muscles in my throat as if someone was trying to strangle me.

"Sam?" I called. It came out as a hoarse whisper. I cleared my throat a few times. "Sam?" That time, the word escaped a little clearer, but the only sound that rang in my ears was the S of his name. I tried again as I walked down the hall to the main room of the apartment.

A light was on in the prison building. Drawing my eyebrows together, I walked over to the floor-to-ceiling windows and contemplated the light on the third floor. There were never any lights on in the building, at least not in the last two weeks. According to my father, the prison was heavily guarded, but the prison cells were in the basement.

My sharp vision confirmed the room was empty except for a table and one chair. The wall had red spots and streaks on it as if someone had taken a paintbrush and splattered red paint against the wall.

I drew in a breath.

Sam wasn't in the apartment. I didn't know if

Dad was in his room or not. I was staring into a room that might've been used to mutilate someone, using the wall as a canvas for their brutal art. Alarms went off in my head. Something was wrong.

Suddenly, pictures of Sam's lifeless body flashed in my mind. I had to pinch myself, hoping I was dreaming and that the sting of the pinch would wake me up. Nope, I was still in the same spot and still looking at the same eerie scene.

I sagged against the couch, trying to think, wondering whether I should go looking for Sam or try to wake my dad. I had to do something.

I pushed off the couch, and the smell of blood wafted in the air, making me hungry. Silence gave way to the hums of the appliances.

I sniffed. There was definitely blood somewhere, but it didn't belong to a human.

I straightened and moved cautiously into the kitchen. The flame in the back of my throat burned brighter. Out of habit, I flipped on the light but winced at the brightness. I quickly switched it off, and when I did, something shiny glinted on the far side of the counter. I gasped.

I blinked a few times, making sure I wasn't seeing things. Nope, a bloody dagger lay on the counter. The last time I saw a dagger, it had been in my hand, and it had proven fateful. During

Sam's rescue, I had fought one of the Plutariums. The end result had been a Plutarium called Fernando stabbing me with my own weapon.

Careful not to touch it, I examined it. Unlike the one I'd held before, it had a leather handle with two silver bands wrapped around it, spaced a few inches apart, with writing scripted on the bands. I couldn't make out the words—they seemed foreign to me. As I moved my head around, raking my gaze over the instrument, I saw that the edges of the blade were lined with blue. I was definitely not touching it. Dr. Vieira had explained that a vampire's kryptonite was cobalt, not silver as I'd believed.

The cobalt-infused metal was a recipe for death.

Without thinking, I ran out of the kitchen and down the hall to Dad's bedroom door. I knocked hard, but there was nothing. I tried again, banging on the wooden door. "Dad? Wake up," I said, raising my voice as I continued banging. "Dad?"

It was dead silent. I twisted the doorknob. The door was locked, not surprisingly. Maybe he was still in his office.

I ran back into the kitchen, slid into the counter, and picked up the receiver to the house phone, which was sitting near the bloody dagger. I stared at the blade as I hit the button programmed with my dad's cell phone number. I waited—nothing. The other end was dead. I pushed the button on the base a few times, trying to get a dial tone. Still nothing.

I felt my blood snaking through me, causing my cool skin to heat up. The mental image of Sam hurt or dead fueled my adrenaline. I ran out of the apartment and down the hall. My father had given me strict orders to stay inside, but I didn't care. If something had happened to Sam again, I would never forgive myself.

I pushed open the door to the stairwell with such force that the doorknob embedded in the wall behind it. I ran down the steps two at a time, finally reaching the landing to the third floor. As I grabbed the handle of the door leading into the hall, a buzzing sound echoed up the stairwell.

I let go of the handle and peered over the banister, but I didn't see anything. I turned to open the door, and the noise started up again. It sounded like a cell phone vibrating.

Jumping four steps at a time, I followed the sound. As I reached the landing on the second floor, the air around me suddenly became thick, almost stifling with electricity. I moved cautiously, slowing my pace, my heart booming in my head. I definitely had a rapid heartbeat, probably a dead giveaway for any vamp in the vicinity.

When I reached the first floor, I found the door to the courtyard had been torn off its top hinge. I peeked outside but found nothing.

The vibrating sound startled me again. I turned to my right. In the far corner of the small entryway, a cell phone danced across the tiled floor, a blue light flashing each time it vibrated. I picked it up and read the name of the person calling: Webb. I stood there, debating whether I should answer. I wasn't supposed to be out of the apartment, but I needed to find Sam. Besides, I didn't know whose phone I was holding. I tapped the screen.

"Hello?"

The other end was silent.

"Hello?" I said again.

Dead.

I looked at the phone, and the bars at the top kept vacillating between low bars and none at all.

I walked out into the courtyard to see if I could get a signal. The bars were still nonexistent. I spoke into the phone again, but Webb wasn't on the other end. My intuition warned me to go back inside.

Before I could take a step back, the cell phone vibrated again, making me jump. I looked down at the caller ID and tapped the screen once more.

"Dad?" I shouted into the phone. "Can you

hear me?" I walked all around the courtyard to see if the signal would get any stronger.

I waited, but all I heard was, "J... J..." The words were garbled, and static filled the background. Still no bars.

I looked up, placing the phone in my jeans. I stood only a couple of feet from the entrance to the prison. Suddenly, a shadow ghosted across the courtyard at the edge of my vision. I backed away, keeping my focus between the open doorway and the corner of the prison building. Then, in a blur, another shadow darted under the security spotlight in the distance.

Is my vampire vision deceiving me? I swept my gaze over the entire courtyard, which was empty except for a few flowering trees and a picnic table. Then it dawned on me. The door to the prison building shouldn't have been open. My father had said it was heavily guarded, but I didn't see any guards.

A quick check of the room on the third floor showed the lights still on. A voice inside my head warned me to get out of there and back to the main building, yet something pulled me toward the open doorway. The air was electrified in waves, ebbing one minute and increasing the next. Maybe Dad's power was reaching out to me, his way of communicating with me. Maybe Sam and Dad were both in the prison wing.

My decision was made. I took three long strides through the wet carpet of grass. Fear escalated as I stopped at the entrance. My instincts told me to go back, but my curiosity was stronger.

With one foot across the threshold, I glanced over my shoulder and calculated the distance to the main building behind me. I wanted to make sure my refuge point was accessible. If not, I was screwed if something happened and I needed to run for safety. But nothing could go wrong. My Uncle Patrick was behind bars, and so were his cohorts. They couldn't hurt me.

I flexed my hands and fingers, trying to shake off the nerves. I picked up my right foot and placed it beside my left. The smells weren't anywhere as nice as the ones I'd inhaled in the courtyard. The scents of mothballs, urine, and blood clung to the air inside. I covered my nose, but it didn't help.

A trail of blood trickled along the floor on my right, and a metal door had been torn off. It lay on the floor to my left, exposing a stairwell leading down. Something was amiss. I stood in the middle of the hall, deciding which path to take. I could have followed the blood trail, not knowing where it would lead. That room I'd seen from the apartment had to be up there, but I didn't know what I would find—maybe a dead body. I shook off the thought.

Impetuously, I turned left. The power in the air escalated the closer I got to the open doorway. I dodged the door, or at least I tried. My jeans caught on a sharp edge of one of the corners. Bending down, I unhooked the fabric.

With my leg free, I made my way through the doorway. Another round of the same scents burned my nostrils. Covering my nose once again, I peered over the railing. "Hello?" I called.

There was no reply.

I started my descent, the fluorescent light overhead providing a bright and clear path as I made my way down the steps. I guess I'd expected candle-type lights on the walls leading toward an ominous basement. But the area was clean and modern with no dungeon-like fixtures.

Halfway down, my head began to hurt then throb. I winced, trying to erase the pain settling into it. I moved my neck around a few times to see if that would help. As I did, darkness blanketed my peripheral vision, as if I was in a tunnel all of sudden.

"Jo," a voice boomed. "So glad you finally came to see me." It was Edmund's voice, loud and clear.

I spun, looking for the evil vamp, but nothing.

I continued my trek down the stairs.

"Just come through the door. I'm in the fourth cell on your right."

Is he talking in my head? I had yet to experience any vampire talking to me telepathically. I felt lightheaded.

I remembered something one of the solicitors had said. Other than me, there were only two other people who had different eye colors as a vampire. My father was one of them, and Edmund was the other. I remembered that his eyes had changed to crimson when I had met him the first time in the basement of Highland Memorial, and I contemplated the significance of his red eyes. Maybe Edmund had special superpowers too.

"Jo, I'm waiting," he called.

"You're in my head, aren't you?"

I am. Now, what are you waiting for? I won't bite. At least, not right now, although I would love to taste you.

Ew—maybe he was some sort of pervert. It was just my luck to run into another one. The last pervert was my foster dad, Cliff Birch, whom I ended up stabbing after he attacked me.

All my instincts told me to turn around and run, but my inquiring mind kept me moving forward.

Here goes nothing.

I rounded the corner and walked through the open doorway and into a long room with five cells lining either side. The shiny steel doors, walls, and ceiling created a reflected glow, making the room seem brighter than the light overhead. All the doors but one were open.

I poked my head into the first cell on the right. The walls were solid steel with raised round circles on them, like polka dots on a pretty sundress. The organized pattern reminded me of a tic-tac-toe design. I counted ten circles across, lining the top. Another ten circles lined the corner of the wall heading down to the bottom. In all, both side-walls had a hundred circles on each, while the back and front walls had seventy tacked to each.

Don't keep me waiting, Jo.

Flinching at the sound of Edmund's voice, I lost my balance. I grabbed the door of the cell then screamed. Fire burned through me. I raised my hand, and the pain stopped as soon as I pulled it away. I inspected my palm. It was a livid red, but in a matter of seconds, it changed back to white.

What did you do?

Edmund's voice in my head was annoying. Ignoring him for the moment, I walked into the empty cell. I had to find out if the walls were cobalt. The door definitely was.

I touched one of the circles. As I did, a clicking

noise sounded, and a sword lashed out, piercing my palm. I screamed again.

I stood frozen, my mouth hanging open, watching my skin burn.

Just pull it out. You're a vampire. It'll heal.

I had no idea how he knew a sword speared my hand. Holding my breath, I separated my hand from the sword, trying not to pass out. A spine-chilling sensation cut a path down my legs, and nausea churned in the pit of my stomach. I didn't know if my sudden weakness stemmed from the blade slicing through my hand or watching the whole scene unfold.

Once my hand was free, I opened and closed it a few times, catching the blood as it dripped down my arm. As soon as I opened my fist again, the skin quickly knitted back together. Instantly, the pain was gone.

Mesmerized and shocked, I didn't take notice of my surroundings. Then, *whoosh!* Two hundred swords jutted out from the circles on the sidewalls, coming together at the tips, a foot from kissing each other. The design created an illusion of a slatted wall made of polished, sharp blades. The backdrop looked like it belonged on display in an art studio.

So that was how they kept vampires behind bars. I slowly backed out of the cell.

I had to think. As a vampire, my senses would warn me if another vamp or human was down there. I concentrated on the smallest of sounds and smells but came up empty.

If the doors to all but one cell were open, does that mean...?

No, it couldn't. Maybe Dad had Edmund secluded because of his powers. No one could escape, especially a vamp. There were enough swords and cobalt in the cells to cook a vampire to a crisp.

Is everything okay, minha linda? I still don't see you.

I'm not your minha linda, whatever that means.

I was moving backward toward the same door I came through when the phone in my back pocket vibrated. I pulled it out. Webb's name appeared on the screen. I tapped the screen, but it went black.

Your father hasn't taught you anything, has he? The Portuguese language is a beautiful and romantic one. Now, show me your beauty, my pretty one.

Yeah, ain't happening, asshole.

I turned to hightail it out of that scary place when Edmund said, *My team has your brother, sweetheart.*

I froze then thought for a second. Sam wasn't in the apartment, and there was blood splattered on the floor on the first level of this building.

Did you hear me? I know you're still out there. Your lavender scent tells me so.

Where is he?

Show me your pretty face, and I'll tell you.

I didn't believe he would tell me anything, but it was possible that they'd kidnapped Sam again. I couldn't chance it. Besides, a very thick metal door separated us. So I should be fine.

I made my way to the fourth cell on the right. I glanced up at the glass window and met dark-red eyes that drenched my insides with something far worse than fear. I should've run then, but his gaze seemed to freeze me where I stood. It was as if he had control of my brain. Then an oxygen-depleting series of thoughts ran through my mind: *He could have control of my brain—that could be one of his powers. Maybe that's why his eyes turned red.* I shook it off. Impossible, or so I had to keep telling myself.

Ah, tao bonito!

Speak English!

Edmund's black military-style haircut had grown out, and he sported a beard that covered his pronounced jaw. *So beautiful. Look at you. Your long black hair with purple streaks is dazzling. I see your scar is barely noticeable. Just tell me who did that to you, and I will take care of him for you.*

Get in line, creep. That would be kind of hard behind that door.

Tsk, tsk, tsk. You are so naïve. I won't be in this contraption much longer. You don't know the power I have or what I can do. Soon enough, you will learn and watch the master at his game.

Shut up.

You know, your elders will not put up with teenagers who do not mind their manners.

I said, shut up! Where's my brother?

My, my. Jo, please show some respect. I may be behind bars, but I am still one of your elders.

You're just a horrible vamp who tried to kill my brother.

You really should get your facts straight. Your kin tried to kill your brother, not me or my team.

You're still responsible.

He was half right. While Edmund's mission was to change humans who didn't carry the vampire gene into vampires, Uncle Patrick had been on a mission to change himself into a vampire. There were several factors that precluded Patrick from making the change early in his life, and the critical missing piece was his father—my grandfather. Patrick needed his father's blood to make the change, but his father had died before Patrick made the decision to turn vampire.

As a renowned genetic scientist, Patrick had

figured out that if he was going to develop a serum that would lead to his success, he needed to get his hands on as many family genes as he could—in particular, a male family member's human DNA and a family member's vampire blood. Both pointed to Sam and my dad. Patrick had joined forces with the Plutariums to kidnap Sam and use him as a lab rat. When we'd found Sam, he was past the point of no return for my father's blood to change him into a vampire. The only way to save my brother was for me to turn vampire.

A wave of electricity swept through the hall. I looked toward the entrance.

Ah, you feel it too. I told you I wouldn't be behind this door for very long.

Where's Patrick and the other creeps?

They're coming for me.

Fear began to seep into my veins.

Suddenly, human blood wafted in the air. I jerked my head around, but as I did, a deafening blow hit the side of it. I stumbled backward, and large hands grasped my arms.

When I looked up, I saw a tall vampire wearing a blue bandana and staring down at me.

Shit! Jonah? He was the vamp I'd seen beating the cop the night I was in the hospital.

I turned to find Uncle Patrick standing in front of me.

Mindlessly, my fangs dropped, ready to tear into his human flesh, and I lunged forward.

I came up short—Jonah held my arms behind my back. I pulled with all my vampire strength, but his older, preternatural strength kept my arms twisted in a knot.

I didn't move, making sure I had control of myself. As a new vampire, I should have had some enhanced physical strength—stronger than a human, at least—but I didn't know how to fight.

"What's the matter? You're not strong enough yet, are you?" Patrick asked.

Either that, or I was just plain scared. Clearly, my brain hadn't changed into that of a fearless vampire. That part of my anatomy was still very human.

Tilting my head, I sized him up. His brown hair looked wet as if he'd been sweating. Dried blood was caked at the edges of his mouth and on his neck. His scent was still human—there weren't any signs that led me to believe he was a vampire. Then again, he couldn't have been. He needed my father's blood to successfully change—at least that was what Dr. Vieira kept telling us.

I tried again to pull away from Jonah. I wanted nothing more than to kill my kin.

"What's wrong, little one? Yes, I'm still human, but in due time, I will return as a vampire."

"You'll never get your hands on my father's blood," I spat.

"Oh, you're so mistaken, Jo," Patrick said. "You underestimate your enemy." His lips stretched into a sinister grin.

I wanted to wipe that smirk off his face. Fury propelled me forward. I slipped from Jonah's grip, tackling Patrick to the floor. I latched my mouth on to his wrist.

He grabbed me by the hair with his free hand and yanked hard. I didn't budge even an inch. My fangs were rooted deep into his flesh, and the harder he pulled, the tighter I clamped down, hitting bone. I wasn't letting go. I might not have known how to fight, but I would take advantage of the one weapon I had.

"Don't move, Patrick," Jonah commanded. "She'll tear you apart." Jonah's voice sounded desperate, as if Patrick were a precious gem.

Sucking hard, I drew in that first rush of blood. The taste was better this time, sweeter. When I had bitten him at the hospital, his blood had tasted bitter, probably because of the drugs in his system. Dr. Vieira had been right. Human blood was tasty, even if it did come from my enemy.

I continued to draw the life out of him, pondering how I could drain him of all his blood like he'd done to Sam.

"Get her off me!" Patrick bellowed.

His heartbeat slowed. I wasn't sure how much my stomach could take, but I didn't care. I didn't care if I puked every drop of it, as long as I destroyed that monster.

A whoosh of air swept over me. Suddenly, a pair of hands grabbed my ankles, yanking me. Patrick squealed like a wounded animal, but I stood my ground.

Heavy footfalls sounded in the distance.

"Jonah, guard the door," Edmund commanded.

Is he still in my head?

As I peered through lowered lashes, sucking the arm of my enemy like a baby suckling her mother's breast, Edmund bent down. His lambent power covered me. I wanted to scream, but my fangs were rooted in flesh.

Edmund stared at me with his red eyes, pinching his eyebrows together in quiet fascination. "Quite beautiful," he said.

I tilted my head, the blood still spilling down my throat, coating my insides.

He mimicked my move as if we were two puppies curious about each other.

"Violet suits you." His voice hitched up a notch, sounding excited.

"Sir, we need to move," Jonah said. "We don't have much time."

Edmund snapped up his head, looking at Jonah.

My fangs retracted before I realized it, and Patrick rolled away. Edmund turned toward me, making eye contact. I knelt on the floor, blood dripping from my lips, each of us waiting for the other to make a move. Before I could do anything, Edmund blurred then snatched me from the floor.

"Patrick, get out of here," Edmund barked. "There's a secret door behind you. Just push the metal circle, and it'll open."

I strained against Edmund's hold to see what he was talking about. I didn't see another exit.

Patrick pushed the raised circle on the back wall between the cells, and I vaguely wondered whether a sword would pop out of it. As the thought skated across my mind, a door slid open, disappearing into the wall. In a sudden flashback, I remembered that Edmund used to be a Sentinel, which must have been how he knew.

As soon as Patrick was through the opening, it slid shut. Not wasting any time, Edmund carried me to the first cell on the block, the one with the kissing swords. I tried to break free, but his hold on me was super strong. He angled my body into the small space between the tips and shoved me against the blades in one fluid motion.

A guttural sound escaped me, a sound I didn't

even know I was capable of. Intense pain and fire rushed through my body. I coughed, and blood dripped to the floor.

I glanced down. The tips of several blades had punctured my stomach, inches below my chest. The room began to spin, and bile rose in the back of my throat.

Tears streamed down my face as I tried to move. The swords had me pinned in place. I couldn't move.

"The more you move, the closer you are to death," Edmund said with a smile.

"Screw you."

He pushed me deeper against the blades.

I wailed, the sound muffled by gurgling in the back of my throat as blood oozed out of my mouth.

"I warned you about manners. I am one of your elders, like it or not." His eyes flamed bright red. "Your father is going to love this one. Retribution at its finest, don't you think?"

I spat at him, and blood splattered the side of his face.

He wiped it off then licked the blood with one stroke of his tongue. "You taste better than I imagined," he said.

"Pervert," I countered.

The mere act of speaking shot a searing pain through me. I was royally screwed. The cobalt burned every cell inside me as if someone had injected me with fire.

"Hurry, sir," Jonah called out. "They're close."

Biting back the pain, I tried not to think about my own demise. I searched within me to find any sense of my humanity, hoping that I still had something to believe in and hold on to. I didn't know if I could die that way or not. One thing was certain, though: if I did get out alive, retribution, as Edmund called it, would be sweet.

"Edmund?" Jonah shouted.

"Sorry, love. Got to run. Until we meet again." He bowed. "I wish I could hang around to see your father's face." He laughed as he closed the door behind him.

"Asshole! I'll kill you!" I cried.

His laugh faded.

Time stood still. Silence reigned in the cell and beyond. There were no footsteps anymore.

I tried to speak but failed. My efforts died when a gurgle of blood came out instead of words.

I hung in the air, tears flowing as I silently swore at my vampire life.

As the tears spilled, anger welled up in me and rose to such a high level that the room blurred for a split second. When my vision focused, the swords were moving from side to side, as if they were trying to get out too. Suddenly, the metal clanged together in unison, creating a harmonic series of different pitches that grew louder as my fury reached a crescendo. The pain became unbearable, and the noise around me was deafening. The light around me faded then brightened as if there had been a power surge in the building.

Before I knew what was happening, I plummeted to the floor, my face hitting a pile of swords. I tried to crane my neck slowly to see behind me, but the pain was unbearable. I glanced up at the metal ceiling and caught a distorted glimpse of four or five swords sticking out of my back. The pain flamed brighter than it had when I was hanging in the air.

Do I dare move and try to stand?

Biting back the pain, I placed my palms flat on the floor next to my ears and pushed up. The weight of the swords slowed my efforts. Not giving up, I managed to rise into a crouching position, but the blades spearing my legs prevented me from bending. I plowed through the pain, pushing off the floor with what little strength I had left in me, but the sea of blades beneath me made me slip, and I fell forward.

I extended my hands out to break my fall, but not in time. My chest hit the floor with a thud, and I wondered whether I'd cracked a rib. My question was answered when I inhaled. The pain stopped me mid-breath.

Cold air replaced the thick, humid air in the cell. Then voices sounded from somewhere.

"In here, sir!" Webb shouted. "Don't move, Jo."

Tears mixed with the blood pooled around me.

"Christ!" Dad said.

"Some... one..."

"Don't speak," Dad told me. "Webb, gently pull this one out first before it does any damage to her heart."

I couldn't see. My face was still planted against the floor.

"This will hurt for a second, Jo. We're going to take the swords out one by one," Dad said in a panicked tone.

Webb removed the first one then the rest. My father was right. It did hurt for a second, but once the swords were out, the burning started to diminish, though I still couldn't breathe that well.

Webb lifted me then set me in a sitting position.

Dad wiped the blood from my face with a swipe of his hand.

The sight of my father overwhelmed me, causing all the adrenaline to gush out of me. I had never been happier to see him.

He plucked a knife from his belt, sliced his

wrist open, then shoved it in my mouth.

I didn't argue. I didn't even speak. I sank my fangs into his flesh and began drawing his blood into my mouth.

His eyes were a pool of liquid silver as he brushed the tears from my face.

Webb surveyed the sea of swords that littered the floor.

"How the hell did the swords end up on the floor?" Webb asked. "We designed these cells so they couldn't be pulled out of the wall."

From his question, I guessed my father hadn't told him about my new ability. It was the first time I'd seen the calm, cool, and reserved Webb shocked. I didn't think anything could rattle him. *Chalk one up for the clumsy teenage vamp.*

I glanced down at my arm. At the same time, my insides started burning. My skin became hot, red, and itchy.

Then my vision blurred. When I glanced at Dad, his face looked as though someone had stretched his cheeks out to the side.

"Webb, get Dr. Vieira, *now!*" Dad instructed, pulling his wrist away from my mouth. "Don't pass out, Jo. Stay with me." He slapped my face a few times. "Jo?"

His voice trailed off as darkness carried me away.

5

My eyelids slowly opened. I blinked a few times as I sat up then glanced around to find Sam sitting in my chaise lounge.

"Sam? You're alive!"

He rose. "And so are you," he said, making his way over to the bed before flopping onto it.

I jumped up and hugged him. "You scared the crap out of me."

"You scared me, too, sis. Don't do that to me again. How do you feel, by the way?"

I examined myself, lifting my shirt. There wasn't any sign that I had been staked by a bunch of swords. My skin was smooth on my stomach and chest. I rubbed my hands over my front and back, searching for cuts. I inhaled several times. It didn't hurt to breathe anymore. I swallowed, once, twice. The gurgling had gone away. I stole a look at the clock on my nightstand: four a.m. *Amazing!* I had healed in four hours.

I lowered my shirt. "There's not a scratch on me. My insides don't hurt or burn. But I should be dead."

"Pops said you came really close. One of the swords punctured a lung, you had several cracked ribs, and another blade barely missed your heart. It's a good thing you're a vamp."

"The last thing I remember" —I inspected my arms— "is huge red spots all over me."

"Yep. Compliments of the cobalt."

"I remember drinking from Dad's wrist. Was it his blood that healed the welts?" I asked.

He shook his head. "According to Dr. V., the cobalt seeped into your bloodstream. Then he gave you some mojo juice, and *poof!*" He snapped his fingers. "They were gone."

"Juice?"

Sam shrugged.

I remembered the solution Dr. Vieira had used on Ben's neck wound that made it disappear and wondered if he'd given me the same stuff.

"So? Where were you?"

He propped up his head in his hand, leaning

on the bed. "I couldn't sleep and went downstairs to Pops's office. Then all hell broke loose."

I leaned back against the headboard.

"It was madness," he said. "Pure craziness. Alarms were going off, radios were blaring, and Pops was barking out commands."

Alarms? I must've been dead to the underworld. "How did the Plutariums break out?" I asked. "Those cells are made of cobalt and swords. Lots of swords."

The memory of my ordeal sent a shiver up my spine.

"Pops suspects foul play. But it all started after he left the prison building. He was questioning Patrick and Dr. Case in the interrogation room on the third floor. As soon as Pops got back to the control room, the radios blared. Some vamp named Jonah and another named Fernando got out of their cells. At the same time, Patrick and Dr. Case got into a brawl in that interrogation room." Sam sighed, shaking his head.

Maybe that was why the walls had blood on them.

After a moment of silence, he continued, "Pops and his team went into action. Pops spotted Fernando coming into this building. So he came straight here to make sure you were okay."

"But Dad wasn't here when I got up."

"He'd gotten word from the control room that Fernando had jumped the stone wall on one side of the base, so he left the apartment to help the Sentinels. A guard was on his way up here to protect you, but when he got here, you were gone."

"What happened to Dr. Case?"

He sat up. "Well, Patrick beat Dr. Case to a pulp. He's recovering in the medical facility."

I didn't particularly like Dr. Case, given that he'd locked me in a coffin and left me to die. It was his idea of revenge—he'd accused my father of killing his sister, Ella. "So how come there weren't any Sentinels guarding Edmund?" It didn't make any sense. I had a permanent crease between my brows.

"There were, but someone took them out too. Tripp found the two Sentinels locked in the tunnels underneath the compound. They were out cold. When one of them woke up, he told Webb that before they could defend themselves, they'd been injected with something. The Sentinel doesn't remember anything after that. Dr. Vieira said they must have been given a strong sedative for vamps to pass out like that. In fact, one of them is still asleep in the medical facility."

"What were they injected with?"

Sam shrugged one shoulder. "The doc doesn't know. He's running tests."

"Where were you in all this?"

"Pop had some SEAL chick, Olivia, babysitting me in the command center," he said as he picked a speck of lint off my comforter.

"Really? She wasn't fighting?"

He shook his head.

I had always thought Olivia was more of a badass than the other Sentinels. I guessed Dad didn't agree. "What happened after I passed out?"

"They all escaped through the tunnels. Pops said something about Edmund being an ex-Sentinel and knowing all the secret passages on the base. And Webb agrees with Pops that there has to be someone on the inside of their team who helped the Plutariums. Maybe even two. He said the job was too organized and that it had to take more than one person."

I let out a deep breath. None of that sounded good, especially with the Plutariums on the loose. Patrick had hinted again that he wouldn't be human for much longer. I wasn't sure how he was certain, though. He needed my father's blood.

"Are you hungry?" Sam asked.

Since he mentioned it, my throat had that scratchy, burning feeling, and my gums were throbbing.

He jumped off the bed with his hand out.

"Come on. Pops, Dr. V., and Webb are waiting for you."

With my hand in his, I stood then checked myself one last time. I'd been speared like a hunted animal. No, hunters seemed kinder to their prey. But I still couldn't wrap my mind around how fast I had healed.

As soon as I entered the hall, a mixture of rain, pine, and vanilla permeated the air.

I walked slowly, looking out the windowed wall directly ahead. The prison building hid in the shadows cast from the lone spotlight illuminating the grounds below its tower, a stark reminder of what had happened just hours before.

I stopped, hesitant to move.

Sam had disappeared into the kitchen. The refrigerator door shut, and Sam poked his head into the hall. "What're you waiting for? Come on."

I shook my head. I didn't want to go near the kitchen. That bloody dagger might still be on the counter.

"What's wrong with you, sis?"

Before I could move, I was cocooned between strong arms.

Looking up, I met green eyes. Dad. Instinct had me wrapping my arms around him. I'd never had a father growing up. Other than Sam, I'd never had anyone to care about me. But there, standing in

Dad's arms, I felt something from the man. His tight hold on me brought tears to my eyes.

"How do you feel?" he asked as he backed away, glancing down at me.

It took me a minute to blink back the tears. "I'm fine."

"Good. I was so worried." He smiled, and the tension in his eyes disappeared.

Sam walked over and handed me a warm mug.

I peeked inside. "You heated the blood?"

"Yep, and it's much better hot," Sam said.

I sipped it then licked my lips. "You're right."

"I know." He gave me a wry smile as he sauntered into the family room.

"Come. Let's sit down. Dr. Vieira wants to make sure you're okay." Dad guided me into the family room with his hands on my shoulders.

I stole a quick glance as I walked past the kitchen bar. I didn't see the dagger.

Dad leaned down and whispered, "That was my dagger. I accidentally left it on the counter when I came up to check on you."

No matter how many times I asked him not to read my mind, he still did. That one time, though, I didn't mind.

I eased onto the couch, folding my legs underneath me, cradling the cup of warm blood in my hands. The mere act of sipping a hot beverage reminded me of my humanity. I could almost pretend that I was drinking a cup of warm cocoa.

Dr. Vieira sat at the opposite end of the couch. I hadn't seen him since Sam had made the change. He looked different—relaxed, as if a weight had been lifted off his shoulders. He'd replaced his thick, black-rimmed glasses with gold specs. It was a nice change. The new frames blended in with his face, so his glasses weren't the first thing I noticed when I looked at him. A question suddenly popped into my head: *if vampires had such perfect vision, why does Dr. Vieira wear glasses?* I made a mental note to ask later.

Webb sat in the lone armchair a few feet away, facing us. I started to think of all the adjectives that could describe Webb's hotness, but with Dad's mind-reading talent... I settled for heart-stopping. His wavy brown hair tickled his shoulders, and his face had the shadow of a day-old beard. It suited him very well, though he looked like he needed sleep.

Dad sat on the arm of the couch, resting his hand on my shoulder. He seemed a little protective.

Sam had flopped onto the chaise lounge behind us near the window.

"Jo? Tell us what happened," Dad urged.

I looked at Dr. Vieira then Webb. Both had

eager expressions as if waiting for some juicy gossip. There was nothing juicy about my encounter with the Plutariums.

"Steven," Dr. Vieira said, raising his hand, "a moment. Jo, do you feel better? The welts appear to be gone. I can hear your heartbeat, and it sounds good. You're drinking blood, also a good sign."

"All good here," I replied. "Sam said you gave me a solution to get rid of the cobalt. Was it the same stuff you used on Ben?"

My father's hand tightened on my shoulder when I mentioned Ben's name—maybe because my heart rate increased. I leaned my head back and made eye contact, and he released his grip.

"No. I'll satisfy your curious mind about the solution at another time. Right now, your father wants to hear what happened."

I bet Dad used his brain phone to warn Dr. Vieira not to tell me.

Dead air hung between us, and all eyes were on me as they waited for me to speak.

"When I woke up, Sam and my dad were gone. Then I found the bloody dagger on the counter and panicked. I tried to call you" —I looked at Dad— "but the house phone was dead. Why?"

"We lost power for a few minutes when the

Plutariums got out, and something happened to the phone lines."

I returned my gaze to the others. "Then I ran out of the apartment and was headed to my dad's office when I heard a vibrating noise in the stairwell. I went down to the first floor and found the phone. Webb called it and then my dad. The signal kept going in and out. Whose phone was it?"

Webb and my dad exchanged scowls.

"It was Kate's phone," Webb said. The vein in his neck bulged.

I hadn't seen Webb's twin sister since I became a vampire. My father had sent her on an intelligence mission to Washington D.C. I didn't even know she had returned. "Is she—"

"Fine," Webb snapped as he glowered at Sam.

I turned to find Sam with his head resting against the back of the chair, biting his bottom lip. "How did her phone—"

Dad squeezed my shoulder. "Jo, continue with your story. We're getting off topic."

I hesitated as shards of power pricked my skin. I peered at Webb through lowered lashes. His eyes had lost their deep-blue luster, blackening to a pool of tar. I would have bet that if he smiled, I would see that his fangs had dropped. I had an inkling there was more to the story. After a few seconds and another squeeze from my loving, mind-reading father, I decided to ask Sam about it later. It seemed my brother had some secrets to dish.

"After I found the phone, I walked outside," I continued. "Then something pulled me to the prison building. I went in, and halfway down the stairs, Edmund was in my head."

"In your head?" Webb asked surprisingly.

"You know, like you get into other vamps' heads."

He narrowed his eyes.

"You sound surprised, Webb?" Dr. Vieira asked.

"It's just, I didn't know Edmund could do that. Or at least he wasn't able to when he was a SEAL."

"You know we all develop secondary powers along the way. And there's more to Edmund. I keep telling you and Steven that." Dr. Vieira cocked an eyebrow at Webb.

"What do you mean, secondary powers?" Sam asked.

Webb ran a hand through his hair. "Natural-born vampires have primary and secondary powers. We all have the primary ones, the enhanced senses and the physical strength. But we inherit different secondary powers we inherit, and our DNA also dictates how many. The secondary powers are categorized as elementals, empaths, healers, telepaths, mind readers, mages, telekinetics, and compellers." Webb's voice was smooth, and his eyes had returned to their cobalt blue.

I wondered whether he ever relaxed. I had yet to see him in a happy mood.

"Which one of them is moving shit around with your mind?" Sam asked.

"Son, proper vocabulary. Please," Dad instructed.

"Moving objects with your mind is called telekinesis," Webb replied.

I knew the term for my new powers, but something else nibbled in my brain. "Aren't telepaths mind readers?" I didn't know why that had popped into my head. Maybe it was a movie I had watched.

"No, sweetie. They're not," Dad explained. "A telepath in our world only has the ability to create a mind connection between two vampires, where they can talk to one another. Just because they're in your head doesn't mean they can read your mind. It takes a lot more skill to read minds. Now, please continue."

I sighed. "Well, as I was talking to Edmund, Jonah came up from behind and hit me. When my vision cleared, Patrick was standing in front of me. He told me he was still human, and my senses confirmed it. But he said he would return as a vampire. I argued with him that he would never get Dad's blood. He told me I was mistaken. I attacked him. And you know the rest."

A hush fell over the room.

"Pops?" Sam said, breaking the silence. "Could Patrick get his hands on your blood? You did say you thought there was foul play."

"How would anyone get ahold of Dad's blood?" I asked. "No one came into the apartment, did they?"

Then I remembered Dad had told Hollings that the rest of his supply was locked up somewhere.

Dad jumped off the couch. "Not that I know of, but I do keep part of my supply in a refrigerated vault in my office." He sprinted into the kitchen then opened the refrigerator. After a split second, he closed then opened the dishwasher before his head shot up. "Webb? I need you to go down to my office and check the refrigerator vault."

"It's impossible. No one can get into that safe," Webb said.

"Humor me. After what happened tonight, I'm not sure what to think. Anything is possible."

Without another word, Webb left the apartment.

"All containers are accounted for. I always count and track every one of them." Dad began pacing in long, furious strides, gnawing the inside of his cheek.

"Dr. Vieira, could Patrick develop a serum to turn ordinary humans into vampires?" I asked.

"My belief in life is that anything is possible. I'm not a genetic scientist. I do know a lot about our kind and how our DNA works, but to engineer a serum to change humans into vampires... I would *like* to believe it is impossible. But Patrick is a great genetic scientist. If anyone can do it, it would be him." Dr. Vieira kept an eye on Dad.

"What would he need to do that?" Sam asked.

"I can only speak to the family genetics. He's been working on serum for a while for himself. As you both know, he wants to be a vampire. He has Sam's human blood, marrow, and DNA. He would need your father's blood to test his theory in the lab. His next steps would depend on the results. I'm sorry I don't have a better answer for you. I'm sure Patrick would go to great lengths to develop a serum, not only for him, but to accommodate Edmund's goals too."

As Dr. Vieira was explaining, I tried to convince myself that science wouldn't allow a concoction to change humans into another species. But then a small laugh caught in the back of my throat as I thought about the absurdity of what I was thinking. After all, I was a vampire, and I hadn't thought a species like us was real or possible.

Dad had stopped pacing and was leaning against the kitchen counter. "What's taking Webb so long?" he asked no one in particular. He let out a sigh.

Webb walked through the door and locked eyes with Dad.

I didn't need to hear the words, as Dad's expression said it all. His power rose instantly, sending out shock waves that made me squirm.

Dr. Vieira joined Dad and Webb in the kitchen.

Sam grabbed my hand. I didn't even realize he had moved from the chaise to the couch.

Webb and Dr. Vieira surrounded Dad as they talked in voices so low, I couldn't hear them, even with my vampire hearing.

Turning to Sam, I whispered, "Who could've broken into Dad's safe?"

"No clue, sis."

After a few minutes, the trio separated.

Looking at Webb, Dad said, "Let's go down to my office. We need to sort through this and gather the troops. The council is going to have a field day with this one."

Dad was right. I remembered how Hollings

hadn't been thrilled with our situation or the risk of having the Plutariums on-site.

Dr. Vieira and Webb said their goodbyes and left.

"I'll be gone for a few hours. It's almost dawn. Get some rest. I'll have a guard outside the door," Dad said.

Sam didn't hesitate. He rose, tapped his heart twice, and left the room.

"Everything will be okay, Jo," Dad said. "We'll find Edmund and his team."

"What if you don't?" I stopped breathing for a moment.

"I can't answer that now. I won't be long."

He kissed me on the forehead and walked out of the apartment, finally leaving me alone with my thoughts. I shuffled through everything I had heard about secondary powers and crazy serums that would change humans, and my brain twisted into a ball of knots. None of it made sense. The vampire world continued to defy everything I thought possible. And I wasn't going to find any immediate answers.

I just hoped Uncle Patrick and the Plutariums didn't change evolution and force a new enemy, a new creature, upon the world.

6

Two weeks passed, and Dad and his team weren't any closer to finding the escaped Plutariums or the culprit who had stolen all of his blood out of the secret vault. He had been scratching his head, trying to figure out how they could've broken into a locked safe. Other than Dad, only Webb knew the lock combination, and Dad trusted Webb completely.

Not taking any chances, Dad had the entire military base locked down. All military personnel had been questioned several times. He suspected that there was more than one person involved in helping the Plutariums, saying that the job was too big for one person to pull off.

In the meantime, Sam and I were once again

confined to the apartment. The incident with the Plutariums had rattled Dad, and he remained overprotective, although he did allow Sam to go to the gym in the same building as our apartment, as long as he was accompanied by a bodyguard.

I didn't care to exercise. I was still tired from my run-in with Edmund.

But at the start of our third week in confinement, my energy had slowly returned. The walls started to close in. My father didn't own a TV, and there were hardly any books to read. I had read the two books I did have, devouring everything in *The Science Behind Vampires* and *The Vampire's Life*. After listening to Webb explain all the categories of special powers, I wanted to learn as much as I could before I started school. Neither book had any information on elementals or any of the other categories. One book taught me more about the pathology and diet of vampires, while the other outlined how to adapt among humans. With nothing to do, I begged Dad to at least let me go to the library, but he'd said no.

Before bed, I figured I would give one last-ditch effort to beg Dad for a laptop at least—anything to link me to more information on the outside world. I knocked on his bedroom door.

"Come in," he said.

I entered his fortress. Steam hung in the air,

and a soapy, clean scent filtered through the crack in the bathroom door.

"I'll be right out," he boomed from the other side of the bathroom door.

I looked around. The last time I was in his room had been the day after my change. The glass cabinets that housed all of his weapons were now empty. I guessed that since Sam had gotten his hands on one of the guns and tried to use it on Webb, my father was a little nervous.

I was leaning against one of the cabinets when Dad walked out of the bathroom.

"Are you going to bed, sweetie?" he asked as he opened one of his dresser drawers and removed a tan T-shirt.

"I am. But I wanted to ask you something."

He turned around, unfolding his shirt, and I tilted my head to one side. The only tattoos I had seen on my dad were on his forearm. Then again, I had never seen my dad bare-chested like I had Sam. My brother was always walking around the apartment with no shirt.

"Something wrong?" he asked.

"Um... I'm sorry—"

He followed my gaze to the front of his left shoulder. "You're wondering about this array of triangles, aren't you?" He sat on the bed. "Come here. Sit with me." He adjusted his position as I sat next to him. "Some of our secondary powers are based in part on alchemy. Do you know anything about alchemy?"

I shook my head. The only sciences I had studied were physics and biology. I wasn't going to take chemistry until next year.

"I'm not surprised. Alchemy is not really studied by humans. In our world, we study it in detail. Some would say alchemy contributed to the development of chemistry and, in some cases, medicine. The basis of alchemy is taking common metals and turning them into gold and silver. Vampires believe the building blocks of the world are based on the four primary elements—earth, air, fire, and water. Each element houses unique properties and characteristics.

"As Webb explained, some vampires are elementals. Those who are classified as air can do things with air that no one in this world would believe would be possible. And the same holds true for the other three elements."

"So, what does all this have to do with your tattoo?" I asked, still staring at the basic triangular markings.

"I have the ability to wield all four elements." His eyes searched mine.

I stared back at him, waiting for him to explain more.

"This marking in the center," he said, pointing to the first of five triangles, which was a triangle with a cross hanging from it, "symbolizes the spirit of life. This one" —he pointed to the one directly above the center symbol, an upside-down triangle with a line through its tip— "stands for the earth. The one right of center, the upside-down triangle with no line through it, stands for water. The right-side-up triangle with a line through its peak, below center, symbolizes air. And the one left of center, which as you can see is a right-side-up triangle, stands for fire. This entire marking is the circle of life," he said, tracing the outer ring of symbols with his forefinger.

I had no clue what he could do with air, fire, earth, or water. From the sounds of it, it seemed he had the ability to play God. Either that, or he was a very powerful vampire wizard. I silently laughed at my own thoughts.

"Don't discount the power of vampires, especially those who can use it to hurt you." Dad narrowed his eyes.

"You're reading my mind again."

"In this instance, yes. This is serious, Jo. As you learn and grow as a vampire, you need to be aware of your enemy. It's no different than with a sports team. In baseball, each player knows his opponent and what he can do on the ball field. The manager knows his own team but also studies other teams. It's the same premise in our world. Learn that quickly.

"Now, I know you didn't come in here to ask me about my tattoos. Something else on your mind?" He stood and pulled on his T-shirt.

I had to think for a second. "Oh. Can I get a laptop? I want to be able to research and surf the Internet."

He bit his bottom lip and shook his head. "No. There isn't anything on the Internet that will school you on our species. The academy will teach you everything you need to know. Plus, it's easy to hack into computers these days, and security is of the utmost importance right now."

I flopped back onto the bed, my hands covering my eyes. "Come on, Dad. I've been trapped in this place. I want to see what's going on outside this compound."

"I'm sorry, sweetie. I can't allow it. Now, it's late. We both need some rest."

I wanted to scream and scream and scream. My father was going to be the death of me.

The next morning, I sat at the kitchen bar, waiting for my dad. He was down in his office, taking care of more paperwork. Later, he planned to escort Sam and me to our weekly blood appointment.

I tapped my foot on the rail of the barstool, thinking about Dad's circle-of-life tattoo and wondering how he used the elements or what any of it even meant. I shook away the thoughts. I really didn't want to know.

Dad walked in, followed by Webb, Tripp, and Sloan.

I hadn't seen Sloan, Tripp's partner in crime, since he'd been hurt in a fight with one of the Plutariums at Ben's house, weeks ago. He looked good. His brown hair was pulled back at the nape of his neck, day-old stubble peppered his strong jaw, and his hazel eyes peeked out from under long lashes.

Dad kissed me on the head. "Good morning, sweetie," he said as he threw his keys onto the counter.

"What's going on?" I asked. "Something happen?"

"No, honey. Webb, Sloan, and Tripp are here to give you some good news."

I hoped they'd found Edmund and his gang.

"Where's your brother?"

I shrugged. "When I got out of bed, I showered then came in here. Bedroom, I guess."

"Sam?" my dad called, not raising his voice. With vampire hearing, no one needed to yell. We could have heard a pin drop in Sam's room if we had to.

Within seconds, my brother sauntered in, pulling on a gray T-shirt. "You rang

"Good news. I'm relaxing my reins, so both of you can have some base privileges, with restrictions. If you violate any of them, you'll be confined to this apartment for the remainder of your quarantine," my father said. Then he nodded at Webb.

"Your dad and I feel both of you could use some physical training. I know, Sam, you've been working out in the gym, but, Jo, you need it more," Webb said.

Sam gave me an I-told-you-so look. "It's about time. She's needed to learn how to protect herself most of her life."

I wrinkled my nose then stuck out my tongue at him.

It reminded me of when Mr. Jackson had told me that I would be attending Coach Welles's self-defense class after school, only I never got the chance to learn anything. That was the day Sam went missing and our lives changed forever.

"See, she loves the idea," Sam said.

"This will be good for you. You need to know basic moves. Your fangs aren't going to get you far against another vampire," Webb explained.

"Especially one like Edmund," Tripp added.

Maybe they had a point. I had silently vowed revenge against Edmund and Patrick. Plus, it would be good to learn how to use my vampire strength.

"So, when do we begin?" Sam asked.

"First, in keeping with the solicitors' orders, Dr. Vieira will draw some blood this morning," Dad said. "Then, Sam, you'll head to sword training with Tripp, who'll be your bodyguard. And, Jo, you can spend a couple of hours in the library. I know you've been bugging me for books and information on special powers. You'll be able to find some of what you want in there. Sloan will be your bodyguard. Then, this afternoon, both of you will attend a basic training class on fight moves with one of the other Sentinels."

I jumped off the barstool, ran around the counter, and hugged him. "Thank you, thank you, thank you."

My father wrapped his arms around me, squeezing me back. "I want you to behave," he whispered before releasing me.

"I will."

"Now, remember," Dad said, looking at everyone, "no human contact. The training won't be a problem, but the library was in question. However, I've closed the library this morning so the other humans on base won't be a problem, including the librarian. Is all this understood?"

"Yes, sir," the Sentinels said collectively.

Sam and I both nodded.

I could barely contain my excitement. I hadn't been so stoked in a long time. I was allowed to roam the base. *What could go wrong?*

7

I walked out of the entrance to the main building, rubbing my right arm from where Dr. Vieira had taken a blood sample ten minutes before. I still didn't understand why I had to give blood once a week. Dr. Vieira had said it was routine for any new vampire. If we had gone to Grayson Manor, we would've had to have given blood there as well.

I tilted back my head, absorbing the sun's rays. The delectable warmth spread through me, and I relished the feeling. I hadn't been in the sun since I was human, and I'd missed it. I hadn't been a sun goddess or anything, but the sun did provide Vitamin D, which all humans needed. As a vampire, I didn't know if I needed Vitamin D, but it didn't matter. All I knew was that I could go out in the sun, and I wanted to take full advantage.

I righted my head and inhaled. The breeze carried a hint of lilacs, and the fresh morning dew smelled as sweet as honeysuckle. Spring had definitely arrived. Memorial Day was only a week away, and the weather was getting warmer.

While I waited for Sloan, I looked up and watched the U.S. flag blowing in the breeze. On base, I'd heard the national anthem blaring through the speakers every morning and every evening. Seemed it was a military custom to raise and lower the flag every day while the anthem played. I hadn't had a chance to witness the flag ceremony, as the SEALs called it. According to Tripp, it was cool. Military personnel marched out of the building and up to the flagpole with the U.S. flag in hand then followed a strict step-by-step process that was coordinated from the first to the last notes of the anthem. In the evening, the steps were reversed.

I turned back toward the entrance and wondered what was taking Sloan so long. Dad had given me two hours of library time, and I wanted to use every minute. I sat on a cement bench against the building. I would've headed over to the library without Sloan, but I didn't know where it was. Besides, my father would've had a bloody fit if I walked alone.

The trees rustled as I waited. Saturdays were quiet, according to Sloan. He had explained on our way to the medical facility that most of the military personnel who lived on base left on the weekends. I imagined they headed off to places like Cape Cod or Newport to bask on the beaches at this time of year.

A hand touched my shoulder.

"You ready?" Sloan asked, pulling his beret out from under his belt and placing it over his dark-brown hair.

I rose. "It's about time. Were you trying to pick up the receptionist?"

He glared at me.

As we walked along the sidewalk, which ran parallel to the main building, the crunch of tires over gravel resounded.

I turned.

"Let's keep walking," Sloan commanded.

I didn't move. The black sedan rounded the island, hugging the curb closest to the building. It stopped between the flagpole and the main entrance.

"Who's in..."

A human was close and smelled as sweet as maple syrup.

He shrugged then grabbed my arm. "We need to go." Sloan's tone had an edge to it as if he was hiding something.

I pulled away, but he blocked me.

"Why won't you let me see?"

He glanced down. "You're not supposed to be within a hundred feet of a human."

"Who is it? Do you know?"

"I don't. And it doesn't matter. Let's keep moving."

His cell phone rang.

"Yes, sir?" Sloan had my right arm in a tight grip, pulling me away from the black sedan, as he held the cell phone with his other hand. "No. Not yet. I got tied up. Yes, sir, I will. We're headed there now. Yes, sir. I understand."

"What did my father want?"

He cocked one eyebrow.

I rolled my eyes. "I'm a vampire, you know. Have you forgotten I can hear just as well as you? If he wanted to talk to you in private, he should've used his telepathic line."

I turned. The vehicle sat parked, looking sinister against the beauty of the sunshine. The windows were tinted. Even my great vision couldn't penetrate that.

"Give it up, Jo. They already entered the building."

Funny, I hadn't heard a car door.

Not knowing Sloan as well as I knew Tripp, I couldn't tell if he was telling me the truth. I guessed it wasn't a big deal, although the scent of a human was tempting. I shrugged it off and kept walking.

As we passed buildings, Sloan explained how the site had been home to an old textile complex. "The military purchased the land many years ago, but it sat empty for the longest time. It's small compared to other military installations, yet strategic in nature. It sits on ten acres of land, and as you can see"—he waved his hand around the open space in the distance—"it's secluded by dense trees and brush, which masks the property from the road. Its proximity to the water and to the military ships and submarines docked at Battleship Cove is strategic for the SEALs and their missions. Plus, the wooded area surrounding the site is a perfect training ground to keep us agile in between missions."

"Why do vampires need to stay agile? I mean, with our superhuman strength, we don't need to train. Or is the training only for the humans?"

He waggled his head. "I can't even remember if I was as naïve as you when it came to vampires. I don't think so. My father was very clear on who he was and what he was. I guess I just answered my own question. Anyway, our species isn't that different. Just because we have preternatural senses doesn't mean we know how to wield those abilities in combat. And it's not as if I knew how to use a weapon just because I'm a vampire. Fighting takes skill for anyone. It's mental as much as physical, and you need to know your enemy. If you can't anticipate their next move, you're dead."

We walked, and he talked. I took in every word, glanced around when he pointed to something, and stopped when he explained landmarks.

"Jo, over here," Sloan called. He stood on a grassy, circular island across from the front entrance of the library.

I'd been so entranced with the history of the place, I didn't realize we had reached our destination until I turned around. I walked across a small strip of asphalt and onto the island. Three flags, identical to the ones at the entrance, hung from the flagpole, with the United States flag on top. Underneath, a blue flag with the words United States Navy rippled in the soft breeze. The third flag had POW-MIA in white letters against a black background.

"What does POW-MIA stand for?" I asked, looking up.

"Prisoner of War. Missing in Action. Two of our SEALs disappeared over a year ago during one of our missions. We did everything we could to search for them, but we still haven't found them."

I stared at a silhouette of a man bowing his head. *How awful.* I recalled the feelings I had when Sam went missing, and a pang of sorrow hit me for the families of those two soldiers. I dropped my gaze and rubbed tears out of my eyes.

Sloan had his head down and a hand on a metal plate attached to the memorial.

"What's this?" I moved next to him, pointing to the inscription:

Viking I
In memory of our fallen comrades.
We are unyielding in our fight.
We are gentle in our love.
We are unwavering in our mission.
We are courageous for our country.

"Who was Viking I?" I asked.

"The Navy has several SEAL teams. The human SEAL teams are identified by numbers such as Team One, Team Two, and so on. The vampire SEAL teams have names such as Viking I or Jupiter Sentinels, although you wouldn't find a human military or government official to explain the differences."

"There's more than one vampire SEAL team?" I asked with raised eyebrows.

He nodded. "On this base, you have the Sentinels and now, Viking II. The other two SEAL teams stationed here are human. Your father likes to keep one human team and one vampire team on base at all times. The others are deployed on missions around the world."

"Why one human and one vamp?"

"Sometimes it's necessary to have humans with us. It just depends on the mission. And you remember our motto? We protect both the paranormal world and humanity. We try to stop things before they get out of control." Sloan's voice had become melancholy. His hand brushed over the names on the steel plate. His eyes were no longer hazel but pitch-black.

"Are you okay, Sloan?" I placed my hand on his arm.

He didn't say a word.

"Did you know those guys who died?"

"I knew every one of them."

I read the memorial again. I stopped on the last name, which I hadn't seen earlier. Then again, I hadn't paid much attention to the names.

I stifled a gasp. The last name on the memorial read *Ella Case.*

"Is that Dr. Case's sister?"

"Yes." His response seemed choked, and he turned and walked toward the front door of the library.

"Did you know her?" I followed, climbing the steps behind him.

Ella had died in a battle in Afghanistan, through friendly fire, no less. According to my dad, one of the Sentinels had accidentally killed her, and I wondered whether it'd been Sloan.

"Let's go inside." He pulled the door open. "We're done with the history lesson for today."

I didn't argue. Since he was going to be my bodyguard, I had a few weeks to ferret information from him. While I was eager to bury my head in books in the library, I couldn't help but think of Dr. Case. I'd asked Dr. Vieira about him that morning. He'd said Dr. Case was doing well. Dad had locked him in a safe house somewhere on base. The Sentinels were still questioning him. I didn't know if I was happy for him or mad that he didn't die.

I sloughed off thoughts of Dr. Case and walked into the building. Cold air rushed past me. Sloan entered, letting the door close on its own.

"The library is up." He pointed to a set of stairs to our left.

I dragged my hand along the railing as I clambered up the stairs. Pictures of fighter jets, aircraft carriers, ships, and submarines dotted the walls, interspersed with groups of military men all bunched together as if taking a high school class picture. As my gaze roamed the picture galleries, I spotted a trophy case on the floor below. Gold statues sat inside, symbolizing wins in football, baseball, and basketball.

"Does the military have their own sports teams?" I asked.

"We do. It's all for fun. One way to exert some energy when we're not deployed."

Sam would love that. I thought of Ben, too, and how he loved baseball as much as my brother did. After all, Ben lived next door to Buster Greene, the catcher for the World Series Black Sox.

"Walk down the hall. The library is straight ahead."

Sloan's voice snapped me out of my brief Ben stupor.

I stopped at the half wood, half glass door that had "Library" stenciled beneath the window.

"You can go in." Sloan stopped and grabbed his cell phone out of its holster.

I pulled the door open and walked inside. The fresh scents of lemon and wood permeated the air. Floor-to-ceiling mahogany bookcases glinted under the fluorescent lighting overhead.

The expanse of the room was incredible. The

library had to have been similar in size to half a football field, filled with computers, tables, chairs, and two floors of books packed, stacked, and ready for me to digest. The top floor wrapped around the main level, rimmed with a wooden spindle railing. Higher up, crown molding edged the ceiling with the infinite number of pi, 3.1415926535, engraved in the wood, framing the room.

Makeshift planets hung from the ceiling and reminded me of the planetarium at Durfee High School. A children's area sat off to my right. Small wooden chairs and beanbag cushions surrounded the main table, where Winnie the Pooh books were displayed.

The door opened behind me.

"Pretty neat place, isn't it?" Sloan asked.

"Neat" wasn't the word I would have used. "Freaking awesome" summed it up for me.

"I haven't seen you smile like this... well, ever," Sloan said. "Geez, I'll have to tell your father to let you come here more often."

I was beginning to really like Sloan. I needed an ally to help me with my father.

"Where do you want to start?" he asked. "We have two hours. I know my way around this place. I usually come here to unwind after a long deployment."

Maybe that was why my dad had assigned

Sloan as my bodyguard. "I'm not sure where to begin."

"Your father said something about vampire special powers. Did he explain the different types?"

"Webb did, but he didn't go into detail. By the way, what's yours?"

"I have a few. My strong one is one of the elements."

I raised my forehead, remembering what Dad had explained last night and the marking on his upper chest.

"I can do things with water," Sloan said.

"Can you be more specific?"

"Let's find you one of the books, and you can read up on it. I have to make a few calls. Webb's been trying to reach me." He walked to the base of the stairs. "Up here."

Following him, I grabbed the banister and stopped as he continued his trek up. I scanned the railing up then down a few times, admiring the ornate design. Whoever had designed the library had a peculiar or fascinating imagination. Geometric three-dimensional shapes decorated the entire banister. A square sat at an angle on one of its corners, creating a diamond shape. I climbed onto the third step. The next shape on the banister was a right-angled triangle, which had a formula underneath it, the Pythagorean theorem. All the way up, different shapes dotted the rail. When I finally reached the fourth step from the top, I paused. The last shape in line was a circle made of plexiglass. I ran my hands over the globe. A bright-red triangle floated inside, bearing the words "Inscribed Angle."

Cool! "Sloan? Who designed this place?"

"A lady Dr. Vieira knows. Ms... oh, what's her name?"

I had one foot on the step above me and one foot on the step below me.

"Ms. Costner. Yeah, that's it."

I lost my balance and stumbled but caught myself.

"I'm sorry. Did you say... Ms. C-Costner?" I stuttered as the words left my lips.

The last time I'd seen Ms. Costner had been in math class, weeks before. She'd been discussing Pythagoras and his philosophy on there being three worlds. If I recalled correctly, the Supreme World was the supreme mind—the soul, as she had explained. The Superior World was home to immortals, and the Inferior World belonged to humans. *Had Ms. Costner been speaking of three worlds in the literal sense? Could she be a—*

I was frozen on a step, holding on to the bannister when Sloan tapped me on the shoulder. "Hey there. You okay? You're pale."

"Yeah." I followed him to the far corner on the third floor. A dozen questions surfaced. *Does she know my father? How does Ms. Costner know Dr. Vieira?* An ominous prickle made its way through me. "Do you know if Ms. Costner is a vampire?"

"Sorry, Jo. I don't. I've never met the woman."

Wonderful! Another mystery to solve. Then again, I couldn't quite pinpoint why Ms. Costner designing the library bothered me. If she was the same person I knew, I wasn't going back to Durfee High School anyway.

Sloan took a badge from his tan cargo pants and hovered it over a grey pad. The orange light on the pad flashed to green, and a door whooshed opened.

"In here." He waved a hand, motioning for me to go in.

My thoughts evaporated. Like the room outside, it was amazing.

"All this is dedicated to our world and species. Your dad keeps it under lock and key. No humans allowed."

I sighed then inhaled deeply, taking in the scent of very old books.

Large bookcases stretched along every wall from floor to ceiling, with a ladder on each bookcase. Several pendant lights hung above while tables, and big, plush chairs peppered the room. The room was larger than any of the foster homes I had lived in.

I spotted a section on the psychology of vampires. I made my way to the back wall, admiring the thick carpeting beneath my feet.

"Jo, is there anything specific you're after? Do you want to read up on elementals first?"

I pondered his question for a second. *No.* Dad's explanation of the four elements was enough for now. "Do you know where I can find info on telekinesis?"

"You'll probably find it under psychokinesis. The terms are similar. Check the back wall in the psychology section."

I trailed my fingers over the spines of several books on the psychology of vampires then pulled one out and opened it to the table of contents. Nothing about telekinesis. I replaced the book and continued scanning the spines. Another caught my attention. I removed the leather-bound book and read the cover—*Dracula Meets Hamlet.* I glanced up at the shelf and chuckled. The book next to the one in my hand read *Shakespeare and the Vampiric Life.*

I turned to ask Sloan, but he was gone, probably outside on the phone. I replaced the book and continued searching. As I scanned the next section, Sloan cleared his throat, suddenly back in the room.

"What is it?" I asked.

"We're headed there now, sir," he said before he holstered his phone. "We've got to go, Jo."

"What, now? We've just got here," I protested.

"Sorry. I have orders. I need to deliver you to Dr. Vieira."

I tore my gaze from the books and looked at him. "What's so urgent?"

"No clue. I don't ask questions. I follow orders. And your father wants you in the medical facility ASAP."

Is there something wrong with my blood?

Sloan made sure the door to the secret room was locked before we traipsed down the stairs to the main library floor. A human heart thudded from somewhere in the building, and my fangs dropped. He went into the hall first then waved me out. "Stay to my right, against the wall. The librarian is on her way up."

"I'm not going to attack her."

"I'd rather not take that chance. Not on my watch."

His phone chirped frantically.

"Why does your phone keep ringing?"

"It's a text."

"Is it my father again?" I murmured.

"No. Your father doesn't text very much. He's old school. When he wants something, he calls or uses his telepathy."

"Then is it the blond receptionist you were flirting with earlier?" I slid a sideways glance at him as we climbed down the stairs.

He raised an eyebrow, glaring at me.

I must've hit a nerve.

"Ms. Simpson? Can you please wait down the hall until we're out of the building?" he asked as we stopped midway down. "She's not supposed to be here," he muttered.

Ms. Simpson looked up. Her red hair was twisted into a chignon with her feathered bangs sweeping to one side of her face. She winked at me before sauntering down the hall and out of view. I inhaled, taking in her orange-and-citrus scent, which made my gums ache.

Sloan placed one hand around my arm and eased me up against the wall.

"Breathe," he whispered. He turned, looking for Ms. Simpson. "When was the last time you fed?"

"She didn't seem afraid," I said in astonishment.

"Answer me." He leaned in so that we were nose to nose.

"This morning."

"You should feed." He pulled me out the door into the bright sunshine.

The sun was high in the sky, and the birds were quiet. Heat radiated off the asphalt, and I removed my sweater. The mornings had been cool, almost cold, but when the sun rose to its peak, the heat did as well.

Sloan and I trudged toward the main building. He wasn't as talkative as he had been earlier, almost as if he was bothered by something.

I rounded the corner a step before Sloan then stopped abruptly and gasped. Suddenly, fire snaked through my legs, burning on its way down. The flames stopped at my knees, locking them in place, as I stared at a familiar figure.

A strong breeze picked up, whipping through his cinnamon hair, sending his scent of burned sugar toward me. I inhaled and closed my eyes.

When I opened them, Ben and I locked gazes, and my heart plummeted to my feet.

My vampire instinct told me to run to him, but my human one told me to run far away. The yin and yang in my head wreaked havoc with my emotions and my hunger. If I ran to him, I might attack him like Sam had... or maybe I would just be the person he'd known as a human.

I mentally slapped myself.

I was raising my right foot, still unsure what I was going to do, when Sloan picked me up, carried me around the corner, and pinned me against the brick wall.

"I want to see him!" I placed both my hands against his chest and pushed with all my vampire strength. He didn't even budge, as if I was trying to move the brick building behind me. My eyes flashed, light fading for an instant. "Let me go!" Glancing up, I met Sloan's pitch-black gaze.

"You will not move," he bit out through fanged teeth.

A car door sounded. *Is Ben leaving? Why was he even here?*

"Let me..." I raised my knee and shoved it between Sloan's legs.

He bent over, hands on his thighs, breathing heavily. I hadn't known if that would work on vampires or not, but, hey, they still had their manly parts.

I ran around the corner at lightning speed, but it was too late. The black sedan had disappeared. I stomped my foot and screamed, letting out an animalistic howl, which sounded more like something coming from an angry lioness who had just lost her cubs.

"Stop, Jo. Stop." Webb whispered after appearing out of nowhere and wrapping his arms around me. "Breathe. Deep breaths."

I inhaled a few times.

"Why did you let her see him?" Webb growled at Sloan. "Jo. Shhh... I need you to breathe, beautiful," he whispered, his breath caressing my ear.

At the sound of his silky voice, my body relaxed, tears spilling down my face. Ben on the base made for another question for which I had no answer.

8

Webb bent down slightly, positioning himself so his retinas could be scanned to unlock the door to the medical facility. We hadn't spoken on our way up, which was fine by me. The voices in my head were still battling. The devil berated me, telling me how much of an idiot I was for not listening to him, and the angel was congratulating me for not giving in to my weakness. But my action or inaction had nothing to do with listening to my inner voices. Sloan had held me back, damn it.

I pushed aside my inner struggle and recalled the image of Ben. He looked good—too good. His hair had grown, falling below his ears, and his dimples... I sucked in a breath.

"After you, Jo," Webb said.

I planted my feet and wiped the remaining tears from my face.

"Look, your father is waiting inside. My advice? Erase whatever is flashing through your mind. He's not in a good mood."

"Neither am I."

He tightened his lips and shook his head. "It's your funeral." He flicked his head toward the door then followed behind me.

My father's tall figure emerged in the window above the double doors to the lab. He stood, leaning against one of the lab benches, arms crossed with a scowl on his face. His brilliant green eyes had silvered.

Uh-oh.

The second set of doors swung open, and a blast of power hit, disorienting me. I staggered to the side, extending my arm, searching for something to anchor myself to. Webb caught me as the floor rose sharply. Dad wasn't just angry. Rage dripped off him in sheets.

"You're damn straight rage is dripping from me. I'm standing here, trying not to strangle you. Was I not clear enough? Did I not tell you to obey the law? Do you want the government to lock us up?" The last few words were punctuated with a growl.

"I didn't do anything!" I yelled. "I wasn't any-where near Ben. And why was he here, anyway?"

Dad combed his fingers through his hair. "Lieutenant London, please check on Sam." The anger in his voice was suddenly supplanted with concern.

I froze.

"What happened to Sam?" I glanced between Dad and Webb. "Where's Dr. Vieira? Is that why you sent for me? Is Sam okay?" When Sam and I had left the lab early that morning, he was on his way to sword training.

"When was the last time you drank blood?" Dad asked.

I tilted my head to one side. "Why?"

"Just answer me." His voice had a feral edge to it.

"This morning."

"Was it mine?"

I nodded.

Fury flickered in his expression once again as his silver gaze seared through me. "Jo, you have a short time left before... the precautionary mea-sures are lifted. Are you trying to get that sentence extended? Because I can extend it without any council approval. In fact, I just... it seems you're not ready to interact with humans."

"Ben is my friend. He's Sam's best friend."

"Humans don't make good friends, Jo."

"You keep saying that. I don't agree with you. Don't you have any human friends?"

"I may command human soldiers, but, no, I don't hang out with humans."

I lowered my gaze and took in a deep breath, tamping down the anger that crept closer to the surface. He was angry, but it had to have been because of Sam and not because I went running toward a car that had driven away.

"And you owe me a flagpole."

I raised one eyebrow. "What?"

"You bent the top of my flagpole. You can't deface government property."

"I don't know what you're talking about."

"I told you not to get upset."

I couldn't remember getting upset enough for my powers to take over. All I remembered was Webb's breath tickling my ear as he whispered the word *beautiful.* I shook it off. I didn't have time to analyze the gorgeous vampire.

I turned to walk away. If I stood there any longer, I was afraid I would destroy the lab and my father. I balled my fingers into a fist. The men in my life irritated me. My father had control issues. Sam kept getting into... I didn't know what. It seemed the universe had other plans for my brother. Webb had an elusive charm. Then there was Ben. Something drew me to him. Whether it was curiosity, his scent, his blood, or all of the above, I wanted to find out. I had to find out, but I could lose my willpower around him and turn into the vampire Dad feared I would become.

"And where do you think you're going, young lady?" Dad asked.

"I'm going to see Sam since you won't tell me what happened. Or maybe try to escape so I can see Ben," I spat.

I assumed Sam was in the room on the far side of the medical facility. Webb had gone in there after Dad told him to check on Sam.

I took one step before my face slammed into Dad's broad chest. He grabbed my chin and yanked it up. A violent storm swirled in his gaze, and his eyebrows were drawn together so hard that the crease in between had to be an inch deep. Fury rolled off him in twenty-foot waves, causing my blood to freeze.

He inhaled. "What is it with you and the Jackson boy? Is there something going on between you and him I should know about?" He raked his gaze over me and no doubt picked through my thoughts.

"My brain is empty right now, so don't waste your time. And no, there's nothing going on. It doesn't matter anyway. Between you and Sam, I don't stand a chance of ever having a boyfriend."

"You're damn right about that. If I had my way, I'd send you off to a convent."

My mouth fell open. It took all the strength I had not to scream.

"That's right."

"You sure you were born in the eighteen hundreds and not the sixteen hundreds?" I spat.

"Young lady…" His grip tightened around my chin. "You're just lucky there aren't any vampire convents or vampire nuns in our world. Though I have a good mind to change that…"

A door opened then closed. Footsteps scuffed across the tile. I turned my head to glimpse the person who approached, but Dad's steel grip restrained me.

"Sir?" Dr. Vieira's voice eased some of the tension in the air, thank God.

Dad let go of me. "How's Sam?"

"He's still under," Dr. Vieira replied.

"Are her blood results from this morning complete?" Dad asked.

"No, sir."

"Is anyone going to tell me what's going on?" I asked.

My angry father began pacing in long strides,

just as he had when he found out someone cracked into his blood vault. Dad didn't seem as mad anymore. His power still ebbed and flowed, but more from what seemed like worry rather than rage.

"Steven, all the boxed blood from our supplier has been removed."

"How could this have happened? Is the blood tainted, or was it too early for Sam to switch to a different blood type?"

"I don't know. Your children's DNA is unique. I don't have all the results ironed out yet. My preliminary conclusions suggest they should continue to ingest your blood as their source of nourishment until I can figure all this out. With that said, however, a couple of younger vampires on-site were sick earlier this week with the same flu-like symptoms as Sam."

"I gave him strict orders not to drink any other blood but mine," he muttered as he continued to pace. "These teenagers are going to..." His voice trailed off.

Then, in an instant, he slammed his fist on top of the granite lab bench, cracking it. The sound drilled through my ears as if a shotgun had fired. "Webb!"

"Commander?" Webb appeared out of nowhere.

"Jo, follow me," Dr. Vieira said in a calm tone, ignoring my father and his choleric temper.

And I owe you a flagpole? Right. I narrowed my eyes and looked at him. *You owe the government a lab bench.* I hoped he read that.

I followed Dr. Vieira to the same room Ben had occupied after he was attacked by one of the Plutariums. My hands trembled. I was afraid to walk in. A mixture of scents greeted me as I looked at Dr. Vieira. Blood for sure, which overpowered the other two, sweat and alcohol.

"You can go in," he said.

I shook my head violently. The images of Sam sprawled across a gurney, his skin pale, arms hanging off, and a breath away from death were still too vivid in my mind.

"He's stable, Jo. He doesn't look like he did when we found him at Highland Memorial," he said as if he knew what I was thinking.

"What happened?"

"Sam passed out in sword training. When Tripp brought him in, he had a hundred-and-four-degree fever."

I gasped. "I'd wondered why he was hot to touch a couple of weeks ago. His hand almost burned a hole in my palm."

"When was this?" Dr. Vieira asked.

"Um...the day we met the solicitors, I think?"

"Mmm-hmm. That explains a few things."

"Like what?"

"We've had a few other personnel sick about two or three weeks ago. Then a couple more this week," he explained. "We're investigating whether the boxed blood we drink has been contaminated."

"Did the other vamps get this sick?"

"No, but they're older, and their immune systems are stronger. Now, go on in. I'll be with you."

Once I was in the room, the air pressure dropped.

Here we go again. I was always walking into a hospital room where a friend or family member was comatose.

I blew out a breath, following the tube from Sam's arm to the IV bag full of blood. He looked peaceful, lying with his arms by his side, breathing in and out in a steady rhythm. Then out of nowhere, a man rose from the chair on the other side of Sam's bed. I did a double take. The man also had an IV in his arm, with blood flowing through a tube into a bag at his side. I froze.

"What's he doing here? Get him out—*now.*" I ran up to Sam's bed and pulled the needle out of his arm. Blood dribbled out, and the small hole in the crease of his elbow closed up immediately.

What is Neil Foster doing in Sam's room? And why is he giving Sam his blood?

"Hey, calm down." Dr. Vieira pulled me away. "It's okay."

"No, it's not! That man's a Plutarium."

"What's all the commotion in here?" my father asked, stalking in like he owned the place.

Dr. Vieira picked up the needle. "Your daughter—"

"Why is a Plutarium giving Sam blood?" I interrupted. "Get him out of here!"

I tried to force back my anger. Releasing it meant my mental powers would surface, causing damage and destruction to the medical facility, and I already owed my father a flagpole. I took several calming breaths.

"It's okay," Dad said, grabbing me. "Look at me. I know you don't understand everything going on around here, but that man sitting in the chair, donating blood, could be essential to Sam making it through this. We suspect Sam has been drinking from the boxed blood in the refrigerators, which may have been tainted with an endotoxin. Dr. Vieira has a lab technician testing every box."

I looked at Dr. Vieira then at Neil Foster then at my dad. "And what's so important about his blood?"

Neil had befriended Sam the day I was rushed

to Highland Memorial Hospital, the same day Sam and I were running for our lives from Jonah. Neil had been kind enough to hide us at his parents' abandoned funeral home, and although he'd been the one to tell Dad where the Plutariums were keeping Sam, I wasn't so sure where his loyalties lay—he had the Plutariums' insignia tattooed on the back of his neck.

Every time I asked Dad about Neil, he told me he couldn't talk about him. A part of me wanted to thank him for helping to rescue Sam, but another part didn't trust him. For some reason, though, Sam had trusted Neil from day one. According to Sam, Neil had been one of the janitors at Durfee High School, although I had never seen him there.

I looked at Neil again. He sat quietly in the chair with the IV tethered to his arm. His diamond earring glistened in his left ear. His appearance hadn't changed, save for a close-shaven beard hugging his jaw.

If Neil had in fact been a janitor at the high school, Sam had to have seen him before that night. If that were the case, then...

Something snaked through the deepest recesses of my brain, pushing its way to the surface. *Did Dad lie about not knowing where we were for fourteen years?* As I stared at Neil, a sinking feeling coursed through me.

"I didn't," Dad said before I could speak.

I lifted my gaze. "You lied to me."

"I—"

"Forget it. I knew I couldn't trust you. Maybe Sam was right. Maybe you're not our father."

"Jo," Neil said. "He didn't lie to you."

"I'm not talking to you," I said to Neil, keeping my eyes on Dad.

His power rose, anger spilling into the air. I'd pissed him off too many times recently not to know his rage.

"If you didn't lie, then why did Sam tell me he knew Neil from school? That would mean Sam and Neil knew each other way before the night I was in the hospital. Given all of that, you lied. You knew where to find us. You knew we were suffering in foster care. You let us live with a pervert like Cliff."

Suddenly, Webb appeared, taking a stance behind my dad as if he knew Dad was about to explode.

Dad released a deep breath. "I didn't lie. I didn't know where you were. One of the reasons Neil is here today is because he has a very special ability—his blood heals."

Dr. Vieira cleared his throat.

"Not now, Damon," my father said, not even looking at the doctor.

"Don't change the subject, Dad. Oh, excuse me —maybe "Dad" isn't the right word."

"Young lady"—his nostrils flared—"let's go." He grabbed me by the arm and pulled me out of the room.

Webb followed as Dad continued to march me into Dr. Vieira's office. When we entered, Dad slammed the door, shaking the walls and everything else in the room.

Webb knocked. "Sir?"

"Not now, Lieutenant."

Webb stuck in his head. "Can I help?"

"I said not now. This is between me and my daughter." He snapped his head and glared at me. "Close the door, Lieutenant. This will only take a minute."

I couldn't tell if Webb worried about me or about my father and what he might do. He closed the door gently.

Dad unleashed his power, zapping my skin. It was as if he was rubbing my arms with a pumice stone.

Webb's apprehension suddenly made me uneasy. I sat on the leather couch while Dad paced the length of the room, thrusting his fingers through his hair then rubbing his jaw. I regarded him with caution, afraid if I said a word, he would... I didn't know what he would do.

"Dad." My voice was soft.

"You don't get to speak right now. I'll do all the talking." He stopped pacing and sighed. "Jo, come here," he said, waving his hand.

I rose from the couch, all my senses telling me to obey the powerful vampire. Dr. Vieira's office window overlooked the grounds in front of the main entrance. The silence grew thick as we both stared out. The breeze had changed into a strong wind, causing the trees to sway from side to side. In fact, since I had entered the building, dark clouds had rolled in.

"Do you remember our conversation the first night you, Sam, and I were together?" His voice had lost a little bit of the angry tone.

"Yeah."

"What did I tell you about why I couldn't locate you and Sam?"

"You said it had a lot to do with Edmund."

"Sure. I told you that with Edmund as my enemy, it was safer not knowing where you were. That killed me more than anything. You may think ill of me for that, but my actions were to protect both of you. Do you think I lied to you?" he asked evenly.

We were both still looking out the window. I'd been watching a squirrel gnaw on what looked to be an apple core.

"I don't know what to believe." I really didn't. Hands down, he looked just like Sam, but I didn't know whether appearance was enough to prove he was my father. I wasn't sure about anything anymore. The only constant in my life was my brother. "Is Sam going to be okay?" I asked.

"He will."

"Is Neil's blood helping him?"

"We don't know. Neil's blood can heal superficial wounds like cuts and open sores, but only in humans. However, we've never had the need to test his blood on internal viruses or infections. It wasn't until the day you came close to being a victim of the endotoxin when Dr. Vieira started experimenting with Neil's blood to see if it could help kill the bacterium that the endotoxin emits. If the boxes of blood were sabotaged with this endotoxin, and Neil's blood helps Sam, we might be able to fabricate a remedy to counteract any effects other vampires have with the toxin. All this could be a long shot, though. It might very well be that Sam is getting better because of his vampire immune system. It just might take longer because he's a young vampire."

"Why did Sam tell me he knew Neil from school?"

The squirrel had eaten the entire apple core and was scurrying up a tree.

"Neil compelled Sam that night to believe he knew him from school."

"You told me you had asked a friend for some help when you found out I was in the hospital. Is Neil that friend?"

"No, sweetie," he said, letting out a breath as if releasing the last effects of his dangerous mood. "While Neil helped, he wasn't the only one. You see, Neil has been undercover in the Plutarium organization for the past three years. Edmund sent him and Jonah to the hospital that night to confirm Dr. Case was telling the truth. When Neil arrived, he found Sam sneaking around the emergency room. Since Sam looks a lot like me, Neil knew he had to be my son. So he called me."

"Is Neil still undercover?" I tore my gaze from my little squirrel friend and looked up.

"No. His cover has been blown." He touched my left shoulder and looked down. "I didn't lie to you. I would never lie to you or Sam." He pulled me into a hug. "I know we're still getting to know each other, but you have to trust me when I tell you to do something. This is a different world than what you're accustomed to. You need to accept that. Your safety is extremely important to me. I can't lose you again. I *won't* lose you or Sam again." He stroked my head.

I stood in his embrace, listening to every word.

I struggled with our father-and-daughter relationship. I'd only known him for a short time, and in that time, we'd had some very tender moments and some serious I-hate-you moments. I didn't know if we would ever build a stronger and better bond. I did want Sam, Dad, and me to be a family, but aside from my brother, I had a hard time allowing myself to feel attached to anyone. After all, foster care had taught me that nothing was forever.

He let me go, turned, and looked out the window. "Did you notice the flagpole?"

I joined him at the window. The pole was bent a few inches below the top, the ball dangling in the air.

"Yes, you did that," Dad said in response to my silent question.

"I don't know how to control it. I didn't get that upset."

"You got extremely upset. Your scream was deep and loud. I heard it from inside here."

"Yeah, but vampires can hear a pin drop."

"While that is true, your scream hurt my eardrums."

I was afraid. I didn't remember getting that upset. I thought I was more nervous than anything. Suddenly, my inner devil poked me in the brain. "I know what might help, but I don't... want you to get mad. Okay?"

He cocked his head to one side.

"Dad, please don't get mad. Promise?" I grabbed his hand.

"I promise."

"Let me see Ben. I just want to talk to him."

He tightened his grip on my hand and I flinched. We stood together in silence, his power climbing up the Richter scale.

"You... promised," I said, trying not to voice the pain shooting up my arm. "Again, there's nothing going on between me and Ben. He helped me get through my shock that vampires existed and kept me from going crazy while Sam was missing. I just want to talk to him."

I couldn't read his thoughts, but I didn't have to. The pitter-patter of his heartbeat changed, rising to a loud thud in my ears. Not to mention the pain he was inflicting on my hand. At any second, the bones in my hand were going to break.

"I can't allow it. You're under Council's orders. Heck, I'm under Council's orders."

I yanked my hand from his. "What's the big deal?"

"Do you hear yourself? Big deal? You haven't come to terms with *what* you are yet. This is exactly why I" —he pointed to his chest— "can't allow it. Until you learn you're not human anymore, you're dangerous around humans. Your mind is still thinking like a human, but I can assure you, your vampire instincts are far from it."

Maybe he was right. At times, I didn't want to believe I was a vampire. I truly didn't know how to accept who or what I was. So many things had changed in such a short time, and I wasn't sure I could process all of it. As a human, I had been trying to find my way in life. Sure, I had been trapped in places and situations I hated to think about, but I didn't yet know if my life as a vampire was any better than my life as a human. At least if I'd attacked someone as a human, it would have been in self-defense. As a vampire, it would be for my sustenance, for their blood.

"So you're never going to let me be around humans?"

He stared out the window as if carefully considering his answer then turned and looked down. "We'll see."

I narrowed my gaze. "I hate this life," I said, tears welling up.

"Jo, I value my job and my position within the government. I also told you I don't want to lose you again. What you're asking jeopardizes all of what I worked hard for. I cannot and will not allow you to see any human right now, especially Ben, a young man you may have feelings for."

I let out a deep sigh. I didn't know if I had feelings for Ben.

"This conversation is over. I don't want to hear another word about Ben or humans. Let's go see your brother." Dad turned toward the door.

I huffed and followed him. I didn't want to push my luck. Besides, it was barely late afternoon, and I wanted to crawl into my bed and go to sleep. A part of me wished I wouldn't wake up until all the council stuff was over.

Webb was standing outside, apparently waiting for us. He had to have heard us. I raked my gaze up and down his tall frame as he peered at me through his mile-long eyelashes. I wanted to laugh, even though my heart flipped a few times and my stomach followed. I wasn't allowed to see a human guy I might have feelings for, but I could be around a deadly vampire one.

The absurdity of my life was probably going to kill me before my father or the Plutariums had the chance.

9

The pad of his foot struck the side of my face. My neck bounced back then forward like a punching bag.

"Easy!" I reached up and placed my hand on my left cheek.

"Pay attention, Jo," Sam snapped. "You need to learn this."

Sam had dragged me out that morning and coaxed me into sparring with him. He had recovered quickly, back to his old self after only two days.

I'd been in some kind of funk. Too much had happened on Saturday. Repeating images of Ben, Sam in a hospital bed, Neil Foster, and the knock-down, drag-out argument with my father had shut my brain down. A mirthless feeling seeped in, and I didn't want to leave the confines of my bedroom.

Once Sam had rested, Dad had slapped him with the Mason Inquisition, firing questions until my brother finally spilled the beans and told Dad he'd drunk a few boxes of blood. Sam had said he'd done it more out of curiosity than hunger.

I'd been surprised Dad didn't try to read his mind. When I asked him why, he responded with several reasons.

"While that's the easy way out, I want to build trust with both of you," he'd explained. "You're easier to read because I don't have to touch you, but your brother requires more effort from me. Besides, I don't like reading minds. There are a lot of sick people in this world, and I don't care to subject myself to their vile thoughts. And the vampire government has placed restrictions on me. It seems a couple of senators in the human government complained and became suspicious when I knew things I shouldn't have. So I don't engage in the act unless there's a dire need."

I'd never thought about the ramifications of reading someone else's mind. I guessed it would be kind of creepy to know another's thoughts, especially if they were crude or sick ones. Still, I was curious as to why he was always reading mine, so I asked.

"For some reason, I have a hard time shutting out your thoughts," Dad had said. "I believe it's because we have a strong connection."

Sam snapped his fingers. "Earth to sis?"

I blinked. "What?"

"Focus."

"I'm just not good at fighting," I replied.

"Stop complaining," Sam said. "Let's go again. Ready your stance. Bend your knees slightly."

I wanted to lie down on the floor, curl up, and go to sleep. The entire room was covered in thick gym mats, and their softness kept calling my name. All I needed was a pillow.

"You need to take that sweatshirt off. It's slowing you down."

I laughed. My brother stood in the center of the room, bare-chested and barefoot, with sweatpants covering his lower half. Sometimes, I thought that my brother would have been content to walk around naked. I erased the thought immediately—it wasn't an image I cared to ponder. He'd pulled a small section of his jet-black hair back from the crown into a ponytail, with the remainder of his hair spilling over his shoulders. It seemed he was ready to expend some energy. Anyone looking at him wouldn't have known he had been in a light coma two days before.

I walked to the water cooler and grabbed a cup

of water. I kicked off my sneakers and removed my sweatshirt. I decided to get into the mood, or Sam was going to force me into one neither of us would like.

I was folding my sweatshirt when Olivia Brock, the only female Jupiter Sentinel and the only female SEAL, walked in. Her brown hair was tied into a long French braid, and her soft brown eyes glistened beneath the overhead light. I had seen her fight against other vampires and admired her for her toughness.

Sam did a double take as she removed her jacket.

"I'm here to work with both of you," she said, placing her jacket on one of the chairs.

"Close your mouth, Sam. You're gawking." I slapped him on the arm.

"Okay, Jo. You first. Front and center, please."

I rose and joined her in the middle of the room. Mirrors lined the two sidewalls, with chairs and benches on the other two. I glanced in the mirror and caught a glimpse of Sam still gawking at Olivia as she flipped the waistband of her yoga pants over then tied the string into a knot. I studied him as his gaze traveled up from her waist and over her six-pack abs to her chest, which was covered in a sports bra, then back down. My eyes widened as his forest-green eyes lost their color and his fangs descended. Uh-oh. Olivia must have been giving off some type of pheromone. Maybe that was how vampires detected their prey.

My brother had a death wish.

It was the first time in my life I'd noticed him looking at a female. He'd never once expressed interest in a girl, at least not to me. I imagined he and Ben probably talked about girls. Heck, girls followed Ben like a swarm of bees. Maybe they had been following Sam too.

Before I knew what was happening, Olivia had him by his throat and shoved him against the mirrors. His head hit with a thud.

"Has no one ever taught you manners?" she said. "I guess not, considering... it's rude to stare. Tuck in your emotions, Sam. Are we clear?" Then she released her grip, and he fell to the floor.

He sat against the mirrors, not moving. I couldn't tell if he was embarrassed or shocked or both. His eyes were no longer vampire-black, thank God. I dropped my gaze as Olivia returned to the middle of the room. She gave off a small amount of electricity, making my skin tingle. If Sam wasn't embarrassed, I sure was.

"Better yet, Sam, join us," she commanded.

Sam stood, adjusted his sweatpants, and walked over to stand next to me.

"Let's sit down. I want to go over some basics of

fighting. Your father wants both of you to be prepared to at least protect yourselves. Despite the fact that you're vampires, your strength will not keep you from getting hurt or killed. After I explain the basics, we'll practice some moves and regroup tomorrow. We only have an hour. Jo, your dad wants to see you in his office when we're done here."

What does he want now? I'd been in my room for the last two days, so I hadn't done anything to piss him off. Sure, I was still upset he wouldn't let me talk with Ben, but I tried to work out my frustrations by sleeping a lot.

The three of us sat on the floor, legs folded underneath us, forearms resting on the insides of our thighs.

"I've been training with Tripp," Sam said. "Jo needs to learn more."

"Sword training is not the same. You need to learn how to fight the old-fashioned way—with your body. You're in no way an expert and won't be for a while. You'll listen and learn whether it's with me, Tripp, or any other Sentinel. Are we clear?"

Sam stared at her with a blank expression, and silence gave way to my thudding heartbeat as I waited for the vibrating tension in the room to stop.

I nudged Sam with my elbow, hoping he would acknowledge her.

He nodded.

"A *yes* is expected," she said.

"Yes, your majesty," Sam said in a sinister tone.

What is it between them? She did babysit him the night the Plutariums escaped—maybe something had happened that night. Either way, the energy in the room was going to suffocate me by the end of the session.

"I've heard about you, Sam," Olivia said. "Your attitude and anger issues are well noted around here. It would benefit you to polish your manners and reel in those inner demons you have picking at you. The vampire society is one that doesn't tolerate outbursts, rudeness, or selfishness."

If I had to hear another person tell me about manners, I was going to puke. She was directing her comments toward Sam, but they were hardly giving me a warm and fuzzy, especially with the first day of school looming. The teachers could be even stricter about manners than the military people.

"Now that we've wasted a good bit of time," she said, glaring at Sam, "I'd like to begin with the three components of the art of fighting. Strength, skill, and strategy.

"Strength is extremely important. This is the

one component that is essential in fighting. You'll build strength through exercise.

"Skill is the moves you learn. How you block, move, turn your body, punch, et cetera. Those two components will require physical training, agility training, and using your brain to put it all together. And we'll get started on some basic strength exercises in a bit.

"The last one is strategy, which is my specialty. Strategy is knowing your enemy, your opponent. Knowing how to anticipate your enemy's moves, the way he may think, and what his strengths and weaknesses are. Strategizing before you walk into a battle is critical."

When Olivia spoke, the timbre of her voice was commanding but gentle. I admired her for her dedication to the military. I didn't know much about how she became a Sentinel, but any woman who made it that far in a SEAL program had to be tough, and I wanted to learn more from her.

For the next hour, Olivia demonstrated several positions that would help in defending against an attacker—how to position our arms, how to protect our faces and stomachs from an opponent's blows, and how to breathe so panic didn't set in. Then, before we practiced any moves, she made us do one hundred push-ups, sit-ups, and squats. By the time I was finished I wanted to pass out and was beginning to think that maybe I had ingested some of the endotoxin. While I struggled with the basic exercises, Sam blew through them as if someone had given him fifty cups of coffee. If vampires were supposed to be that energetic, I had missed the mark.

"Jo, stand up," Olivia commanded.

I threw back my head then rose from the mat.

"What's wrong with you? Why are you so tired?"

I scratched the back of my head when Sam slapped me on the arm.

"What was that for?" I drew my eyebrows together.

He slapped me again. The room disappeared for a brief second. I glanced in the mirror as the room came into focus. A lucent shade of violet glinted off the mirror. It was the first time I had seen my eyes violet. I walked up to the mirror and stared at myself.

"Why do her eyes change to violet?" Olivia asked.

"I don't know. My sister is weird," Sam said.

I blinked a few times. My reflection had me mesmerized. It was odd to see myself with purple streaks running through my hair and a pair of violet orbs to match.

Sam stalked up to me. "Come on. We only have

a few minutes left."

"So? I'm done," I said, tracing the scar on my left cheek.

"Oh no, you're not," he said. Then he pushed me, and my head hit the mirror.

At that moment, my eyes started glowing. I spun around, extended my right fist, and punched him in the face. He flew back, hitting the bank of mirrors on the opposite side of the room.

Whoa! What just happened? Was that me?

I barely had time to process my sudden burst of energy when Sam pitched forward and tackled me to the mat, knocking the wind out of me. "Where did that come from?" he asked, rubbing his jaw.

I inhaled a few times, trying to get the air back into my lungs.

"Get... off... me." I barely squeaked out the words.

He jumped up.

I glared at him as I rose. I turned my head slightly, looking in the mirror. It was still me. My eyes were still vampire violet, and my lovely, creepy fangs had decided to make an appearance. I adjusted my vision.

Olivia joined us on the mat. "Before you two continue, a couple of pointers."

"I'm done for today," I said. I didn't want to do

any of it, but I could feel the adrenaline snaking through me, and my energy level rose.

"No. We're doing this, sis."

Olivia looked at me. "You get to kick your brother's ass. If not, I'll gladly stand in," she said, glowering at my brother. "Now, clear your head. I want you to use your senses, be aware of your surroundings. See if you can anticipate Sam's moves. Fighting is like dancing. Your opponent moves, you move. It doesn't matter how you move, just keep moving. Which leads me to the second point. Footwork is so crucial. You must stay on the balls of your feet. The minute you plant your entire foot on the mat, you're toast." She looked at Sam, then me. "Keep it civil for your first time."

Sam bounced on his feet, moving his head from side to side. "Give me your best shot, sis."

Olivia resumed her position on the sidelines.

Sam circled around me, looking stealthy and animalistic like a wolf sizing up his prey. "Are you going to move or just stand there?" he barked.

I turned to face him, and he jumped into the air, rotated his left fist, and swung. I ducked under his arm, twirled, and jumped backward.

"Good," Olivia called.

Sam froze, cocked an eyebrow, and stared at me.

I narrowed my eyes. "You really want to beat

up your only sister?"

He waved his hand. "Come on. I'm getting bored."

I let out a breath, and he pounced. He scissor-kicked, landing a crushing blow to my stomach. Air rushed past me as I catapulted, landing against the non-mirrored wall. My back hit with a thud, cracking the sheetrock. In one fluid motion, I slid down to a crouching position then leapt at him without thinking, as if a beast inside had taken over, and tackled him to the ground. He grabbed my arms and pushed. My arms buckled, and he flipped me. In a nanosecond, he was on top of me with my wrists pinned to the mat.

"Not bad," he said. "But—"

"But nothing." I raised both my legs and rocked, using my upper chest to propel him off me. He flew backward as I stood up. I might have been weaker, but the spikes of adrenaline sure did help.

We met in the middle of the mat, doing that dancing thing Olivia had just explained.

"Watch him, Jo. Don't let him out of your sight," she instructed from the sidelines.

Girl power. Cool. I have a coach.

Sam smirked and rolled his eyes. "You don't have a chance, sis."

"You're mighty cocky, aren't you?"

In a blur, he jabbed his right fist, hitting me square in the jaw.

"Ow." I cupped my face, anger welling up. *Dance moves be damned.*

I flew at Sam, not even thinking, grabbing him by his long hair. He spun under my arms and punched me in the stomach. Doubling over, I let go of his hair. The pain soared through me—and so did my anger. I raised my right elbow and caught the underside of his jaw. His head bounced back then forward. As he righted himself, he smiled.

Cocky bastard. The blow didn't faze my brother at all.

Before I could step back, he threw a punch, his fist hit my nose, and the bones inside cracked. I closed my eyes tightly as the pain bit me hard. I wiggled it back and forth. The bones snapped back into place, and the pain was gone. When I opened my eyes, Sam's fist was inches from me. I squatted as his arm swept over my head, air whooshing past my ears. I swung my leg in a low sweep, knocking Sam to the ground. His head hit the mat, but he jumped up seconds later. His movements were crisp and precise as he attacked again, throwing another punch and making contact with my right eye. I returned the gesture, only to his left eye. I wasn't trying to follow the eye-for-an-eye cliché, but I guess the universe had a way of making it happen.

"Okay, you two. Break it up." Olivia walked toward us. "That's enough for today. I don't want either of you expending all your energy. We have a lot of work to do tomorrow."

As though we didn't hear her, Sam and I kept punching each other. When Olivia grabbed my arm, Sam's fist hit the left side of her face. Suddenly, Olivia's eyes blackened. She let go of my arm and pushed me out of the way.

"You don't want to fight me, big guy. You won't come out of this clean."

Sam grinned and lunged at her, but Olivia disappeared behind him. I didn't even see her move.

Sam whirled around. "What the hell?"

"I told you, you're too young to fight me. There's no point in engaging you," she said. "Now, class is over for today." She looked at me. "Jo, nice job. You still have a long way to go, but it's a good start."

"By the way, sis, not bad," Sam said.

"Um, thanks."

"You okay?" Sam asked, sitting next to me. "I want you to learn this. You need to learn this."

"I know. You've been saying it all my life. Hitting another person is weird, that's all. And it hurts."

"Once you build up your strength, the pain won't be as severe," Olivia said. "Tomorrow. Same time." She bent to pick up her jacket.

Sam settled his gaze on Olivia again. The vibe I got was a little anger and a little...

I punched him on the arm.

"What?" he asked, feigning an innocent tone.

I shook my head. "You really do have a death wish," I said in a hushed whisper, hoping Olivia couldn't hear me. "Besides, it's gross."

"Looking at a girl is gross? Like you looking at a boy isn't."

"I don't look at boys. Either you or Dad would cut my head off."

"Well, you're right about that. But I've seen the way you look at Webb, so don't preach to me."

"Then maybe I should cut *your* head off," I added.

He laughed as he wiped the sweat from his brow with his T-shirt.

Boys were lucky. They could get away with so much more than girls. It was okay for them to look at the opposite sex, but it wasn't for a girl. And boys could remove clothing and show bare skin without anyone batting an eye. Hell, when a girl did the same, showing her midriff, boys would stop what they were doing and ogle. It happened all the time in gym class. Some of the other girls at school would wear a sports bra and short shorts to gym class, and the boys would stand around like zombies, staring at them. I sure wasn't one of those girls. The most skin I put on display was my bony legs and arms, and only because I had to wear shorts in gym glass.

I took inventory of the room, wiping the perspiration from my face. The mirrorless wall had a dent in it, courtesy of my backside and Sam's vampire strength. Adjacent to the large indentation, a crack snaked up the sheetrock, all the way to the ceiling. The wall of mirrors on the sidewalls had come away unscathed, thank God. I didn't want seven years of bad luck. I realized after a few pats of my fingers and a quick glance in the mirror that the skin below my nose was tight with dried blood. I was picking at it when the door to the training room opened, and a familiar figure walked in.

Her brown hair hung freely around her shoulders, while her navy-blue eyes glistened. I couldn't figure what Kate London, Webb's sister, was doing there. I hadn't seen her in what seemed like forever. She reminded me so much of my best friend, Darcy Rose, whom I hadn't seen since Webb removed me from school the day Sam went missing. I could only imagine Darcy was going crazy wondering where I was. If I had been in her shoes, I would have been. I'd wanted to call her, but she'd have too many questions that I wasn't prepared to answer.

As she sauntered toward us, Sam lifted his gaze, and his heartbeat picked up speed. Kate had on a white buttoned-down blouse with three-quarter sleeves, belted at the waist, and a pair of blue jeans painted on her legs. Peeking out from her white blouse was a bright-orange camisole. Her scent of cinnamon wafted toward us as she approached.

"What happened in here? The room looks like a cyclone hit, and it stinks." She wrinkled her nose.

Sam's heartbeat was racing, and if I wasn't mistaken, his cheeks flushed redder the closer she got.

"They were sparring," Olivia said, throwing her gym bag over her shoulder. "See you two tomorrow."

I acknowledged Olivia, but Sam didn't. His gaze was riveted on Kate.

"It's impolite to stare like that," I whispered in his ear.

Sam's demeanor around Kate was vastly different. Around Olivia, he was cocky and confident, but the encounter with Kate led me to believe Sam had a shy side—or a scared one. He started gnawing the inside of his cheek.

Boy, what I would have given to have been in

Sam's head just then.

"Hey, Jo. Long time no see," Kate said, standing in front of Sam and me.

"I know. My dad sent you on some assignment." I nudged Sam. "Do you know Webb's sister, Kate?"

He didn't move. He didn't speak.

"We met the night the Plutariums broke out," Kate added. "Isn't that right, Sam?"

He nodded.

Ah. Her phone in the hallway. That's right. I'd forgotten to ask Sam about it. "What're you doing here?" I asked.

"Sloan's tied up, so your father wants me to escort you up to his office."

"Now? I need to clean up."

"He said to bring you straight away."

I finger-combed my hair then flipped it into a messy bun of sorts. I rose, grabbed some water from the fountain, splashed it on my face, then wiped it with the hem of my T-shirt. I surveyed myself one last time. *Yikes.* My right eye was blackish yellow, but it seemed like the color was disappearing even as I stared back at myself. Oh well. If my father got mad, then he got mad. After all, it had been the SEALs' idea to have me learn how to fight, anyway. Turned out I kind of liked going a few rounds with my brother. Of course, I didn't like the pain that came with it, but I enjoyed the freedom of moving around like that.

"Okay. I'm as ready as I'll ever be without a shower," I said. "Sam, are you going back to the apartment? Oh, wait. Where's Tripp? Isn't he supposed to be here to escort you back?"

"He's on his way," Kate said. "He'll be fine."

I turned to Sam, who was frozen like a mime.

"Kate, can I have a minute with my brother?" I asked.

"Sure," she said. "I'll be right outside." She walked backward, looking at Sam.

Once she was gone, I turned to him. "Is this about her phone?"

"No," he snapped.

"Then what's going on? Why are you so freaky? She said you met her that night. What happened?"

"I don't want to talk about it," he growled, throwing his head into his hands.

"I've never seen you like this. You like her?"

I wasn't an expert on emotions. I couldn't even decipher my own unless I was angry or sad. Still, my vampire senses were extremely sensitive, and Sam gave off a nervous energy.

"No way. She just scares the shit out of me." His voice was muffled.

"Wait. Kate scares the shit out of you, but Olivia doesn't? I don't get it."

He raised his head. "I don't know how to explain it. Kate's emotions change around me. Her heart speeds up, and her body temperature rises. She gives off a weird vibe. Olivia just gives off this outright rage and I'm-better-than-you vibe. I get that."

I laughed.

"Don't start, sis, unless you want to go another round."

"Do you hear yourself? You're the one who has the speeding heartbeat. You're the one who gives off the nervous vibe. Besides, Kate was as calm as the water in a bathtub. Maybe there's fire between *you two*."

He jumped before I knew what was happening and tackled me. I guess he didn't like his own words thrown back at him. He had me pinned to the mat in one of those wrestling moves. With my back digging into the floor, he gripped my neck and upper arm and locked it under his left armpit, cutting off my airway. I kicked my right leg up, then my left, rocking back and forth on my lower spine. Once I had momentum, I somersaulted backward, and Sam's body came loose. I landed on my knees, gasping for breath. "What the heck?"

"What's all the commotion in here?" Kate asked, peeking her head through the door.

"Nothing. Just a brother and sister squabble." I

stood.

Sam rose, turned his back to me, and picked up his shirt.

"Are you going to be okay?" I asked as I straightened my shirt and sweatpants.

He cast me a look over his shoulder. "I'll see you upstairs. Now, go before Pops sends out the troops."

I tapped my heart twice and walked out.

That whole hour had been quite bizarre. I was stunned I could even throw a punch but wasn't surprised that I didn't have strength to match Sam's. I was going to have to work hard if I wanted to learn how to fight. Sam's odd behavior around girls concerned and puzzled me. His actions toward Olivia were unlike him—at least unlike the boy I knew. Then there was Kate. Sam's whole personality instantly changed when she walked in the room. I had never seen him so timid before—ever.

Sam didn't fluster easily. The only thing my brother knew was anger, usually resulting in a fistfight with some bully or boy who came too close to me. Never had he been intimidated by anyone. Maybe girls were the answer to curing him of his anger. Maybe our old principal, Mr. Jackson, had had it all wrong. Sam didn't need an anger-management class. It seemed he needed a female challenge.

10

I trudged through the basement of the SEAL compound. The space housed many rooms, ranging from the weapons room, which was completely off-limits and barricaded from everyone except those with a high security clearance, to different types of training rooms. It was nothing like the sort of basement I was accustomed to with dirt, darkness, and creepy crawlies—it reminded me of all the other floors in the main building, bright, clean, and sterile. The tile floor had a sheen to it that almost blinded my sensitive eyes as I made my way through the hall to the exit.

My father wanted to see me. God only knew why. But he didn't figure in my thoughts as much as Sam's behavior.

"Jo, slow down," Kate said, tapping me on the shoulder.

I was so deep in thought that I had forgotten she was escorting me.

I stopped. "Huh?"

"You're in another world. You okay?" she asked.

"Sorry. I was thinking about my brother." I raised my gaze to meet hers.

"He'll be fine. He's a big boy." She looked away as if hiding something.

"Do you want to tell me something?"

"Like what?" Her gaze was glued to the wall.

"Like why I found your phone in the stairwell when the Plutariums escaped? And what my brother has to do with it?" I studied her body language, searching for some sign she was concealing something.

She inclined her head to one side. The air suddenly grew thick and almost soup-like. I sensed a change in her chemistry. Her cheeks reddened as if embarrassed.

"Did Webb tell you that?" Her voice rose, echoing in the hall.

I raised my brows. "Webb didn't tell me a thing. What was he supposed to tell me?"

She didn't know her brother didn't talk to me just for the sake of it. Not Webb. That wasn't his style.

She fidgeted, playing with her belt. "You can't read minds, can you?"

Irritation unfurled inside me. "What would I find if I did?" I didn't know Kate that well. She seemed to care about her brother. But at times, she gave off mixed messages about her feelings toward him. One minute, she ragged on him for his militaristic attitude, and in the next, she praised him for his decision to save her life. Webb had turned vampire to save her, much as I had for Sam. Still, a disconnect sizzled between her and Webb. One I couldn't quite figure out.

"You're getting upset. Don't. Sam and I had a little run-in that night. When the sirens went off, I dropped my phone on my way into the building. I didn't realize it until later," she explained.

"What kind of run-in?" I crossed my arms over my chest.

The stairwell door opened, and Tripp and Sloan emerged.

"Jo, there you are. Your father is waiting," Sloan said.

"Why didn't you escort her up?" Tripp asked, glaring at Kate. "Never mind. Webb needs you in the control room. Is Sam still in the training room?"

"Yeah," I replied.

Kate was definitely hiding something. I

couldn't put my finger on it, but she gave me a strange vibe. Whether she was going to tell me or not, I was going to get to the bottom of it.

"Let's get you upstairs, Jo. The last thing I want is to incur your father's wrath," Sloan said.

I walked through the doorway with Sloan in tow. I climbed the stairs to the first floor then kept going, thinking of Kate and Sam. I'd made it to the third level and placed my hand on the door when Sloan grabbed my arm.

"Wait."

"What?" I asked, turning, practically snapping my jaws at him.

"We have some unfinished business. I haven't seen you since you almost crippled me."

"Oh, yeah. That." I bit my bottom lip.

"Well?" he asked.

I liked Sloan. He was a little more open with me and talkative, unlike Webb, who hardly carried on a conversation with anyone. And Tripp was affable but getting him to talk was like trying to pull a hungry vampire off a human. Sloan had been patient with me. He didn't deserve my crankiness. I imagined my father gave him enough discord, especially since he was my bodyguard. Babysitting the boss's daughter had to have been a pain in the ass.

I wrinkled my nose. "I'm sorry I kicked you in the crotch."

"Don't ever do that again. I'm not your enemy. Now, get rid of the attitude before you go in to see your father. I don't know what happened between you and Kate, but you're dripping with anger. Between you and your father, I can feel another tornado brewing."

I raised an eyebrow. "Why? What's going on?"

"Your father is just irritated about an incident. He snapped at me before I came down to get you. It's just a warning. Take it or leave it."

I hadn't seen much of Dad in the past two days. He and the Sentinels had been even busier trying to gain more intel on the Plutariums since two of his undercover vamps had spotted Jonah and Fernando at a medical supply store near the state line. I wasn't even sure Dad had slept. I knew he wasn't anywhere in the apartment when I awoke in the mornings. Ever since the Plutariums got out, I had a habit of opening up my senses as I woke, checking for two heartbeats, his and Sam's.

"It's not you. Take the worried look off your face."

I let out a breath. A reprieve for a day. It wasn't me. I pulled open the door and walked through. A blast of warm air, a vast difference from the cold basement, brushed my face as I turned right and headed down the hall.

The third floor of the main building was split into two sections with the enlisted barracks and the mess hall taking up one half and offices for all the naval bigwigs comprising the other half. The only officer who didn't have an office on the third floor was Webb. His office was on the second, next to the war room and the command center. He said it was necessary to be close to both, just in case of an emergency.

Since my father was the big bad vampire in charge of the entire base, he had a corner office on the third floor. I had yet to step foot in it and only knew its general location in the event I needed to find him.

I stopped outside his closed door and slid down the wall, parking my butt on the floor. I was drained from all the physical training and really just wanted to go up to my bedroom to shower and sleep.

Voices trickled through the steel door. I concentrated to see if I could hear the conversation and gauge my father's mood. It wasn't that I didn't believe Sloan, but what he considered a bad mood, I might not have. After all, I was learning my father was one moody vampire. Then again, I could set him off more easily than any of his soldiers. I propped my head against the wall and closed my eyes.

"Young man, you fucked up," Dad said, the tenor of his voice rising.

"But, sir, it wasn't…"

"No, buts. This is life or death we're dealing with. Screw up again, and I'll put you on desk duty. Understood?"

My eyelids flew open. Dad actually swore, even after all those times he had reprimanded Sam and me for our language. I had to file the moment away for a rainy day.

Slowpoke Sloan finally joined me. He raised his eyebrows and shrugged as if trying to tell me he told me so. He rapped his knuckles against the door.

Suddenly, pain pierced my forehead then my ears. I grabbed the sides of my head and squeezed my eyes shut.

"Hey, what is it?" Sloan asked, pulling me up off the floor.

I blinked a few times as the blackness closed in, and the pain compressed my temples. It was as if someone had placed my skull inside a trash compactor. After a few seconds, Dad's voice burst through the darkness.

I'll be just a minute.

I winced as the pain spread to the back of my

head. I couldn't catch a break. First, he was reading my mind. Now, he was talking in my head.

"Are you all right?" Sloan asked again.

"My father's voice." I kept my hands glued to my skull, waiting for the pain to go away.

"He's in your head, isn't he?"

I nodded, rubbing my temples.

"Odd feeling, huh? It gets easier. The pain won't grab you so much after a while."

Ooh, lucky me. I hate this life.

Easy, young lady.

Really, Dad? Get out of my head.

Silence.

The door to his office opened, and a young vampire walked out. Blond hair and moss-green eyes met my gaze as he nodded. *Cute.* I moved to the side to let him pass, while Sloan moved to the other side. I twisted my mouth, and Sloan just shrugged one shoulder.

"What happened?" I asked.

"He screwed up on a job," he whispered.

I didn't think he wanted my father to hear him, low as his voice was.

"Jo," my father called out loud.

Sloan nodded for me to go in. "I'll be right outside," he said as if I was going to need his help.

I walked in and squinted from the bright light shining through the windows. My father's office looked to be half the size of the apartment. He had a couch, two chairs, and three tables that made up a sitting area. Nothing fancy. The furniture didn't look comfortable at all. A large steel desk sat in front of three medium-sized windows, which banked one of the longest walls in the room. Bookcases stretched along the far wall, and a door was framed in the corner. I couldn't make out whether it was a closet or a bathroom.

Dad sat behind his desk, closing a folder. "Have a seat."

His voice had an irascible edge to it. Maybe it was just the remnants of his outrage with his soldier. If not, the consequences for either him or me wouldn't be good. I slid into one of two wooden armchairs in front of his desk.

He looked up. "Christ, what happened?"

"Is my eye still black? I wasn't sure how fast I would heal on my way here. It was yellowish-blue when I left."

"It's yellow, and you've got blood all over your nose."

I wiped my nose again with my fingers. I still had a small amount of dried blood crusted underneath.

He rose from his chair, tucked in his shirt, and adjusted the belt on his khaki uniform. I couldn't help but stare at all the military ribbons pinned to his upper left chest, above a pocket. He had several of them, all with different colors and patterns. I had no idea what they were for, but it was the first time I had seen my father in a full military uniform. Normally, the Sentinels wore their cargo pants and a T-shirt.

He stepped around his desk. "Let me see. Tilt your head back."

I did as he ordered, keeping my gaze focused on his ribbons while he surveyed the damage. "You can thank Sam for the nose," I said. "He cracked it earlier."

"It looks like it hasn't set right. Don't move."

He pinched the bridge of my nose and squeezed tightly, moving it back and forth. The bones cracked once more, and again my eyes watered. *Damn it.*

"That's better," he said as he leaned against the desk. "Did you learn anything with Olivia?"

"You called me up here to chat?" Boy, that would have been a first. I rubbed my nose. The pain slowly dissipated as the bones fused back together.

His desk phone beeped. "Commander," a sweet female voice said.

"Yes, Ruth?"

I recognized her voice. It was the blond receptionist who sat behind the circular desk at the main entrance. Sloan had been flirting with her the other day.

"Your guests are here."

"I'll be a few minutes. I'll let you know when I'm ready."

"Yes, sir."

My father leaned over and hit a button on the phone then resumed his position.

"I got a call from Hollings yesterday." He gazed down at me. His lips tightened into a thin line. Then he bit his bottom lip, let go, and continued. "He got a call from a government official within the human government. It appears the Jackson boy's father has some friends in high places. He's worried about you and Sam. He hasn't seen you two since you left school with Lieutenant London and his team. And since we kept Ben here for a few days, it seems Mr. Jackson has been curious about us."

"Is Ben okay?" The sheer mention of his name sent sparks flying through my veins.

He nodded. "Ben is fine. I've invited Mr. Jackson to take a tour of our facility to dispel any suspicions he may have. And Hollings feels we should allow you and Sam to see Ben. This will also extinguish some of Mr. Jackson's concerns about your well-being. Of course, I don't agree with any of this."

"Really? I can see Ben?" I wanted to jump out of my chair and scream for joy.

"Did you hear what I just said?"

I drew my eyebrows together.

"I said, I don't like it. Not one bit." He glared at me.

"You don't like it. I get it. So why are you telling me any of this, then?"

It was all I could do not to strangle my father, who seemed to be trying to torture me.

"Jo, this is a serious situation you haven't thought through. There are many things about the human-and-vampire relationship that don't mesh well. And I have many more concerns about this now that Mr. Jackson has gotten the attention of government officials. Humans aren't prepared to know we exist. Sure, we have some humans within the government who work with us. There aren't many, though. And we have control over those humans. The elders within our vampire government are getting nervous. So, while you think I might be the worst dad in the world, I'm laying down demands to protect our species and to protect you as well as the Jackson boy. Having feelings for a human, when you're a young vampire, can be deadly. I don't use the last word lightly. Do you understand what I'm telling you?"

I dropped my gaze.

He leaned down and raised my chin. "I need an answer."

I met his eyes and swallowed. "As a human, I struggled with my identity and where my life was headed. Now that I'm a vampire, life has only gotten more complicated. I'm not aware of everything about vampires or all the government stuff you talk about. I'm just a teenager trying to find my way in life. And why do you keep saying I have feelings for Ben? He's just a friend."

"You're telling me you don't have feelings for the boy?"

I couldn't believe I was having a conversation with my dad about boys. I let out a deep breath. "I've never had a boyfriend. So how would I know?"

My father scratched his head. "This is one of those times I really miss your mother."

"Don't worry. I'm not going to ask you about the birds and the bees. Way too awkward."

"Look, Jo." His tone was calm now. "You'll meet with Ben under my supervision. However, after this one meeting, you're not allowed any contact with him, either on the phone or in person. You need to do everything in your power to put distance between you and him and forget the young man, whether you have feelings for him or not. His father has made too many inquiries. I'm extremely nervous. We have too much going on right now with the Plutariums for me to worry about any other issue."

"I can't see Ben after this one meeting? Like, ever?" I held my breath. He had to be insane.

A barren expression etched on his face. "That's correct." He didn't look mad or concerned and wasn't emitting any of his power surges that followed a state of rage. It was almost as if he had locked down his emotions.

"You really are a mean dad." The words tumbled off my tongue.

"I still want an answer," he said, ignoring my comment.

"Does it matter what my answer is?"

I didn't agree with him. I didn't know what I agreed with anymore. I did want a normal life, to be an ordinary kid in a normal family who had normal friends, but I was living in a different world where I was a stranger myself. My brain seemed human, the way I thought, my feelings, my beliefs were all still as if I had my humanity intact, but maybe all of that would change and my father would make me into something he wanted me to be. I didn't know the answers. I might have been giving up one fight, but I wasn't giving up the battle.

"It would be nice to hear that you agree.

Clearly, you don't, which just makes the stakes that much higher."

"Huh? You're reading my mind."

He gnawed the inside of his cheek, the first sign of his patience waning. "It's kind of hard not to. Let's move on. Mr. Jackson and his son are downstairs, waiting to come up. This is your only meeting."

"He's here now? Seriously?" I started tapping my foot. I hadn't even thought about what I would say to Ben, and Dad had just soured my mood. "Why now?"

"This was the only time he had. Mr. Jackson said Ben's been busy with baseball. They've made the regional finals, and he's getting ready to go out on the road for the next week. Plus, I don't have time for all this. We have a war brewing."

"Can I at least talk with him first without Sam in the room?" I didn't want Sam around. I didn't want anyone around. Sam would probably dominate the conversation. After all, Ben was his best friend, and they had a lot of catching up to do.

Dad nodded. "I will be here, though."

A girl's worst nightmare. Suddenly, nerves took over. *Does Ben even want to see me? What will I say with my father watching us?* All that time, I had been longing to see him, but now that the time was here, I wasn't so sure. My physical state was in question. I'd just gone a few rounds with my brother. It wasn't the look a girl strives for: loose sweatpants, blood on my shirt, a just-fixed cracked nose, and hair as disheveled as if I had walked out of a hurricane. Not to mention the sweat leaking from me. I didn't have to smell my underarms to know I stank like a wet dog.

"You smell fine," my father said.

"Okay. Some ground rules. I can't have you in my head while I talk to him, Dad. I just can't. Are you sure you want to stay while I talk with Ben?"

"I don't like it any more than you. The last thing I want to do is listen to my daughter talk with a boy. It's bad enough I can read your thoughts." He pushed off of the desk, went around to his chair, and grabbed his cell phone. He punched a few buttons. "Lieutenant, I need you in my office," he said.

"Why did you call Webb up here? He's not staying in the room with us, is he?"

My father holstered the phone to his belt.

"While you and Sam are talking with Ben, I need two people to take Mr. Jackson on a tour, and I need one other person in here as backup."

Just fantastic. I had to talk to a human boy I might like in front of a vampire boy I might like. I honestly couldn't catch a break. "Do you seriously think I'm going to attack Ben and drain all his blood?"

"I've seen it done before, sweetie. It's not a pretty sight."

I wasn't even going to ask. I was already a basket case. I didn't need to know about my father witnessing a crazed vampire draining some human, although the memory of my brother attacking Ben did come to mind. I rose from the chair to get the blood circulating through my legs. I paced the length of his office, thinking hard about what I would say. I stopped in my tracks then walked over to the door in the corner and peeked in. I let out a sigh. It was a bathroom. *Thank the Lord.*

Without hesitation, I barricaded myself in and stuck my head in the sink, letting the cold water run all over my face. After a minute or two, I patted my face then examined myself in the mirror. My eye had a hint of yellow, but my nose looked straight. I pulled out the band in my hair, combed my fingers through it, then twisted it into a bun before securing it with the band.

I drew in a breath, relieved that I looked halfway decent. My stomach lurched. Piranhas and butterflies vied for attention inside me. I splashed on more water, breathing in and out slowly. I wiped my face again.

A soft knock on the door made me jump.

"Are you coming out of there?" Dad asked.

"Is he here?" I sniffed the air.

"No."

He was right. I didn't smell any humans yet. I opened the door to find Dad standing there, holding a stainless-steel container.

"Much better," he said. "Here, drink this."

"I'm not hungry."

"I don't care if you're not. Drink it. It'll take the edge off."

I took the container as Webb's woodsy scent drifted in, tickling my nose. Then his voice filled the hallway.

I drank a few swigs then decided to down the whole thing. I hadn't realized how thirsty I was. When I finished, I handed the bottle back to my dad and wiped my mouth with my hand. At that moment, Webb walked through the doorway, dressed in his standard black cargo pants and black T-shirt that clung to his well-toned chest.

The day just kept getting better and better. I looked like hell, I smelled like swine, and my nerves were about to explode. I didn't think I could do it. Dad, Webb, and Ben all in the same room with me. Watching me. Listening to me. These guys were insane. No way would I be able to say one word. I had to focus, to tune out at least Webb.

While I might have been a bit embarrassed with Dad there, it was going to be worse with Webb in the room. *Focus, focus.*

Dad looked at Webb before sweeping his gaze over me as confusion set in. "Is there something you want to tell me?" Dad grabbed my arm.

I scrunched up my nose. "No."

"Sir?" Webb's voice diverted Dad's attention away from me.

"One moment, Lieutenant," he said, letting go of my arm. "Young lady?"

"Let it go, Dad. If you're going to read every thought of mine, then I suggest you take a few valiums. I'm a teenager. Get used to it."

He shook his head and walked over to his desk.

I silently laughed as I recalled the last of my thoughts about Webb and wondered whether that was what Dad was reacting to.

"Lieutenant London, as you know, Sam and Jo will spend some time talking with Ben Jackson today. He and his dad are waiting in the lobby. I need you to select two Sentinels to give Mr. Jackson a quick tour of the grounds."

"Sure, Commander. I'll have Olivia and Sloan give the tour. Olivia is down in the lobby with them right now. Do you need me to stay? The Jackson boy can be rather excitable. It took two of us to restrain him at one point when he got out of control with me."

Please say no. Please say no.

"I'll need someone here with me, so, yes," my father replied.

I was so screwed.

My father pushed a button on his desk phone. "Ruth, have Olivia escort them up, please."

"Yes, Commander. Will do."

My father hit the off button then looked at me. "I don't want you to get upset," he said. "The last thing we need is for Ben to see your new powers."

I wasn't promising him anything. I couldn't even promise myself I wouldn't get upset. I had no idea how I was going to react to any of it.

Voices sounded as soon as they exited the elevator. Mr. Jackson was telling Olivia how she looked just like one of his students at school. My heartbeat ramped up slowly. Anticipation was a bitch. Their footsteps grew louder, and so did the beat of my heart.

My eyes flashed to vampire violet.

Webb snapped his head, glaring at me. "Commander, this isn't a good idea."

"I'm not comfortable with it either. Let's stay alert."

They both sounded like they were getting ready for battle and their enemy was close. Dad leaned against his desk. Webb had taken a stance behind one of the wooden armchairs, Sloan stood at the door, and I settled on the edge of the other wooden armchair, my knees shaking.

A plenitude of power filled the room as Webb continued to stare at me. His deep-blue eyes swirled in a mad storm, turning, shifting, flickering, and finally settling into deep, dark shades of black with specks of what looked to be red flames inside.

"Both of you, get yourselves under control, please. Lose the vampire eyes," my father commanded.

Webb tore away his gaze. I dropped mine, taking in a few deep breaths to quell my nerves. Olivia poked in her head, and my father nodded. She came in, followed by Mr. Jackson then Ben.

As soon as Ben walked through the door, his heady masculine fragrance of burned sugar with a hint of spice trepidation just about knocked me out. I could almost taste his fear, his hesitation. He peered at me through lowered lashes. His brandy-colored eyes glistened as he smiled, highlighting his come-to-me dimples. His hair was crazy messy, the ends curling at the edges. He wore a short-sleeved Black Sox T-shirt that showed his muscular arms.

"Hey, Jo," he said.

"Hi," was all I managed to get out before Webb's touch distracted me.

I broke my gaze from Ben and cocked an eyebrow at Webb. He moved his head back and forth ever so slightly as if to tell me something or distract me.

"Mr. Jackson, welcome. We've spoken a few times on the phone. I'm Steven Mason, the twins' father."

Mr. Jackson extended his hand. The two men exchanged a handshake.

"Nice to finally meet you. I want to thank you for allowing Ben to spend some time on campus here. While I didn't particularly agree with the timing of it, he got a sense of what the SEALs are all about. He's been dreaming of becoming a Navy SEAL since he was a little boy. Hopefully, he's learned a thing or two," Mr. Jackson explained.

Yeah, he had no idea what Ben had learned when he was here. If he did, he would have run like hell.

Then Mr. Jackson looked at me. "Jo, how are you? Are you doing okay?"

I swallowed. Mr. Jackson looked the same, not that I was expecting him to look any different. He still had the goatee he had grown during spring break. His coiffed brown hair was styled neatly atop his head, and he wore a black suit, sans tie, with his white shirt unbuttoned at the neckline. He must've come straight from school. He, too, gave off a hint of fear, although he looked more relaxed than Ben.

"I am. I just got through working out. Sorry for the appearance." It was the truth at least.

"Where's Sam?" Mr. Jackson asked, looking around.

"Sam will be up in a minute. He's finishing a class. We've been kind of homeschooling Jo and Sam," my father replied.

Yikes. Dad was telling a white lie.

"Mr. Jackson, if you don't mind, Olivia and Sloan will give you a tour of the grounds while the kids here get reacquainted. We can meet back in the officers' lounge later."

"Ben, is that okay?" Mr. Jackson asked. A little excitement tinged his voice.

"Yeah. I'll be fine." Ben's voice was silky and deep. It sounded different than what I remembered.

My heart sped, my hands became clammy, and my head throbbed. Suddenly, I wanted to crawl into a corner and hide.

Mr. Jackson left with Olivia and Sloan.

"Ben, don't be afraid. Have a seat." My father waved his hand toward the wooden armchairs as he closed the door.

Ben moved deeper into the office, nearing the chairs, getting closer to me.

Webb took his place near the door, taking his place beside my father.

I pushed off the chair and made my way over to the windows. I couldn't be close to him. Not just because Daddy dearest would get nervous, but because Ben's scent was driving me crazy. The sun's rays warmed my arms as I gazed out into the courtyard. The lawn looked pristine, as if it had just been mowed, with diagonal lines cutting in opposite directions. I kept breathing—barely. I searched for some object in the distance to center myself. It had always worked in public speaking class. This wasn't public speaking, though. This was a conversation between a boy and girl. My erratic heart rhythm was having a good old time inside of me.

I found two squirrels chasing each other near a large oak tree at the far end of the courtyard. One went up a tree while the other waited at the bottom as if he knew his partner was going to crawl back down.

Christ! What am I going to say to Ben? All I could think about were squirrels. There were a lot of them on base. *Get a grip.*

I'd wanted this day to happen—like, forever. All of sudden, I wasn't the same person I had been a month ago. Heck, I wasn't even the same species. My new world wasn't Ben's world.

As much as it pained me to think about my lost humanity, I couldn't turn back the clock. I hoped Ben could accept me for what I'd become. My throat tightened and suddenly burned at the sound of his breathing. Tears stung the back of my lids. I blew out a breath, trying to clear my mind. Then I blinked a few times, hoping the tears didn't spill. *I can do this.*

"Are you okay?" Ben asked in a whisper.

I swallowed and turned around. "Hi again," I managed to squeak out in a voice I didn't recognize.

His eyes widened, and he took one step forward. Out of the corner of my eye, I glimpsed Webb take two steps then stop. Ben rested his hand on the back of the wooden armchair in front of my father's large steel desk. *Thank the Lord for furniture.*

"What happened to you?" Ben asked.

I raised my hand to my right eye. "Oh, Sam and I got into a small fight."

"A fight? Are you okay?" He raised both eyebrows in concern.

"Yeah. You should see Sam." I smiled.

"You hit Sam? And he let you?" He laughed. "How is he?"

I didn't want to talk about Sam or my eye. "He's good." I swallowed hard. "What about you? How have you been?" I asked, not taking my eyes off him.

"Good. I've been playing a lot of baseball." His eyes were soft as he held my gaze. "We made the regionals."

The small talk was definitely awkward with Dad and Webb in the room.

"So why were you here the other day?" My voice was still a little shaky.

"Well, Dr. Vieira wanted to see me. I thought I would've had a chance to talk to you and Sam that day too. But Dr. Vieira said you guys were busy."

I was so enthralled with his looks and what I was going to say that I totally forgot about the injuries Sam and the Plutariums had given him, probably because his scent erased some of my short-term memory. My gaze traveled down, resting on the smooth, tanned skin around his neck. His artery bulged, his pulse beating rapidly. I licked my lips. My fangs jumped out of my gums. *Breathe.* I swallowed hard again, mashing my lips together so my fangs wouldn't show.

"The mark's gone now," Ben said, noticing my stare and placing his hand over his neck where he was bitten.

Whew! Thanks for covering it. I'd have hated to

have been the one to ruin the smooth skin Dr. Vieira worked so hard to heal. Ben had been through enough with the Plutariums trying to mutilate him then Sam trying to suck him dry. He didn't need me following in Sam's footsteps. But the sound of his heartbeat was pulling me toward him. Every brain cell screamed at me to jump over the desk and claim my prize. *Get a flippin' grip!*

When he dropped his hand and exposed his carotid once again, I shook my head a few times. The movement seemed to help. For a split second, the angel within stilled me.

"Jo?" Ben said.

"I'm sorry. I didn't mean to stare."

"Do they have to watch us?" he asked, nodding at Webb and Dad.

I looked at the duo, both standing with their hands cupped together in front of them, staring straight ahead. I almost laughed at the sight of Dad chewing the inside of his cheek. He looked as if he was trying extremely hard not to look at me or even fidget. I had a strong feeling the whole scene was bugging him. Plus, if Dad was reading my mind, he was well aware of the war that raged inside me. I had a sneaky suspicion he was letting me suffer to see how strong I was.

"I'm afraid so." I returned my gaze to Ben. "I

distracted you earlier. Were you going to say something else?"

He ran his fingers through his hair. "I thought..." He shoved his hands in his jeans pockets and shifted his stance. "While I was here... well... that... maybe... um... the May dance at school is..." He looked past me.

My blood froze. His heart raced like a thoroughbred sprinting to the finish line. *Is he trying to ask me out?* I blinked a few times, hoping my eyes wouldn't shift. Although Ben had seen that before, he had yet to see them turn violet, and I wasn't ready for him to see that change. It would only open up a boatload of questions I wasn't prepared to answer, and I was certain Dad wouldn't be enamored with explaining it either.

"Would you like to go with me?" Ben asked finally, his eyes locking with mine. "It's this weekend."

My joints locked in place, and I stopped breathing. I'd never been asked out by a boy, *ever*. I didn't know what to say. My eyes began to burn. The tears were getting ready to spill. *Oh God. I can't cry.* I didn't dare look at Dad or Webb.

Ben's pulse was surging to astronomical levels. I could sense his anxiety, his butterflies. His scent grew stronger as his heart thudded, echoing in my ears. I wanted to run to him—but only because the predator inside me willed me to attack. I wanted to taste his blood so desperately that a fire ignited in the back of my throat.

My devil friend decided to make an appearance. *You want him, Jo. Go to him. Taste the sweetness of his blood, his fear.*

I couldn't give in. I just couldn't. It would confirm the animal inside me, and I couldn't handle that. I couldn't allow my father to be right. I closed my eyes, taking in a deep breath, counting to ten, willing my fangs to retract. I opened my lids, and a tear escaped. *Damn it!*

"Jo?" Ben whispered.

"She can't," Webb said in a caustic tone.

Ben kept his focus on me. "I know it's short notice, but..."

He completely ignored Webb. Ben and Webb had a tense relationship, similar to the one Sam had with him. Ben had gotten into several arguments with Webb before I made the change, even to the point where Webb almost took off his head. As nervous as Ben was in that moment, he stayed true to who he was, refusing to let a powerful vampire like Webb change what he'd come to do.

I shot daggers at Webb for answering for me. Before I could say or do anything, pain shot through my head. I grabbed both temples and bent forward. Suddenly, Dad's voice broke through.

Remember our conversation. My demands. You need to end it now.

Bloody hell! Get out of my head, Dad.

"What's wrong?" Ben's scent grew stronger and his voice louder.

Please don't be near me. I didn't trust myself.

Take your shot now, said the devil in me. *You know you want to. Taste his blood.*

I grabbed my ears and fell to my knees. I wanted to kill the bloody devil inside me then my father.

A hand touched my back. "Jo?" Ben said.

I didn't move. I couldn't. If I did, I would attack him, just like Sam had.

A strong current of air whipped past me.

"Lieutenant," Dad called.

I couldn't look. My head hurt as if someone was beating me with a sledgehammer.

"Sweetie." Dad's hands grabbed mine. "Hey, I'm sorry. I forgot how painful it could be when I use telepathy on someone. Let's get you over to a chair."

"No. Where's Ben?"

"Hold on," Dad said, letting go of my hands. "Lieutenant, stand down."

I peered through my fingers and gasped. Webb

had Ben pinned to the desk with his hands around his throat. I jumped up. Ben's face was tomato red. It looked like he couldn't breathe.

Dad struggled to peel Webb off Ben. "Take Jo out into the hall for a minute."

Webb stumbled backward and froze. His eyes were full of rage and as black as a starless night sky.

"Ben was just making sure I was okay. Are you an idiot?" I bristled. The vampire was certifiable.

My heart went out to Ben. Dad helped him over to the couch, where he sat and rubbed his neck.

"I said to take Jo out into the hall, Lieutenant. *Now!*" Dad commanded.

Webb pushed me out into the hall.

Cold air rushed over me, and a shiver crawled up my spine as I wondered what was going on. The only terrible thing about it all was Webb being there. Dad never should've allowed him in the room.

"And you were worried about *me*." I stalked up to him and pushed him against the wall. "You're an asshole."

"Not now," he snapped, grabbing my wrists.

"Lieutenant, have Tripp bring Sam down," Dad instructed from the doorway. "Sweetie, you can come back in."

Terse seconds passed before Webb conceded to Dad's command, let go of my wrists, then took out his phone.

On my way back into the office, I flicked a murderous look Webb's way. Sadly, though, it was wasted since he had his back to me.

Ben's fear hit me, erasing any irritation I had at what Webb had done.

"I'm sorry, Ben," I said.

He raised his head. "No worries. I know he was protecting you." He nodded toward the door. "Are you all right, though?"

I nodded. "I'm fine. I get these headaches sometimes. They're painful. They happen instantly with no warning," I explained, glowering at my dad.

"Son, you're sure you're fine?" Dad asked.

"Yes, sir."

Dad leaned in and whispered, "End this now."

Webb came in. "They're on their way down."

"Ben, I have to go. I promised my dad... anyway, Sam will be here in a minute."

"Jo?" The softness in his voice brought tears to my eyes again. "The dance?"

My father groaned.

"I'm sorry... I... can't," I replied.

Ben slouched on the couch as if I'd just deflated a balloon. He peered at me through lowered eyelids. His eyes ached with a soul-deep sadness that shattered my heart, and I looked away.

Sam sauntered in, followed by Tripp.

"Ben, dude. What's up?" Sam's voice leaked with excitement.

As Ben rose from the couch, Dad planted himself between them.

"I'm fine, Pops."

Dad studied Sam for a second before stepping aside.

The two best friends did some type of fist bump while my father inched his way closer, just in case Sam's bloodlust wasn't under control.

"So, tell me all about baseball. How's the team? Is Mr. Asshole still being an ass?" Sam rattled off, sitting in one of the lone leather chairs.

"Jack Powell has been okay. He's changed a bit since you've been gone," Ben said, sitting back down on the sofa. "Wow. Look at you. You really have changed. You're like bigger, more muscles. Dude, we could use you on the team."

Ben didn't seem frightened, even though my brother was one of the vampires who'd attacked him before. It was amazing how Ben's demeanor changed with Sam. With the two of them talking sports, I didn't need to be there anymore. I didn't have anything else to say to Ben. Plus, his presence, his emotions, and his scent still overwhelmed me. I needed to get out of there.

I slipped into the hall. I couldn't believe he'd asked me out. I had never once been to a high school dance. Darcy wanted me to go this year with Jack Powell, the pitcher of the high school baseball team who Sam and Ben had just mentioned. I didn't know him, and he probably didn't know me. It didn't matter anymore, though. I was beginning to believe humans weren't in my future, and that just downright sucked.

"Jo." Dad followed me out. "Where're you going?"

"Upstairs. I'm tired."

No lie in my answer. Exhaustion weighed me down. My body had been pummeled a few times. My nose had been broken, and my emotions were wreaking havoc inside me. Aside from that, I just wanted to be alone.

"Lieutenant."

"No problem, Commander. I'll take her up," Webb said.

Great, another moody vampire. I didn't have to handle my father, but I still had to deal with Webb.

"You have a key, right?" Dad asked, looking at me.

"No. I didn't take it with me to the training room," I replied.

"I'll use mine," Webb said.

I ran up to the fourth floor, leaving Webb a good distance behind me. Then I leaned against the wall, waiting for the Sentinel. I closed my eyes and replayed the exchange between Ben and me. His muscular frame, his silky voice, and those dimples had melted me all over again. I let out a breath. Shock still rippled through me as I thought about Ben's nervousness and how he'd stuttered to get out the words to ask me to the dance—and in front of my dad, no less. And the image of sinking my fangs into him hit me like a category-five hurricane.

Maybe Dad was right. Maybe humans and vampires shouldn't mix, but maybe not all humans were as mouthwatering as Ben. I thought back to Highland Memorial, when I went looking for my dad and ended up inside a blood lab run by humans. The scents there were certainly enticing— sweet and heavenly. But while Ben's burned-sugar scent also made my gums ache, it was different. It set off other feelings inside me, feelings I couldn't quite figure out.

Webb's footsteps pulled me out of my stupor. I opened my eyes to see him striding down the hall.

His long, crescent-moon lashes framed cobalt eyes that glistened every time he stepped under a hall light. He placed his hand in his pants pocket and withdrew a set of keys. Fingering through the clump of metal, he readied one in his left hand. He stopped, inserted the key into the deadbolt, and twisted. Before he could open the door, I pushed him out of the way and beelined for the bathroom. I wanted to barricade myself in and never come out.

I slammed the door behind me then locked it. I grabbed a small cup off the sink, filled it with cold water, and downed it. I took several more drinks then dropped the lid on the toilet and sat. My tear ducts opened, and the waterfall began. I couldn't stop crying.

"Jo." Webb knocked on the door. "Are you all right?"

"Go away." I grabbed several tissues and blew my nose.

"Can I come in?"

"I said, go away." I managed several breaths between sobs, trying to figure why he wanted to come in. It would have been funny if the irritating vampire wanted to talk or give me boy advice.

"Please, I want to make sure you're all right." His voice had a soft timbre to it.

Everyone was concerned about me, but it

wasn't like I was queen of the compound—far from it.

"Jo?" He pounded on the door.

"You're not going to leave me alone, are you?"

"Not until I make sure you're—"

I flipped the lock. The door swung open with an ominous creak. "See, I'm fine. Now go away." I blew my nose again.

He stepped into the small space, and I scooted backward, even though I wanted to lean into him, nestle in his embrace, and have him tell me everything would be okay. He took another step forward. The bewitching intensity of his soul-stealing blue eyes kept me from moving. I couldn't look away. He raised his hand and wiped away my tears with the pads of his thumbs.

Suddenly, my mouth became dry. He was close to me, touching me. I had no way to get around him. I closed my eyes. My face was hot. My nose was running like a waterfall, and I couldn't stop crying. I was a complete mess.

"There's no need to cry. Your father is doing what's best. Look at me," he whispered.

I couldn't pry my eyelids open. If I had, I would have crumpled even more. I was in the middle of an emotional breakdown. I wasn't about to bare my soul, let alone talk about Ben, with a vampire who made my insides twist with excitement. I was so thankful he couldn't read minds.

"Hey there." He lightly rubbed my scarred cheek with the back of his fingers. "Open. Let me see those stunning eyes."

My stomach did somersaults. More tears spilled. I couldn't wrap my mind around his words, his voice, his touch, and his scent. Confusion snaked through me. While his scent didn't make my throat burn the way Ben's had, it sure did a number on the butterflies having a field day inside me.

I opened my eyes slowly, blinking away tears, and met his gaze. He searched my face as if he was cataloguing every pore, every hair, and every facial detail. His gaze finally landed on my lips, and my pulse jumped.

Damn that vampire.

His presence radiated strength and power.

My hands started shaking. He had to have heard my heart racing and sense my anxiety—or maybe it was excitement. He had my mind in a jumbled mess, my arms covered in goose bumps.

He moved even closer, which I didn't think was possible.

I couldn't breathe. *Oh my God!*

He dragged the backs of his fingers over my

scar again. "You know, the man who did this to you will pay." His voice was soft, breathy.

I really didn't want to hear about my scar. It was the last thing on my mind and a horrific reminder of a night I never wanted to remember *ever* again.

"Breathe." He leaned in, and his hand disappeared behind me.

I stilled, my heart beating uncontrollably. *What is he doing?*

He grabbed the band out of my hair, and my freaky mane tumbled down, falling around my shoulders. He grabbed a few strands and placed them behind my ears. Darkness threatened the edges of my vision as his fingers tangled through my hair.

He lowered his head and whispered, "Life will get better. I promise."

Shock hit me at his promise and the notion that maybe one of his special powers was reading the future. I wanted to scream. I was standing in a small bathroom with an imposing creature who unnerved me, confused me, and made my pulse race with delight all at the same time. Maybe Sam was right, and there was fire between us.

I shivered, and Webb wrapped his arms around me and pulled me to him. His heartbeat pounded in my ear as my body melted into his. *This can't be happening.*

Silence gave way to footsteps. I tried to pull away, but he was strong and kept me nestled against him. It was as if he didn't want to let go.

The door to the apartment clicked, and I tried to pull away again. Webb wasn't moving. I stood in his embrace, listening to his racing heart.

"Jo?" Sam called. "Jo?" His voice grew louder.

"Webb." I slid my hands between us, rested them on his muscled abs, and tried to push him away. "You okay?"

His eyes vacillated between blue then black as if he was trying to get control of himself, his feelings.

"There you—what the heck is going on in here?" Sam asked.

I peered around Webb to see that Sam had a look of horror etched on his face. Webb kicked shut the door and locked it.

I leaned against the sink. "What're you doing? He's going to have a fit. Open the door!" I pleaded.

"Webb? Get away from my sister," Sam growled, banging against the door.

"We'll be out in a minute. I'm just talking with Jo," Webb replied.

"Like hell you are. You lay a finger on her, and I'll kill you," Sam said.

Webb leaned against the door. We stared at each other.

"Sis, are you all right?" Sam asked.

"I'm fine. I'll be out in a minute." I wasn't fine. My insides were in a complicated knot. I didn't know what was going on between Webb and me, what he wanted from me, or if he felt sorry for attacking Ben.

"If he touches—"

"Sam, chill. Webb and I are just talking," I replied. Okay, we weren't actually talking, but if I knew my brother...

A thump sounded, as if Sam had plopped his butt down outside the door.

"You better open the door," I said to Webb in a low voice. "My brother isn't going to let up until you get out of this bathroom."

"I know," he said as if he didn't care.

On the outside, Webb had always been the hardcore soldier. I had only seen him pissed once when Ben lashed out at him. Something in his behavior had me a little baffled. The steel shield that he erected around himself seemed to be thinning —maybe he was trying to open up to me. Maybe he cared. I immediately erased that thought. He was way out of my league—I was just a measly teenager who didn't know the first thing about the male species.

He pushed off from the door, and within two steps, he was standing close to me again. My damn heart was getting one hell of a workout. Between Ben and Webb, I was going to pass out from emotional exhaustion.

I looked into what seemed like a dark-blue ocean. "What do you want from me?" My voice quivered.

He raised a hand to my face. "I want to make sure you're okay. You've been through a lot and... I'm sorry. I know you like Ben. I didn't mean to... I really was trying to protect him. I could feel your bloodlust."

"Is... that... all?" I didn't believe him. Something else was going on. Webb had never acted like he cared, let alone spoken to me in a soft, husky tone.

He lightly rubbed his thumb over my bottom lip. "No." He breathed before his gaze dropped to my lips once again.

My pulse pounded louder than twelve drummers drumming. *Oh my! Is he going to kiss me? Please don't.* I had never been kissed by a boy, and while I was excited about him being so close to me and touching me, I was confused—no, I was dumbfounded.

A knock on the door shattered our connection. Webb raised one eyebrow as if our guest outside irritated him. In one move, he turned and opened the door. He fell backward, his body pinning me against the sink. Sam barreled in, throwing punch after punch, hitting Webb on one side of the face then the other.

"Stop it, Sam," I yelled, my voice piercing my own eardrums.

I tried to push Webb off me, but he swung out his arms, trying to shield me. He didn't move while Sam punched the crap out of him. Bones cracked, and blood sprayed in all directions.

"I mean it, Sam. I'll kill you if you don't stop," I cried.

I peeked around Webb, and Sam's fist hit me square in the nose. My head snapped back then forward. My eyes watered, and tears spilled. *Son of a bitch!*

Instantly, Webb made his move, grabbing Sam by the arms and pushing him out of the bathroom. They tussled like two wrestlers in a championship match. Webb elbowed Sam in the jaw. Sam returned the blow with one to Webb's stomach. Webb didn't even flinch.

I ran out of the bathroom, holding my nose, which was gushing blood, horrified by their exchange. Webb grabbed hold of his Sentinel sword. They were about to kill each other.

I gasped, ran to Webb, and grabbed his wrists with my free hand. "Don't! Webb, please stop it."

Webb let go of his sword and looked at me. "Damn. Let's get you into the bathroom," he said, ignoring Sam, who was about to throw another punch.

"What's going on here?" Dad asked, stalking toward us.

I hadn't heard the door to the apartment open. I looked past Sam, and Dad's face reddened. Webb pulled me into the bathroom, also ignoring my father.

"Sit down," Webb commanded, his deep, military voice returning. No more sultry and silky tone.

When it was over, I was going to kill my only brother.

11

After the brawl between Webb and Sam, I tried to make sense of what had happened between Webb and me in the bathroom, how he'd run his fingers over my lips, and the silkiness of his voice. I still couldn't make any sense of it.

I also tried to figure out how I'd felt after seeing Ben. He certainly looked good, but I was still confused. I'd struggled not to jump over the desk and suck the very life from him. Dad's constant reminder of how vampires shouldn't be friends with humans screamed in my head. I didn't want to think what could've happened if Webb and Dad hadn't been in the room when I was talking with Ben. It was clear that Ben hadn't understood that there was a predator lurking within me, clawing to get out. *God help me! What have I become?*

My head swam from all the emotions raging through me. Night after night, I tossed and turned, dreaming about Ben and Webb or other things I couldn't make sense of. An old man haunted my sleep, trying to tell me something. He spoke in gibberish. I was surprised that I remembered any of it when I woke up. It was as if my subconscious was melding into my conscious. Sometimes, I couldn't tell what was real and what was a dream.

After a week of avoiding me, Sam was finally brave enough to enter my room.

"Time to get out of this dungeon of yours," he said, stalking in. "You can't lie around for the rest of your immortal life, sis."

"Did you drink some brave juice?" I sneered. "Get out."

"You need to get your ass out of this dungeon. Olivia wants you down in the training room," he said. "You can take your frustrations out on me down there. It'll be good for you." His eyes were pleading.

Maybe he had a point. Using Sam as a punching bag sounded like a good idea. Plus, I was getting tired of being in the apartment. I wasn't going to figure out my boy problems in there, anyway.

Sam took three strides toward me and extended his hand. "Come on. It'll be fun."

I acquiesced.

He pulled me out of bed then hugged me. "I love you. Now, get dressed. I'll meet you downstairs." He started to walk away.

"Sam?"

He turned.

"Love you too."

He tapped his chest then closed the door on his way out.

I donned yoga pants and a T-shirt then met Sam in the training room.

Nickelback blared from the speakers as I entered. Olivia raised an eyebrow as she turned down the volume, clearly surprised at my sudden appearance.

"Glad you could join us, Jo," she said. "I hope you're ready to work." Forewarning tinged her tone.

I was screwed.

I barely had one foot on the mat, and she started barking out orders. Suddenly, I regretted my decision to join my brother.

With a deep sigh, I did every exercise as she instructed, whining and complaining only silently. The littlest outburst of complaint would have

Olivia in my face, or even worse, pushing me until I couldn't stand anymore.

The first few exercises were excruciatingly painful to every limb and muscle in my body. After five hours of jarring my arms and legs and subjecting my body to a hell where two hundred sit-ups, push-ups, and other torturous moves rendered me immobile, I wanted to crawl back into my so-called dungeon and not come out for a month.

But then, on about the fourth day, my adrenaline kicked in. Training with Sam helped to take my mind off of everything, at least during the day. He'd been right. The physical exertion helped tremendously. The routine became an outlet for me—a way to push aside all the crap swimming in my head. Another added benefit was my increased strength. My body grew stronger, my limbs were more flexible, and my muscles began to like the feeling of pain.

Equally surprising, I learned moves I didn't even know my body was capable of. With the help of Olivia, Sam and I also learned how to tune into our surroundings with our heightened vampire senses, learning what to look for when we walked into a room in a combat situation and how to assess everything in detail in a matter of seconds.

When I wasn't training, Dad allowed me to

spend time in the secret vampire library, where I researched vampire history and looked for any knowledge on secondary powers. I read as many books as I could, absorbing everything about my new species. Dad said I could trust the data in the library. All of it had been written by well-known people within the vampire community.

School loomed in the near future, giving me hives if I dwelled on it too much. I hated the idea of adjusting to a new school with new teachers, new kids, new friends, and new bullies. I had one thing going for me, though—I had a few fight moves under my belt and could stand up to any bully. I just prayed I wouldn't have to.

Aside from my anxiety over school, several questions raced through my mind: *Is a vampire school any different than a human high school? Do human teachers work at the school? Will the kids be nicer?* The uncertainties twisted my stomach into a million knots.

Before we could even attend school, we had one last meeting with the Council of Eternal Affairs to fit the last piece into the puzzle, which had me a little unnerved—they would inject a chip into my butt. I was far from thrilled about it, but Dad had his, and so did every vampire SEAL. That didn't make me feel much better, but Dad had said there were more important things to be concerned about. Plus, it was for our safety and protection. I didn't know if I agreed with him, but I had no way around it. If I wanted to be a free vampire, I had to get the chip, plain and simple. Probably one of the reasons my stomach was in an uproar when I should have been focused on training.

Like every day since I'd started training, Olivia was bellowing out commands. Sam and I were in the middle of practicing a new move, using a wooden pole to spar. Olivia explained the prop helped to build stamina and balance, and it was one way to get used to having a weapon in our hands. Just as Sam came forward and lifted his pole, I froze when the door to the training room creaked open. The pole hit me under my jaw, and my head flew back.

"What the heck, Jo? Pay attention." Olivia snapped her fingers. "This is exactly what I've been trying to teach you. You need to know your surroundings. You cannot let distractions break your concentration with an opponent. Now, go again."

It was easier said than done. I hadn't seen Webb since our quiet exchange in the bathroom, and there he was. I'd avoided him at all costs. Luck had been on my side. If he showed up at the apartment unannounced, I made a point to leave the room when he walked in. If I was in my room and

I heard his voice in the apartment, talking to Dad, I made sure I didn't come out. I still wracked my brain endlessly, trying to understand what happened in that bathroom between us. The quiet exchange we shared had me wanting to jump off the nearest cliff and into his arms at the same time.

The door closed with a thud, making me jump. It was the first time Webb had come to observe Sam and me. In fact, it was the first time Sam and I had an audience.

My brother stood in front of me with his hands on his pole and his gaze fixed on Webb. Then, in an instant, the air thickened. I held my breath. Even though several feet separated them, it didn't matter. The two males might not have been in a physical fight, but both were wielding their energy like two out-of-control electrical wires whipping back and forth. One electrical charge dared the other one to start a brawl. Maybe it wasn't power. Maybe it was just plain, raw testosterone, egos on display to see who would triumph as the alpha male.

Olivia's voice finally snapped the tension. "Lieutenant, is there a reason you're here this morning? If not, I'd appreciate it if you'd leave. Your presence has obviously rattled these two for some reason."

"Rattled" was the understatement of the century. From her last statement, it was clear she didn't know the tension that strangled Sam or me when Webb was around—of course, for different reasons. I lifted my gaze and peered at Webb. His expression was deadpan, and his eyes pierced a hole clear through to the other side of my back. My heart pounded furiously. Unlike in the apartment, where I had other rooms to hide in, there was no option in the training room. He blocked the only exit to freedom.

"Petty Officer Brock, I hear your request, but I'm not leaving. I'd like to see what you've accomplished with Jo and Sam." He sat in one of the chairs against the wall.

I blew out a breath. I broke my gaze with Webb and glanced at Sam. Several creases were stitched in his forehead, not to mention that the animosity dripping off him was about to choke me.

"Very well, then," Olivia replied, walking onto the mat. "Okay, you two. Concentrate. Jo, look at me." She snapped her fingers again.

I turned my head.

"You need to focus. Remember what I taught you about using your senses. If you freeze in a real altercation, you'll be hurt or end up dead. Now, both of you meet in the middle, poles in hand, and bow before you begin."

Of all the people who could have walked in, it

had to be him. I sucked in a breath and let out all the air in my lungs. Then I stepped to the middle of the mat. Sam was still going through his calming routine. Olivia had taught us about breathing and quieting our minds. It usually worked for me, but not today. Images of Webb holding me undulated with every intake of air and release of breath. His touch, his scent, and the way he made me weak at the knees cemented me to the mat. I wasn't sure I could move. I closed my eyes and shook my head a few times, hoping the images would disintegrate—and quickly. I opened my eyes slowly and focused on Sam. His hands were clasped around the pole in front of him, his eyes closed, and his nostrils flaring.

A haze settled around my brain while I waited. If he didn't hurry, I was going to lose it. I adjusted the pole in my hands and brought my feet together. Sam let out a long breath, opened his eyes, then took two steps and met me in the middle.

"Don't pay him any attention, sis." Sam's eyes were hard. The green luster had lost its shine, and his expression screamed of a predator ready to kill.

I was screwed. It was bad enough that I was nervous as hell with the irritating, drop-dead gorgeous vamp sitting on the chair watching us, but I also had to battle my brother, who had conjured up his predatory muse to spar with me just because his kryptonite sat a few feet away.

"Look who's talking? You sure you don't have daggers coming out of your eyes?" I asked in a whisper.

"Acknowledge your opponent," Olivia commanded. "We're wasting time."

Oh, this is going to be a riot. Not.

Sam and I bowed then stepped back. He adjusted his pole, and as he did, I made my move. I lunged with the weight on my right leg then twisted my upper torso to the left and stumbled, my pole grazing Sam's left arm.

"You're doing it all wrong," Olivia barked. "When you step with your right foot, your torso shifts right, not left, Jo."

As soon as I righted myself, Sam lunged forward. He twisted and turned his pole upward, hitting air as I bent backward in a move that any gymnast would have been proud of. I snapped back.

Sam stopped for a split second, his mouth hanging open. Yeah, I was just as shocked. He regrouped then lunged. That time, his pole clacked against mine. He charged. Then I charged, our poles connecting with each lunge. The last swipe of his pole connected with my shins. The pain stopped me in my tracks.

"Jo, you can't stop. Push through the pain. Move!" Olivia commanded sharply.

Easy for you to say. I bounced on the balls of my feet and caught a glimpse of Webb staring at me.

I barely registered a voice grunting when, out of the corner of my eye, I saw Sam's pole headed toward my head. Before I could move, a large body stood between Sam and me. I blinked a few times and saw that Webb had grabbed Sam's pole, stopping him from swiping it against my head.

"What the—" Sam glared daggers at Webb.

"Lieutenant London, what're you doing?" Olivia jumped to the center of the mat. "You have to let them learn. Jo has been in another world since we started training. You helping her isn't going to teach her anything."

Webb didn't move, but my insides sure did. My stomach flipped.

"Lieutenant," Olivia called, "remove yourself from this mat." She bristled as she inched closer to Webb.

I stole a glance in the mirror. Webb's eyes had blackened to a pool of molten onyx, and Sam's did the same. Drops of power sparked off Webb. Before it got out of control, Olivia clutched Webb's arm. He let go of the pole with a calm deference, but not before he struck me with a look that shot a bolt of lightning through me. Then he resumed his position in the chair.

"That's enough for today," Olivia announced. "Put the poles away and cool down." She stalked over to Webb.

I collapsed on the mat, sweat dripping off me not from hard training but from nerves. I had barely moved at all. My brain had endured more of a workout than my body.

Sam parked his butt in front of me.

"The vampire irritates me," he whispered, crossing one leg under the other.

Yeah, he had no idea how the gorgeous vampire unnerved me too. I stretched every limb I could, hoping it would relieve some stress. After a few yoga poses, I uncurled my legs and rose from the mat.

Sam completed his cooldown before following me to the water fountain.

"Why do you hate him so much?" I asked as Sam took in a few gulps of water.

"I told you, there's something I can't put my finger on. I feel it every time I'm around him," he muttered.

"Like that fire thing you think is between me and him?"

"Sis, it's not just fire. There's a volcano brewing inside him. He tries to control it, but he's getting weaker."

"What the heck are you talking about?"

"I don't know. I don't know why I sense what people are feeling."

"You can feel what other people feel? Like emotions?" I dropped down on the wooden chair next to the fountain, my brain firing like crazy.

"Sometimes. I don't know. Why? What's wrong? You look like you just saw a ghost."

With all the research I had been doing on vampire history and special powers, a link connected in my brain. *Could Sam be... dare I even think it? Could he be an Empath?*

I recalled the text I read in one of the many books on secondary powers. An Empath was referred to among our species as an *Energy vampire*. Any vampire who possessed this power could drain the life energy from anyone, including humans, and use it to their advantage. They could also sense feelings like fear, love, rage, creative energy, and sadness. However, the only way to exercise this type of power was through the sense of touch, and Sam wasn't touching Webb.

I rubbed my temples. "I believe I might know what your secondary power is," I said, leaning back in the chair.

Sam stood in front of me with his hands on his

hips and his brows raised. He blocked my view from you-know-who, thank God.

"Remember all those categories Webb mentioned about secondary powers?"

"Yeah, yeah. Just tell me."

"I read up on a few of them the other day, and you might be an Empath."

"What's that?" he asked.

"You can sense others' feelings or emotions. That's why you can sense something with Webb. Didn't you have some feeling about Kate too?"

He sat in the chair next to me, biting his bottom lip. He fidgeted, pulling his cheek to one side and gnawing it, a muscle in his jaw ticking as he did. All I could think was *like father, like son*. So many similarities between the two.

"Well, say something."

"Did the book say anything else?" Sam asked, pushing his fingers through his hair.

"Yeah. I'm not sure I can recall all of it, though." I extended my hand and placed it on his knee. "An Empath has to be touching someone for them to tap into another's emotions. Try it."

He placed his hand on mine.

As we sat in silence, Webb and Olivia were still in a heated discussion. Olivia shook her head as if disagreeing with Webb. I strained to hear what they were talking about. Vampires had a way of whispering so other vampires couldn't hear. My throat suddenly burned, and my stomach gurgled, the sounds echoing in the somewhat quiet room.

"Well, can you feel my emotions?" I asked.

"I can hear your emotions. Are you hungry?"

"Duh. Anything?"

"Not a thing. You're empty, sis."

"Good to know, I guess."

"I don't think I have any powers. Not yet, at least. Pops did say it would take a year."

"Yeah. You could see them early like I did, though," I added.

"Maybe," was all he said.

I didn't push the issue. My stomach growled. If I didn't get upstairs soon, I might have snacked on someone in that room.

The door clicked closed, and Olivia walked over to the mat. "Nice job today. Let's go. I'll escort both of you upstairs," she said.

One more day, and our quarantine was over, which meant we could be around humans. I couldn't wait.

The three of us trudged upstairs in silence. I kept thinking about Sam, how he could be an Empath, and how he might drain the energy out of another person. I made a mental note to do more research on it.

Sam opened the apartment door and bumped

into a blond-haired, green-eyed vamp, the same one my father had been yelling at in his office the other day. He was tall and young-looking, with a straight nose and a dimpled chin. Like the other Sentinels, he had an aura about him that was all military.

"Sorry, dude," the blond vamp said to Sam. "Nice to see you again, Jo."

"I'm out of here," Olivia said as she turned and walked down the hall.

"You know this guy?" Sam asked in an irritated tone, flicking his thumb behind him as he bumped into Dad on his way into the kitchen.

"Not really," I replied, following him. "He was in Dad's office the other day."

"We were never formally introduced," the blond vamp said. "I'm Kodiak Snow. I'm one of the new Sentinels. I just finished training and—"

"Snow, don't you have someplace to be?" Dad asked.

"Sorry, sir. Nice to meet you both." Snow nodded, turned on his heel, then closed the door behind him.

"Son, are you angry about something?" Dad sidled up to the counter.

I almost laughed. I guess Dad hadn't paid much attention to the war between Sam and Webb.

"Not a thing," Sam replied rather flippantly, opening the fridge.

Dad's jaw clenched. "I want to go over a couple final details on school and our meeting tomorrow with the solicitors. Why don't you both get cleaned up and meet me back here in the family room." He ignored Sam's comment.

I volleyed my gaze between them, waiting for whatever argument or explosion was about to take place. Dad had one eyebrow raised. Sam ignored him, plucked a bottle of blood from the fridge, then stalked out of the kitchen.

I let out a sigh, thankful that the quiet little quiet exchange, or whatever it was, hadn't erupted into something more violent between them.

Dad's cell phone rang, so I headed to my bedroom.

I flopped on the bed while I waited for my turn in the bathroom. A hot shower would really do the trick. My body still wasn't used to all the hits, scrapes, and cuts Sam inflicted on me. Olivia said it would take a few months or more for our threshold of pain to increase. The pain would always be there, but it wouldn't feel as intense. I didn't believe her because the blows hurt like hell. But the pain was mild, though, compared to when Edmund had staked me with those swords.

I grabbed a pillow, buried my face in it, and

tried not to think about Edmund and his gang. A sudden shiver crept up my arms. Aside from some Sentinel scuttlebutt about spotting Jonah and Fernando at a medical supply store, I hadn't heard any other whispers of Plutarium sightings around the base.

My mind drifted. An image of Ben asking me to the dance popped into my head. A smile tugged at my lips as I remembered how nervous he'd been. Then, *poof,* my smile turned into a frown. The dance had come and gone. Maybe he had asked Darcy. After all, they were friends, and she had a huge crush on him. As I replayed the scene over and over again, Ben's image morphed into Webb's. I dug deeper into my pillow and screamed as loudly as I could.

A hand touched my back. "Hey, Jo?" Dad called. "You all right?"

I picked up my head. "Yeah."

"You want to talk about it?" he asked.

I rolled over and sat upright. "No way I'm talking to you about boys."

The bed dipped as he sat down on the edge. "I didn't see boys in your thoughts. Is there something you want to tell me?"

Busted. "Uh, no."

"You weren't thinking about the Jackson boy, were you?"

"What did you see?" I asked, quickly trying to change the subject.

"You were thinking about Edmund." He placed his hand on my knee. "I know we haven't made headway on finding them, but I don't want you to worry. You'll have a bodyguard escorting you to and from school. Once you're inside the school grounds, St. Anne's Academy has a tight security team to look after you."

"So that's all you read?" I asked.

"When you started screaming, my cell phone rang again. I lost the connection to your thoughts."

I blew out a breath, thankful that his phone had averted an argument between us.

"Wait. Rewind. We're still going to have bodyguards? You know, Sam and I are old enough to drive ourselves."

We were, but we didn't have our driver's license. We had never bothered to take any driver's education classes, largely because we didn't have any money when we were in foster care. Besides, living in the city meant there was public transportation to get around.

"Doesn't matter. I'm not letting you out into the city with the Plutariums roaming around."

"Can't we just get our licenses?" I asked. "Sam and I never had the chance before."

"We'll talk about it another time. Right now, I

can't risk it. With potential moles, your uncle testing whatever serum it is he might have developed, and Edmund..." He shook his head. "Edmund is a loose cannon. The man is driven by power, revenge, and greed. And I don't want you anywhere near him, ever. Do you hear me?"

"How would I go near him? It's not like I'm going to—"

"Promise me, Jo."

"I promise, Dad. Have you found the spies? Is it any of the Sentinels?" There were two vampire SEAL teams and two human SEAL teams on base. Aside from the Sentinels, I didn't know whether the other teams were deployed.

"No," he said emphatically.

"How do you know?"

"I just know," was all he said, rising from the bed.

"Did you use your mind-reading ability to find out?" I asked.

"Jo, first, the Sentinels have been cleared since each of them had an alibi. Second, I can't read everyone's mind. The act alone would literally kill me if I had to read everyone's minds on this base. You let me worry about all that. Right now, it sounds like Sam is out of the bathroom. Get cleaned up. Don't take too long. I have a meeting tonight." He left the room in a huff.

The last thing I was going to do was dwell on Edmund or my Uncle Patrick. I had more pressing concerns, especially with school next week. As the time grew closer, my nervousness grew, inch by maddening inch.

12

Thirty minutes later, after my shower, I donned a pair of jeans and a plain old tank top then padded down the hall. Sam was relaxing on the couch, flipping through a sports magazine.

"Where's Dad?" I asked, jumping onto the couch next to him.

"He said he'd be back in a few minutes. He had to get something from his office." Sam kept his nose buried in the magazine.

The lock on the door clicked, and Dad strolled in, hands full. He unloaded two garment bags, flinging them over the barstool before placing his keys, a newspaper, and two folders on the counter.

"What's all that?" I asked.

He removed his jacket and picked up the two

folders before sitting down on the edge of the chair across from us. He rubbed a hand along his jaw. A vertical line was etched between his eyes. He looked like he was struggling with what to say.

Sam set his magazine on the coffee table before we exchanged curious glances.

"Before I hand you these files with your birth certificates, I want to say how sorry I am that your lives didn't work out better for you. I never meant to hurt you or abandon you." He swallowed. His hands were shaking. "In these folders, you'll find... well, I'll let you read through the contents. I have a meeting to get to. We'll talk when I get back." He handed Sam one folder and slid the other across the coffee table to me. "Tripp is outside the door in case you need anything." He rose then left.

Sam slowly opened his folder while I glared at the cover of mine. I didn't know whether I wanted to open it. My father's apology appended me to the sofa, and *my* hands were shaking. I had thought I would be excited to see proof of who I really was, but...

Pressing my lips together, I peered at Sam. His doleful expression and his racing heart made my chest tighten. It was as though he had just lost the last game of the World Series. Oh, that wasn't good.

I pushed aside my hesitation. It was now or

never. I picked up my folder and placed it in my lap. I held my breath, and with a slight touch, I gently opened it.

The eight-by-ten black-and-white picture instantly brought tears to my eyes. I swallowed and ran my hand over the glossy photo. A gorgeous dark-haired woman stared back at me. Her elegant evening gown draped over her slim body in the shape of a bell. It gathered in all the right places and widened as it tapered to the floor. A diamond-studded belt was gathered at her waist, sparkling as the light glinted off it. She wore elbow-length white gloves with a diamond bracelet covering her right wrist. Her hair was eloquently twisted up behind her head with wispy strands framing her face. More tears clouded my vision as I kept absorbing every detail of the woman I never knew and would never know. She'd died of leukemia when I was just over a year old.

I blinked a few times to clear my eyes. Dad stood by her side, dressed in a formal military uniform. A few rows of ribbons lined his left breast. There weren't as many as he'd worn on his uniform the other day. His black hair was tied back, and a smile lightened his eyes. Despite the age of the photo, Dad looked exactly the same.

Before I got too teary-eyed, I stared at it one

last time then flipped it to see what other papers lay underneath.

I scanned my birth certificate. It listed my name, time of birth, date of birth, and my mother and father's signatures. I looked it over in more detail. This piece of paper indicated I was seventeen, not sixteen, and we were born in December, not February. I went to ask Sam if his paper said the same thing, but he wasn't sitting next to me anymore. His folder sat open on the coffee table.

"Sam?" I called, looking around the immediate area.

He didn't answer.

Rising from the couch, I headed down to his bedroom and knocked on the door.

"Sam, I know you're in there. I can hear your heart racing." Easing open the door, I peeked inside. "Can I come in?"

"You're already in," he said. He was lying on the bed in the dark with his hands behind his head, staring at the ceiling.

"I didn't hear you leave. What's wrong?" I asked, leaning against the doorjamb.

"Nothing."

"Really? Why don't I believe you?" I flipped on the light switch.

"Turn it off," he said, covering his eyes.

Wow! "Are you crying?" I'd never in my life

seen my brother shed a tear. Those papers or the picture must've spooked him. I did as he wanted and switched off the light. Then I made my way over to the bed and sat down. "Why are you upset?"

I waited for his response. Silent seconds turned into silent minutes before I decided to give him his space and not press the issue.

Standing, I glanced up at his patched quilt, the same as the one I had hanging over my bed, only his name was embroidered at the top—Samuel Jove Mason. We were still waiting for Dad to explain how he and our mom came up with our names. In fact, Sam and I found it odd that we even had a middle name. Over the years, the social workers who had been assigned to us had never indicated that our paperwork had one listed.

"I'll be in the family room." I made it halfway to the door.

"Jo... wait. Do you think Pops is really our father? I know he gave us our birth certificates, and I saw the picture of Mom standing next to him, but..." He sat up. "I also feel his emotions around us, and he hurts every time the three of us are together. He's hiding something."

My brother had never been one to trust anyone except me, so I wasn't surprised to hear his questions. But I didn't share his distrust. Sam was the spitting image of my father. They were both tall and well built, and they had the same dimpled cheeks, the same nose, the same color eyes, the same smile, and even the same mannerisms. It would have been hard to convince me that Steven Mason wasn't our father.

Plus, the most critical piece that proved it was our DNA. Dr. Vieira had tested mine to make sure I was truly my father's daughter before I made the change. Granted, I hadn't seen those results, but I trusted that Dr. Vieira was telling the truth. For that matter, there was also the fact that we had even become vampires. Everyone said that could only be done with a father's blood.

"If he's hiding anything, it's something to do with his feelings," I told Sam. "Besides, you saw his name on our birth certificate. And there's no way I could've turned vampire if he wasn't our father. Our DNA had to match in order for us to change."

"Sis, don't be so naive. How do you know they weren't lying? We're on a government compound. The government can do or say anything."

"You're not listening. This has nothing to do with the government. Science doesn't lie. Now you know that he's really our father. Maybe it's the reality of it that sucks."

Sam jumped off the bed and stood in front of me before I could blink.

"The only family I will ever have is you." He leaned down and kissed my forehead then walked out.

Whoa! What just happened? He was acting extremely odd. I shook my head. I wasn't going to worry about Sam's hang-ups. Steven Mason was our father, and until someone proved otherwise, I would continue to build a relationship with the man, even if it took an eternity to work out our differences.

I retreated to the family room and continued sifting through the papers in my folder. Aside from the picture of Mom and my birth certificate, there were a couple of pictures of Sam and me as babies. Sam was decked out in a blue outfit that had a baseball embroidered on the T-shirt, and I was wearing the exact same outfit, only in yellow.

I was about to get off the couch and join Sam on the chaise when Dad walked in. He placed his keys and cell phone on the kitchen counter before easing onto the cushion beside me.

"Did you look through the folder?" he asked.

"I did," I replied.

"Do you have any questions?" Dad glanced over his shoulder at Sam. "What's wrong with your brother?"

I shrugged.

"Can you tell me about Mom?" I asked.

"Scoot over here," he said, patting the cushion.

Curling my legs underneath me, I leaned into the crook of his arm. He placed his arm on the back of the couch.

"Your mom was a strong woman," he began. "A little feisty, like you. You remind me a lot of her. She loved life and loved being pregnant with you two."

"Did you love her?"

His heartbeat picked up.

"I loved her dearly. I still do. She was the only woman…" His voice trailed off as his pulse raced.

"I'm sorry, Dad. I didn't mean to stir—"

"You didn't," he whispered.

"The only woman who what, Pops?" Sam asked snidely. "Who put up with your shit?"

The only sound in the room was Dad's fangs clicking as they descended. I grabbed his arm to hold him down, but he was far stronger than me.

He flew off the couch and stood toe-to-toe with Sam. The power around us escalated.

Why, oh why, is my brother being an idiot?

"You will not disrespect your elders," growled Dad. "And you will never speak to me about your mother in that way. Do you hear me, son? I'm trying to let you air out your issues, and I've even ignored some things to try to help you, but I will not stand for disrespect."

I ran over to them, but before I reached Dad, he stuck out his arm. "Stay away, Jo."

"No! I know he can be an ass, Dad, but have you ever stopped to consider how he feels? Just because you handed us a piece of paper with your signature on it doesn't mean that all our issues are over." I held my breath, afraid he would yell at me.

After several long seconds, Dad walked away.

I let out all the air in my lungs as I went over to Sam.

He dropped onto the chaise. "Get away, sis," he snapped, throwing out his hand and hitting me in the face.

"You asshole. I'm not your enemy here. I'm your sister. What happened to what you told me earlier? Now you're hitting me? Both of you are insane." I hated when my brother was a jerk. He seemed to know just what buttons to push with Dad.

Why couldn't we finish a decent conversation? Or even have a conversation, for that matter?

Dad came toward me as I was headed to my room. "Jo, calm down. Sit." He guided me to the sofa. "Sam. On the couch," Dad commanded, pointing his finger at the space next to me.

Sam obeyed then wrapped his arms around

me and buried his face into the crook of my neck. "I'm so, so sorry, sis. I'm an ass. Please forgive me."

I pushed him away, and a tear streamed down his face. His green eyes slowly faded to black. It was just too freaky. For the second time in barely an hour, my brother was shedding tears. We were seriously screwed up.

"Let's start over," Dad said. "What questions do you two have?"

Really? He's going there again?

Sam kicked his feet onto the table.

I leaned back against the couch. I did have a few more, and if Sam screwed up our getting answers, he and I were going down to the training room to have it out. "What about our middle names? Where did they come from? Why didn't we know we even had them before?" I glared at my brother, daring him to interrupt.

Dad claimed the spot next to me. "Your mother believed in the power of the universe." He hesitated as he gazed at Sam. "She believed names held power and that their meaning shaped a person. She may have been human, but her spirituality electrified the people around her. Her aura was what drew me to her. Anyway, she knew the strength your grandfather had as a vampire and the power that I have, and she knew in her heart that both of you would live to do great things in this world. She studied astrology and astronomy and found the two sciences interrelated. Her main focus was how the astrological phenomena behind the universe linked to events in the human world. Of course, the scientific community has a host of reasons why astrology is not worthy of being considered a formal science. That didn't matter to your mother, though."

"So how did she come up with our names?" I asked.

"I'm getting to that, sweetie." Dad swallowed. "Through her studies, she found that the planet Jupiter signified good fortune. She believed, as others did and still do, that Jupiter is the guardian and protector of the sky. Astrologists will tell you Jupiter is the ruling planet of the sign Sagittarius, and in Roman mythology, Jupiter was considered king of the gods."

"Wait," Sam cut in. "Is that why you guys are called the Jupiter Sentinels?"

Dad nodded.

I raised my fingers to my lips. A thought grabbed me. I remembered in space science class, sitting in the planetarium, looking up at the fake sky, listening to Ms. Lewis explain that Jupiter, Neptune, and Pluto were all very powerful gods. The three brothers were reputed to have presided over one of the three realms of the universe.

Jupiter governed the sky, Neptune controlled the waters, and Pluto was considered the god of the underworld. The hairs on the back of my neck stood up straight as pins—the Plutariums had to have been named after Pluto.

"Your mother was superstitious," Dad continued. "Since your astrological sign is Sagittarius, and your ruling sign is Jupiter, she thought the symbolism behind the name Jupiter fit perfectly for you, and that the name would bring both of you good fortune. So she and I decided on your middle names of Jove and Juno. And if you don't know, Jove is synonymous with Jupiter."

"Where does Juno come in? There's no planet Juno." I struggled to recall anything Ms. Lewis had taught us about other planets. All that came to mind were the popular planets in the solar system.

"Well, you're right," Dad said. "But Juno is an asteroid. In mythology, though, Juno was believed to be the sister of Jupiter, his twin. She was a goddess known for her protective nature."

"Um, Pops, wasn't Juno the wife of Jupiter?" Sam asked. "At least, that's what I remember from my literature class. I think one of the girls in class did a paper on Juno."

I laughed. "Wife? I'm not marrying you."

A smile twitched at Dad's mouth. "It depends on the interpretation. Your mother found the same thing, and we discussed it at length. Regardless, she was dead set on the correlation of the names, since you are twins."

"Great. I was given a name as the wife of my brother."

"Now, Jo, let's not dwell on that part." Dad rubbed my head. "While your mother is not here today, I'm beginning to learn that she may have been on to something with her beliefs, looking at the way both of you are growing into adults. Of course, time will still tell what lies ahead."

"So why do our birth certificates say we're seventeen? That would mean Sam and I will be eighteen in a few months. It also says we were born in December and not February like we were told."

Dad kissed me on the head. "Very astute, sweetie. All vampire babies are born at home through a midwife. Our society can't allow any newborns who carry the vampire genes to be born in a human hospital. Too many tests result in too many questions. When a baby is born with a vampire gene, our government completes all the paperwork for both our world and the human world, only the data they list on the human birth certificate doesn't necessarily match with the vampire one. We change things like your birth date, middle name, and your mother's name. The reason we do this is to protect our world from humans. If the human government ever compared notes or documents with our government, they would be hard-pressed to put two and two together. It helps conceal our identities as vampires. The documents in your folders are your real vampire birth certificates. I don't have your human one, which I know, Jo, is your next question. You don't need your human one, not right now. I am your father, even though Sam has more than a ton of doubt in him about me. But for now, that's all you're going to get. Any other questions?"

An infinite amount. But it was getting late. Sam and I weren't going to get very many answered, at least not tonight.

"You know, Pops," Sam said, sitting up, "I know there's a lot you're not telling us. Granted, I get the vampire government stops you from telling us everything, but I want you to know that if you're lying to us and you ever hurt us, I will do everything in my power to make sure you pay, regardless of whether you're family or not. Are we clear?"

Spoken like a true Mason. I was in awe of my brother.

My father didn't move, didn't even flinch. He just stared at Sam as though he was the son and Sam was his elder. I couldn't tell whether Dad was proud or pissed.

Several moments of silence gave way to Dad

clearing his throat. "Son, I wouldn't have it any other way." He pushed to his feet.

I let out the deepest sigh, relieved they hadn't gotten into a brawl.

"Now, one more thing. In preparation for our meeting with the solicitors tomorrow, I want to ask you both something." Dad sat on the coffee table so he was facing Sam and me.

Sam and I gave him our full attention. Maybe because Dad never asked us anything so much as told us.

"As you both know, you'll have a chip placed in you with all your personal information on it. The procedure on how it's done will be explained to you tomorrow. The chip is not an option. However, I would like to give you the choice to have a tattoo placed on your body at the same time. It's a tradition in the Mason family to have a symbol that represents who we are tattooed on us. I have one here," he said, pointing to one of the tats on his forearm.

The tattoo was a circle with an arrow jutting out from the one o'clock position.

"What does that stand for, Pops?" Sam asked.

"Well, in addition to your mother, my family also believes in the power behind the universe. They gave me the birth name of Steven Mars Mason. They thought it was appropriate for me. Mars is considered the god of war. Were they right? I don't know. My role is to prevent wars, not start them. Nevertheless, I wanted to follow in the family tradition, and your mother agreed that if we had children, they would do the same.

"However, I don't want to force this one on you. I know that you have concerns over the chip. Frankly, I don't blame you. I had the same issues. But the chip is nothing more than a way to police our world. In addition, being a legal vampire does provide some benefits like stipends for everyday living. Some vampires can't work among humans, but they still need to live. Our government provides a way for them to do that so they're not out robbing places or killing humans for their next meal."

"Why not just have vampires carry something like a social security card instead of a chip?" I asked.

"We tried that many years ago. It was too confusing to keep things separate from the humans. Plus, we want there to be as little as possible physical evidence to prevent humans from finding out about us. With technology evolving every day, the process is easier," Dad explained.

I guess it made sense, although I still wasn't enamored with having a chip implanted under my skin.

"What do you think about getting a tattoo?" Dad asked.

"I'm cool with it, Pops," Sam said.

"And sweetie, what about you?" Dad looked at me.

"I guess it depends on what it is," I said, shrugging.

"Well, your tattoo would represent your middle name of Juno and for Sam, Jove. Juno's symbol is an upside-down cross with a seven-pointed star at the top. And, son, yours would be the Jupiter symbol like all the Sentinels have." He pointed to his forearm. "But there would be a slight variation. Instead of the straight stem of the symbol, yours would have a lightning bolt instead, to make sure there's a distinction between you and the Jupiter Sentinels."

I bit my bottom lip, thinking about all this. I didn't have any hang-ups about tattoos. I liked Dad's. I just didn't want a ton like he had.

"Why don't you think about it overnight? If you're keen, think about where you would want it on your body. Now, it's getting late. I'm going to bed." Dad stood and kissed me on the head then patted Sam on his shoulder before he left the room.

Sam and I sat in silence. After a few minutes, I

turned to face him. "So, what do you think of all this?" I asked.

Sam and I hadn't really discussed much in the last week or so—we hadn't even discussed how we felt about the computer chip or school or anything else. All we'd been doing was working out, training, and sleeping.

"I guess there are bigger things in life to be concerned with than a chip and a tattoo," Sam said. "So the vampire government tracks their people. So do the humans, just in a different way. I don't see that the vampire government is doing anything bad. If it's a way to police us, as they say, then what's the harm? I asked Tripp about his, and he said it's no big deal. Pops has one too. As for the tattoo, I was getting a couple anyway as soon as I could."

I'd always trusted my brother. Perhaps Sam was right.

"Why the face, Jo?" he asked.

"I didn't realize I was making a face."

"You look deep in thought."

"I am. I've been struggling with the chip more than anything. You know, it reminds me of the chip that one of the foster families we lived with had implanted in their dog? Do you remember them?"

He nodded. "So?"

"Well, I feel like a dog."

"Sis, I hate to break it to you, but we are vampires. Things are different now, and this is one of those differences in our lives. It's really not as bad as you're making it seem. Let it go. Choose important things to fight about."

"You're probably right."

"Well, are you going to get that tattoo?" he asked. "I think it would look good if you got it on the back of your shoulder. Not too big though."

I laughed. "Why is that?"

"Guys think it's hot to see a woman with a nice tattoo on her shoulder."

"Oh yeah, who says?" I poked him in his side.

He flinched. "I do."

"You know, I'm your sister," I snorted.

"That's why I'm looking out for you. It's tasteful to have it there."

"Since when did you become the expert on tats, huh?" I grinned.

"Since I'm a guy, and I know what guys like." He attacked me, tickling me.

"Sam, stop it!" I snorted between fits of giggles.

He stood up after torturing me into a state of laughter. "I'm going to bed. See you in the morning."

I followed him. "'Night, Sam," I said.

I was exhausted from the entire conversation

we'd had with Dad. Computer chips, vampire government, humans, tattoos, middle names, our mother, and the symbolism of it all—my brain hurt.

Flopping onto my bed, I decided that I would get the tattoo. I just didn't know where yet. It didn't matter. I would think about it in the morning.

13

Tiny pinpricks of light lit up the night sky. The air around me was cold and crisp. Odors of dirt and rot hung in the air.

I had no idea where I was.

Snowcapped mountains rose in the distance. Rolling green hills spread out for miles. Dew sparkled on the blades of grass, thanks to the millions of stars shining down. I inhaled, and a scant scent of eucalyptus hung in the night air.

A gust of wind blew, and I shivered. Then a blinding light flooded the area for miles, followed by a sharp, booming sound as if someone had shot a cannon into the midnight sky. I threw my hands over my head and crouched to the ground. After a few seconds, the echoes from the noise died, and I stood. The hillside was steeped in darkness, but a warm, yellow glow ignited at the base of the mountains, making visible the silhouette of an older man with a large black cat at his side.

My eyes widened as he began to walk toward me. Something told me to run, but my feet wouldn't move.

"Do not be afraid, child. I won't hurt you." My sensitive ears picked up his soft voice as if he'd been shouting.

The light followed him as he walked, as though a thousand angels shone flashlights from overhead to help light his path. His slender build, black hair, and pale skin sent a warning message to the deepest part of my brain: *Get the hell out of here.*

I tried to pick up my bare feet, but they were firmly planted in the soft carpet of grass. I peered down just to make sure a creature hadn't popped out of the ground to hold me in place. No eerie, clawed hands came out of the ground. Nothing was around my ankles. But I still couldn't move.

Satisfied that at least I wasn't strapped to the earth, I lifted my gaze.

The old man was draped in a red robe, and a gold sash hung around his neck. It reminded me of what priests wore for Sunday mass. He held out his hands as if he wanted me to run to him.

I cocked my head to one side.

"I am your protector, my child. I come bearing a message."

Is he reading my thoughts?

"I most certainly am, though your thoughts are not of a world with which I am familiar."

Where the heck am I?

"You are between heaven and Earth. A place where time doesn't move, where humans don't age, and the sanctity of my world is preserved. A world where you're safe from harm," the old man said. "Don't worry, child. I will not hurt you."

I sucked in a sharp breath. *If heaven is real, does that mean hell exists?*

"Many worlds exist, my child. Heaven is truly real, but hell exists in many places around the Earth, even places you least expect it," he said.

I tried again to move, but my body seemed to be locked down.

The only thing moving was my agitated stomach. I was certain my eyes still had the oh-my-God look—and not because of the old man, but because of his companion. It wasn't a black cat—it was a black panther, a magnificent creature with a shiny obsidian coat that covered his entire body, except for a white marking between his eyes. His irises were equally stunning, deep yellow with pink undertones. I felt like I was looking into expensive topaz stones.

The old man stopped five feet in front of me. His companion did the same before sitting on his haunches.

"No need to be afraid of me or my friend here," he said, nodding to the panther. "He will not harm you. His name is Serapis."

At the old man's last word, the panther bowed his head then dropped down to drape his long, sleek figure along the ground as though he understood the old man's words.

"We don't have much time," the man continued. He raised his left hand then his right high above his head as he closed his eyes. "The God of Light and the God of Darkness will merge. Take mercy on her world, my liege, as this child before me will forever be steeped in battle. Protect her while she lives among the enemy."

I stood in awe of the words he spoke.

The old man continued speaking, but his English changed into a language I didn't understand.

Serapis sat up on his haunches and looked around, shifting his head in all directions as if sensing something. The old man chanted as if casting a spell.

I followed the panther's lead, opening my senses

to my surroundings. All I could pick up was a faint breeze that carried a mild scent of honeysuckle. The strong scent of dirt no longer permeated the air.

The bright light that had guided the duo to stand before me suddenly dimmed, and the old man stopped chanting.

"Now, that's better," he said, opening his eyes as if he had cleansed his system of some bad energy. His silver eyes glowed as he stared at me. He extended his hands. "Come to me, child." His voice was soft and vaguely familiar.

I shook my head violently.

"I told you I would not hurt you. Now, take my hands."

As if my body had a mind of its own, my feet decided to move. Before I could get my brain to work, I was standing in front of the old man with my hands in his. I closed my eyes, blinked several times, then opened them. Nope. He was still standing in front of me, and so was Serapis.

I met the man's gaze. His silver eyes changed to green then to violet—it was as if I was looking at myself in a mirror

"Wh— who... are you?" I managed to say.

"Who I am bears no importance here. For there is light and darkness. Both will challenge you, challenge your beliefs, and create a place that can be far worse than hell. The darkness will be like no other that your world has ever seen. Your soul still lives with shades of humanity lingering, though not for long. You must be mindful of those around you. Do not let the shadows consume you." His eyes changed from violet to green then back to silver.

"I don't understand," I whispered.

Then he squeezed my hands so tightly that I gasped. "You must not let humanity suffer at the hands of"—he looked over his shoulder—"protect what is left, my child. Come, Serapis. We must get back to the others."

"Protect what?" I shouted as they walked back toward the base of the mountain.

Serapis stopped and turned, his yellow eyes glowing, lighting up the area around me.

Before I knew what was happening, my legs gave out. I dropped to the ground as if I'd been drained of every ounce of blood. I looked up, and the dark-haired man and his companion were gone, as though they'd disappeared into thin air.

My eyelids were heavy. A fog blurred my vision. All I could think about was sleep. I nestled into the soft bed of grass, curled into a fetal position, closed my eyes, and inhaled. When I released a tiny breath, a noise like a door slamming jarred me from the heavy sleep that tugged at me.

Open your eyes, a voice in my head whispered. *You must wake up now.*

My eyes fluttered open. The pristine night sky had bleached into a wall of stark whiteness. I gazed around and was met with furniture and pictures in a room. The green, rolling hills were gone. In their place was my goose-down comforter, bunched into mounds on top of me.

I rubbed my eyes before blinking a few times. I must've been dreaming. I knew it. It wasn't the first time I had seen the old man in my dreams. I lay still, thinking. It was the first time the old man spoke to me, though. *What did he mean by "shadows"?*

Dad's voice echoed outside my door. A quick glance at the clock on my nightstand told me it was seven a.m.

"Sam, get dressed. We have to meet the solicitors in an hour," Dad said as the door to my bedroom creaked open. "Jo, good. You're awake."

I buried my head under my pillow. "Go away."

Dad pulled back the covers. "It's time. You need to get ready."

I stiffened. "I'm tired."

I felt like I hadn't slept at all. My body was as limp as if I'd run three marathons in one day.

"Sweetie." Dad picked up my pillow. "Now is not the time to lounge."

"I don't want to go."

"Today is your induction into being a legal vampire. You should be excited."

Far from it. I dreaded the whole thing. I wanted to sleep and try to make sense of my odd dream.

"Please, please don't start. And what dream?" he asked, reading my thoughts.

I let out a breath and sat up. "It's nothing." Maybe I shouldn't have been so concerned about a dream. After all, it was only my subconscious at play.

"Sometimes you should listen to your dreams. As vampires, we can have insight into the future through them," Dad said.

"What? How?"

"I don't know how. Only a few vampires I've known have had glimpses into their future. I've never been one of them."

"Who were they?"

"We can talk about it another time. Now, shower. Meet me in the kitchen. Oh, and Jo? I want you on your best behavior today. Understood?"

I met his gaze and nodded as he walked out.

The old man had said I would always be steeped in battle, but nothing else in the dream made sense.

I shook off those thoughts for the time being. I

had to get ready for my big day, which I was not at all excited about.

I showered then dressed in yoga pants and a T-shirt. I figured if I had to strip down for the event, my workout clothes would be easiest to shed. I slipped into my flip-flops then walked into the kitchen.

As I did every morning, I grabbed a container out of the refrigerator and a coffee mug from the cabinet. After Sam had turned me on to warm blood, I got into the habit of heating it up any chance I had, especially in the morning. The microwave dinged. I removed the mug then cradled it in my hands. I took the first sip and stilled, letting the warm fluid coat every cell inside me, igniting my system. I took another swig then sat at the bar.

To take my mind off the upcoming ceremony, I set the mug down and picked up the morning newspaper. I flipped it open and scanned the headlines. In the bottom left-hand corner, a small caption read, "Local High School Pitcher Believed to Be Missing." My adrenaline picked up. I skimmed through the few lines in the article looking for a name. My gaze landed on the last line. *Mr. Jackson, the principal of Durfee High, said the school is doing everything they can to cooperate with authorities and Jack Powell's family.*

"No way!"

"What's wrong?" Sam asked, securing his hair behind him with a leather strap.

I slid the paper to him. "Bottom left."

His eyes widened as he read. "Shit!"

I took another swig from the mug.

"Are you two about ready?" Dad asked, checking his pockets as he rounded the corner from the hall. His hair was still damp from a recent shower. Like Sam, he secured it with a leather strap at the nape of his neck.

"Pops, I need to talk to Ben," Sam said.

At the sound of Ben's name, the mouthful of blood I had just taken got stuck in the back of my throat. What a way to start off the day, and I had been doing so well. Nothing like thinking about Ben to get me energized first thing in the morning.

"You're not seeing the Jackson boy today."

Thank you.

"I don't want to see him. I want to talk to him. You know, on the phone. Can I at least do that?" Sam asked.

"What's so urgent?" Dad was still looking for his phone and messing with his uniform.

"This," Sam said, pointing to the article on the front page of the newspaper.

Dad ambled over to Sam and read the article.

"Well, Pops?"

"What do you want me to do?" He grabbed his cell phone from the coffee table.

"I want to talk to Ben to find out what happened. That's all I'm asking."

"We have the meeting with the council. We'll talk about this later."

Sam mumbled a few choice words before grunting.

"Son, do you want to say something else?" Dad's brow furrowed.

Here we go. It was too early in the morning to sit through another one of their arguments. But only silence followed, and I let out another thankful sigh. As I slid from the stool, the old man's words flashed in my mind. *For there is light and darkness. Both will challenge you.* I didn't know what he meant by that, but for some reason, my intuition told me I was about to find out.

14

I paced around Dr. Vieira's office while we waited. He'd gone down to the lobby to retrieve Atherton and the council's resident medical technician. Sam and Dad sat on opposite ends of the sectional sofa.

"Why are you pacing?" Dad asked me. "This should be a breeze."

"Really, Dad, if you hadn't noticed, I'm not all that thrilled with this."

"Sis, I told you to pick your battles. This won't be bad."

I just growled at my brother, showing my fangs.

He laughed then buried his nose in the newspaper again.

"You know, you can read that fifteen more times, and it isn't going to tell you how Jack went missing," I said. I needed to get out of there. Instinct was urging me to run.

"Have both of you decided on the tattoo?" Dad crossed one leg over the other. He looked really relaxed—or maybe my nervousness made him appear that way.

"I have, Pops," Sam said. "I want mine in the same place where Jo gets hers."

I stopped cold. "What? Why?"

"Well, for one, we're twins. Two, I know this whole thing makes you nervous, so call it solidarity. Three, chicks will love it."

Dad laughed. The man actually laughed. I wasn't sure if I'd ever heard him laugh before.

I rolled my eyes. "What if I don't get a tattoo?" I speared a look at Sam as I advanced a few steps to stand over him.

"You will," he said, not looking at me.

"Cocky." I kicked his foot.

He raised an eyebrow in challenge.

"Jo, are you going to get a tattoo or not?" Dad asked.

Not taking my eyes off Sam, I said, "Yes, I guess so."

Sam smirked. "She doesn't like needles, Pops." His gaze didn't waver.

I blinked when Sam reached up and pulled me down onto the seat beside him. His hands immediately grabbed my sides.

"Sam, don't you dare." I wiggled, trying to get up.

"Now, I wouldn't move if I were you." His voice was light, playful.

"Is that why you're nervous?" Dad asked.

"Nah, I just love the feel of sharp objects poking me," I spat.

"Where, sis?" He squeezed my sides a little tighter as a warning.

"Back, right shoulder."

Sam smiled mischievously. "Good. That's where I wanted it."

He was about to tickle me but released his hands from my waist at the sound of Dr. Vieira's voice.

Thank God.

"Back room. Far corner," Dr. Vieira said.

Dad rose from his seat. "I'll be right back."

"Don't worry about this, sis. Think about something nice when you're on the table." Sam hugged me tightly before letting me go.

"Jo, you're first," Dad said, standing in the doorway. "Son, I'll be back for you."

I stood, smoothing my hair. "Wish me luck," I said, looking at my brother.

All he did was tap his heart twice.

Sam really did take away some of the nerves. He always had a way of doing that, especially when I was really freaky about something. As Dad and I walked to the operating room, a small amount of fear coursed through me. Sam was right. I didn't like needles. But it was more than just that. Alongside the fear was an empty feeling, as though my emotions were about to be taken from me.

As I walked into the freezing operating room, I realized that all my worry over the chip and becoming a legal vampire was more about my feelings of losing my humanity than anything else. Maybe that was what the old man had meant when he said I still had my humanity, but not for long.

I relaxed a little, but I still hated needles.

The scent of alcohol hung in the air. Three operating beds were centered in the room. Around each was an array of machines, rolling stools, cabinets, and a cart housing medical instruments. Completing each station was a large halogen lamp hanging over each table.

"Jo, over here," Dr. Vieira called.

I made my way to the middle table as Dr. Vieira and the tall redheaded male vampire arranged several items, which included brightly colored paints and one large bottle of gold-speckled glitter, a small computer chip, and a picture of an upside-down cross with a seven-pointed star at the top—the symbol that represented Juno.

I guessed Dad had presumed that I would say yes to the tattoo.

Once the items were arranged neatly on the cart, Dr. Vieira introduced me to the redhead.

"Jo, meet Corpsman Wheeler. He'll be inserting the chip and drawing the tattoo."

"Hi," I said.

"Pleased to meet you, Jo. You can call me Wheeler." The man had a face full of freckles.

"So, what kind of first name is Corpsman?" I asked.

"Corpsman is not his first name, honey," Dad said. "The enlisted medical personnel in the Navy are classified with the title of Hospital Corpsman."

A familiar man walked up. "How are you, Jo?" Atherton asked. His auburn hair hung loose around his ears, and he was dressed casually in a pair of blue khakis with a white polo shirt. He looked like he was on his way to his weekly golf game.

"Good," was all I said.

"Well, let's get started. I do have another induction other than Jo and Sam today," Atherton said.

Good to know Sam and I weren't the only ones.

"Very well. Here's how this is going to work," Wheeler said. "The chip will be placed in your lower back on the right side, just above your buttock. I will insert it using this device." He pointed to a small gun-like instrument. "It will take a second. You will feel a sting, much like a very bad bee sting, but nothing more. Once the chip is in, it will begin to adhere to your tissue. This isn't like the animal chips that they place in dogs or cats where it's inserted just under the skin. This chip will become part of you, molding and adapting to your body."

"I don't understand," I said.

"While this chip has your personal information on it, like your name and other basic info, it will also store your body's temperature, blood pressure, heart rate, et cetera, and will record them on a constant basis," Wheeler explained. "This will help in medical emergencies. Not that vampires have very many medical issues. However, there are vampires among us that do."

"It's helped us pinpoint some problems with vampires before they've occurred, and in others, it has helped to identify what went wrong prior to them getting ill. While it is very rare for vampires to get sick, our immune systems are not perfect," Dr. Vieira added.

Sam had been sick, as well as other vamps in

the building. Maybe the chip was good for something, after all.

"Jo, have you decided where you want your tattoo?" Dr. Vieira asked.

"Yes. Back, right shoulder."

I glanced at Dad, who stood next to me, and he smiled in a way that said he was proud.

"Very well. Any questions before we get started?" Wheeler asked.

I shook my head.

"All right. I'll start with the chip then do the tattoo. Lie down on your stomach, please, and fold down your pants," Corpsman Wheeler said.

I folded down the top of my yoga pants then swung my legs up onto the table to lie on my stomach.

Dr. Vieira washed the area on my lower right side with a solution of alcohol. Then, before I could blink, Wheeler had pressed the gun-like instrument against my skin. True to Wheeler's word, a sting grabbed me, then it was over.

"That's it?" I asked, astonished.

"Yep. All done. Next, what do you have under your T-shirt? You'll have to remove it," Wheeler instructed.

"No worries. I came prepared," I said. I was wearing a racer-back sports bra, so my shoulder was completely exposed.

As I removed my T-shirt, Dad moved around to the head of the table, grabbed a rolling stool from the bench against the wall, pulled it to him, and sat. I couldn't see where Atherton was standing or what he was doing.

"So, how's a tattoo going to stay on my skin if we're vampires and all? Doesn't our skin heal quickly?" I asked.

"It does," said my dad. "What Corpsman Wheeler is using isn't your ordinary tattoo ink."

I stared at Dad, waiting for him to elaborate, but he said nothing. He glanced beyond me and shook his head.

"What?" I asked.

"Steven, full disclosure," Atherton said from behind me. "Every new vampire must learn our ways. You know this."

I sensed that Dad was hesitant to tell me since he had just learned that I didn't like needles.

"The ink is muriatic acid-based," Dad said. "The acid helps to cut through your skin, allowing the ink to penetrate the top layer under the dermis. This is the only way to tattoo a vampire."

I hadn't taken chemistry yet, but I still knew that acid was bad news.

"I'm going to start, Jo," Wheeler said. "I want you to remain still. Any sudden jerks will only make this process harder and longer. Initially, you'll feel an intense burning sensation. That will die off as I continue inscribing the design into your skin."

The chip procedure went well, so I couldn't imagine the tattoo would be that bad. At least I wasn't watching the needle poke me.

Dad tapped my head. "Look at me, sweetie. I'll talk to you while he's working."

I lifted my gaze to Dad.

The tattoo machine started, and a humming noise tickled my eardrums. A hand touched my shoulder. I sucked in a breath.

"Okay. Here we go," Dad said. "Breathe."

My body vibrated as soon as the needle pricked my skin. Suddenly, an inferno erupted, sending tendrils of searing pain through my body. I threw back my head and wailed. The vampire within came roaring to the surface, my fangs jumping out of my gums.

"Deep breaths, honey, deep breaths," Dad whispered, holding my hands.

"Don't move," Wheeler snapped. "This will not go well. Commander, please, hold her down."

Dad let go of my hands and grabbed my wrists. "Put your head down," he said, scooting closer to the table.

I did as he instructed.

He rested his head against mine. "Now, think

of something pleasant. The pain will go away shortly."

Gritting my teeth, I only succeeded in drawing more blood as my fangs dug into the softer side of my lower lip.

"Breathe," Dad whispered.

Corpsman Wheeler had resumed the engraving. I didn't think the pain could get any worse, but it climbed ever higher. My vision started to blur, and not from my eyes shifting. All I could think about was killing the man standing over me and everyone else in the room.

"Relax for a minute, Jo. I need to change needles," Wheeler explained.

Dad let go of me and moved back. Sweat beaded on my forehead. I was about a second away from passing out. I relaxed the muscles in my body and took in several breaths. I couldn't wait to see how Sam would react.

After a couple of minutes, I raised my head and turned. Dr. Vieira was fanning my shoulder, the coolness of the air providing a little relief from the burn still snaking through me. Wheeler was preparing the tattoo machine, filling it with the gold paint.

"Sweetie, lie down," Dad said.

"Okay. Last part," Wheeler announced.

The cool breeze died, and my muscles tensed

at the sound of Wheeler's voice. Then the needle pierced my skin. The room spun in an instant. Fire raced through every limb. Pressure built somewhere inside me, creeping along my stomach into my chest. All of sudden, pain stabbed me in the back of my head, as though someone had just driven a nail into my skull.

"Get it off!" I yelled as tears dropped onto the white paper underneath me. I looked down to see drops of crimson coating the table.

"Dr. Vieira. Get over here, *now*," Dad commanded. "Wheeler, stop what you're doing."

"Commander. I still have to—"

"I don't care whether you have another dot to color. Put the fucking machine down."

"Steven," Atherton said, walking up to stand beside Dr. Vieira and Dad. "There's no reason to sw—oh, shit. What the—?"

"Exactly, Matthew," Dad confirmed.

"Someone want to tell me what's going on? Other than the explosion that's about to blow off my head from the inside out." Tears streamed down my face.

Another rivulet of red liquid coated the white paper.

"Her skin. She's having a reaction to the gold," Dr. Vieira said.

Darkness clouded the edges of my vision. My

heart rate increased, and a million lighted matches pricked my skin from head to toe.

"Well, do something, Damon!" my father snapped.

"Turn her over. Sit her up," Dr. Vieira instructed.

Wheeler grabbed my legs, and Dad grabbed my shoulders, turning my body, and I sat upright.

Dr. Vieira pulled out his stethoscope and pressed it against my chest. Atherton had a wad of paper towels, and he placed them over my nose.

"Her heart is racing," Dr. Vieira said. "I need to get her heart rate down. Steven, please hand me the syringe from that table over there."

I made eye contact with each vampire surrounding the table. Panic was carved in each expression.

"Are you going to sedate her?" Atherton asked.

"Yes and no. The solution in the syringe is a remedy for cobalt poisoning. And it also has a mild muscle relaxer in it. I'm going to see if it works on whatever is going on inside her. Some vampires have a reaction to the acid. I have yet to see anyone have any reaction to the gold. Then again, this is Steven's child, so anything is possible," Dr. Vieira said as if I wasn't even in the room.

Before I could protest or speak, Dr. Vieira inserted the needle into my left arm. Within a few seconds, a warm and fuzzy feeling seeped through my body, erasing all the fire and pain wreaking havoc inside me.

"Ah, yes. Her skin is clearing up. How do you feel, Jo?" Dad asked.

"It's not burning anymore, but the pain is still in my head," I replied. "I don't want that tattoo needle anywhere near me. No way."

"Jo, we need to finish," Dad said. "Damon, can you give her a sedative so she doesn't tense up?"

"What about my allergic reaction?" I asked.

"You'll be fine now," Dr. Vieira said. "I just gave you a healthy dose of prednisone mixed with Neil's blood. Interesting. I can add gold reactions to the list of ailments remedied by this solution." He turned to his clipboard. "Jo, you probably have enough of it in your system to complete the marking process. If not, I will give you another dose."

"Let's finish up. I'm only here to witness the chip insertion, and I need to be elsewhere in an hour," Atherton said.

"Roll over, please, Jo," Wheeler instructed.

My muscles had loosened, and the burning sensation abated. I rolled over and Dad sat down in front of me once again. The tattoo machine started humming, and then Wheeler resumed carving into my skin. I waited for the pain, the burning sensation, but nothing came. It seemed that the solution Dr. Vieira had administered was working.

Before long, the sound of the tattoo machine stopped.

"Jo? It's over. You can get up." Dad released a sigh.

Yeah. I was relieved, too, that the small battle was over. However, if the old man in my dream was right about me being forever steeped in battle, it was just the beginning. I had an inkling I was on the precipice of something more, something bigger that would test not only my physical threshold for pain but my metaphysical limits as well.

15

The first thing Sam had done after we left the medical facility was try to get ahold of Ben, but he hadn't had any luck then or since. Dad tried to call Mr. Jackson at school. He, too, struck out, only reaching his voicemail. Sam asked Dad whether he could visit Ben since we were free to be around humans, but Dad wanted him to wait. The Sentinels were deployed on a mission for a few days, and Dad didn't have the manpower to have anyone accompany Sam to Ben's house.

I spent the rest of the week in the library, reading some newish novels. I'd thought the chip would physically bother me, but I could hardly tell it was there. On the other hand, the tattoo did take a couple of days to stop being sore, even with my vampire healing ability.

After Wheeler was finished, he'd rubbed some type of salve on the tattoo and sent me away with instructions to keep it moist with the salve for a few days. I couldn't stop looking at it in the mirror every chance I had. It did look neat—the gold specs outlined the star, while the cross was blue and red. Sam's looked even cooler than mine. His tattoo had a red lightning bolt as the stem of the fancy four that represented the Jupiter symbol. It looked good on him, too, especially when he flexed his muscles. Sam hadn't experienced any allergic reactions like I had, but he didn't have any gold ink in his tattoo.

On Sunday evening, the night before school, Sam and I were sitting in the family room. Dad walked in, carrying two garment bags.

"Why do you have those in your hands again?" I asked.

"I forgot to give these to you earlier in the week," he said, laying them over the armchair.

"What's in them?" Sam asked.

"Your uniforms for school tomorrow," Dad said. "I had them dry cleaned."

Sam and I did a double take at the same time.

"What the..." Sam rose from the couch.

I couldn't speak. *Uniforms? Is he kidding?*

"No, I'm not kidding, sweetie," Dad replied.

I guessed one good thing about school was that I wouldn't have anyone around to read my mind. The thought of being alone with my own thoughts excited me.

I bit one of my nails, waiting to see what the circus costume looked like.

Sam removed a cranberry-and-navy-plaid uniform. "I think this one is yours, sis. I'm not wearing a skirt," he said.

My jaw dropped.

"So why the uniforms?" Sam asked, pulling a pair of navy-blue pants and a white shirt from the other garment bag.

"Uniforms show politeness. Plus, they put every student on the same playing field. No one is singled out because of what they wear," Dad said.

I silently laughed. It was never my clothes that spoke to others. I was the outcast of Durfee, the one they called Moonbeam because of my silver eyes, thanks to Blake Turner. Now that I was a vampire with purple streaks through my hair, I suspected I would probably stand out even more.

I held the plaid skirt and blue sweater in my hands, cringing inside. I hated showing any bare skin, and I would have to show my bony legs. I hated school already. I set down the uniform.

"Where are the pants?" I asked, glaring at Dad.

"No pants. All the girls wear skirts," he said as though I should have known. He really was showing his true age.

"Do all the kids in school wear this crap, Pops?" Sam asked, holding up a plaid jacket I hadn't seen earlier.

Ignoring Sam's question, Dad said, "Enough of the uniforms. I was able to speak with Mr. Jackson today."

Sam and I dropped the uniforms and wasted no time sliding onto the stools at the bar.

Dad stood on the other side of the counter. "Mr. Jackson said Jack Powell has been missing for two weeks. He disappeared shortly after one of the last road games. He doesn't know what happened. The police are doing everything they can to search places they think he might be, and they've been interviewing everyone on the team, including the students at school."

Sam raked his hands through his hair and let out a deep sigh. "Can I talk with Ben?"

"Use the house phone," Dad said.

A sharp pain pierced my temples. I narrowed my eyes at Dad.

Why don't you get your things ready for school?

Sam rose, picked up the receiver on the house phone, and dialed.

Jo?

I wasn't trying to ignore my father. I was glued to my seat, waiting to see if Sam was able to get ahold of Ben. Okay, maybe I did want to hear Ben's voice. Maybe if I did it, it would help me decide if there was something more between us. After all, he wasn't in the room, so I couldn't lust over his blood or his scent. Maybe it was a way to level the field to be between boy and girl, and not boy and vampire.

The line rang five times before someone answered.

"Hello?" Ben said.

"Hey, buddy. It's Sam. What's up?"

"Sam?" Ben sounded surprised.

"Yeah. You know, your best friend."

Dad moved from the counter to the sink, where he rinsed out empty containers from earlier in the day.

At the sound of Ben's voice, my pulse began to race. I stared at nothing as I listened.

Ben told Sam all about the baseball team and the state championship game. It was the second year in a row Durfee High had won, bringing home another trophy to be displayed in the school's award cabinet. Regardless, the trophy or the fact they'd won wasn't what froze me. No. It was the huskiness of Ben's voice and how it sent tingles to my stomach.

Ben's voice trailed off, supplanted with Sam's.

"What happened to Jack?" Sam asked.

"We're not sure. He was on the bus when we got back from our last road game. His girlfriend was waiting for him. He said goodbye to the team and left with her," Ben explained.

"Jack has a girlfriend? I thought he swore off girls during baseball season?" Sam asked.

"I know. He met her at one of the games or something. She's hot, dude—long brown hair, deep-blue eyes, and legs to die for," Ben said. "She kind of reminds me of Webb's sister."

Whoa! I wasn't ready to hear Ben describe a girl right down to how great her legs were. I rubbed my arms, trying to rid my body of the tiny thorns coating my skin.

Dad cleared his throat. "Why don't you get ready for bed? Tomorrow is going to be a long day."

I narrowed my eyes at Dad as a sharp pain skated across my brain.

This is exactly why I don't want you around the Jackson boy. Your thoughts are not making me comfortable about you being around humans. Is every human boy going to be like this?

I dropped my head to the counter. *Leave me alone. I just wanted to know what happened to Jack. Besides, I haven't violated any of your rules.*

I know that. The question is, will you? I told you, having feelings for a human is not healthy and can be downright dangerous.

Are you serious? Mom was human, wasn't she? You married her and had children with her. What's the difference?

When I met your mom, I was a very old and mature vampire. I'd learned how to control myself around humans a long time before that. Your willpower will be tested many times during the next few years, but you will never be more dangerous to humans than right now.

So why are you letting Sam talk with Ben?

Your brother is vulnerable, too, but he doesn't have feelings for Ben like you do. Those feelings just add another layer of danger that could cause you to lose focus. We have a deal. I expect you to honor it. If I find out you've seen Ben at any time while you're off this base, I will take action you won't like. Is that understood, young lady?

Dad waited for my answer as he stood between Sam and me.

The phone clicked.

"What're you two doing?" Sam asked, walking back to his seat at the counter.

"Nothing. I was just leaving," I replied.

"Young lady?"

"Yes. Okay. Is that good enough for you?" I stormed out of the kitchen. *Stupid vampire life.*

I slammed my bedroom door then plopped down on the bed. I had done so well during the past few weeks, not thinking about Ben, and in one minute, all my resolve shattered. Maybe Dad was right. Maybe it wasn't good for me to be around Ben.

16

The next morning, the first day of school, I jumped into the back seat of a black sedan. My adrenaline was all over the place. After hearing Ben's voice the night before, I still had trouble settling my mind enough to sleep. When I finally did, the darkness whisked me away into a freakish nightmare about creatures that roamed the halls of the vampire school. I prayed Dad wasn't right about vampires' dreams predicting the future. If so, I was screwed.

I took a deep breath, adjusting my skirt that was making my backside itch like hell. I scratched the back of my leg and thought about the day ahead. Sure, I was super stoked to finally get off the military base, but I was also paranoid about meeting other vampires. I didn't want my first day at St. Anne's Academy to be like my first day at Durfee. I kept my fingers crossed that there would be no vampire bullies roaming the halls. I shivered at the thought.

As I waited for Sam to get in the car, my mind drifted. Ben's voice filled my head. Before my thoughts could wander, Dad slid into the front passenger seat.

"What did I tell you about human boys?" he asked as he closed his door.

I was so looking forward to not having him around me. My thoughts would be my own for an entire day.

"Jo, stop it. You would think by now, you'd be used to the mind reading," Dad said, capturing every word in my head.

"You're kidding, right?" I asked, my mouth agape. "How would you feel if someone could read every thought you had?"

"Frankly, I'm tired of your whining. If you want to find a way to block me, then find a way. Otherwise, I don't want to hear another word about how you hate me reading your mind. Understood?" He turned. Fire flickered in his eyes.

Well, two can play this game. I narrowed my eyes in return.

Sam climbed in and froze. "What's going on

already? The emotions floating around this car are suffocating, and I haven't even sat down."

"Nothing. You look like a geek," I said, trying to change the subject. "I just love the plaid jacket. Where's your bowtie?" I giggled, but it came out as a grunt.

He punched me on the arm when he finally sat and strapped himself in.

I was thankful for the interruption. I didn't want to go a few more rounds with dear-old Dad that morning. I wanted to be in a good mood for my first day of school. If I was going to be meeting people, I didn't want to come off as a lunatic or a bitch.

"I looked through the paper this morning," Sam replied. "Three more human teenagers have gone missing in the last couple of weeks. Jack isn't the only one."

"The police are looking into it," Dad added.

"Don't you find it odd that three more are missing?" I asked.

I thought back to a picture of body bags Dr. Vieira had shown in the war room a few months ago. He'd mentioned then that humans were disappearing. Maybe the news was just hitting the newspapers.

"Dad? Do you think the Plutariums have something to do with it?" Sam asked.

"Highly unlikely. Edmund wants soldiers, men who can fight. It wouldn't do him any good to enlist teenagers into his plan."

"Why, Pops? The vampire SEAL program likes them young. You even said so."

"Sure. But I've had time to train and mold the Sentinels. Edmund is a very impatient vampire. He wants immediate results. That means men who can physically fight and who have experience using weapons."

Dad might have been right. Still, a sense of foreboding gnawed at me.

"I don't want you two to worry about Edmund or the Plutariums. I want you to concentrate on school," Dad stated.

Webb climbed into the driver's seat.

"Everything okay, Lieutenant?" Dad asked.

Sam mumbled something under his breath that I couldn't quite make out. I ignored him, stealing a glance in the rearview mirror. Webb met my gaze. His eyes were shifting from blue to black. Something was wrong.

After a second, he looked away and answered Dad. "Yes, sir. Things are fine."

The tone of his voice told me otherwise. He was hiding something.

"Let's get moving and stay alert," Dad commanded.

I didn't like Dad's tone either. I imagined he and Webb were communicating telepathically.

I relaxed as the car began to move. I hadn't seen Webb in over a week. He'd only returned last night from a brief scouting mission with the Sentinels. It had something to do with the Plutariums. When I'd asked Dad about it, he said the mission was classified. In any case, it was good to see Webb.

I snuck a peek into the rearview mirror. One by one, tingles zinged through me, butterflies fluttered inside me, and every glance from him infused me with warmth that made my pulse speed up. I had to clear my mind, especially with Dad so close.

We drove past three military men who were preparing for morning colors. One of the men had the flag resting between the palms of his hands, while the other two fiddled with the rope on the flagpole. I checked to see whether Dad had the pole repaired from when I accidentally bent it in one of my telekinesis tirades—yep, the pole was straight with a shiny new gold ball at the top.

I had yet to witness the ceremony for morning colors. I'd always enjoyed listening to the national anthem. To me, it was a very emotional song. Without thinking, I began humming it in my head. Halfway through the song, I stopped. My damn plaid skirt was itchy, and my legs kept sticking to the leather seat. I grabbed the hem of my uniform, wiggling, trying to pry my legs loose.

Once I was comfortable, I started the song from the beginning again, glancing out the window. Branches on the trees swayed from one side to the other. Fallen flower blossoms littered the edges of the road, and every now and again, something hard hit the roof of the car.

By the time we turned out of the base, I had hummed the national anthem three times. It was then that I realized I hadn't thought about one thing since singing the tune. My pulse wasn't racing, my head seemed clear, and the tingles and goosebumps were no longer taking control of my body. Excitement stirred—maybe I could use it as a tactic to clear my thoughts. I made a mental note to try it again.

I cracked the window, letting in some fresh air. The closed space was a bit stifling, especially since Dad's temper still lingered.

I sniffed, taking in the first scents of the city. The human world buzzed with all sorts of smells and sounds. Engines roared to life as we passed other cars in the street. The smell of cooking grease wafted in but was quickly replaced with exhaust fumes. Sometimes, I hated that I could smell everything right down to the molecule.

As we approached an intersection, the variety of scents took a backseat to the fresh, sweet scent of honey, of human. I flared my nostrils like an animal seeking out my first meal of the day. Oh yeah—it was heaven. My fangs descended, and I licked my lips. I waffled in my seat. I wanted to tear the skirt from my body and jump out of the car.

I glanced out through the windshield. *Bingo!* A group of humans stood in line, waiting to board the bus that was stopped in front of us. All thoughts faded from my mind, except one—sinking my fangs into the soft flesh of any or all of those humans, a busload no less. I'd definitely hit the lottery. It was like a buffet line for a vampire.

Sam took my hand, killing my mouthwatering excitement. I shot him an evil glance. He shook his head ever so slowly. He was trying to tell me something, but my mind was concentrating on the bus. Suddenly, my throat burned. I squeezed my eyes shut. I tried humming the national anthem. That didn't work. The scent was too strong to think about anything except sweet, sweet blood.

My resolve for the very thing that I needed as a vampire was being tested. I was failing miserably at self-control, so I closed the window.

Sam clamped down on my hand. His eyes were obsidian. He seemed to be fighting the same demons that were plaguing me.

I suspected Dad was in my head. I didn't know for sure. I didn't care. I wanted one thing, and if Webb didn't get the car moving soon...

"Do you honestly think I'm not in tune with your thoughts?" Dad asked, breaking the silence.

"It doesn't matter. Just get me out of here," I replied.

"This is just what you need to test your willpower."

"You're loving every minute of this, aren't you?"

"Both of you need to learn restraint from your weaknesses. Today will not be the only time your self-control will be tested. Now, lock it down." Dad's tone was resolute.

I knew of one way, and that was jumping out of this car.

"I said, lock it down, young lady."

"Pops, lay off her," Sam said. "I don't know what you're reading in her mind, but this is hard for her and for me. We're young vampires with a lust for blood. We're on our way to a new school, and... well, just remember your training, sis. If anyone picks on you today, you're trained now to protect yourself."

I could always count on my brother for his support. He'd always fought my battles, and while I wasn't thinking about school, he was right. I had a few protective moves under my belt.

"You two better not fight anyone in school," Dad said.

"We do what we have to do to survive," Sam said.

Dad whipped around. "Young man, if I find out about a fight or I get a call from the school, you and I will be in that training room tonight." His bristling temper flared.

"Looking forward to it, Pops," Sam chided.

Dad's eyes flashed silver, and the vein in his neck strained against his skin.

Now whose resolve is being tested?

"I will not—" Dad's cell phone rang. He grabbed it and tapped the button while he glowered at Sam. "Go," he barked into the phone.

Sam and I both leaned back as Dad turned to face forward.

As he talked, I realized we were no longer stopped behind the human buffet line anymore. The sweet scent lingered, but it wasn't as strong.

Webb zipped down one side street then another.

The burn in the back of my throat had eased, so I relaxed and stared at the houses and buildings whizzing by.

After a few more turns, Dad said, "We're almost at the school. A few instructions before we arrive. Jo, I don't want you getting upset. I don't want anyone to know about your telekinesis. Sam, control your anger. Webb will return for you this afternoon. I have to head to a meeting at the Navy base in Newport, Rhode Island, today, so I won't be available. I don't want to get any calls from the headmistress or the security office. Son, I want you to take care of your sister. Is that understood?"

"Pops, I always take care of my sister—long before you ever came along too—so don't worry about that." Sam's voice was even and calm.

Dad turned in his seat. I thought he was going to reprimand Sam for his comment. Instead, he looked at me. "Young lady?"

"What?"

His emerald-green eyes began to shift. "An answer. Do you understand?"

"Yes. I get it, Dad. I'll behave."

What did he think I was going to do? Sure, I had been called into the principal's office a few times, but I wasn't the one he needed to worry about.

Before long, we were traveling along the edge of Mount Hope Bay. The water glistened under the morning sunlight. A few sailboats drifted and swayed, while two large yachts powered down the waterway. After a few twists and turns on the winding road, we came to a dead end. To our left was the bay, and to our right was a pair of large, black, wrought iron gates. Aside from the two men inside the guardhouse, there was no other sign that life existed beyond the gates, not even a plaque displaying the name of the property.

Sam and I bent our heads at the same time, trying to look out the windshield. In the distance, atop the hill, sat a large six-story building that looked like one of the mansions in Newport, Rhode Island.

The car rolled to the gate, and Webb rolled the window down.

"Mason," was all he said to the man who had walked out of the shingle-and-glass building, wearing a black cargo uniform, military boots, and fingerless gloves.

The guard looked down at his clipboard and flipped through sheets of paper. After a few seconds, he scribbled something before placing the clipboard behind his back. He dipped down and peered into the car. His chocolate-brown eyes became black.

"Wait one," the guard said then went into the guardhouse.

"Vampire," Sam muttered.

"He is," Dad confirmed. "He's also a Guardian."

"Is that like a Sentinel?" I asked.

"In the human world, he'd be equivalent to the local police," Webb said.

We sat at the gate, waiting. I guessed the Guardian needed to get approval for us to enter.

Webb poked out his head slightly. "Are we clear?"

A different Guardian stepped out, twirling his forefinger in the air as he approached. The vampire was massive. He stood well over six feet and had to have weighed a lot. His chest was sculpted in all the right places. His long, wavy blond hair was tied behind his head. But his good-looking features weren't what had me in awe. The beast was a walking tattoo shop. Both his arms were covered in colorful designs.

"Commander, Lieutenant, Ms. Lawrence will meet you in her office. There's visitor parking in front of the building," he said, pointing toward the main entrance. "Head up the stairs and through the main doors, and two Guardians will be inside to meet you."

Webb nodded as the gates in front of us opened.

"Have a good day," the Guardian said, backing away from the car.

I glanced behind me, still in awe of him, and noticed one tattoo I did recognize. The Jupiter Sentinel symbol was tattooed on the back of his neck.

"Is that guy... a... Sentinel?" I asked, my gaze still peeled behind me.

Sam turned to look again.

"He is," Webb replied. "He's one of my team members."

"How come I haven't seen him on base?" I asked.

"We have a few Sentinels working for the Guardians," Dad said. "That's all you need to know."

Sam and I faced forward. The road from the gate to the main entrance was fairly steep and winding, which felt like a metaphor for my life.

17

A carpet of pristine groomed grass spanned the grounds, spilling out to the edge, where a large fence bordered the property. In the distance, across the bay, homes dotted the hillside. The boats I saw earlier were mere dots from where we parked, high atop the hill.

Dad slid out first. He seemed to be in a hurry, taking the stone steps two at a time. Webb followed.

Sam waited for me at the bottom of the steps, fidgeting with his tie.

I hesitated for a moment, inhaling the salt air drifting up from the bay and feeling the warm sunshine against my skin. It was nice to be somewhere other than the base.

"Jo!" Dad shouted. "We need to go."

When I walked up to Sam, he was still messing with his tie. He looked uncomfortable as hell. It was the first time I'd ever seen my brother in a sports jacket and dress pants. Heck, I'd never worn a skirt, for that matter. While in foster care, we'd had to take what we could get, which meant hand-me-downs. Jeans and T-shirts, sometimes new and sometimes well worn, were all we had to choose from.

"You ready?" Sam asked, smoothing back his hair.

"Not really." I looked at my brother.

Sam had grown a few more inches since he'd turned vampire. He was taller than Dad. "What's wrong?" he asked.

"Aside from your geekiness in that plaid jacket, you look good."

He rolled his eyes and climbed the steps two at a time.

The building before me was enormous. It looked like something out of medieval times. Pointed-arched windows lined the building from one end to the other. Each window had a pane of stained glass, all symbols and shapes that I couldn't quite make out. It reminded me of a church, only there weren't any religious figures painted on the glass.

"You coming?" Sam called.

I shrugged. Part of me was stalling. Reluctantly, I climbed the steps, stopping when I reached the massive columns that supported the archway. Two large wooden doors were open. Above them, "Ye who enter shall respect the power of their destiny" was inscribed in stone.

Dad stood to my right with his arms crossed over his chest. "Let's go," he said. "We're late."

The four of us entered.

Suddenly, my tattoo flared to life, pins and needles prickling the area around it. *Hmm.* Maybe the gold-speckled paint was still reacting with my skin, or maybe it was that freaking itchy uniform. I decided it had to be the uniform since my legs were itchy too.

The Guardians on either side of the corridor inside wore the same uniform that the big badass dude at the gate was wearing—a full black cargo uniform, military boots, and fingerless gloves.

Both greeted Webb and Dad, and the one on the left instructed them to stand with their arms out to their sides. Once they complied, the Guardians patted them down as though they were criminals.

"Sorry, sir. You can't have this inside," the Guardian on my left said, pulling Webb's sword from his belt. The sword beeped and vibrated in the Guardian's hands.

"Hand that to me, please," Webb commanded. "I'm the only one who can touch it."

I guessed they weren't part of the SEALs or the Sentinels. Otherwise, they'd have known that Sentinel swords couldn't be handled by anyone except their owners.

The Guardian handed it back. "Drop it in this bin, then. You can retrieve it on your way out."

Webb did, and Dad did the same with his Sentinel sword.

Sam and I were next. Instead of frisking us, they each waved a wand over our bodies. They didn't beep, so Sam and I were free to enter.

"Ms. Lawrence will be out shortly. Please have a seat on the bench," one of the Guardians said, motioning to the left wall.

While Dad and Webb sat, Sam and I stood, checking out our new school.

The floor between the headmistress's office on the left and the admin offices on the right had a seal imprinted on the honey-colored wood floor, a large circle spanning the entire width of the hall. Inside it, words were written around the perimeter of the circle: "Education is the key to unlocking your journey." Embedded in the circle was another circle. Inside the inner one was the same marking that Dad had on his arm—the circle of life and the symbols for earth, water, air, and fire. Scattered between the two circles were other symbols that looked to be astrological signs.

I was convinced that the vampire world lived by symbols and believed they held power. Hopefully, the one on my shoulder would give me the power I needed to get through life. Okay, maybe not life—maybe just that day.

"Dad?" I called, my voice echoing in the hall.

"Yes." He raised his head.

"This is the same marking as you have on your arm, right?"

Sam tore his gaze from the trophy cabinet.

"It is. As I mentioned to you, our powers are based on alchemy."

"What the heck is alchemy, Pops?" Sam asked. He focused on the floor beneath his feet.

"You'll learn about it soon enough."

The door to the headmistress's office opened. A tall, slender woman with brown hair and eyes walked out. She was dressed in a black pencil skirt that covered her knees, a form-fitting black jacket, and a crisp, pink-collared shirt. Her hair was tied back at the crown, leaving the remaining strands of hair spilling around her shoulders.

"Steven," she said, extending her hand. "It's so

good to see you. It's been quite some time. You look well."

"Ms. Lawrence, always a pleasure," Dad replied, taking her hand in both of his.

Sam and I were standing on the circle when she turned and glided over to us, her low heels clicking against the hardwood.

"I've heard so much about both of you." She took a handful of my hair, scanning my features. "So pretty. You do look like your mother. Beautiful." She stepped in front of Sam. "Wow. Steven, the resemblance between you two is remarkable. Anyway, I'm Ms. Lawrence. I'm pleased to finally meet you both. Now, why don't we all go into my office? We have a few minutes before orientation begins. Most of the students are in the auditorium already, but I'm still waiting for a couple of stragglers who are also running late this morning."

Sam and I looked at each other then back at Dad.

"Well? You heard Ms. Lawrence. Let's go inside," he said, his voice deepening slightly.

Webb walked in first. Dad followed. Ms. Lawrence held the door, waiting for us.

I'd taken one step when searing pain hit me square in the temples. *Christ!*

"What is it?" Sam lightly touched my elbow.

"Didn't you know Dad could now get in my head?" I pressed my fingers to my temples.

"Sure. I know he reads your mind."

"Um. No. I mean now he can talk to me telepathically. Hasn't he been in your head?"

"Once. I try to stay away from Pops. I don't want anyone in my head."

I guess I hadn't really noticed, although since Sam mentioned it, he wasn't around Dad as much as I was. When we were on base, Sam was either in his bedroom or the training room. He mostly ventured out of his bedroom when Dad wasn't around. Maybe I should take note and follow his lead.

Young lady, I'm warning you. Now, grab your brother and get into the office.

"Come on, Sam. Dad is about to blow a gasket."

Ms. Lawrence's office was rather large. The room was all wood—wood floors, a wooden ceiling, wood-paneled walls, a wooden desk. The only furniture not made of wood was the couch and chairs in the sitting area, just off from her office.

The lady is high on wood.

"Please, have a seat in the sunroom," she said, waving a hand at the arched entrance to my left.

Dad sat on the couch, and Webb took a position on the opposite end. Sam leaned against the wall while I stood between Ms. Lawrence's office and the sunroom. She made her way to a bar area, where she grabbed a cup and poured coffee into it.

"Can I offer any of you a beverage?" she asked.

"No, thank you, Ms. Lawrence. We're fine," Dad replied.

"Very well," she said, sitting in the chair by the window, which overlooked the grounds and Mount Hope Bay. "A couple of welcome items, and then I'll have the children escorted to the auditorium."

"That would be appreciated," Dad said.

Webb didn't say a word. Neither did Sam or I.

Ms. Lawrence directed her attention at Sam and me between sips of coffee. "First, welcome. I'm looking forward to having both of you in school. I'm excited to see how you progress during your time here. The next few weeks are mainly a refresher of your last year at the human high school. The summer is a good time to catch up on the classes you missed recently and prepare you for the fall semester. Students in school this time of year are new vampires, like you. Today is dedicated to meeting your fellow students and finding your way around the school. It will only be a half-day. A full day of classes will begin tomorrow. Questions?"

I shook my head. The onset of a bad headache loomed.

A verbal answer is expected.

Dad, it hurts when you do this?

Obey your elders, young lady.

Crap.

Dad scowled at me from where he was sitting.

"No, ma'am," I replied.

Ms. Lawrence looked at Sam.

"Son, answer Ms. Lawrence."

"No, ma'am," Sam said.

"Good. I'll have Mr. Banks escort you to the auditorium, then." She placed her coffee cup on the bar and left the room.

Dad let out a deep breath. "I'm warning you two. Politeness and manners are expected. If I hear you've been disrespectful—"

"We get it, Pops," Sam said.

Ms. Lawrence walked back in with Mr. Banks.

"Now remember what we talked about in the car," Dad warned. "Webb will return for you later. Are we clear?"

"Yes, Dad," I replied.

"Yes, Pops," Sam said.

"Follow me," Mr. Banks said.

I glanced over my shoulder at Webb. He nodded at me before standing. He didn't even need to speak to get my insides dancing. Before I could even think another thought, I started humming the national anthem. I had to keep my mind blank until I was out of Daddy Dearest's range.

Mr. Banks, a medium-build vampire dressed in a black suit, led us to the auditorium.

Sam fiddled with his jacket as we passed a string of lockers on both sides of the hall.

"Are you nervous?" I whispered.

"No. Why?"

"You were playing with your tie, now your jacket," I replied.

"I hate this uniform," he whispered.

I just shrugged. I didn't know what to say. I was just as uncomfortable. My bony knees were on display for the world, and I hated it, and the skirt had to have been wool because it was still making my legs itch like bejesus.

After a few turns down a couple of halls, we were in the auditorium. Theater-style seats rose from the stage at the bottom and spanned back underneath a U-shaped balcony that hung above the entire auditorium. Blue velvet curtains draped the large wooden stage, which had a podium in the center and two large television screens hanging from the ceiling on each side.

Mr. Banks waved a hand toward the seats. Sam and I followed his silent directive as he disappeared behind the blue curtain. We made our way to the middle aisle, passing a few vampires seated in the front row, texting on their cell phones. Others gathered in small groups, talking to each other. A few glanced our way. Most didn't. Sam settled for seats in the fourth row, behind everyone else. Most of the other vampires had taken seats in the first two rows.

A man fiddled with wires at the podium on stage, and a couple of women talked just behind him. After several more minutes, a short, red-headed woman took the podium. She had pale skin, and her hair was twisted into a neat bun. Her navy-blue jacket fitted her chunky waist, and she wore a pink scarf around her neck.

"Welcome," she said. "Please, take your seats. We have much to do today. My name is Ms. Chapman. I'm part of the administrative staff on campus. I will be your go-to person for any questions on schedules and paperwork. Before we get started, I would like to introduce you to Mr. Banks."

Mr. Banks emerged from behind the curtain and grabbed the microphone. His bald head shone brightly beneath the stage lights.

"Some ground rules." His voice was deep and boomed through the speakers around us. "All of you sitting in this room are new vampires. You're here to learn the ways of your new world. My role as head of security is to keep each of you safe while you're inside this building and on this campus. My Guardians are here to protect you against any threats or harm. I don't expect to have any problems, but times are changing."

The crowd started to whisper. Sam and I looked at each other. Dad had said the place was safe and well protected, but my stomach suddenly tightened.

"While you're here, you will follow all our rules and regulations," Mr. Banks continued in a pithy tone. "Emergency exits are posted in every classroom, and the staff is well versed in emergency procedures in the event there is one. My only advice to you is to keep your head down. Stay out of trouble. I don't want to see any of you in my office unless you're there to say hi." He inclined his head toward Ms. Chapman.

"Thank you, Mr. Banks. Now to the fun part. Today is a short day. It is set up for you to explore the campus, pick up your schedules, meet some of the teachers, and get to know your fellow students. The thirty of you sitting here will be graduating in two years as a class, so get to know one another. This is the beginning of a fantastic journey for each of you." She nodded to another person standing at the edge of the stage. "Ms. Weston will be giving you a guided tour. Gather down in front of the stage. I will see everyone shortly."

The vampires stood, grabbed their belongings, and slid out of the aisles, talking all the while.

Sam and I followed the crowd to the stage area. Immediately, a girl about my own height turned to me, smiling.

"Hi. I'm Zea Yangstrom," she said, extending her hand as I walked up. "I don't remember seeing you at Grayson Manor."

Jeepers! Doesn't this vamp believe in personal space? The only thing between us was two inches of air. My claustrophobia kicked in before I could step away.

"Something wrong?" she asked, dropping her hand.

At least her breath was minty. "No. I'm Jo Mason and this is my brother, Sam," I replied, taking a couple steps back.

"As in the daughter of Steven Mason?" she asked, eyes widening.

Did I hit a nerve? Or did I say something I wasn't supposed to? God, please don't let Dad's name be the death of me here at school.

I stared at Zea. Her curly dark-brown hair was pulled back from her face with a red headband. She had a smattering of freckles, and her cheeks were flushed with a shimmering pink.

"Yes, Steven Mason is our father," Sam chimed in. "Why?" he asked in a distrustful tone.

"Oh my. He's a powerful vampire. One of the most powerful." Her voice oozed with admiration or maybe something else—I couldn't tell, but she might have been gushing over my dad. And okay, he was handsome, but he was *my dad.*

I drew my eyebrows together. "Do you know our father?"

"No, I've never met him. My dad has been trying to get a meeting with him," she said, shaking her head.

"Meeting?" Sam and I blurted out at the same time.

"My sister is really sick. My father spoke of some breakthrough medicine that your father developed."

Sam chuckled. "I think you're mistaken. Steven Mason hasn't developed anything."

All hope drained from her face.

Perhaps she was referring to the concoctions that Dr. Vieira had whipped up in his lab for cuts and open wounds, or the solution to counteract the effects of cobalt. "What my brother is trying to say is that our father is not a doctor."

"Oh. I..." Her voice trailed off.

"Is your sister a vampire?" I asked.

Zea nodded. "She turned the same time I did.

She's older than me and wanted to wait until I decided whether I was going to turn. We either wanted to do it together or not at all. We did all the right things: the paperwork, the council, and then Grayson Manor. Then something happened while we were at Grayson Manor. She woke up one night, puking, and had a high fever. Since then, she's been in a coma." Tears formed in her brown eyes.

"I'm sorry about your sister," I said.

Zea pulled a tissue from her purse and patted her eyes.

Sam diverted his attention toward the stage. I imagined Zea crying was making him a bit uncomfortable.

Ms. Weston cleared her throat. "Listen up."

The whispers and voices died, and the group gathered closer to the stage. Zea dropped her head and walked over to the group.

"What do you think she's talking about?" Sam asked.

"Maybe the miracle drug is the solution Dr. Vieira uses for the cobalt reaction. Or even Neil's blood. It supposedly helped you."

"Dr. V was never able to confirm that Neil's blood did anything," he said.

Zea's description of her sister's symptoms reminded me of what Sam had experienced when he drank the tainted boxed blood. Dr. Vieira had the blood sent to the lab to have it tested, but I hadn't heard whether he'd received the results. Maybe Grayson Manor had experienced a similar incident. "I'll ask him when we get home later."

"Sis, don't get involved. We have enough shit to watch out for."

Sam was probably right. Still, I wanted to know more about the boxed blood, especially if that was going to be our steady source of blood in the near future.

"We'll be taking a quick tour of the school. As we walk, I will fill you in on some of the history of the grounds and the building," Ms. Weston said.

We began our tour immediately outside the auditorium.

"The pictures here" —she pointed to a wall of portraits— "are of the founders of the school. You'll learn all about the others in your vampire history class, but for this tour, we'll focus on the man at the top."

The vampire she was referring to looked to be in his twenties. His large nose blended well with his strong jaw and deeply set green eyes. His black hair was pulled back, and he had one dimple showing on his right cheek.

"This is Lord Charles James. He's not only the

founder of this school—he's also the leader of our world."

I nudged Sam. "Isn't that the guy Dad mentioned a few times?"

"I guess," was all he said.

I vaguely remembered his name coming up. I moved closer to the crowd. I definitely wanted to learn more about the dude.

"He kind of looks like your brother," Zea whispered.

I jerked my head in her direction then up to the picture of Lord James. I studied it for a long minute. Maybe a hint of resemblance, but I didn't really see it.

"Lord James is a very old vampire," Ms. Weston continued. "He's one of the first vampires in our history who was able to withstand the sun's rays. In fact, you could say he was the first natural-born vampire."

A boy in front of me raised his hand.

"Yes, young man?"

"Is it true he's sick and dying?" the boy, who had whitish-blond hair, asked.

"I wouldn't believe all the rumors you hear," Ms. Weston replied.

She continued to talk about the school's history. Her tall, lanky figure towered over most of us. Aside from Sam, only two other male vampires dominated the crowd in height. The majority were average, and the mixture of male and female was split down the middle.

The door to the auditorium opened, and Ms. Chapman poked out her head. "Ms. Weston, a moment, please."

"Talk among yourselves. I'll be right back." She disappeared into the auditorium with Ms. Chapman.

"I hear Lord James and your father are like best friends," Zea said, leaning in.

Boy, she sure knew more about my father than I did. I might have known more if Dad talked to us. Maybe it wouldn't be a bad idea to become friends with Zea. I could use a girlfriend since I couldn't see Darcy, and I could learn a lot about what was going on in the vampire world.

"Where did you—"

Heels scuffed against the floor behind me, creating a loud echo in the hall.

"Crap. Um, sis? You may want to turn around." Sam moved closer to me.

Now what?

"Mason? Is that you?" a very familiar voice asked.

"Don't talk to him. He's the devil, you know," Zea said quietly, looking at the source of the voice. "Vile and disgusting."

"Is that Moonbeam?"

All the blood rushed out of me when I heard that name. It couldn't have been him. It just couldn't. Rage, shock, and fear thrummed through me.

I spun around. My mouth fell to the floor. *How in this stupid world, in my screwed-up life, is Blake Turner a vampire?*

"You can close your disgusting mouth," Blake Turner said. His gaze slid over my body.

I wanted to jump in the bay to wash off the slime. The fish were cleaner than him.

Dad was going to love this one. I promised I'd be good, but with Blake standing in front of me, all my promises went over the cliff.

Sam grabbed my hand.

My breathing became shallow.

"I see you still have your brother doing your dirty work." Blake's malevolent tone flipped a switch inside me.

I took one step forward, knees trembling. I wanted to show him I wasn't afraid of him. Even if I was.

Sam stopped me from moving any farther, which was probably a good thing since my legs were about to fail me.

I dug deep into the recesses of my mind, willing my knees to stop shaking. My body was on the verge of convulsing, but maybe it wasn't out of fear. Maybe it was just pure rage. I would have liked to get hold of the scumbag who drummed up this scenario to ruin my life.

Sam squeezed my hand tighter. Knowing he was by my side made me relax a fraction. But to add salt to the wound, the little devil inside my head kept coaxing me to punch the shit out of Blake. My yin and yang were fighting for control. As I stood cemented to the floor, all sorts of thoughts ran rampant through my head. However, one stuck out clearly. If he was a monster as a human, I could barely imagine how much of a jerk he would be as a vampire.

Blake's eyebrows were scrunched as he stared at me. He looked like he was in pain, and his forehead was coated in a sheen of sweat. He stood a head taller than I remembered. His eyes were no longer yellowish-brown, but a deep golden yellow. They almost reminded me of the beady eyes of the wolves I'd confronted in the forest weeks before. His fangs were descended, and his aura said danger, predator, and enemy.

I pulled free from Sam's grip and moved closer to my kryptonite. My heart thumped erratically. As I drew closer to him, holding his gaze, something shifted inside me. Rage obliterated the shock and fear, and bloodthirsty malice consumed me. The room began to spin. My eyes flashed vampire. Then my fangs shot out of my gums, and at the same time, my body writhed as that little devil took control.

Glass crashed in the background.

"What's wrong with her?" Blake asked. His menacing grin waned.

"Jo, you need to calm down. You're in *Carrie* mode," Sam whispered in my ear.

I narrowed my gaze, stalking toward Blake. I wanted to rip out his heart.

He stumbled to the left then backward, almost falling on his ass. Sweat dripped from his forehead.

"Make her stop," Blake shouted. "She's hurting me."

A small, cold hand touched my arm. "Jo." Zea's voice was soft. "He's not worth your energy."

She had no idea how long I'd waited to torture that scuzzbag.

Blake grabbed his head and bent over.

"Sis, stop. I think you're actually hurting him. I don't know how. Take some deep breaths. Remember to breathe." Sam's voice resonated somewhere in the back of my mind. "Christ, Jo. Pops is going to have our heads. Please," Sam begged.

I'd never heard my brother plead before. I wanted to take revenge on Blake more than anything, and a part of me wanted to prove to Sam that I could take care of myself.

"Please, sis. Blake will get his day, I promise, but not in front of these people," he whispered. His tone was raw with desperation.

"Um... Jo? Ms. Weston is coming," Zea whispered.

I took in some air. Maybe he was right. I swallowed and blinked several times. I unclenched my fists and dropped my shoulders.

Sam and Zea caught me before I fell to the floor.

"Young lady, what've you done? You've destroyed school property!" Ms. Weston said, glancing at the broken window then at me. "And you almost hurt that boy."

She had no idea how much I wanted to destroy him. I wanted payback for all those times Blake had bullied me.

"Weird as a human and even weirder as a vampire," Blake barked. "What are you, Moonbeam?"

"Stuff it, Turner," Sam warned.

"Me? I should be asking you that," I shot back, pulling away from Sam and Zea's grips. "Something's off with you." I was face to face with him.

"You almost killed me," he sneered.

"You're being a bit dramatic, asshole," I said.

"Enough, all of you," Ms. Weston said in a

sharp tone. Then she looked at me. "We do not swear in this school. Now, apologize to the young man not only for calling him a name, but for hurting him," Ms. Weston ordered.

I glared at her. Like that was going to happen. In her vampire dreams.

Blake's lips curled into a smug grin that I wanted to punch into a frown.

I bit my lip, and before I could say anything, three loud blasts pierced the air.

"Into the auditorium!" Ms. Weston shouted above the noise. "This is a drill. Don't panic."

"Why inside?" some vamp in the group asked. "What if it's a fire?"

"The fire alarm is a different pitch. This alarm means to gather the students and take them to one of the safe zones inside the building," she said, raising her voice again.

All the students scattered, including Blake.

"Come on, Jo." Sam pulled me.

"Let's go. Hurry!" Ms. Weston barked, her eyes turning black.

I ran, keeping up with Sam. Zea was ahead of him. All of us flew into the auditorium. The scene was pure panic, even though Ms. Weston had told us not to panic. Maybe my interaction with Blake had frightened them.

Whispers floated in the air from those on their

cell phones. I needed to talk with Dad about getting a phone. Then Sam and I could call for help when we needed it.

"Okay, I need everyone to get down near the stage," Ms. Weston instructed.

The group scurried, following her instructions. Several of them had their hands over their ears.

"Again, this is just a drill. We're going to our safe room behind the stage," she shouted above the alarm.

"Can't they turn the alarms off?" shouted a male vampire.

"They will," Ms. Weston replied.

"Come on, sis," Sam said.

"I'm not getting in a safe room with Blake," I said, surveying the crowd.

Every single vampire had black eyes except for one. Blake's were still a deep golden yellow.

Before I could process this observation, Blake leaned into Zea and buried his fangs into her neck. Her eyes widened, her fangs dropped, then she let out a loud shriek that reminded me of nails clawing a chalkboard. I shivered.

Sam ran toward the crowd, barreling through a handful of vamps. When he reached Blake, he extended his right leg, twisting his torso at the same time. The pad of his foot connected with Blake's chest, and both Blake and Zea fell to the floor.

The vampires crowded around Sam, and I couldn't see what was happening. I shook off the shock that consumed me and ran over to my brother.

Blake's fangs were still clamped on to Zea's neck, drawing her blood into his disgusting mouth. Her eyes were closed. It looked as if she wasn't breathing.

Anger rose, and without thinking, I slammed my foot onto Blake's ankle. His mouth fell away from her neck, and he let out a guttural growl.

The students backed away.

Blake jumped up, and before I could move, he flew through the air. His fangs were dripping with blood, and his eyes had turned from yellow to the color of the sun on a hot summer's day. He resembled a fireball, soaring through the air.

I crouched into my fighter's stance, waiting. My adrenaline surged. The predator in me was ready as though she had been waiting for this moment all her life.

He landed in front of me with his knees slightly bent, blood sliding down his chin.

Without hesitation, I sprang forward, twisting my upper torso and planting a roundhouse kick that connected with his jaw. Blake fell back into Sam with a look of surprise on his face.

Sam twisted Blake's arms behind his back.

Every ounce of me wanted to leap forward and tear off Blake's head, but a slight shake of Sam's head stilled me.

But then Blake smirked. That was all I needed to finish what I started.

I lunged, and in one fluid motion, I extended my right arm, twisted my wrist, and threw out my fist. Bones cracked. Blood sprayed in all directions. And I realized too late it wasn't Blake's blood. Ms. Weston had walked into the fray. I shook my head, trying to clear the haze. After a second or two, I glanced down at the scene on the floor. Ms. Weston was flat on her back, blood gushing from her nose and dripping onto Blake, who was pinned under her.

Oh shit!

The alarm and horns had stopped. The voices in the room sounded frantic.

One of the male vamps ran over to her then dropped to his knees, shock plastered over his pale features. Then the doors in the auditorium burst open.

Students scattered as the Guardians moved deeper into the room. A flash of bright light blinded me, as though someone had snapped a picture, causing me to stumble. Catching me before I fell, Sam was by my side.

"Kraft, take the Mason children to Ms.

Lawrence's office," Mr. Banks instructed. "Frost, Skane, take Ms. Yangstrom and Ms. Weston to the nurse's office. And this one too."

I imagined Mr. Banks was referring to Blake.

"Let's go, sis," Sam said, guiding me toward Kraft. "You know we're in a world of shit. Pops is going to have our heads."

At that moment, I didn't care about Dad. Of course, Sam was right, but I had been trying to save Zea from Blake. I was tired of him bullying me or any other girl. My heart went out to my new friend. I just hoped Sam and I had gotten to her in time.

Every fiber inside me wanted to see Blake take his last breath. While I was enraged with his imperious attitude and still stunned Blake Turner was even at my school and in my life again, I couldn't shake the knowledge that he was a vampire. Something about him kept nagging at my intuition. I couldn't make sense of it.

My mind was still in shock, but a cold, painful shiver slid down my spine. The old man in my dream had been right. Hell existed in many places in this world, and school was one of them.

18

I fidgeted in Ms. Lawrence's office as I waited for either Webb or Dad to arrive. Sam and I had been sitting in her sunroom for the past two hours. Meanwhile, Ms. Lawrence informed us that Zea and Ms. Weston were going to be fine. I figured that Ms. Weston would be okay since she only had a nosebleed, but I wasn't so sure about Zea. Atherton had explained that a vampire could go brain-dead if their blood was drained.

My mind was still processing the fact that Blake Turner was a vampire and at my stupid school. My life was ruined. Dad and I were going to have a long, drawn-out talk about it—Durfee was looking a whole lot better to me. Its large student body meant at least I could hide there. At the vampire academy, no way. I stuck out like a bad zit.

Sam sat in one of the plush chairs, staring out the window. He hadn't said a word since the badass Sentinel-Guardian, Kraft, had hauled us out of the auditorium.

"You haven't said much," I murmured.

Sam turned his head. "Pops is going to be furious."

I rolled my eyes.

Sam sighed. "I'm learning the more I'm able to feel emotions, the more it sucks. His temper will rub off on me. I'm trying to control it or block it, but I don't really know how."

I scooted my chair closer to him. I didn't want Ms. Lawrence to hear about our family problems. I had learned in Durfee that the walls had ears, and this place was worse. Vampires could hear a flippin' pin drop from five miles away.

"What do you mean? Does it physically hurt or something?" I asked, wrinkling my forehead.

He leaned over, dropped his head to his hands, then rubbed his face. "When Pops gets mad, he exerts this energy that somehow sends sharp pain to the base of my skull, and then it radiates out into my head. And sometimes, yes, it's painful."

"Maybe he's trying to get in your head. Maybe

it doesn't have anything to do with his emotions," I reasoned.

"No," he said, his voice muffled. "It's definitely his emotions." He raised his head. "When I got into the car this morning and you two were arguing, I got a headache instantly."

"Everything I read about Empaths said you had to be touching someone to really absorb their emotions."

"Obviously, whatever book you've been reading is wrong." He leaned back in his chair.

Then something dawned on me. "Did you feel anything when I was in *Carrie* mode earlier?" I studied him.

Sam had removed his tie and his jacket. The sleeves of his white shirt were pushed up above his elbows. The front of it was peppered in blood. His hair was no longer in a ponytail but hung freely around his shoulders. "That's the thing—no. All the rage and fury you were clearly throwing out at Blake, and I didn't feel any of it. It seems I can feel everyone else's emotions but not yours. This whole thing is driving me crazy."

"Huh." Nothing about vampire powers applied to me, it seemed. Dad could read my mind without touching me, but no one else's. I had the power of telekinesis, but no other vampire in our world did. Oh, and my eyes turned violet when my emotions changed. I was beginning to wonder if I'd been born with a faulty vampire gene.

A car door shut. Sam and I exchanged glances. He straightened, steeling his shoulders. I stood then peered through the window.

Dad didn't waste any time getting out of the car. He jumped the stone steps four at a time. His caustic expression made my blood gel. Webb followed on his heels, his hair whipping around him.

Dad's voice rumbled in the hall as his boots scuffled along the floor. Suddenly, the air pressure dropped in the building, a clear indication that a very bad storm was headed our way.

"You ready?" I asked.

"Whatever. I'll have to take a bottle of aspirin when this is over."

We were both going to need more than just aspirin. "I'm the one who did the most damage. Dad won't be mad at you."

"Yeah, right." Sam laughed. "Where there's an opening, Pops will find it. He'll blame me for this."

Maybe he was right. After all, Dad did instruct him to watch out for me and make sure I didn't do anything wrong.

"Where are they?" Dad's voice boomed with rage.

"Steven, please wait," Ms. Lawrence pleaded.

She was trying to calm Dad. *Good luck with that.*

"I appreciate what you're trying to do, Elizabeth, but I—"

Webb walked into the sunroom, breaking my concentration on what Dad was about to say. Probably a good thing—then again, maybe not. My stomach did the flip-flop dance it usually did when Webb was near.

"What happened?" he asked with a slight grin on his face, almost mockingly.

Sam stood to face Webb, anger instantly etched on his face.

They were going to exchange either words or punches—I wasn't sure which. I touched Sam. "Put up your shields or whatever it is you can do." The last thing we needed was for Sam to get into a fight with Webb. "Not here, Sam," I warned.

"Don't worry, sis. I'm not going to. His emotions are telling me he's calm, not angry or—"

"What's telling you?" Webb asked.

"We think Sam is an Empath," I blurted out.

"Do you, now? And how do you know that?" Webb's eyes swirled with curiosity.

"Because I feel your freaking emotions when you're around my sister. That's how."

Webb was on him in a flash.

Here we go. Leave it to my brother to stir up trou-

ble. Eye color changed, fangs sparkled, and the electricity in the small room became unbearable. I was about to stop them from getting into a brawl then decided against it. The fact was that I was super curious how Webb was going to answer. I sat and crossed my right leg over my left. If popcorn had been available, I would've bought a bucket for the show. Excitement stirred within me as I waited anxiously for the words to spill from Webb's kiss-me lips.

"And what do you think my feelings are for your sister?" he asked.

Okay, I didn't think that would be the first question out of his mouth. Like Sam, Webb threw caution to the wind, which was unusual for the reserved vampire. *Yeah, Sam. What are his feelings for me? Come on. Tell him before Dad comes in.*

In the distance, Dad and Ms. Lawrence were finishing up their conversation.

The two vampires matched each other in height. Mere inches separated their noses, and while the power in the room was choking me, I didn't care anymore.

"What are you two doing?" Dad asked. "Lieutenant, stand down."

Bummer.

Webb took two steps back, glowering at my brother.

"Lieutenant, we're not here for you and my son to get into it. Are we clear?"

"Yes, sir." Webb pulled his cell phone from his belt.

"Lieutenant, meet us outside," Dad said.

Webb strode into Ms. Lawrence's office, and they engaged in conversation. Then their voices trailed off and were just a whisper after the door closed.

Dad stood with his arms crossed over his broad chest. The silence in the room was unbearable as silver and sparks of red banished the emerald green in his eyes.

My blood turned from gel to pure ice, frozen solid. I'd seen Dad's fury before, but never that intensely. It was as though he were about to shift from vampire to devil.

"What do you have to say for yourselves?" he asked no one in particular. "I thought I had made myself clear in the car and in this very room earlier today. Did I not?"

Sam only moved an inch before Dad grasped his arm.

"Wait." My voice was just a crackle. I cleared my throat. "Dad."

He whipped around. His eyes were a pool of molten lava, shifting between red, black, and silver —colors I had yet to see from the powerful vampire. His gaze met mine, his hard glare turning my frozen blood to stone.

A sharp pain grabbed the base of my skull, radiated slowly upward, and spread into the deepest recesses of my brain. I winced as my fangs descended and my eyes shifted. *What is he doing?* I placed the palms of my hand against my face, willing the pain to stop.

"You're hurting her. Stop!" Sam said.

I closed my eyes, dropped my hands to my side, and inhaled deeply through my nose. With each release of breath, I pushed, forcing out the tendrils of pain one by one. When only a small, dull ache remained, I opened my eyes and met Dad's gaze.

His eyes were muted silver. Gone were the sparks of fury.

A warm feeling barreled through me, and my blood slowly melted, allowing me to move my limbs.

"Impressive, young lady," Dad said as his shoulders relaxed.

To my horror, Sam was slumped in the chair with his head in his hands as if Dad had drained all the energy out of him.

"Sam? You okay?" I asked, kneeling down in front of him.

"What's wrong with him?" Dad asked.

"Your boiling anger hurts him," I replied as I rubbed Sam's knee. "Hey, look at me, Sam."

"I'll be fine." He raised his head. His green eyes had turned black, and deep lines creased his forehead. "But this was the worst I've had it."

First chance I had, I was going to research Empaths before it killed Sam.

"What?" Dad asked, sidling up to me. "Is that true? Is Sam an Empath? Son?"

"We think so," I said. I kept my eyes focused on my brother.

"So, you feel what others around you feel?" Dad's tone had morphed from anger to concern in an instant.

"What's wrong, Dad?" I kept one hand on Sam's knee.

Dad walked over to the window, rubbing his jaw. A late-day shadow painted his face, even though it was only late morning.

It was then I realized he wasn't in one of his black cargo uniforms or the khaki one with all the ribbons. He was wearing his dress blues, the uniform he'd worn in the picture with Mom.

I tilted my head to one side, remembering the picture as if it were in front of me now. Then, for some reason, Zea popped into my head. She'd seemed to be infatuated with Dad for his power, but it wasn't just power that oozed from him. Underneath his power and confidence lay a father who was worried about his children. At that moment, I was proud to be the daughter of Steven Mason, even though he had just tried to shatter my brain cells. Seeing him in that uniform reminded me of his words about how he loved my mother, although he had yet to tell me he loved me.

"Well?" I stood, and so did Sam.

We met Dad at the bank of windows. In the distance, across the bay, smoke billowed from a stack that rose high in the air. The water rippled from east to west, a clear indication the wind was still as strong as it was earlier this morning.

"Empaths... let's just say the ability to feel other people's emotions can ruin a vampire."

Sam growled. He seemed to be biting his tongue.

"If you don't control how you filter others' emotions, it will consume you, especially in battle. It's the worst of the special powers to have." Dad crossed his arms as he continued to stare out the window.

"Just great, Pops," Sam spat.

"You're going to learn to control it, Son."

"How?" I asked.

"There are ways. It's all up to the individual to learn how to block them. Just like you did with me.

Somehow, you threw up mental shields to push me out of your head. Sam will need to do the same. Sometimes, vampires who are Empaths can also manipulate air, one of the four elements. This helps to shield them from strong emotions that are emitted. Some Empaths can also channel emotions and use them to their advantage."

"Huh?" Sam quirked an eyebrow.

"Look, son, time will tell if you'll acquire the ability to manipulate air or any of the elements. Until then, you'll have to find a way to filter other people's emotions."

"I've been able to handle it so far. It's *your* emotions that cause me pain. It seems you're a walking time bomb, and when you get into one of your moods, I get a searing pain in my head."

Dad rubbed his face again. "Look, we've gotten off track. You two have managed to change the subject of why I had to leave a very important meeting in Newport to race over here. Now, who wants to start?" His gaze swept over me then Sam.

"It was all my fault. I'm sorry." I wanted to atone for my mistakes, shield Sam, and make Dad understand the severity of the situation with Blake.

Sam gave me a what-the-hell look, but I would clue him in later.

The muscles in Dad's jaw relaxed. He looked

equally as shocked as Sam. If I was a betting teenager, I would wager all my chips that Dad expected a fight, and a nasty one at that.

"I see. So, what happened?" Dad placed his hands in his pants pockets.

"She helped a friend," Sam replied before I could get out any words.

"I'm listening." Emerald threaded through the silver in Dad's eyes, as though he was trying to reel in his emotions.

"There's this boy—"

Dad growled.

I rolled my eyes. "It's not what you think. This boy is a bully who picked on me at Durfee. Now, he's a vampire and up to the same old tricks. He attacked my new friend, Zea. Sam and I stopped him from draining her. We were only helping."

"By using your telekinesis? Ms. Lawrence said you destroyed school property."

"Oh, that." I dropped my gaze to the floor.

"Yes, that," he repeated. His tone changed, becoming uneven and less calm.

"I hate him, Dad. I just hate Blake Turner." I was starting to sound like Zea.

Dad commanded troops. He was a leader among vampires. *How would he ever understand?*

He came closer to me. "I do understand," he said in his commander tone, deep and rough. "The need to protect yourself and others is in your blood. I will not fault you for actions you take to protect. But heed my words, young lady." He tipped up my head and the silver in his eyes won out over the green. "You will not use your powers whenever you feel it is convenient. We have laws in our world, and just because a boy taunted you does not—I repeat—does *not* give you the right to retaliate to the point where you almost took his life. You will learn restraint and learn when to take action. Are we clear?"

I stilled for a moment, processing his words. *Did I almost kill Blake?* A stir of excitement laced with fear coursed through me. *Can I do that with my telekinesis?*

"Answer me." Dad squeezed my chin tighter, no doubt reading my thoughts.

I shuddered a breath. "Yes."

"Very well, then. Let's go home. I need to take care of a few matters that I didn't get to finish today."

Since it was a short day, and we had only about an hour left before school let out, Ms. Lawrence decided to send all students home early.

As fast as he'd stormed in, Dad stormed out with Sam and me in tow. The sun's rays shot a beacon of light at me as I stood under the portico, the heat from it warming my cool skin.

Dad looked around, spotting Webb in the distance.

"I want to see Zea," I said to Dad.

"You can see her tomorrow. She's still resting in the nurse's office. Her dad should be here shortly. We need to go." He made his way down the steps.

Sam followed Dad at a leisurely pace.

Not me. Standing on the top step, I inhaled as several students glanced my way.

One boy who sat on the side ledge midway down the steps said, "You did the right thing by protecting Zea."

A girl who sat next to him said, "Thank you."

I was shocked. I thought I'd be the laughing-stock of the school after what happened.

I nodded. "Thanks."

Several others nodded at me as they waited curbside for their rides. A few cars trickled in.

"Jo," Sam called, waving his hand.

I was starting to walk down when a blue car pulled up to the curb and a tall brunette got out of the back seat. Her brown hair spilled down past her breasts as she tipped down her sunglasses, meeting my gaze.

I cocked my head to one side.

Her knee-high boots covered blue jeans, while a white tank top hugged her midriff, showing off toned arms and a toned stomach. Several of the male vamps who were waiting for their ride gawked. Sam even turned to gaze at her.

The hackles on the back of my neck went up as her strawberry scent wafted toward me. I had my right foot on the step below me when Blake's voice blared behind me: "Moonbeam."

I went to turn when he pushed me. Too late, I threw my arms to the sides to balance myself. I dove headfirst down the stone steps. Gravity took control, flipping me several times before I landed at the brunette's feet.

"Jo?" Dad's voice echoed in the distance, followed by Sam's.

A large hand grasped my arm and helped me up. I jerked away, the predator in me stretching awake. I whirled around to face Blake, to draw blood, but Webb stood between Blake and me.

"Get out of the way, Webb," I snapped.

Blake was not going to keep doing this. The asshat needed to be taught a lesson. He had always bullied me in front of everyone. Well, no more. I didn't care what my father had just warned me about. Laws, restraint, or whatever was not on the table in that moment. I was tired of being bullied.

Webb edged out of the way as Sam and Dad flanked me on each side.

"Young lady?" Dad said.

I stared at the beast in front of me. His eyes

turned from a deep, ugly yellow to that fiery orange I had witnessed earlier. His heart raced, keeping time with a mouse in his wheelhouse. He definitely was nervous. His face reddened, and blisters began to form on his face as the sun beat down on him.

The brunette barged through, pushing Dad and me away. She grabbed Blake by the arm and dragged him toward her.

I stuck out my foot in the hope he would fall.

Instead, the brunette caught me. She narrowed her gaze, moving closer to me. "I wouldn't do that if I were you," she said threateningly.

As she released a breath, I inhaled. That was when it hit me. She was human. *What is Blake doing with a pretty human?* "You dare to step foot among vampires?" I asked. My fangs dropped.

A car horn blew, breaking the electricity between us.

"Get in the car, Blake." She shoved him toward the vehicle before stopping in front of me. "Are you trying to scare me?" She poked her finger into my chest.

Webb grabbed her shoulder while Dad slid his arm between the brunette and me.

"You don't scare me either," she said, shrugging off Webb's hand. "I've been around your kind for far too long." She bumped my shoulder and pushed Dad out of her way. She stopped at the car door and turned. "Watch your back, Jo." Then both she and Blake jumped into the back seat.

"What was that all about?" Sam asked as the car sped down the driveway.

"Webb, find out who she is, and the boy," Dad commanded.

I blew out a breath. *How did she know my name?*

Ms. Lawrence and Mr. Banks came running down the steps.

"What's going on here?" Mr. Banks asked, grabbing his phone. Before he pushed any buttons, three Guardians stalked down the steps.

"Okay, students, it's over," Ms. Lawrence said. "Steven, a word, please?" She motioned to an area down the sidewalk away from the crowd.

Webb and Sam both stared at me. Both had a grin from ear to ear. Both made my heart melt for different reasons. The sister in me was proud of my brother, and the female in me wanted to run and jump into Webb's arms. I wanted to feel his touch again.

"Jo, are you hurt?" Sam asked.

Warm liquid seeped down the back of my shirt. I placed my hand at the base of my neck to find it was in fact blood.

Webb grasped my hand.

My body froze.

Sam lifted up my hair and examined my neck. "It's healing," he said.

Webb guided my hand to rest on his abs. My gaze shot to his. A blast of nerves exploded, sending fire to every cell in me. He pulled out his black shirt from the waist of his pants, wrapped the end of it around my hand, then wiped it clean.

My mind went blank, the earth spun, and my heart fluttered so hard I was sure Dad would notice.

"Dude, you can let go of my sister's hand." Sam punched Webb on the arm.

Webb growled deeply.

Oh, please. No fighting. At least they had been cordial to one another when they thought I was hurt.

"I'm proud of you, sis. You stood up to Blake in front of Dad. Now he's seen what a jerk Blake is and that"—Sam licked his bottom lip—"that woman."

I pushed him with my free hand. "Did you like her?"

"She is pretty... she's also human. How can I not notice that?" he said as his fangs dropped.

"Sam, control yourself," Webb said, his attention still on me. "You stayed calm, Jo. You handled yourself well in spite of the anger that took control of your body."

I almost collapsed at his feet when he let go of my hand. His touch, the sparkle in his eyes, and the deep timbre of his voice were enough to erase all the hell that had broken loose.

It seemed the world had shifted several times in the span of six hours. However, that one moment, standing in front of Webb, was worth the wrath of my father, the sight of Blake Turner, and the pain I had at the base of my skull. I willed the gods to freeze time as I inhaled Webb's alluring, clean, soapy scent.

Jo, in the car—now. Dad's order roared in my head, shattering the dreamy spell Webb had me under.

I blinked a few times then turned.

Ms. Lawrence still had Dad's attention.

As Sam, Webb, and I made our way to the car, I tuned in and listened.

"Steven, I can't have any more of these outbreaks. What if the entire student body was here? This would've been a disaster."

"Let's not forget that the Turner boy is the common thread in all this. He did attack the girl. Since when do you have vampires sinking their fangs into others?"

"He's new. We will deal with him."

"That's not what I asked. Let me rephrase the

question. Since you've been headmistress at this school, have you had any students bite another?"

She shook her head. "No. But—"

"You don't get to stand up for a student. You said yourself this morning that you're a fair person. I'll give you that my two need to atone for what happened here today, but I will not let that boy get away with what he's done. I saw him push Jo down the steps too. So don't try to blame my kids for all this."

"You're right. I apologize. I wasn't trying to take sides here. Your daughter has powers we haven't seen in our world in quite some time. I'm afraid she may be more of a handful than my staff can handle."

"Elizabeth, you and I have been around a long time. You know that this school will be good for her. Heck, it'll be good for both of them. Your staff can help her rein in some of her energy."

"I don't have anyone on my staff who can do that. Unless..."

"Unless what?" Dad asked.

"I've been trying to get her to join our staff for years. I wonder..." Ms. Lawrence wrapped her left arm around her waist, then folded her right arm so her hand rested under her chin.

"I'm not following."

"Alia Costner. She's a fantastic teacher and

would be able to help Jo with her telekinesis. For some reason, she doesn't want to leave her current employer. You see, she teaches at the human high school."

I coughed then choked. Ms. Costner's name kept surfacing, at the library and now here.

"A vampire? Teaching at Durfee High School?" Dad asked in a skeptical tone.

I held my breath.

"She's a half-breed. She didn't want to make the change. Over the years, she has developed her magical skills, though, and I think that would help with Jo's powers."

"She still carries a human scent. That may pose a problem here," Dad added.

"No, not at all. Her family has unique abilities that have helped her to shield the scent."

"Then why doesn't she want to teach here?" Dad tilted his head a fraction.

Ms. Lawrence shrugged. "She wouldn't tell me."

"Look, Elizabeth," he said, "my kids are trying to find their way in this new world of theirs. They've had a hard road, and that's not your fault, I know. I need you to help me help them. They're both showing signs of powers that have me scratching my head." His tone had dropped to a soft whisper.

"I can help. However, I need you to ensure that no outburst like today's happens ever again."

Dad grabbed hold of Ms. Lawrence's hand. "I will do my best. And you need to take care of the Turner boy. He's trouble. Even I can see that."

She nodded once.

"Thank you. I need to go. I have a pressing matter with my superiors that I need to take care of." He let go of her hand.

"Steven," she called out as Dad walked toward the car. "Is there any way you can have a chat with Alia Costner? I can give you her contact information."

"I'll see what I can do," he said, pulling out his cell phone.

My mind reeled from what I'd just heard. Ms. Costner, part vampire or half-breed. I had to wonder what that meant, whether she carried the vampire gene, and what magical abilities she had. Maybe she even had some of the special powers Webb had told me about, but I couldn't figure out how, if she wasn't a fully-fledged vamp.

Sam blew on my ear. "You coming?" He waved his hand toward the open door of the car. "You sure that hit to your head didn't do something to your brain? You look like a zombie."

"Ha, ha." I stuck my tongue out at my brother then jumped into the back seat.

Webb was already in the driver's seat. Dad slid in on the passenger's side.

We'd made it through a very rough first day. My head hurt, and not only from the fall—my brain rioted with question after question. *Who was the brunette with Blake? What did Ms. Lawrence mean by her statement that I was a handful? How will Ms. Costner be able to help me? Will Zea be okay? Blake is a vampire. His spooky orange eye color isn't what bothers me. No. It's his scent. It hints of human. Sure, I saw his fangs, but...*

Only time would reveal the true answers. For the time being, I leaned back against the soft leather seats, released a sigh, and silently prayed. If Blake was going to be there, I needed all the help I could get. Or maybe it was the other way around.

19

———————

The next morning, my nerves were more than a little on edge. I plain didn't want to go back to that school. I didn't want to see Blake again, and I sure didn't want to don the uniform that insisted on irritating my butt. When I'd changed out of it the day before, the backs of my legs had a severe rash, and my behind itched like hell. I was still itching as I made my way down to the idling black sedan.

Webb stood on the driver's side with his hands on the hood, and Sam was in the back seat—he'd beaten me that morning. I had taken a few minutes extra in the shower, mainly to soothe my rash, but part of me was stalling too. But when I thought of Zea, I realized I wanted to see if she was all right. I really liked her, even though she seemed a little clingy.

The last person to show up was Dad. He'd worked in his office all night. When I woke up around three, he was just getting home. He emerged from the building with his cell phone to his ear. The dress blue uniform had been replaced by the Sentinels' standard-issue black cargo ensemble. He was listening intently to whoever was on the other end of his phone, who had to have been speaking in a whispered voice—I couldn't hear a thing. Then again, with Webb watching me, I really wasn't concentrating.

Dad twirled his finger in the air with his free hand, his bicep bunching as he did. He looked intimidating. A few of his tattoos glinted in the sunlight, his black hair was tied back at his nape, and the sharp angles of his face enhanced his emerald-green eyes. I hoped I wouldn't see them turn silver that day. It was never good when Dad's eyes were silver.

Once Dad was in his seat, Webb didn't waste any time getting on the road. As soon as Dad hung up, he and Webb engaged in conversation about a few military things. I tuned it out. All that military stuff bored me.

"By the way, Commander, did Dr. Vieira talk

with you this morning about the lab results on the boxed blood?"

My ears perked up.

"He did indeed. Jo, Sam, I want to remind you not to drink any boxed blood that the school may have or anyone's blood except mine. In fact, I need to speak to Ms. Lawrence about her supply."

"What's going on, Pops?" Sam adjusted his tie.

"The lab results finally came back from the supply that we had when you got sick, son. It was definitely tainted with the endotoxin."

Shock ran through me. *Someone laced the boxed blood?*

Dad responded to my silent question. "Yes, sweetie. Someone is trying to make our lives miserable."

"Any idea who?" I asked.

"We still haven't gotten any closer to who the enemy among us is," Webb replied.

There were a lot of people on base. It could have been anyone. Maybe one of the humans was angry and wanted to harm vampires.

"No sense in worrying about it," Dad added. "You two drink my blood, anyway."

He might have been right. Then a sudden thought occurred to me: *Zea's sister.*

"Dad, my friend Zea's sister is in a coma at

Grayson Manor. She seems to have the same symptoms that Sam had."

"Did she drink any boxed blood?" Webb asked.

"I don't know," I replied.

"Grayson isn't supposed to have any of that crap on-site, since the place is designed for new vampires, mostly. And all their blood is given by the fathers," Dad explained.

"So can you look into it to see if she did?" I asked. I wanted to help Zea if I could.

Sam glared at me. "Stay out of it."

"No. What if she's sick like you were from boxed blood? If we can help, we should," I said to Sam.

"I'll have Dr. Vieira make some calls. I can't promise anything," Dad said, texting on his phone.

"Did Dr. Vieira confirm if Neil's blood helped Sam get better from it?" Maybe it would help Zea's sister.

"Dr. Vieira is still running lab tests. Preliminary results look promising," Dad said. "But let's move on to another subject that you should be worrying about, and that is school and staying out of trouble." The terse inflection in his tone left no room to question his directive.

By the time Dad uttered the last word, we were on campus in the parking lot.

Climbing the stone steps, I took in several deep

breaths, trying to quell my nerves. I didn't know how I was going to react to Blake. After we left the school the day before, Dad had headed straight to his office, so Sam and I hadn't had a chance to talk with him. I didn't even know if Webb was able to find out who that lady with Blake had been.

When we reached the portico, Dad stopped. "I need to speak with Ms. Lawrence this morning. Do you think you two can behave today?"

I closed my eyes. A slight breeze sent a shiver up my skirt. *Damn uniform.*

"Pops, we'll try," was all Sam said.

I opened my eyes and met Dad's gaze. "I will, but..."

"No buts. Do your best." He barged through the large wooden doors.

The halls were quiet. Classes didn't start for another thirty minutes, but I figured we would see students in the halls. Only the two Guardians were around, standing sentinel at the door.

All of us went through the same routine as the day before. Webb and Dad dislodged their Sentinel swords from their belts, and Sam and I were wanded before entering.

Before Dad disappeared into Ms. Lawrence's office, he bent over and kissed me on top of my head. "Try to behave. Both of you," he said, glancing at Sam. "Webb will pick you up this afternoon. I have unfinished business to attend to." On his last word, he opened the door then was gone.

Webb lagged behind for a second, stealing a look behind him. His long, soft lashes danced as he winked at me. Then he, too, disappeared.

Wonderful! That should get me through the day. Or so I hoped.

"We should find Ms. Chapman. Isn't she the one with our schedules?" Sam asked, pointing to the admin offices.

I shrugged. As Sam pushed in the door, Zea came running down the hall.

"Miss, no running," a Guardian called.

She slowed, the heels of her Mary Janes making a soft echo.

"Hey, are you okay?" I asked.

I was stunned that Zea was even there. She looked great. Her hair was pulled back with the red headband in the same style she had worn before. Her cheeks were rosy, and her chocolate-brown eyes had specks of blue dancing in them.

"Yeah. It was a rough night. When my dad picked me up yesterday, he was furious. Between my sister still being sick and then the incident yesterday, I thought he was going to explode."

"Speaking of your sister, I spoke to my dad this morning."

She squealed. Her voice bounced off the walls.

"Miss," the Guardian warned. "Shhh."

"Really," she whispered. "You really did that for me?" Her brown eyes shimmered as brightly as chocolate diamonds.

Sam narrowed his eyes at me. "He's not promising anything."

"What's your problem?" I asked.

"Don't give her high hopes."

"I'm not."

"Sam, don't worry. I get it," Zea said. "Just talking to your dad means a lot, though. Thank you." Zea threw her arms around me, practically choking me.

"Jo, we need to get our schedules," Sam urged.

Zea let me go.

"Did you get yours, Zea?" I asked.

She nodded. "I got here early, and Ms. Chapman gave me mine. I'm dying to see if we're in the same classes. They split our class into two groups." She followed us into the offices.

A hint of fresh pine filled the room.

"Ah, the Mason twins. There you are." Ms. Chapman rose from her desk behind the counter. "Here are your schedules. We split you up."

"You can't do that," Sam argued.

"I'm sorry, Mr. Mason. Orders from your father," Ms. Chapman countered.

"What?" Sam drew his eyebrows together, several creases lining his forehead. "Ms. Chapman? My sister and I need to be together."

"It's okay, Sam. It's not Durfee, where we'd be miles apart. This place is small. We'll be fine." I tried to convince him.

Black seeped through the green in his eyes—his anger was rising.

"We don't need another day like yesterday," I whispered in his ear. "It's your turn to calm down. We'll meet between periods and at lunch."

As soon as the words left my mouth, I experienced a moment of panic. The last time we'd said we would meet at lunch, Sam had disappeared. Maybe he was right. Maybe the school wasn't safe. That female with Blake had threatened me the day before, and Blake's presence certainly threw a curveball into the whole mix.

"What about Blake?" he whispered.

I shrugged. I didn't know how to answer that. Heck, I didn't know how I was going to react to seeing Blake again.

"Are you talking about the Turner boy?" Ms. Chapman asked.

"He's vile," Zea whispered under her breath.

I was going to get to the bottom of why Zea hated Blake.

Sam nodded to Ms. Chapman.

"The Turner boy has been placed in your class,

Sam. It might interest you to know that Ms. Lawrence has instructed that one of our Guardians shadow Mr. Turner," she said.

The word "shadow" reminded me of the old man's warning message: *"Don't let the shadows consume you"*. I still didn't know what he meant by that, but my stomach tightened all of sudden.

Sam's shoulders relaxed. He lost the wrinkles in his forehead. I didn't think Sam was comfortable with us being apart but having Blake in his class and not mine seemed to ease some of his tension.

With the situation with Blake settled for the moment, Ms. Chapman gave Sam and me our schedules.

"Well?" Zea asked. "Are you in my class, Jo?"

"I don't know. How can I tell?"

She read through my schedule and let out a soft squeal. "Yep. You and I are together. Thank God. I didn't want to be anywhere near that disgusting beast, Blake."

"What's up between you and him?" I asked. I couldn't wait any longer.

"Not here. I'll fill you in later. Let's go to the cafeteria."

I barely read my schedule. I guessed I would have time once I was able to sit down and breathe.

Zea was a ball of fire. Maybe her dad had given her some speed to perk her up this morning.

"Sis?" Sam called. "Wait."

The three of us walked in the direction of the cafeteria.

"I have math first. What about you, Jo?"

"Jo and I have vampire history," Zea answered with excitement ringing in her voice.

"I thought we were going to play catch-up on our classes from Durfee?" Sam queried.

"You will. I still have to catch up on the subjects I missed at my school. Ms. Chapman told me that part of the summer program for new vampires is to take two subjects related to our new world, and the rest will be the basics—math, science... you know the rest."

"Where did you go to school?" The only high schools in the city were Durfee and an all-boys school.

"I went to a school in western Connecticut. We lived on the border, close to New York City," she explained.

"So did your family move here?" Sam asked, holding open the cafeteria door for Zea and me.

"Yeah. It's the only vampire school in New England. In fact, it's the only one in the Northeast." Zea walked into the cafeteria first.

"Are there other vampire schools in the country?" I asked, following behind her.

She stopped short and turned. "You're kidding, right?"

My eyes widened. She was inches from my nose. I made a mental note to tell her about personal space. I eased back, bumping into my brother.

"She's not," Sam added, his hand guiding me around Zea.

"Where have you two been hiding?" She turned and walked alongside me.

If only she knew that Dad had kept us locked up on base. I guess it wasn't any different than Zea staying at Grayson Manor, although Dad and the Sentinels weren't that forthcoming with information about the vampire world. It seemed Sam and I found things out either as we violated vampire laws or when it was convenient for Dad to tell us.

As we walked deeper into the room, my training kicked in. Olivia had taught Sam and me how to assess a room in a few seconds. It wasn't a large room, so it was simple. Tables and chairs were scattered around. I let out a relieved sigh when my final evaluation came up empty—Blake wasn't there. The cafeteria was buzzing, though, with other vampires hanging out and talking.

Whispers and the drone of voices died as we

walked by. Heads sprang up. Several pairs of eyes followed us as we passed tables.

"Ignore them," Zea advised.

"What are you looking at?" Sam asked no one in particular.

The vamps at the tables ahead of me dropped their gazes, as did the others behind them.

My brother was rather intimidating with his height and broad shoulders. If they'd known what I knew about Sam's anger issues, they would have known not to piss him off.

Zea stopped, perching her hands on her hips. "Mind your own business," she said, sticking each vampire who looked her way with a hard glare.

It was as though she had blossomed into a feisty vamp overnight. I was beginning to think there was more to Zea.

"Let's find a table outside," she said. "The sun's out, and it'll warm the chill in here." She dropped her hands and resumed walking.

A light breeze tickled my face as I scooted around cement tables and a large water fountain that sat smack in the middle of the courtyard. The ornate structure rose high with several peaks and valleys, creating a geometric downward cascade of water into the circular basin. Several flowering plants and shrubs surrounded the edges at the bottom.

I sat, closed my eyes, and tipped back my head, letting the sun beat down on my face, warming me, relaxing me. As I absorbed the rays, I inhaled the salt lingering in the breeze from the bay. I loved the smell of the ocean. It reminded me of those few times Sam and I played in the sand when we were around eight years old. We'd been fortunate to live for a time with a nice foster family who loved the beach as well.

"It's great out here," Zea said, cutting short my reminiscing.

My eyes fluttered open.

"I could get to use this," she said, sitting down.

"Don't get too used to it. The bell is about to ring. Sam, move. You're blocking the sun."

He took off his jacket before dropping into the seat next to me.

"So, Zea, are you going to tell us how you know Blake?" I asked. I hated to even say his name, but I had to get the skinny on the creep.

Sam's head jerked toward me, his eyes wide. He raised his hand, fingers together, and slashed them across his neck, his way of telling me to shut up.

Zea fidgeted in her seat, dropping her gaze.

"It's okay, Zea. You don't have to talk about it," Sam said, breaking the long silence.

"I haven't told anyone..." She lifted her gaze.

"I... hate the sight of... blood. And I panic when I see... fangs."

I gulped. Shock rippled through me. *A vampire who hates the sight of blood and fangs? Holy moly! How can that be?* I placed my hand on top of hers. "Hey, it's okay." My pulse sped. The mere mention of blood made my mouth water.

"No, it's not okay," she said. "I'm a freaking vampire. I shouldn't pass out when I see fangs or blood."

"Do you like the taste of blood?" Sam asked.

"Not really," she replied, wiping a tear from her cheek with the back of her free hand.

"Huh?" My mouth fell open. I could hardly speak. I loved the sticky red stuff. My throat suddenly became dry just thinking about it.

"I know. Crazy, isn't it?"

"Crazy? More like screwed up," Sam blurted out.

I slapped him on the arm.

"Well, it is. That would be like a human not liking food," he added.

He was right. It still didn't answer the question. "What does this have to do with Blake?" I removed my hand from hers, trying to get to the heart of the matter before I ran looking for blood.

"He tortured me while we were at Grayson Manor. My sister was trying to help me take my mind off drinking our dad's blood. It didn't work. I passed out. Blake got wind of it and every chance he had, he picked on me. He'd take vials of blood and spill them in front of me while he shoved his fangs in my face. He's gross and an asshole." She hiccupped.

My blood began to boil as she told the story. I hated Blake as much as she did. My adrenaline surged. I dug my nails into my palm, trying to prevent my fangs from descending. The predator in me wanted to find him right that instant and kill him.

"Jo, why're your eyes purple? All vampires have black eyes when they change. Well, of course, not that vile beast, Blake." Zea stared at me. "Are you like him?"

"What do you mean, 'like him'?" Sam asked. A deep frown line formed between his brows.

"His eyes are that strange orange when they change. Dr. Grayson was fascinated with him because of that. He'd never seen any vampire with a color other than black." Her smooth forehead wrinkled.

"Did Dr. Grayson say why his eyes were orange?" I asked, swaying the conversation back to Blake and not me.

"No. He was going to run tests on Blake. Then a man pulled him out of the Grayson program. In fact, the Council of Eternal Affairs is investigating why he got pulled early."

"His dad?" My instincts kicked in.

There was something awry about Blake that I couldn't quite pinpoint. However, one thing was certain: hanging around Zea was proving to be a good idea. She was a wealth of information.

"The man didn't look like he could be Blake's dad. Anyway, it's your turn. You never answered my question yesterday. How come you two weren't at Grayson Manor?" Zea asked.

The bell rang. How appropriate that we were literally saved by the bell.

Sam's shoulders relaxed, and so did mine. It wasn't that I didn't want to tell her. It was just Sam and I had a weird story. Besides, I didn't think Dad would like us telling her about the Plutariums and my uncle Patrick.

"Zea, if I can get my dad's permission, do you want to hang out sometime?" I asked as we walked into the building.

"Ooh. I'd like that," she replied.

Sam raised his eyebrows.

I shrugged. I wanted to make friends. I had to make friends. Hanging out on base with my brother was great, but I needed a female friend, and I liked Zea.

When we reached the end of the hall near the

cafeteria, there were two teachers, one male and one female, directing students to their classrooms. The woman was a tall vamp who reminded me of Ms. Weston. I didn't even think to ask about her this morning. I made a mental note to track her down and apologize.

We stopped at the crossroads of the halls. The female teacher read through Zea's schedule and pointed her in the right direction. The male vamp glanced over Sam's. All classrooms were on the upper floors. The first floor was dedicated to the auditorium, cafeteria, and anything administrative.

We climbed the stairs to the second floor. A framed sign tacked to the wall adjacent to the hall door indicated that this floor was home to all subjects related to English.

We made our way to the third floor, for all things history.

"This is us," Zea said.

"I have math. I guess I'm going up." Sam pointed toward the upper stairwell.

"Come on, Jo. I want to get a good seat." Zea held open the door.

The halls were quiet, a sign that most of the other vamps were in their classrooms.

"You go ahead." I flicked my head to the open doorway. "I want to talk to my brother."

"I'll wait for you in the hall. Hurry," she said, closing the door.

"Are you going to be okay, sis?" Sam's gaze roamed over me. Since he couldn't read my emotions, the lines on his forehead were telling me he was struggling to find something to clue him in.

"I'll be fine. You're the one who has to put up with the asshole."

"Blake doesn't bother me. I'll meet you at lunch at the same place we sat earlier."

I nodded.

He turned to climb the stairs.

"Sam?"

He glanced over his shoulder, holding on to the railing.

I tapped my heart twice.

"Love you, too, Jo. See you at lunch."

I had my head down when I barreled into the hall and into Ms. Weston. *Oh, crap!*

"Jo, come on! We're going to be late," Zea called in a panicked voice. "We have two minutes before the final bell."

While that might have been true, I had another matter to attend to.

"Yes, Ms. Mason, you're going to be late," Ms. Weston repeated, staring down at me.

"Ma'am, I'm so sorry about yesterday. I didn't mean to—"

"Enough. You'll make up for it during your time here." Her calm, even tone did nothing to mask the threat behind her words.

"I truly am sorry."

She moved to my right. "Off to class, Ms. Mason." Then she walked away.

Zea waited, fidgeting where she stood. Clearly, she was worried about being tardy. I was more concerned about Ms. Weston's subtle threat than being late to class. I for sure wasn't starting school on the right foot.

Zea and I made it to vampire history with thirty seconds to spare. She frowned when she walked in. Only two seats were left, both at the back of the classroom.

"I wanted to sit in the front," she whispered as we took the remaining seats.

I hunched my shoulders forward, shrugging. There was nothing we could do about it unless we kicked out the overachievers in the front row. That wasn't going to happen.

Zea pouted while we waited for the teacher to turn around. He was writing a few things on the whiteboard.

"Okay, settle down," he said as he placed the cap on his dry-erase marker. "My name is Porter Hale. When called on, I expect you to answer the question followed by 'sir.' If you haven't learned any manners by now, then you don't belong in this school."

I silently harrumphed. I was quickly reminded of Dad and the solicitors. Everything in the vampire world was about manners. However, unlike the solicitors, Mr. Hale didn't believe in tailored black suits. Instead, a pair of plaid pants and a plaid jacket covered his tall, skinny frame. His hair was slicked back with tons of oil, and his skin was pale white.

He glanced around the room. "For the next two months, you'll learn the basics of vampire history. As you move into the fall semester, you'll continue with this course where we left off. This is only an introduction. We'll talk about the important vampires that have shaped our world and how it all began. Before we do, it is prudent to discuss some of the myths and fables that humans believe to be true about our world.

"We'll have quizzes every Friday, and you'll have homework every night. This is a fast-paced class. At the end of August, you'll be given a final —one essay question. So make sure you do your homework and pay attention in class. Participation on your part counts a great deal as well. Any questions before I get started?"

The room was silent.

"Very well, then, I'll take that as a no." Mr. Hale

pointed to the whiteboard. "We'll start by discussing the history of this school. This will be a good starting point since there's quite a bit of history in this building alone."

I leaned back in my seat as he spoke. He explained that the building, which had been a convent for nuns, was purchased from one of the large church organizations in the city. Over the years, the church downsized as the nuns migrated to other churches around the world. It had seemed to be the perfect location, away from the dense population of humans in the city. Each floor was dedicated to a subject, as Sam, Zea, and I had found out. English was on the second floor, history on the third, math on the fourth, and science on the fifth.

When he drew in a breath, a female vamp in the front row raised her hand.

He nodded. "State your name first then your question."

"My name is Sarah. Aren't there six floors in this building? I also understand that there are tunnels under the school that lead to secret places around the city. Is that true, sir?"

Mr. Hale tilted his head to one side. Several lines formed under his eyes and on his forehead. "Wherever do you children learn this stuff? First, the sixth floor is dedicated to electives you choose to take during your time at this school. And the astronomy lab and observatory are located on the sixth floor too. You'll have a chance to tour the observatory this week. As for the tunnels, that's a myth." He leaned against the front of his desk.

I was curious whether he was telling the truth about the tunnels. The military base had tunnels. That was how the Plutariums had escaped. Then a question pinged in my brain. *If there are tunnels, is this school really as safe as Mr. Banks and Dad said it was?*

Mr. Hale droned on about the history of the school, and before long, the bell sounded. Unlike Durfee, the tone of the bell was very low. I imagined the school staff had programmed it that way for vampire hearing. Whoever had thought of that should have been given a medal.

The fifteen of us piled out of the classroom and into the hall.

I looked to Zea to lead us to English, which was on the second floor. I'd hoped to at least pass Sam on his way down if he had history. I'd forgotten to ask him what he had during the second period.

We had only ten minutes between classes, so Zea and I traipsed down one flight of stairs and found the English classroom. She wanted to pick her seat early this time, but I decided to head to the girls' bathroom to freshen up. My legs were burning, and I thought dabbing them with some cold water might take away the sting of the rash. I was beginning to question my vampire body. I healed quickly from stab wounds but couldn't get my freakin' skin to heal from a stupid piece of fabric. It didn't make any sense.

After tending to my legs, I wadded up the paper towel and threw it in the trash. Then I smoothed my skirt, rubbing my hands down the front then the back. I glanced one last time in the mirror. I was running my fingers through my hair, fluffing it at the roots, when the door to the ladies' room creaked open. Her strawberry scent hit me before I could move.

"What're you doing in here? You don't belong in school." My fangs shot out of my gums.

The brunette who had been with Blake yesterday stalked up to me. "Are you going to bite me, Jo? You want to sink your fangs into me, don't you?"

Her heart pounded in my ears. Each pump of her blood through her veins sent a burning sensation to the back of my throat. My gums ached. I couldn't breathe.

"Hard to control yourself, isn't it?" She was taunting me. "I told you yesterday. I'm not afraid of your kind." She pulled a dagger from her back pocket.

Fear gripped me, my muscles tensing. "Who are you? And what do you want with me?"

"Who I am is none of your business. What do I want with you? Well, I can't ruin the surprise." She inched closer to me.

I followed her steps, keeping an eye on the dagger in her hand. It looked like the blade was cobalt.

I assessed my options. There was only one way out of the girls' bathroom, two if I counted the window. I was on the second floor, so it couldn't have been too far down if I had to jump.

Olivia had taught me not only to assess the room but my opponent as well. She had a weapon. I didn't. She was human. I was a vampire. There were laws in my world that stated I couldn't harm a human.

The whole scenario screamed disaster.

"Looking for a way out? I'd say you're screwed. You have to go through me," she said with more than a little haughtiness.

The human thought she could stop me, with a dagger, no less. Anger bubbled to the surface, slowly neutralizing the fear that had settled in my veins.

"You realize that dagger can't kill me," I said through gritted fangs.

A sinister grin painted her thin pink lips. Her soulless blue eyes swept over me. Death would not be my fate that day unless I took my own life.

"If I stab you through the heart and tear it to shreds, it will," she countered.

We glared at each other. Seconds or minutes passed. I wasn't sure which.

"You plan on using that dagger, or are you just going to stand there?" The dare rolled off my tongue before I realized it. Oh, well. Time to find out if all that training would pay off. "You realize I could kill you in a second." I smiled widely, exposing my fangs. The idea of sinking my canines into her was enticing. A thrum of excitement coursed through me, and my throat burned hotter at the thought.

Her pulse still beat rapidly. Inside, she was scared. On the outside, she was doing a bang-up job of masking her fear.

The door flew open with a thud.

"You started without me," Blake said, his eyes bright orange, his fangs protruding well below his bottom lip.

What the hell?

"Where have you been?" The girl whipped around to face him.

At the site of Blake, my anger morphed into a rage that zipped through me, awakening the predator in me. She clawed to get out, to attack the ugly beast in front of me. I silently apologized to Dad. Then again, the game had just changed. I couldn't be held responsible for defending my life against a human and a vampire.

But he seemed different from every other vampire I'd met. His fangs reminded me of a lion's—thick and yellow—and blood stained both of them. It seemed he'd had a snack before arriving at the party.

"I had to take care of the Guardian. The fucking school thought they could have one of those morons babysit me." Blake sidled up next to the brunette.

The Guardians I'd seen were well over six feet tall with chests and arms that could crush a human easily. While Blake was tall and stocky, I didn't think his height and weight would match a Guardian's.

The bell rang.

"Get rid of her before they come looking for her," the brunette barked, inching backward, her knuckles white around the handle of the dagger.

Oh yeah. This is going to be fun.

Blake ripped off his school jacket then threw it on the floor. "I've been waiting for this moment for a very long time, Moonbeam." His voice dripped with slime.

The door to the bathroom opened.

"Jo, what's taking—" Zea poked in her head. Her jaw dropped.

The brunette jumped her, pulled her into the bathroom, and held the dagger to her neck.

Oh boy. Not Zea. Not again.

Adrenaline erased the fear. I met Zea's gaze. Her chocolate-brown eyes had turned to pools of tar. Red sparked from them, much like Webb's when he got mad.

I shook my head slightly, trying to tell her not to move. The point of the dagger was poised on her jugular.

"Well, now, if it isn't the vampire who hates blood. Now, *you*, pretty one, just became my dessert," Blake growled, licking his disgusting lips.

Pervert. I couldn't let anything happen to Zea. I'd been staked in a room full of swords. If I could survive that, I could survive a brawl with that jerk. After all, they didn't have any weapons, at least Blake didn't. It was just him, me, and our vampire strength.

"Take care of the blood-hating vampire, Jewel." His eyes turned fiery red.

Without hesitation, I flew into the air, knocking him to the ground. I landed with my feet on either side of his hips. Before I could drop down to pin him to the floor, he swiveled his waist then kicked upward, hitting the back of my head. I fell, and our heads collided. He raised his hands, grabbing me at my waist. In one fluid motion, he threw me forward. My palms landed on the tiled floor, and I somersaulted into a standing position. I turned when he lunged and raised my right knee, pushing him with all the strength I had. He soared through the long bathroom, cracking the tiles under the window.

He cocked his head to one side as he slumped to the floor. "Impressive, Moonbeam," he barked, jumping to his feet. "But you can't keep me down."

"Oh no?" I stomped closer to him. My arms shook as the rage inside me neared a crescendo.

Blake ran at me with his head down, as if he was going to tackle me. I jumped in the air, landing on the other side of him.

He turned, brows drawn together.

"Is that all you got, asshole?" I growled.

He shook his head, his fangs dripping with saliva. "Not in the least."

"Kill her already, Blake," yelled the brunette, or Jewel, or whatever her name was.

He snarled. His fangs seemed to be growing longer.

We were at a standstill, sizing up each other,

waiting for the other to make a move. I stole a glance at Zea, who shot me a kill-the-vile-creep look. Then she nodded, the dagger scraping along her neck.

As though time had frozen, Zea whipped around, pulling the brunette's hands away from her neck. Before I could blink, she sank her fangs into the woman. The brunette gasped.

Blake and I ran at each other.

He jumped in the air. His fist hit my nose as he dropped to a crouch. Blood arced out in all directions.

I pushed away the pain and planted a round-house kick to the side of his face. Before he could react, I twirled around and kicked his other side.

He rose, parrying my blows with one hand then the other. As I raised my leg, he caught my foot, pulling me toward him. I scooted on one leg, trying to stay upright. Balance and grace were my friends.

With my right foot between his hands, he twisted, snapping my ankle, then pushed me. I bit back the pain as I fell, my butt landing hard on the tiled floor. Balance and grace were gone, replaced by sheer clumsiness. My skirt was high above my waist, my undergarments on display for Blake to see. He didn't seem to notice, though. I rose, putting all my weight on my left leg.

Blake grinned as if he had just won the fight, but it wasn't over. Not even close.

I stood on one leg before the beast, afraid to put pressure on my right. His eyes swirled with a vehement excitement that made my muscles tense.

I lowered my right foot, and in a flash, I lunged. I punched him with my right fist then my elbow. His head didn't even move.

Blake laughed, and the sound called up the animal inside me. Flames of fire blasted through my veins. I bit down on my lip, my fangs drawing blood.

Then something sharp stabbed me in my left leg. Before I could process what was happening, pain gripped my stomach too. I glanced down then up. The brunette held the dagger in her hand, my blood dripping from the tip.

I looked past the brunette and saw that Zea was gone. Hopefully, she ran for help.

With a clang, the dagger fell to the floor, then the brunette. Her eyes rolled back into her head before she passed out.

The room began spinning. Faucets turned on, toilets flushed, and glass shattered. I held out my hands, palms facing up, drawing all the energy I had inside me to the surface. Power, darkness, and hatred consumed me. My concentration was focused solely on the monster in front of me. The energy flowing through me controlled my movements, even my brainwaves. My nostrils flared when I inhaled the scent of blood—my own blood.

I suddenly wanted death, not for me, but for the boy standing before me, that beast who wasn't deserving of humanity or vampiredom.

I slid my left arm out to the side then back. The water from the faucets shot out. I clenched my left hand into a fist, and droplets of water formed into golf-sized balls. I squeezed, and the balls of water turned to ice, swirling as they hung in the air. Then, in one motion, I dropped my left arm, opening my hand. Hundreds of ice balls flew through the air, hitting Blake in a torrid storm, drawing blood as they pelted him.

He threw his hands over his head. "Stop it, you bitch!"

I bit down harder, sucking in my bottom lip, my fangs hitting bone. I clenched my fists. My vision blurred. The room spun as I clutched the sides of my skirt. Fabric tore as heat rippled up my arms.

I relaxed my left arm, and the ice balls stopped. The faucets turned off. But my power still flowed.

Blake dropped his arms, his eyes widening. Suddenly, his face reddened, and he grabbed his throat. His face turned ten shades of red before turning blue. He let out one large yelp then collapsed onto the floor.

A loud thud resounded, and then Mr. Banks's voice filled the bathroom. His brown eyes quickly changed to black. "What happened in here?" He raked his hands through his hair. "Kraft, get in here now!" he shouted.

I stood frozen, unable to move. Not because I didn't want to—my limbs wouldn't move. I was on the verge of collapsing. Every muscle in me hurt. My head was on fire, and my lips were burning.

"Ms. Mason, what have you done?" Mr. Banks bent down to check the two bodies on the floor.

He was pulling a two-way radio from his belt when Kraft stormed in as if he owned the place. The large, hulking Sentinel was intimidating with his tall stature and arms as big as tree trunks. "Holy crap! What happened? Did a bomb go off?"

"That's enough, Guardian. Help Ms. Mason, would you, please? I need to see if these two are still breathing," Mr. Banks barked before he pressed a button on his radio. "Skane. Frost is down in the boy's locker room. I need you to check on him."

"Ms. Mason. Jo. You have to let go of your skirt. Your hands are turning blue." Kraft's voice was deep but delicate. He took hold of my hands.

His strength sent a wave of warm tingles skittering up my arm. As if by magic, the tingles spread. My muscles loosened. He brushed the hair from my face. Sweat dripped down the sides of my temples. My knees wobbled, and my body suddenly became a ball of putty.

Kraft slid one of his large hands behind my legs and the other behind my back as I fell into his arms. Before I knew what was happening, he was carrying me out of the bathroom.

"Kraft, take her to the Guardians' medical office. I don't want these kids in the same room, and Ms. Lawrence will have a fit if blood is spilled in her office," Mr. Banks instructed.

"No problem, sir."

With every pound of his heavy boots against the wooden floor, my head lolled from one side to the other. My eyelids were heavy, my body was numb, my ankle was throbbing, and my head hurt as though I'd run into a brick wall.

In a matter of minutes, Kraft kicked open the door to the Guardians' office, walked past several rooms, and reached a room with two cots. Glass cabinets lined one of the walls, and peeking through were boxes of cotton balls, Band-Aids, syringes, gauze pads—everything in a first aid kit, only on a larger scale. It wasn't Dr. Vieira's medical facility by any means, but it was well stocked to take care of someone who needed it.

He set me down on one of the cots and placed a blanket over my frayed skirt. He rummaged through a few drawers while I stared at my hands. The blue dissipated slowly.

"I don't need any Band-Aids," I said, my voice barely a whisper.

"You let me determine that. Your leg has a deep stab wound, and your stomach is oozing blood. And I wouldn't look in the mirror right now if I were you."

I raised my hand to my mouth then pulled it away. A small amount of blood stuck to my fingers. Suddenly, my stomach lurched. My throat was on fire. I dipped my bloody fingers into my mouth and licked. It wasn't enough. I needed more, lots more. "Kraft? I don't need bandages. My throat..."

Before I could finish speaking, he stood in front of me, removing his watch from his left wrist. "You need to feed." He raised his arm, setting his watch on the cot.

Dad's words from this morning rang in my head. "No, I can't drink your blood."

"You have to. You'll heal faster, and it will take away the urge to attack. And we don't need any more excitement right now. This is not up for discussion." He stared at me, his mahogany eyes swirling to black.

I usually didn't need to feed at that time of day.

Normally, Sam and I had our elixir in the morning and then again before bed, unless we'd trained hard. Yet, Kraft was right. I remembered my dire need for blood after I was staked by the swords. Dad had given me his wrist, and his blood had helped the healing process. Still, Kraft wasn't Dad.

I lifted my gaze from his wrist, meeting the storm brewing in his eyes. I swallowed hard. "I have to drink my father's blood." I pushed away his arm even though my throat started to burn.

"Drink," He intoned then shoved his wrist into my mouth. As he did, his muscles flexed, and the tattoos along his arm danced.

His scent hinted of sage mixed with vanilla, causing my nostrils to flare and my fangs to descend. Without another thought, I placed both hands around his wrists and bit, sinking my fangs into his tough skin. I suckled, drawing his blood onto my tongue. I savored the sweet flavor for just a moment. As I swallowed, the room darkened, and images of a young woman flashed in my mind. She had auburn hair that spilled past her breasts and the greenest eyes I'd ever seen. She was standing in what looked like a penthouse suite overlooking a city that had skyscrapers in the distance. The sky was dark, and rain pelted the windows. She was crying and pacing behind a white couch that stood out among the black and red fixtures around it. Kraft stood, leaning against a shiny black countertop, watching her. *I wanted to go to her to tell her I was sorry, but I didn't know what to say. It broke my heart to see her in tears, to see her porcelain skin red with sadness. But I had no choice. It would never have worked between us.*

Suddenly, a hand tapped my head. "Jo, that's enough."

I blinked a few times, drawing my last mouthful. The young woman disappeared from my vision. The lights brightened around me, and I saw Kraft peering down. I must have been losing my mind.

"Are you okay? Your eyes dilated as you were drinking," he said.

I quirked an eyebrow. "What?"

"Your eyes rolled around, then changed from silver to violet then to copper before dilating. Strange. You zoned out."

The whole day was strange. "I'm fine. I must've spaced for a second. I saw..." He would think I was loony if I told him.

He stared at me as he wrapped his watch back around his wrist. "Well? You saw what?"

After what had just happened in the girls' bathroom, he probably thought I was crazy, anyway. "When your blood hit my tongue, I had a vision of a lady. She had long auburn hair and dark-green eyes. She was standing in an apartment, crying while you were leaning against a black counter, watching her."

His eyes grew wide.

"Do you have visions? Is that one of your powers?" Sweat popped up on his forehead.

I shook my head. "No." I hoped not. It would suck if every time I drank blood, I had a vision of someone else's life. I couldn't make sense of it and wasn't even going to try. I was too tired. "Do you love her?" I asked.

As his blood made its way through my cells, a warm tingle spread throughout my body. My eyelids were getting heavy.

"It's not important," he said. "Let's get you cleaned up." He picked up a gauze pad and a bottle of alcohol. He tipped the alcohol and soaked the gauze before he gently wiped the area around my nose and mouth. "Does it hurt?"

I shook my head. The pain had gone away as I drank from him. In fact, the stab wound on my leg had knitted together, and the balloon around my ankle had deflated, the skin turning a yellowish blue. I grabbed my nose, moving the bone back and forth to make sure it snapped into place. My nose had been broken twice before, and I hoped that I wouldn't look like one of those boxers on TV who'd had to have the bones removed from their noses because they'd been broken so many times.

"What happened in the restroom?" Kraft asked.

I pondered his question. I wasn't sure what happened. Dad had mentioned something about it being possible to harness the elements of earth, water, air, and fire, but I had no idea how I'd done it.

My mind and body had been through too much in such a short time. Sleep took control of my muscles. My eyelids drooped, and I yawned, my fangs retracting.

"Where's Zea? I need to see her. I want to see my brother too."

"You didn't answer my question, Jo," he said, patting the skin around my mouth.

I tipped my head down slightly so I could look at him. "I don't know. I was wiping my hands, heading back to class when they came in. Is Zea okay?"

"Zea?"

"The girl who ran for help?"

"I didn't know someone got help. I wasn't in Mr. Banks' office. Sorry."

"Do you think the other Guardian, Frost, is okay?"

"I don't know that either. I was at the front gate when Banks radioed for help."

He finished cleaning the blood from my face then pulled out his cell phone. He punched a few buttons. The phone rang a couple of times before the caller picked up.

"Lieutenant London. Kraft here. We have a situation. I think you'd better get to the school ASAP."

"Not again. What the fuck happened?" Webb asked. Irritation resonated in his voice.

"Ms. Mason has been in a rather destructive fight. I'm not sure of the boy or the woman involved. Both were out when we arrived. And we have a Guardian down."

"A Guardian? How is that possible? Never mind. I can't get there. I'm in the middle of something. Bring her here."

"Yes, sir. One more thing, Lieutenant?"

"What?"

"Banks is pissed. This isn't going to go over well with the commander," Kraft said.

"What else is new? Whatever you do, do not call the commander," Webb snapped.

"The headmistress already did," Kraft warned.

"Fuck." Then the line went dead.

I guessed it was good to have vampire hearing. At least I was warned of the impending doom ahead—and not just from my dear old Dad, but from the reserved Webb London as well.

"I need to clear this with Mr. Banks before I can remove you from school. Wait here. And don't move." Kraft pinned me with a glare.

Arguing with him wasn't on my agenda. Sleep was all I could think about. I tried to fight it as my eyelids fluttered. I needed to find Zea. I needed to make sure she was okay. Plus, I wanted to see my brother. But I had to lie down, just for a minute. I felt as if I'd been given a sedative. I swung my legs up onto the cot and stretched out, placing the blanket over my lower body. I would probably have to wear the darn thing since my skirt was practically in shreds, but I couldn't remember how it had gotten that way. Fog clouded my brain.

I positioned the flimsy pillow under my arm, thinking of Zea. I hoped she was all right. I fluffed the thin pillow as best I could, resting my head on it. I needed to thank her.

I replayed the scene in my head as my muscles relaxed. *What did the brunette want with me? What is her relationship with Blake?* I silently screamed at the thought of his name. I curled into a fetal position and closed my eyes. *Think of something else, anything but this school and the evil that's in it.*

I let out a sigh.

Kraft's voice lingered in the background.

"What do you mean?" he asked, but I didn't know who he was talking to.

Darkness began to swirl around the backs of my eyelids.

Silence.

"How? There were no deadly wounds on him. I just don't get it." Kraft sounded stunned.

Blackness seeped into my veins as Kraft's voice trailed off. Then all sound faded into nothing.

A musty scent wafted in the air as I opened my eyes. Pain shot through every brain cell. My ears hurt too. Wincing, I grabbed the back of my neck as I sat up. I squeezed my eyes shut a few times before my vision cleared. As I looked around, fear gripped me then bit as if a shark clamped down on my chest, taking all the air from my lungs. Lots of buttons peppered the steel walls. I swallowed a scream, choking in the process.

What am I doing in the prison cell? Swords flying out from the walls and stabbing me flashed before my eyes. I had been in there once before. I had to get out immediately.

The door in the distance was open. I stood and wobbled, dizziness taking over my equilibrium.

Blowing out a breath, I tried to run forward, but my knees gave out, and I fell flat on my face. I pushed up on my hands then stood upright, swaying the whole time. I tried again to run to freedom, away from that death trap. Plowing through the open doorway, I hit an invisible barrier that was supercharged with electricity. It threw me back, I hit the back wall, and several swords answered in return. Instinct took over, and I fell forward, flattening my body as the swords jutted out above me. Like a snake in the grass, I slithered my way to the middle of the room. Once I was free of the blades, I made my way to the door again but stopped just before the doorway.

"Hello?" I called. My voice sounded muted against the steel enclosure.

My mind scrambled for some sense of clarity, but a haze blanketed my brain, not to mention the pounding inside my skull. Maybe I was dreaming. That was it. I was dreaming. I had to have been.

"Anyone there?" I called again. My voice was barely audible.

I let out a scream then muttered all kinds of swear words. Fear and anger sat on top of my confusion. My body froze. *Did I do something wrong?*

The door in the hallway opened, and Tripp walked in.

"Tripp? What's going on?" I asked.

His sandy-blond hair seemed to have grown a bit since I last saw him. The wavy tips were brown, offsetting the lighter portion. I hadn't noticed that before.

His lips were moving, but I couldn't hear him.

I cocked my head to one side.

Then he pushed a button on the wall, and his lips moved again.

"Jo, you're awake?" He seemed startled.

Thank God. I started to walk through the door.

"No, don't move," he said emphatically.

Too late. The electrical charge zapped me again. Only that time, my right leg took the impact. A burn skittered straight up to my stomach. I bent over, staring at him.

Tripp ran to the door, stopping inches in front of it. He touched his right ear. "Lieutenant, she's awake," he said. Then silence. "Yes. Okay."

I straightened, blowing out all the air in my lungs, which helped to ease the pain.

"Jo, step back from the doorway."

"What's going on?" The blood in my veins began to pump faster through my system. My heart sped, thumping against my ribs.

"The door has an electrical barrier that prevents you from leaving that room."

"No shit! Why am I in here?"

"Webb will be here in a minute. He'll explain," Tripp said as he stood next to the door in the hall.

"No, I don't want to wait for Webb. Tell me, please." Tears stung the back of my eyelids.

Tripp's bronze eyes projected a sadness I had yet to see on the vampire SEAL.

"Did I do something wrong?" The dam opened, and tears flowed.

"I'm sorry. I've been instructed to keep quiet. You have to wait for Webb."

It was one of those times when I didn't want to wait for anyone. I wanted to get out of there. But Tripp was the good soldier, always following orders. No matter how hard I pressed, he wouldn't budge.

I turned from the door then glanced down. I wasn't wearing my school uniform. *Who in the world changed my clothes?* A sudden chill whispered along my spine. *Oh my. Did Webb change my clothes?* I shook my head. I couldn't think about that. I needed to figure out why I was even in that place.

Turning back to face Tripp, I asked, "Where's my brother? Can I see Sam?"

Tripp shook his head. "Sam's not back yet from school."

"What time is it?"

"Two in the afternoon," he said, glancing at his black-banded watch.

I inhaled. *Do I dare ask what day it is?* On second thought, I didn't want to know. *None of this can be good.* I began pacing, staying clear of the swords that stuck out from the back wall. I dipped back into my thick brain, looking for a memory that would tell me what happened to put me in a vampire prison cell.

My bare feet slapped against the cold steel floor, the only surface that wasn't cobalt. Images of Blake, the brunette, and Zea came into focus. We were all in the bathroom at school. I fought Blake, the brunette stabbed me a couple of times, and Zea drank from the brunette. So far, so good. Then Mr. Banks came in. Kraft carried me to the Guardians' quarters, then I plunked down onto the cot and drifted off to sleep. That was it. *What am I missing? Think, think.*

Tears continued to flow, but I stopped moving, combed my fingers through my hair, and leaned against the sidewall. A succession of clicks in the cell drew me out of deep thought.

Uh-oh. Quickly, I pushed off the wall. A sword protruded, nearly missing the base of my neck. *Stupid swords. Stupid room. Stupid life.* With a sigh, I shuffled toward the middle of the room.

"You're lucky you weren't stabbed," Webb said

as the large steel door scraped against the floor then clicked closed.

I didn't hear him enter.

All the air whooshed out of the cell. Suddenly, I couldn't breathe.

He stood by the door, sweeping his gaze over me.

Something was terribly wrong.

A tickle slithered around in my stomach as I held his gaze, two predators waiting for the other to make their move. He wasn't there to fight. He wasn't even there to argue. He was there to deliver bad news. How I knew that was beyond me. Maybe it was the sadness in his eyes. Like Tripp's, Webb's blue eyes didn't have their usual sparkle.

A voice whispered in my head. *Calm down.* Webb's voice.

Everything in me stilled.

No freakin' way! I can't have him in my head. I just can't.

I stared at my bare feet peeking out from my jeans.

Are you okay?

My neck snapped up, meeting those damned mesmerizing eyes of his.

"How did you get in my head?" I asked out loud.

It was just a matter of time. He was still using telepathy.

"Why doesn't it hurt like when my dad gets in my head?" I asked aloud.

He smiled, white teeth shining beneath the muted lights overhead, causing the butterflies to flutter wildly inside me. Oh, the panic and pain were still there, but those damn butterflies had a mind of their own.

"Your father tends to barrel into people's heads when he's pissed. In turn, he draws pain in the process. There's a way to be gentle when using a telepathic connection," he explained aloud, his tone gentle.

It figured that my dad just took command and control of anything he wanted, whenever he wanted it.

"What am I doing in here, Webb?" I dropped onto the cot, which I had just realized was in the middle of the room, away from the walls.

He walked a few steps toward me. "Do you remember anything that happened today?"

At least days hadn't gone by. "Sure. Where's Zea? Is she okay?"

Webb stopped in his tracks. My heart stopped beating.

"Tell me." My voice quivered.

"She's missing. What went on in the bathroom?"

"Wait, how can she be missing?" I assumed she'd gone for help.

"They're still looking for her. Sam is helping in the search. Now, the bathroom."

I explained the entire story to Webb, from the time I entered the bathroom until Kraft took me to the Guardians' medical office.

He stood feet away as I talked, not showing any emotion. In fact, he didn't move a muscle at all. The black in his eyes fought for control over the blue whenever I mentioned Blake's name. When I finished my side of the story, silence sucked even more air out of the cell, if that was even possible.

After a few minutes, he blew out a breath and sat next to me.

"I don't understand how Zea can be missing." I kept my gaze down, staring at the floor. I was afraid if I stole a glance, I would crumple, not from his presence but from his sad eyes. "She was holding the brunette back one minute, but when I looked again, she was gone. I assumed she went for help because a few minutes later, Mr. Banks barged in and radioed Kraft for help."

"I'm sorry. I don't know any more at the moment," Webb said. "Your father sent me down here to get you. He's waiting in his office."

"Why didn't he come?"

It was so unlike Dad not to barrel in and take control.

"He's on the phone with the solicitors and the Master of Elders."

"What? Why?" I jumped off the cot. "Solicitors? What do they want?" I paced furiously in front of the folding bed, staying away from the freaking walls.

Webb rose, grabbing me. His arms circled around my shoulders, drawing me to him. His fingers tangled in my hair as he pressed my head against his hard chest.

I couldn't breathe. I tried to push him away. He only held me tighter.

I drew in a breath. I wanted to melt into him and feel the heat of his body, the safety of his arms, the reassurance of his heartbeat. I wanted to lose myself in his embrace, but it wasn't the time or the place. I planted both palms against his chest and pushed. "Let me go. What did I do?"

He just held me tighter.

"Webb? You're scaring me."

"Shh."

"No, damn it. What happened, already?"

He loosened his hold on me, easing back a fraction. He peered down. His eyes were swirling black, a true sign his emotions had taken over.

"Blake Turner is dead."

My knees wobbled, my chest tightened, and my vision clouded. He couldn't be dead. He just passed out, and so did the brunette. My body went numb. "I... didn't... have any weapons that would..." I couldn't bring myself to say the word. I didn't have any cobalt weapons to stab him through the heart. I didn't cut off his head, and I didn't set him on fire. Those were the only ways I knew to kill a vampire. I fell to my knees as tears cascaded like a powerful waterfall.

"Dr. Vieira will be conducting an autopsy. Based on your actions yesterday and today, using your telekinesis, the school is speculating that was the cause of his death." His voice was soft.

I killed someone? Oh, my God. This can't be happening to me. I hated Blake and wanted to strangle him, but...

Webb pulled me up.

"I didn't do it. I couldn't have. I just couldn't have." I shook my head several times.

He wrapped his arms around me. "We'll get to the bottom of this."

I didn't have any witnesses. Zea had left the bathroom before Blake passed out, and now, she was missing.

"The solicitors will figure it out," he said as if

he'd read my mind. "We need to get you upstairs to see your father."

Oh no. Dad. I was deathly afraid to move. Maybe it was better that I stayed in the cell rather than face him. My body began to shake.

"Look at me, Jo," Webb whispered.

I lifted my gaze.

He wiped away the tears with the tips of his fingers. His touch was gentle, calming. I closed my eyes and inhaled, taking in his male scent of earth and power.

"Open your eyes, beautiful," he whispered.

My heart stopped beating at the last word. Time froze, as did every muscle in me.

I followed his command and slowly opened my eyelids.

His soft lashes framed a picture of molten onyx that I could stare at forever.

"Ah. Your eyes are a window to a field of vibrant lilacs." He raked his gaze over my face. "You've grown so much since you turned vampire. You're taller, more beautiful, and stronger," he said in a husky tone. "You're stronger here." He placed his hand on my heart. "You're stronger here." He placed two fingers on my temple. "I know you didn't intentionally kill Blake. But your powers rival anything I've ever seen in my time as a vampire. Do you remember the mess you made in this room?" He flicked his head to the side without breaking eye contact with me. "To destroy hardcore steel without any physical effort is unheard of, especially since you've only been a vampire for a short time." His thumb traced my bottom lip as he lowered his gaze.

My mouth grew dry. Fire raced through me. All sense of where I was became a blur.

Then his hands cupped my face as he lowered his head, his hair falling, brushing against my cheek.

Oh God. My heart was pounding so hard it was bruising my rib cage. The blood flowing in me boiled. Heat rose, pinching my cheeks. Then, before I could blink, his lips touched mine, soft, electric, warm, and...

I shivered. Not from a chill, but from pure excitement coursing through me. Tingles pricked my fingers, my stomach, and my toes. My body stiffened. In that moment, my world exploded, shattering into a million colorful stars. Then my body began to shake again.

He placed one hand at the base of my spine, holding me, drawing me in. His hold was gentle yet firm. He pulled his lips from mine and tangled his fingers in my hair.

"You need to learn to use your powers wisely." His deep, husky voice caressed my ear. He eased back, obsidian black eyes gazing down at me. The sadness I had seen earlier was now replaced with something else, but I couldn't be sure what. Heck, I couldn't even think straight, and my body was pure freaking mush. My brain was rioting with fear and excitement at the same time. I mean, he just told me Blake Turner was dead then kissed me. Webb London, gorgeous vampire, kissed me. My first kiss, no less. I should have been running around, jumping up and down for pure joy, but I couldn't move. All I could think about was how morbid it was that I had to kill a boy to get my first kiss.

He touched his ear. "Yes, sir. We're on our way." He touched his ear again. "We need to go." He grabbed my hand. "Between here and your father's office, think about control. Control your emotions. Otherwise... well, you know your father by now. Remember, you're strong, but decide when to fight."

I had no idea what he was talking about. I was still processing that spine-tingling kiss.

"Jo? Did you hear me?" he asked, brushing the back of his hand down my cheek.

If he kept touching me, my brain wasn't going to be able to function. "My father. Yeah. I get it."

I really didn't. Or maybe I did, and I just didn't want to even think about Dad. I was sure he was going to rip into me, no matter if I was angry or I pleaded the fifth. His rage already seeped into me. I didn't have to go to his office to know that he was furious. The fact that he didn't bother to come down to the jail was proof in my book that my father was trying to calm down before he even talked to me.

"Is Blake really dead, Webb?" My lips seemed to be working, although they were still tingly from that kiss, which I so wanted him to do again.

With a nod of his head, he said, "Yes."

I still couldn't wrap my mind around Blake's death. I let out a deep sigh as I followed Webb to the door. I hated the creep. Sure, part of me wanted Blake out of my life, but not by death. It just didn't make any sense to me how my telekinesis could have killed him.

As we walked past Tripp and up the stairs, I silently prayed for mercy. I was about to face the most powerful vampire in my world. I was going to need more than prayers to get me through Dad's wrath.

Dad was sitting behind his desk with the phone stuck to his ear. His silver eyes flashed anger my way. I stopped near the door, not wanting to go any farther. Power I didn't want him to use on me emanated from him. The need to run tore through me. My skin itched to retreat, to hide, but there was nowhere to go. The base was a fortress. Besides, I wouldn't have gotten five feet down the hall before Webb or Dad was on me.

Webb had walked in ahead of me. He didn't seem to be bothered by Dad's power, but he wasn't the one about to get his head cut off by the angry vampire. For a mere second, I took comfort that Dad wasn't paying any attention to me. I needed to keep calm. I closed my eyes and breathed slowly, trying to keep nausea from rising.

No luck. My hands started to shake. Several questions skittered through my head. *What will happen to me? What do they do with vampires who murdered others? Webb said the solicitors were involved. Like in the human court system, will I be prosecuted?*

I wasn't looking for any of those answers. I was just trying to defend myself against an asshole who wanted my life. As I stood waiting for Dad to finish his call, I went through the scene one more time. I still couldn't figure out how I'd killed Blake. Then there was the brunette who had passed out. I'd forgotten to ask Webb about her. It didn't matter—I was more worried about Zea.

I swallowed several times to quell the uneasiness building in my stomach. I kept my lips tight so Dad wouldn't see my fangs. The vampire within was taking over. At any moment, my telekinesis would take center stage, and I wasn't sure I could tamp it down. It seemed whatever drove my powers had a mind of its own. Sometimes, it seemed as if I had ten different personalities.

All I kept hearing in my head was *Stand up for yourself, Jo. Don't be a weakling.*

I clasped my hands together so Dad wouldn't see them shaking. *Get it together*, I repeated.

Webb had told me to control my emotions. Yeah, right. There was no way, not with a lunatic screaming in my head. I couldn't find my little angel voice, but no matter. Neither was going to help me.

Dad slammed down the phone, jarring me from my inner turmoil. I jumped as reality smashed into me.

"Sit, young lady," he said in an unyielding tone.

Oh boy. He was furious. He only used the term "young lady" when he was mad at me.

I bit my bottom lip.

Obey your father. Don't make this harder for yourself.

I shot daggers at Webb as his voice resonated in my head.

A stabbing pain hit me in my temples. *Really? Dad too?*

Did you hear me, young lady? I gave you an order. Now sit your ass down before I drag you to the chair. Flames of anger flickered in Dad's eyes.

This should be so much fun.

Are you sassing me? I told you to sit. Now, move.

I glared at the blue-eyed vampire then the furious silver-eyed one.

My brain silently waged a war. I really did need to see a shrink.

You're going to need more than a shrink... Dad

rose from his chair, stalked over to me, and peered down from his six-foot height. For some reason, he appeared much taller than usual. His anger seemed to add five inches to his broad build.

I craned my neck and met his gaze, not saying a word, trying to keep my mind blank.

We stared at each other for what felt like years. Then Dad grabbed me by the arm and pulled me to the chair. "When I say do something..." he growled.

He released my arm then resumed his place behind his desk, only he didn't sit. He stood behind his tall leather chair with his fingers wrapped around the sides. His knuckles were white. *I told you to decide when to fight. Why do you insist on irritating your father?*

I dropped into the chair, ignoring the hunk next to me. I desperately wanted to tell him to shove it in one breath and...

I suddenly stopped thinking. I'd almost forgotten that Dad could read my mind. I erected a mental shield around my brain the fastest way I knew how—I silently started singing the national anthem in my head.

Dad looked at me, a vertical crease between his eyes.

A long silence filled the room.

The national anthem blared in my head,

helping to take my mind off the impending doom hanging between father and daughter.

"Do you like singing the national anthem?" Dad asked. His voice still rumbled with power that teetered on the edge of destruction.

I hesitated to say anything, but the words just spilled out. "It's the only way... I can keep you... out," I whispered.

"Do you know what you've done, young lady?" he asked evenly.

My brows shot up. "You already reached a verdict? You think I killed that jerk? Whatever happened to innocent until proven guilty? Oh, right. You're the law too." I sat on my hands, hoping to keep my anger under control. "Is that why you threw me in the prison cell? Because you're judge and jury?"

Jo, you need to stop. Webb's voice rang in my head. *I told you to control your emotions. Your eyes are changing from light purple to deep violet. Anger isn't going to win with your father. He's trying to hold in his rage, but you're not helping. If you think you've seen him angry, think again.*

"I put you in that cell to knock some sense into you. Now, I have to answer to my superiors and try to get you out of this one." Rage was clear in his voice, and hard lines cut into his forehead.

"Don't do me any favors. I didn't kill him. I will

stand up for myself." The tension inside me snapped. I wasn't going to listen to him accuse me of something I didn't do. I stood and ran into the hall, where I plowed right into my brother.

"Hey, what's wrong?" Sam asked, grasping my shoulders.

I started crying. "I didn't do it. I didn't do it."

"Shhh." He hugged me. "It's all right. We'll figure this out." He pulled away, regarding me. "We always do. I promise, sis. I won't let anything happen to you."

I took comfort in Sam's promise. I loved my brother more than anything in the world, human or vampire. His humanity might have been gone forever, but his resolve would never waver. He would do everything he could to protect me, but even Sam couldn't fight the law.

My tears poured, and I morphed into all-out sobbing, to the point where I couldn't breathe. I closed my eyes and shuddered several breaths before tiny bits of tension eased. My muscles relaxed. Sam *was* my protector. I wanted to stay safe in his arms, but...

"Get away, Webb," Sam snapped as the other man approached.

"Jo," Webb said gently. That tone would normally have made me melt, but I wasn't in the mood for even the gorgeous vampire. I wanted to stay with my brother, the only real family I knew.

"Webb, I mean it. I said to get away from her," Sam said through gritted teeth.

"Son," Dad said. "Bring your sister into the office."

"Why? So you can yell and scare her to death? She didn't kill Blake Turner. She's not capable of hurting anyone. Christ, Pops, can't you for one minute get to know us instead of always telling us what to do? If you knew—"

"Stop." Dad's tone gentled. "I need to know what happened."

Sam eased back. "Hey, I'm here now." He wiped the tears from my face with his tie. "Dad's right. We need to hear about it. Okay?"

"You're taking his side! No, I'm not talking to him. He doesn't know how to talk. He's an ogre," I spat before running down the corridor.

I got as far as the door to the stairwell before a hand grasped my arm.

"Jo," Webb said in a breathy whisper. "I know your father has his own way of handling things. And if I know him, he's regretting his actions. When he's extremely angry, he acts without thinking. I'm not saying I agree with him, but he's been on the phone all day, trying to keep the solicitors from taking you into custody. He needs to know your side of the story now."

I didn't turn around. One look into Webb's eyes, and I would have caved. Hell, his husky voice had already cut through my wall of anger. "Well, he should think before he acts. And I'm not going back there. He's insane," I said in a low tone.

He turned me to face him.

Don't look at him. Just don't look at his heart-grabbing eyes or his kiss-me lips.

"Beautiful, would you do it for me? I'll be in there with you." His tone was breathy, silky.

He called me beautiful again. He just didn't play fair. *Damn vampire.*

With my gaze glued to the shiny tiled floor, we stood in the hall in silence. I didn't want to go anywhere near my father. I was just as angry as he was.

Webb broke the silence. "Please."

He had to have known, somehow, that he had an effect on me. I let out a breath. "One condition." I lifted my gaze to his.

He raised both eyebrows.

"If my father lashes out at me, plays judge and jury, or yells, I'm out of there, and I won't talk to you, him, or anyone about what happened. In fact, I might be better off with the solicitors than staying here."

"I can't promise you any of those things. As you must know by now, no one controls your father. But it's a start. If he does any of those things, I won't stop you from leaving. And Jo..." He pierced me with a look that scared the crap out of me. "You are far better off with your father than with the solicitors."

I had no idea what he meant by that last statement and, frankly, I didn't want to know, at least not just then. Something told me I would find out eventually, anyway.

Reluctantly, I went back to Dad's office with Webb. Sam sat on the couch, and Dad was settled in the armchair opposite him.

Sam patted the seat next to him. "Come here, sis. Sit with me."

I didn't hesitate. I eased down next to my brother.

"You okay?" he asked.

"Just peachy."

Webb took the remaining armchair.

Dad scrubbed his face with both hands.

Silence gave way to the desk phone beeping.

"What is it?" Dad said loudly.

Ruth's delicate voice came through the speaker. "Sir, you have two visitors in the lobby who want to speak with you."

Dad rose from his chair, made his way to his

desk, then picked up the receiver. He listened for a minute before saying, "I don't have time. For what? Why? Hold on." He lowered the receiver and glanced in our direction. "Webb, where's Kate? Is she on the premises?"

Sam stilled and tightened when Dad mentioned Kate's name.

"She was earlier. She helped Jo with her clothes. But she asked for two more days off, so I granted it. She isn't leaving until this evening."

I guess that answered my question about who'd changed me into the jeans and T-shirt.

"Call her. Ask her to check in with Ruth and speak with our guests," Dad said to Webb before lifting the receiver to his ear. "Ruth. Yes, Kate will be down in a few minutes to address our guests. Yes. Thank you." He placed the phone on its base.

Webb walked out, tapping on his cell phone.

"Who's downstairs, Pops?" Sam asked.

"It's not important," he said. "Now, I need to hear what happened."

I folded my legs under me as I found a comfortable spot on the couch.

"Jo." Dad's voice was even. "This is serious. A boy is dead."

I straightened my spine. "And it's your flippin' daughter who stands accused! I'm not one of your soldiers. I don't know how to handle this!" My control was faltering, and my powers teetered on the edge.

"I'm sorry. You're right. I was too consumed with rage when I found out the boy was dead. Please... tell me what happened."

"Are you saying you were more worried about your reputation than your own daughter?" I wasn't letting him off the hook. He was certifiable.

He glared at me, no doubt reading my last thought. I didn't care, not one bit.

He took four long strides before sitting next to me. "I'm truly sorry." He pulled me to him, but I pushed him away, hard.

He raised his hands in a placatory gesture.

We locked eyes. I was certain mine held anger. His made me freeze. My father, the powerful vampire, had water in his eyes. I blinked twice. More water muted his shifting eyes.

He cleared his throat. "I'm not going to make excuses. I was wrong. And I know no matter what I say right now, it isn't going to take away the sting. I can be an ass, plain and simple."

My jaw hit the floor. I didn't have a reply to his tears or him calling himself an ass.

I looked at Sam, whose eyebrows were practically in his hairline.

"Look, Jo, this is serious. I don't want to see anything happen to you. You are my daughter, and

I will stand behind you. If you say you didn't kill the Turner boy, then I believe you. We'll face the solicitors together."

"Really?" I asked.

He pulled me into a hug. "Really," he whispered.

Suddenly, the window shattered, spraying glass everywhere. The building rocked beneath our feet, and there was a deep booming sound somewhere in the distance.

Dad jumped into action, sprinting to his safe. Webb ran back in. Sam covered my head with both arms.

Then another explosion rocked the building, shattering more of the windows in the office. Alarms blared, and red lights flashed.

"All personnel, man your stations," a voice thundered over the loudspeaker. "All personnel, man your stations. This is not a test."

Dad's cell phone blared. Webb's beeped.

"Lieutenant, get downstairs. I'll meet you in the control room."

Webb ran out, his cell phone to his ear. "Report." Then he was gone.

"I need you two—"

The desk phone rang. Dad took two strides before picking up the receiver. "What? Shit! Lock it down. Too bad. They can't leave right now."

"What's going on, Pops?" Sam stood, tugging me along.

Dad picked up a tiny earpiece from his desk then inserted it and pressed the outer edge of his ear. "Tripp? Come in."

He stood in his black cargo uniform, waiting for Tripp to respond.

"I need you to get down to the lobby, Tripp. I'm sending Sam and Jo down there now. You need to keep an eye on things. We have two guests with Kate. Send Kate to the control room." He stopped talking for a few seconds. "Yes, the Sentinels at the main door have locked down the building. Make sure Ruth is okay too. Yes." Then he touched his ear lightly. "How are you two on your hunger?"

"I'm fine," Sam replied.

"I'm okay," I added. "Why?"

"Our guests are human. I need you to meet Tripp down there. Mr. Jackson and a female friend of Ben's are downstairs. They'll feel more comfortable being with people they know until I can give the all clear for them to leave. Right now, I need to head to the control room."

Sam and I looked at each other, eyes wide. "What is Mr. Jackson doing here, Pops?"

"I don't know. He wouldn't tell Ruth. All he said was that it was urgent, and he needed to speak to me."

"Who's the female?" I asked.

"Don't know." Dad opened a five-foot safe. Within the large safe were two smaller ones, one sitting on top of the other. Dad fiddled with the combination of the top one, then it opened. "Here." He handed me a small container of his blood. "Son, take one just in case."

Sam grabbed one from him.

As we drank, Dad spun the combination lock on the bottom safe before pulling out three daggers, all in leather sheaths, a gun, two clips, and a wide leather wristband that held several bullets.

"Jo, Sam, remember—no emotional outbursts. They don't know you're vampires or that vampires exist at all, at least not that I'm aware of."

"What is that?" I asked, pointing to the wristband.

"Cobalt bullets."

I froze.

"Are the Plutariums—"

"Not sure. Both of you, get moving." He adjusted the Sentinel sword on his belt.

Sam pulled me to the door. "Pops, I can help." His eyes sparkled with excitement as he watched Dad strap one dagger belt around his right leg and the other around his left. He pulled the extra dagger out of the sheath and placed it between his belt and his cargo pants.

"I need you to stay with Jo this time. Don't worry. You'll get your chance."

He had everything he needed, so he closed his safe and guided us out the door. The three of us jogged to the elevators. Sam and I waited for it while Dad took off toward the stairwell.

The alarms had stopped, but the red lights still flashed, creating an ominous atmosphere. Then the elevator doors opened, and Sam and I jumped in. The door slid shut, and Sam pushed the lobby button.

As we rode the elevator, several things went through my mind. *Are we under attack? If so, why? Does it have anything to do with the Plutariums? And what is Mr. Jackson doing here? What help does he need from Dad?*

"Jo?" Sam touched my arm.

I blinked away my thoughts and looked at him.

"Pops is right. We can't display any emotions in front of Mr. Jackson and whoever else is with him."

"Yeah, I know, but it's not that easy. They're humans. Whether I'm hungry or not, their scent still tempts me."

"We both need to stay in control, Jo." He shoved his hands into his pants pockets.

The elevator bell dinged, and the doors slid open.

Tripp blocked Sam and me as we exited then herded us to a small room adjacent to the elevator.

Once in, he closed the door then studied both of us.

"Is there a problem, Tripp?" Sam asked, standing eye to eye with the tall Sentinel.

"No, I just want to make sure you two are in control." Tripp touched my chin, tilting my head. I met his metallic brown eyes. His expression was blank. I wasn't surprised. Tripp had a mysterious aura about him that always concealed his true emotions. "No trouble," he said, staring at me. "Smile. I want to see your teeth."

"Huh?" I was dumbfounded.

"No fangs. Now show me."

I smiled. My extended canines were tucked in, at least for the time being. I couldn't promise they wouldn't pop out again.

"Your turn, Sam," Tripp said.

"We just had blood," Sam said.

"I don't care if you had ten pints of the stuff. There are two humans out there with scents that drive even me crazy. And I've been around a hell of a lot longer than both of you. I can't teach you how to control your urges, but you must do whatever it takes. We've got a ton of shit going down right now. We don't need any more, especially where humans are involved. Do I make myself clear?"

"Tripp, we'll do our best. Chill," Sam said.

I nodded.

"Good. There's a young lady named Darcy Rose with Mr. Jackson. I take it she's a friend of yours, Jo?"

"Darcy's here? Why?" I asked.

"I don't know. Mr. Jackson wants to speak with your father. It has something to do with Ben."

"What about Ben?" Sam asked, his voice hitching.

"Again, I don't know. Look, you two, I know it's hard. Control it. Your eyes can't change, and no fangs," Tripp warned.

"We get it. Do you have a backup plan just in case?" I asked. *What if my fangs drop on instinct? What if raw emotion takes control when I'm talking with Darcy or Mr. Jackson?*

"Look at me, Jo," Tripp commanded. "Take a deep breath. Here's what we're going to do. I'll stay close to you at all times. If you feel yourself losing it, I want you to touch me. My healing powers might help subdue your emotions."

"Will it work?" Sam asked.

"Don't know," Tripp admitted. "So do your best."

"Wait, what about Sam?" I asked.

"Tripp's not touching me," Sam said with a snarl. "No offense, dude. You're not my type."

Tripp laughed. "Good to know, Mason. Don't worry. I'd bet Sam is better at control than you, Jo."

"Huh?" I felt as if I had "weakling" imprinted on my forehead.

"I'll be fine, Jo. Tripp's right. You seem to have a stronger pull to the blood than I do. Don't ask me why."

He might have been right. Anyway, I needed to focus on me, not on Sam.

The three of us walked out into the lobby.

Ruth was seated behind a circular desk, and she appeared to be reading something on her computer screen.

Two Sentinels stood guard at the main doors of the building with rifles around their shoulders. Both of them wore unblinking expressions and reminded me of statues in a museum. The area was cold, which was no surprise to me. Since the first day I'd walked through the main doors, the chill had grabbed me— not just a cold chill, but an ominous one.

Mr. Jackson and Darcy were sitting on the padded bench that lined the left wall. Mr. Jackson had one leg crossed over the other, while Darcy fidgeted in her seat. She seemed nervous.

When she saw me, she jumped off the bench. I hadn't seen her since Sam disappeared months ago. Her blond hair was pulled back into a low ponytail. Her skin glowed as though she had recently spent time in the sun. She wore a pair of tan capris, flip-flops, and a black tank top. It seemed her hiatus from school suited her well.

"Jo? Is that you? Whoa! What happened to you?" Her eyes grew wide as she fired off the questions. Then she looked at my brother. "Sam?" Her big brown eyes got even bigger. Her throat rippled, and so did her jugular.

Then her cotton candy scent wafted my way and stirred the vampire in me.

Focus. Damn it. All I needed was to sink my fangs into my best friend.

Tripp was right behind, almost touching me. He leaned down and whispered, "Breathe. Your heart is racing."

No shit!

"Jo. Sam. How are you?" Mr. Jackson asked as he stood.

I nodded. "Nice to see you, sir."

He slanted his head to one side. "It looks like both of you have grown since I last saw you a couple of weeks ago. It must be late puberty for you both."

I wanted to laugh. Our vampire puberty, or whatever it was that caused growth spurts, was at its peak, and so was the bloodlust. I gritted my teeth as the tasty humans stood in front of me, mentally scolding myself.

"Well? Are you going to answer me, Jo?" Darcy asked. "What happened to you?" She hadn't changed. Her demanding attitude and feisty temper were still there.

I swallowed. "I'm sorry I haven't called. Things have been crazy since my father came back."

"That's not what I meant. I know why you haven't called—Ben told me you two were trying to get to know your dad—but you're taller, your skin is like porcelain, you've thinned out, and your hair... you highlighted your hair purple?"

She didn't even take a breath between sentences. That was Darcy.

"Mr. Jackson, what brings you here? Where's Ben?" Sam cut in, saving me for the moment.

Darcy stared at me then at Sam. While her mouth seemed to operate normally, her appearance gave me reason to pause. With the light above spraying down on her at just the right angle, it looked like she had been crying. The whites of her eyes were red, and dark patches were tattooed beneath them.

Mr. Jackson let out a frustrated sigh. "That's why I'm here. I need to ask your father for help."

Sam's heart raced, and I suddenly wondered if

he could feel any emotions from Mr. Jackson or humans in general.

Tripp placed his hands on my shoulders. I didn't need his help yet, but the warm sensation flowing through me relaxed my muscles. My brain was alert, though. If I wasn't mistaken, a sad tone colored Mr. Jackson's voice.

"Did something happen?" Sam asked.

I stole a glance at him and saw that black was beginning to weave through his green eyes.

"Ben is missing." Darcy's voice cracked. Tears dropped from her eyes.

I sucked in air, clasping my hands over my mouth. That poor boy had been through hell with the Plutariums, and... I couldn't think. I couldn't move. I couldn't even speak. Life came to a stand-still. The past couple of days had been hell, but that news was something else. I blinked a few times, trying to control my emotions, but the tears were building, my control was wavering, and the vampire within itched to get out. "Is that true?" My voice was muffled since I had my hands glued to my mouth.

Tears filled Mr. Jackson's eyes. "I'm afraid so."

"When did he disappear? And from where?" Tripp asked.

His healing hands never left my shoulders.

Good thing. If they had, I might have been passed out on the floor already.

I wondered how he could have been missing, whether there was any correlation between Jack Powell's disappearance and Ben's, and why Darcy was there to tell us. My heart began to ache.

Tripp raised one hand. I turned and met his gaze. His expression was one of shock. I knew my eyes must have shifted as soon as he raised his hand, which he placed back on me. The room around me disappeared for a split second then cleared.

It was a good thing Mr. Jackson had walked away from us. I imagined he was trying to gain control of his emotions. I could relate. On the other hand, Darcy just stood there, watching Sam and me.

"What's wrong with you two?" she asked.

I furrowed my brows. "Nothing. Why?"

"Your eyes. They just changed colors."

Tripp slid his hands down to my arms then squeezed. Meanwhile, Sam walked over to the two Sentinels at the door. I imagined he also had to get control of himself. If the vampire world was smart and didn't want humans to know we existed, they should have invested in research to develop a pill to quell the eye color change or even in colored contacts.

"Their eyes do that. Some sort of genetic family phenomenon," Mr. Jackson explained as he walked back.

My breath caught in the back of my throat. I wasn't expecting that. Either Ben had told him a lot, or the man had witnessed our eyes changing colors and rationalized it.

"I've never heard of that," Darcy stated.

"It's not important," I said. "Now, tell us about Ben."

Darcy and Mr. Jackson sat on the bench. Mr. Jackson nudged Darcy.

"Ben and I went to see my aunt in the hospital at Highland Memorial. We came out and were walking through the garage to Ben's car when a tall, scary dude with black hair came out of the shadows like he'd been waiting for us. Ben and this guy talked. It seemed he knew Ben. Ben called him by name, but I can't remember it. So I walked toward the car while they talked. It seemed like no big deal. Then my phone rang, and I talked to my mother. When I hung up, Ben wasn't around, but his car was still there. I looked all over the garage. I even went back into the hospital, but I couldn't find him." She dropped her head into her hands.

Mr. Jackson rubbed her back.

"How long has he been missing?" Tripp asked.

Sam still hadn't returned. I didn't think he

could handle their emotions in addition to trying to overcome his own.

"Two days," Mr. Jackson replied. "I've contacted the local police, even my friend Chief Garrett. No luck. Ben takes the total to five missing kids from Durfee now. I can't lose him. These past two days have been..." He looked away, more tears welling up in his eyes.

"Darcy? Did you see anyone else around the garage at the time?" Tripp asked.

She shook her head. "No one."

"Can your father help?" Mr. Jackson asked.

I craned my neck to look at Tripp.

"As you can see, Mr. Jackson," he said, "we're in the middle of a crisis that we've not yet resolved. It seems there was an explosion in the shipyard, which is why the building rocked. Commander Mason is busy trying to take care of matters and make sure people are safe."

"I'm not leaving until I can speak with him," Mr. Jackson said.

"I understand. We couldn't let you leave yet, anyway. Once the building is locked down, we can't do anything until we get the all-clear sign. I do need to get the twins back to their father, though. Can I get you both anything to drink while you wait?"

"No, we'll be fine," Mr. Jackson replied.

"Ruth is here if you need anything. Someone on my team will check on you shortly."

"Thank you," Mr. Jackson said.

"Sam, let's go," Tripp called.

"Jo." Darcy seemed to struggle to say my name.

I met her human gaze. I couldn't read her emotions, but I didn't have to. The tears said it all.

"I miss you," she said.

"I've missed you too." I held back my own tears.

Sam stood near the elevator.

"She has to go," Tripp said.

"I'll see you soon," I added. "I promise."

She dropped onto the bench as I glanced back at her.

I might have just lied to her and questioned how I could hang out with her if I couldn't be honest.

We left the humans in the lobby as we got into the elevator. As soon as the door closed, I collapsed on the floor of the car. My fangs shot out of my gums, and my eyes changed instantly. Between their human scent and learning that Ben was missing, my body gave out.

Tripp tried to help me up, but I needed to sit. My muscles were too weak to stand. I hugged my knees to my chest, letting out several short breaths.

"Sam, are you okay?" Tripp asked, pushing the button for the fourth floor.

He nodded. "I will be. Their emotions were too much to handle. I thought vampire emotions were rough on me, but they're nothing compared to humans'. Not only were their scents distracting, but Mr. Jackson's fear, sadness, and anger stabbed me in the gut. I didn't have to process the news about Ben. Mr. Jackson's agony was plenty for me."

"Sam, I'm sorry, man. Empath is the hardest of the powers to have," Tripp said. "But it can also come in handy when you learn how to use it."

Sam straightened. "How?"

"It'll take practice. When we have time, I'll work with you. I'm a weak Empath. My healing abilities sometimes counteract others' emotions, as you saw with Jo just now."

Sam dropped his head back against the wall, slid down, and sat on the floor next to me. "Thank you, man," he whispered.

I looked up at Tripp. "Hey, I thought you had to stay down there?"

"I did. Then I made a command decision to get you two out. It was getting a little too emotional for me, and Sam was struggling. Jo, you did well."

"Thanks to you."

Sadness crept in as I thought about Ben, whether the Plutariums had anything to do with his disappearance, and what my father could do to help Mr. Jackson. Given all that had happened at school and the explosion, I didn't think Dad was going to be open to spending time trying to find Ben. I was afraid if I even mentioned Ben's name, he would have a cow. Sam and I would need to figure out if there was something we could do to help. The problem was that I had no idea where to start.

By the time we got off the elevator, Sam and I were like two zombies, but for different reasons, I imagined. For me, it had been a day of both heaven and hell—though mostly hell. The scary part was that the day wasn't even over yet.

22

Tripp had radioed Dad to let him know that we made it to the apartment. There wasn't much Sam and I could do to help Dad or the Sentinels with the explosion or Mr. Jackson with finding Ben. So parking my butt on the couch sounded like a good idea, though I wasn't sure I could relax, knowing that Ben was missing.

Sam heated two cups of blood while I made myself comfortable on the couch.

"Here." Sam handed me a mug of warm blood with a splash of pepper on top.

"Since when do you season it?" I brought the mug to my nose and sniffed it.

"It's good." He sat next to me, sipping his.

Hesitating with the mug in my hands, I took

one last sniff before tasting it. I shrugged. "This isn't bad. It has that sweet-and-spicy taste that I like."

"I told you."

Looking around as I drank, I spotted a large crack that zigzagged down one of the windows. It must've happened during the explosion. The apartment had fared twenty times better than Dad's office—that was the only damage in the whole place.

Tripp strode in, brushing his hand over his head. "Are you two going to be okay?"

"We'll be fine," Sam replied. "Sleep sounds good right about now. Feeling someone else's emotions is draining."

"Did my father say what happened?" I asked.

"There was an explosion on one of the military ships down at the docks. It's contained now." Tripp grabbed the doorknob.

"Anyone hurt?" Sam asked.

"Not sure yet. I need to get down to the control room. Your father wants both of you to stay in the apartment. He needs all military personnel on this matter, so you won't have a bodyguard standing outside." Tripp flicked his head, motioning to the hall. "The buildings and the base are locked down anyway."

His phone rang, and he answered it.

"Yes, sir," Tripp said. "No, they're fine. Yes, I will. I'll be down in five. I already explained that to them." He pushed a button then holstered the phone. "Do not leave the apartment. Is that understood?"

"Where're we going to go?" I yawned.

"Your father said to call him if you need to. Otherwise, he'll be up as soon as he can." With that, he opened the door then was gone.

"Sam?"

"Mmm?" He set his mug on the coffee table.

"We need to find Ben."

"How? We can't get off this base. And if we did, where would we even begin to look?" He let out a sigh.

"Do you think the Plutariums have something to do with Ben going missing?"

"Maybe. I don't know. Pops said that Edmund wanted men who could fight, not teenagers."

"Yeah, but don't you find it odd that Jack Powell is missing, and now Ben? Not to mention that Mr. Jackson said that there are a total of five Durfee students missing. And... Zea is missing too."

It was hard to think that Zea was missing. She was a vampire, so it was hard for me to get my head around who would have taken her or where she had gone. My mind struggled to believe that the Plutariums would kidnap a vampire. If they had, that meant they had access to the school.

He rested back against the sofa. "Oh, I forgot to tell you. The Guardians found Zea. She was hiding in the boys' bathroom, puking her guts out."

I let out a huge sigh. "Is she okay?"

"I stopped by the nurse's office before I left school. She was definitely pale. It seems she really can't handle her blood." Sam shook his head.

I was still shocked that any vampire didn't like blood. Regardless, I was relieved that Zea was safe. "What about Ben?"

Sam propped his feet up on the table. "Jo, there's nothing we can do right now. We're on a military base that's in lockdown. We don't need to be pissing off Pops."

He had a very good point. Ruffling Dad's vampire feathers wouldn't help my case. Besides, I wanted more time to bask in the fact that not but an hour before, the powerful vampire had laid out his feelings in front of Sam and me.

I thought about Ben, which was much better than revisiting all the bad stuff that had happened to me that day. Ben had been through too much with vampires, and his life had been spared more than once. Still, instinct whispered to me that luck might not be on his side, especially as time whittled away.

The door swept open, and Dad walked in.

I jumped up. "Is everything over with?"

"For now." He headed into the kitchen.

"What about Mr. Jackson?" Sam asked. "And Ben. He's missing."

"We'll have to discuss that later. I wanted to make sure you two were okay. Then I need to get back downstairs," he said, washing his hands.

"You don't trust us, do you, Pops?" Sam muttered.

"It's not that. We suspect that the Plutariums are involved in the explosion at the shipyard. I'm not taking any chances." He wiped his hands.

My heart stopped. "Did the Plutariums get on base?"

"We spotted Jonah outside the compound." He grabbed a mug from the dish rack.

"What about Ben?" Sam asked. "Do you think—"

Pounding on the door stopped the conversation.

All three of us jerked our heads in that direction. Sam jumped over the coffee table and ran to my side. Dad placed the mug on the counter then strode to the door, growling. "This better be good," he muttered.

Their scent gave them away before Dad even opened it. Humans stood on the other side of the steel door. Mr. Jackson had said he wasn't leaving until he spoke to Dad.

"I insisted that Mr. Jackson leave. I'll talk to him later," Dad said in response to my thoughts. He opened the door, and cold air rushed in.

Two large men dressed in military police uniforms stood behind Webb.

My heart stopped. Maybe the solicitors called for them to take me away for killing Blake.

"Commander?" Webb nodded. "These two men need to speak to you." His voice had a strange, nervous timbre to it.

Dad cleared the way for the men to enter then closed the door. Sam grasped my hand. Webb fixed his gaze on me. Confused anguish flickered in his eyes. I clutched Sam's hand tighter.

"What can I do for you, soldiers?" Dad crossed his arms over his chest.

I couldn't tell them apart. If it hadn't been for their nametags, I would have sworn they were twins. They both wore navy uniforms with wide blue bands plastered on their left arms, the initials *MP* in white letters. Their hats were tucked under their right arms, and they both had shaved heads. The only difference was their eye color. One had blue eyes, the other brown. The one with blue eyes was apparently Carter, and the brown eyes belonged to Peterson.

"Sir, I'm afraid you need to come with us," Carter said.

Dad creased his eyebrows together. "Explain."

Webb had made his way to stand by Sam and me, so I was sandwiched between the two imposing vampires as though they were my bodyguards. If Dad had to go with them, it wasn't about Blake. I relaxed a fraction but then worried about why Dad had to go with the human military police.

"Sir, the Secretary of the Navy has been murdered. You were the last one with him today. The Chief of Naval Operations has requested your presence for questioning," Peterson explained.

I gasped, covering my mouth with my free hand.

Webb sidled closer to me.

Dad unfolded his arms, dropping them to his side. Then he ran both hands through his hair, pulled out the band secured at his nape, then rubbed a hand over his mouth and jaw. Power rose around him. I didn't think the two humans could feel it, but they sure seemed nervous. I wondered whether they knew Dad was a vampire or that he could kill them in a flash.

Without thinking, I let go of Sam's hand and ran to Dad, standing between him and the MPs. In a blur, Peterson lunged toward me. I moved back into Dad, and we fell to the floor. Immediately, Dad and I jumped up to find Sam and Peterson fighting. Webb was trying to break it up. Carter walked over to Dad and me.

"Stand down, soldier," Dad barked. "Sam, stop." Dad's voice growled with anger.

Webb managed to separate Sam from Peterson. I had no clue what had just happened or what the MP was trying to do. I only wanted to be near my dad.

Webb grunted. "Sam, step aside." I could tell his eyes were on the verge of changing as he glared at my brother.

Dad touched my shoulders before he leaned down. "Are you okay?"

I nodded.

"Petty Officer Peterson, apologize to my daughter." Dad's voice had a deep timbre to it, not one I'd heard before.

Peterson bent down and picked up his military cap. He brushed off the white fabric lining the top.

"Why would you attack my sister?" Sam spat.

"I-I'm sorry. I thought she was going for the dagger in Commander Mason's leg holster." His voice cracked as he looked at me with soft eyes.

"That's our father, you idiot," Sam barked, pacing back and forth, struggling to keep his vampire caged.

"Son, his soldier instincts kicked in as they're supposed to." Dad kept his hands on me.

"Screw instincts. He had no right to come into our home and think Jo was going to attack." Sam's deep, commanding voice resonated.

Webb pulled Sam into the kitchen.

With the misunderstanding out of the way, Dad turned me so I was facing him. "Look, I need to go with these folks," he said. "It's protocol. I'll be back as soon as I can." He struggled to keep his eyes from changing to silver, the deep green in them slowly fading. "I'm also sorry about earlier today. I know I told you that already, but... we'll talk more when I get back. Okay?"

I nodded, trying to keep from tearing up. Dad's voice held so much regret, and I didn't think it was just because he'd had me thrown into a prison cell out of blind rage.

Then something clicked inside me. I wasn't sure whether it was the buzzing in my head or if my heart somehow locked into place. Our relationship was far from solid. Hell, it had been a wild rollercoaster ride of decent moments, tender moments, and fiery moments. But a chill settled in me, and I didn't want him to leave with those men. "No, I don't want you to go." I hugged him tightly. The little girl in me wanted her daddy even as the teenager in me wanted to be strong. I was caught in a storm of confusing feelings.

He wrapped his arms around me and rubbed his hand up and down my back. "It'll be okay. I know a lot is going on, but I must go with them, sweetie." He took one step back. "I promise, I'll be fine."

A tear slid down my cheek.

"Hey." His broad hand swept the side of my cheek, taking the tear with it. He wasn't as gentle as Webb, but nonetheless, tenderness sparked through his fingers. "Nothing is going to happen to me. You're strong. You're a Mason. I'll be back as soon as I can."

Dad turned to Webb. "Lieutenant, we need a team down at the shipyard. Make sure you have Snow and Viking II accompany the Sentinels. Also, I want Tripp and Sloan interrogating the young brunette woman. Find out everything you can about what she wanted with Jo. I shouldn't be long." Dad began removing all his weapons.

I stiffened. "The brunette is here... on base?" I grabbed Dad's hand before he walked away.

"She is." He turned his attention back to the MPs. "I need to lock these up," he said, indicating his weapons. "I'll be just a second."

"How? She was at school the last I saw her." I looked at Webb.

"We had her brought back from the school to question her," he replied.

Dad didn't give the MPs a chance to respond, nor did he give me a chance to ask more questions about the brunette. He just walked down the hall into his bedroom. The MPs followed him and stopped at the door, which Dad slammed in their faces.

One of the MPs tried to open the door but to no avail.

They weren't getting through that door.

The air in the room grew thick. An ominous tickle slithered along the back of my neck. The bitch of a brunette was on base. My mouth watered as images of her flashed in my head—not sugarplum versions, either, but pictures of me strangling her that had my pulse racing with excitement.

The door to Dad's room opened, and pain stung me.

You will not go anywhere near her. Do you hear me, young lady?

Gone was the regretful, sorrowful voice that he'd used earlier. In its place... soldier, commander, and strict father.

Dad strode toward me with the MPs right on his heels. He stopped at the small table near the door and picked up his keys.

She stabbed me, I told him.

And you think that warrants revenge? You have a lot to learn in this life. I expect you to listen to Webb while I'm gone.

"Sir, we need to frisk you before we leave," Peterson said.

Dad glared at me. "Go ahead, MP."

Don't worry, Dad. I won't touch her. But I will protect myself, just like I did in the bathroom at school. Unless, of course, you want me to stand there while others beat on me.

He growled, raising an eyebrow.

Yeah. I didn't think so.

"Lieutenant, you have my permission to utilize Sam's combat skills. He's ready. I don't want Jo out of your sight. Are we clear?"

"Yes, sir," Webb said.

"You know where I'll be. Again, I shouldn't be long," Dad said.

The MPs pulled his hands behind his back, locking his wrists in human handcuffs, and without any struggle, Dad allowed himself to be escorted out of the apartment. I wanted to laugh at the act. The two human soldiers clearly had no idea that Dad could snap those handcuffs in two if he wanted. Nevertheless, he had to abide by human laws when he was working alongside the human government.

As soon as the door clicked shut, I bent over and immediately sat on the wooden floor, wondering what was happening to my life. My world was crumbling around me. My brain swam with confusion. I'd been accused of killing Blake, Ben was missing, Dad had just left in handcuffs, and oh, I got my first kiss, all in the span of a day.

I traced my lips with the tips of my fingers as I sat pondering my last thought. My first kiss. I recalled how Webb's hair had tickled my face as he bent down to touch his lips to mine, ever so lightly. Goose bumps pebbled my arms.

A hand touched my head. I glanced up and into what looked like the deep waters of the Caribbean Ocean.

Webb extended his hand. "Come on. Sit on the couch."

I looked around the apartment.

"Where's Sam?"

"He went to change."

I grasped his strong hand as he pulled me upright. "Is he really going to help the Sentinels?"

"Your father's right. Sam is ready. He's been training nonstop since he turned vampire. He's going to be a great fighter."

I had no doubt. Our training sessions were always intense. His focus was sharp. His precision was exact, and his moves were executed with the grace of a panther, lithe and sleek. While a part of me was excited for my brother to jump into battle, I was downright scared that something would happen to him. It *was* time for him to stop protecting me, though. I believed he needed to take the next step, though it wasn't a step my heart was ready for.

Webb guided me to the couch. His alluring scent instantly erased all worries from my head.

I dropped onto the cushion, keeping my eyes on him. Heat skated through me. It was just us. There were no swords to worry about or cell doors to break through.

Suddenly, I was scared, not that Webb would hurt me but that he would kiss me again. While I could still feel his lips from the last kiss, I was afraid that I wouldn't know how to kiss him back.

He sat next to me, breaking me from my thoughts and that soul-stealing stare he had me locked into.

"Who's the Secretary of the Navy?" I asked. I was an idiot to ask about some Navy guy. I wanted to ask him to kiss me again.

"The secretary is in charge of the entire Navy. Your father had a meeting with him and some of his colleagues today." He scooted closer to me.

"Do you think my dad... you know?" My hands

trembled, and not because we were discussing Dad.

He draped his left arm over my shoulder. A frisson of excitement coursed through me.

"No way. Your father is the most upstanding man I know. He is and has always been honest, and he cares about protecting people. He would never take someone else's life unless it was in self-defense."

The word "self-defense," the idea, slapped me in the face. I sure hoped Dad remembered it when we resumed our conversation about Blake. "Why is all this happening to us, Webb?"

He lightly tugged me to him. Like iron being drawn to a magnet, I rested my head against his chest.

"I don't know. We'll figure it out." His fingers traced a path up and down my arm.

His heartbeat thrummed against my ear, lulling me into a world I was beginning to like very much. "How? When?" I placed my left hand on his stomach, the same stomach I'd touched at school when he was wiping the blood off my hands with his shirt.

Oh heaven. I wanted to feel more of him. My heartbeat kicked into high gear, pounding in my ears. *Christ!* What was I doing? I immediately raised my hand. He caught it and placed my trembling hand on his chest then guided it down to those strong, hard abs. My world stopped again. Everything around me faded, except him.

"I don't have all the answers," he said, still caressing my arm.

Like his lips, his touch electrified me. "Dad said the Plutariums might be responsible for the explosion. Do you think they have something to do with Ben missing too?"

His body stiffened.

Does he know something about Ben? Or is it something else?

Then he relaxed. "I'm not sure."

"I hope not," I whispered.

"Me too."

I looked up at him with wide eyes.

"What? I don't want to see him hurt, Jo."

"Really," I said.

Boots scuffed against the wooden floor, and I sat up when Sam appeared in the family room. He was dressed in all black. His green eyes sparkled with a wildness—a need to fight.

"Where the heck did you get that uniform?" I asked.

Sam growled.

"What?" I looked at Webb, then down. My hand was on Webb's thigh. "Oh, don't start, Sam."

Webb rose, making his way to my brother.

"First, you need to get over your angst about me being close to your sister. I know you've protected her. I know you love her. But now you're entering into a world where your mind needs to be clear. Your sister is strong. Stronger now than when she was human. She can take care of herself. If you're going to help out, I need you focused. Is that clear?"

Webb was right. I could take care of myself. But he might not have known that Sam and I shared an extremely strong bond, one no one could break, as brother and sister.

"Oh, we're clear. My focus will be solid. But like I told my father, if he, you, or any of the Sentinels hurt Jo in any way, that person will have to answer to me. Are we clear?" Sam glowered at the gorgeous vamp.

"You have my word," Webb responded in an unwavering voice.

"Hey, I'm right here, you know," I said.

My words died when the building rocked for the second time that day. Windows rattled. Kitchen cabinets opened.

"Son of a bitch," Webb snapped, tapping his right ear. "Report."

Sam strode over to me. "Will you be okay, sis?"

Nerves made me laugh. His voice brought tears

to my eyes. My brother was about to go into battle or whatever it was Webb wanted him to do.

I frowned. "I'll be fine."

"I don't have to go if you don't want me to," Sam whispered.

"It's not that." I swallowed. "It's just... our lives are changing. And, yeah, I'm a bit nervous."

The building shook again, harder than before.

"Lock it down. I'm headed there now." Webb tapped his ear communicator again. "We need to get down to the control room."

The day had been a doozy, and I wasn't sure I could handle anything else, especially since Sam was dressed to kill.

23

The NASA-like control room buzzed with activity. It hadn't changed since the last time I was there. Small and large computer monitors sat on top of desks and tables. The most impressive thing about the room was the large wall screen that was divided into sections, each with a different picture. Five sections showed various places around the base, and five others showed different views of the shipyard. One picture, in particular, focused on a ship with a large hole in its side.

Sam and I stood behind a solid waist-high divider elevated behind the entire command center. We were instructed to remain behind the barricade until Webb got a handle on the recent explosion.

Sam and I scanned the room. It had become a habit for us to assess a room when we entered. Vampires typed frantically on keyboards, some talked on the phone, and two scribbled pictures on a whiteboard in the far corner. Kate had done the same thing not that long ago when they were preparing to rescue Sam. I swept my gaze back and forth, looking for her. She wasn't there—Webb had given her two more days off. I wanted to thank her for helping me out of my uniform and sparing me some embarrassment.

As I diverted my gaze from the frantic activity on the floor to the adjoining outer rooms, I stilled. Tripp and Sloan were in one of the glass-walled rooms, talking with the brunette.

I nudged Sam. "Look in the glass room to your right."

He turned just as the brunette smiled in our direction. Both Sloan and Tripp then turned toward us and closed the blinds.

Webb stood below us, behind a vamp seated at a computer terminal. "Where's Viking II?"

"They're in the war room, sir," the vamp said, not even turning to look at Webb.

"And Snow?"

"Same place, sir."

"How about Kate?"

The vamp stopped typing. "Sorry, sir. She left thirty minutes ago when the commander gave the all clear. By the way, is the commander going to return? Is everything okay?"

Webb placed a hand on the vamp's shoulder. "The commander will be back shortly. No need to worry. Just a misunderstanding."

God, I hoped he was correct. I didn't really want to have the Blake conversation with Dad, but I was worried. After sixteen years of not having him in my life, I wanted to at least get to know him before...

"Any word on where the AT4 was fired from?" Webb asked, looking at the screen.

The vamp's fingers flew across the keys, and in an instant, a cluster of ships floating in the middle of nowhere came into view.

I leaned into Sam. "What's an AT4?" I wasn't sure if he knew, but he had been working with Tripp on weapons.

"The AT4 is what the military calls a LAW, which stands for 'light anti-tank weapon.' It has a range of over two thousand meters," he whispered, not taking his eyes off the computer screen.

Okay. I was thoroughly impressed that he knew.

"It couldn't have been fired from there." Webb

pointed at the screen. "Those ships are way out of range for the AT4 to reach the shipyard."

"You're right, sir. Our intel shows that the warhead was fired somewhere between these mothballed ships and our docks." The vamp planted his finger on the screen, showing Webb the exact spot.

Webb pulled out his cell phone then dialed. "Kate, where are you?"

Sam straightened.

I opened up my senses while I kept focused on my brother.

"What is it with her?" I leaned into Sam.

"Shh."

A fire sparked within me. *He told me to be quiet? No way.* "Hey," I snapped.

"Jo?" He raised both eyebrows and brought a finger to his mouth.

I would play along for the time being.

"I need you back here," Webb said into the phone.

I heightened my hearing.

"I can't. I'm halfway to Boston," Kate said.

"You told me you weren't leaving until this evening. We have a crisis. I need you back here now."

"Too late, brother. I'm almost to Nicki's place."

Webb stiffened then growled. "I didn't know

you were going to Nicki's. I told you to stay away from her."

"You don't get to tell me what to do. Besides, it sounds to me like you're still in love with her."

Silence.

Sam and I exchanged surprised looks. Heck, the look on my face had to be one of shock. The blood rushed to my feet. Suddenly, I wanted to run far away. In fact, I had to get out of there before my heart stopped pumping. Tears stung my eyes.

"Damn it, Kate. Get your ass back to base —now."

"Sorry. I'm a big girl. I don't answer to you any-more. You've protected me long enough."

"Kate, I'm warning you."

"See you soon."

The line went dead.

"Damn," Webb muttered, raking his hands through his hair. He tapped his ear. "Tripp? I need you and Sloan in the war room. ASAP."

I tried to take a step back to get away from the anger dripping off him, but my hands seemed glued to the partition I was standing behind. I was afraid that if I let go, I would fall over from the shock galloping through my body like a thorough-bred racing around a track. Webb London was in love with someone. It shouldn't have surprised me.

He was gorgeous. Heck, the more I thought about it, the more I was surprised he didn't have a girlfriend. Still, hearing the phrase "in love" about Webb hurt.

He turned, glancing up at Sam and me. "Sam, in the war room." He flicked his head to the right. "Something wrong, Jo?" He leveled those cobalt-blue gems at me.

Something was definitely wrong. Hell if I was going to tell him, though. He'd only kissed me once. That one kiss didn't give me the right to take his head off just because he might be in love with another woman. I steeled my shoulders, straightening my posture. "Nothing is wrong," I replied in a tone that would melt butter. "I'm going to the ladies' room."

"Do you know where it is?" he asked in his rough and stoic soldier's voice.

I remembered it was in the hall on the same floor as one of the entrances to the war room. "Yep."

He cocked his head to one side. His expression softened as if looking for something in my face. "Don't go too far," he said. "My meeting in the war room won't take long."

I nodded then stalked toward the exit. I had my hand on the handle when Sam stopped me.

"You okay?"

"Fine. I'll meet you in the war room. I'm only going to—"

"Mmf. The last time you went to the bathroom, all hell broke loose."

"Blake isn't here. The brunette is locked in with Tripp and Sloan. I'm safe."

"Five minutes," he said.

"Look, Sam. Webb's right. You need to stay focused if you're going to work with them. You need to concentrate on keeping yourself safe. Besides, Webb will be here."

He mashed his lips together. "You trying to piss me off?"

"Get over Webb. Or do you want to have a conversation about Kate too?"

"There's nothing going on between me and her."

"Maybe not, but your body reacts when you hear her name."

"Five minutes. Then I'm coming to look for you," he said abruptly before walking off.

I exited through a door that dumped me into a stairwell. Irritation scraped across my skin like a bad rash. My brother could be just as frustrating as Dad.

As I climbed the stairs, I shook off thoughts of my brother, thinking about Webb and that girl,

Nicki, instead. I wondered who she was and whether he still loved her.

I opened the door and had barely made it into the hall when a hand covered my mouth while an arm encircled me, locking my arms in place. My eyes flew open as I tried to scream. I craned my neck to get a view of my attacker.

He leaned down. "We meet again, sunshine," he whispered, his breath caressing my ear.

Jonah. I squirmed, kicking him in the shins.

"That won't work this time." He dragged me into the ladies' room. "She's ready," he called as he closed the door, not letting me go.

Kate London walked out of a stall.

My eyebrows flew deep into my hairline. If Jonah's hand hadn't been plastered to my mouth, my jaw would've hit the floor.

I shook my head, refusing to believe Kate would have anything to do with the Plutariums. There was no reason for her to betray her brother, her family.

I swallowed hard then tried to scream, but Jonah's grip grew tighter around my mouth. I had to get out of there.

Kate made her way to me with tape in one hand and a needle in the other. She whirled the syringe in her hand like she was twirling a baton on the high school drill team.

I had at least one second, if not two, between when Jonah would release his hand and the tape would seal my fate.

"Shocked, I see." Her lips curled at the edges.

I grunted, groaned, kicked, and squirmed. I had to stall her for five minutes before Sam came looking for me.

She placed the needle on the sink then unrolled the tape. The sound was ominous. "Ready, Jonah?"

He released his stronghold on my mouth. I tried to scream again with no luck. Kate was too quick with the tape, banding my lips shut.

"Hands next," she said.

Jonah loosened his grip around my right arm. I counted to three.

"Don't try it, Jo." Kate's voice had changed from the sweet girl I'd first met to something more sinister.

I swung out my right arm, clenching my fist. Before Jonah could get control of my right side, I lashed out, punching Kate smack in her left ear. I kicked, and the toe of my shoe connected under her jaw. Her head flew back.

"Shit, Jonah. Get control! She's a hundred pounds wet," she barked, sliding backward a few inches.

I lunged forward when Jonah's fangs clicked

into place. I turned and looked up at the large vampire. Before I could react, the crazy vampire bit me in the shoulder. I threw back my right elbow, hitting him in the gut. It didn't even faze him. He just kept sucking the blood out of me.

"Jonah will rip you to shreds if you don't stop moving," Kate said.

I grunted again, but it was futile. My moans died against the tape.

Kate laughed. "Looks like he's rather enjoying the sweetness of your blood."

I lunged forward again, taking Jonah's fangs with me. My skin ripped, and blood dripped down the front of my shirt.

"Keep trying. It's fun to watch you panic." Kate wrenched my hands together in front of me before wrapping the tape around my wrists several times. "Jonah, enough. I need to inject her with the sedative."

Jonah released his fangs. "Very sweet, sunshine. I could get used to tasting you." His tongue licked my ear.

Sicko.

"We need to move before my brother comes to her rescue," Kate said to Jonah.

My brother was going to have her head for dinner.

Tears clouded my vision at the mention of

Webb. My mind scrambled to make sense of it all. She was Webb's sister. She couldn't possibly be siding with the Plutariums.

Why? Why? Why?

With my hands and mouth taped, she pushed up the sleeve of my shirt. "Jo, the fun is just beginning." Then she jabbed the needle into my arm.

Warmth seeped through my veins. The room spun. Images of Webb, Dad, and Sam flashed before me. I blinked several times, trying to keep my eyes open. "Your... brother. Family. You... can't... do... this." The words were lost under the tape.

My body went limp. Then there was only darkness.

24

The sound of Beethoven dragged me awake. I stretched slowly, raising my arms over my head. I slithered, slinked, and squirmed against soft cotton sheets. My muscles ached as I stretched each limb, one by one. The music caressed my ears but did nothing to soothe the blazing headache I had. It was as though I had a hangover from a wild night of binge drinking, not that I would have admitted to knowing what that was like. I kept my eyes closed, breathing slowly in the hope that it would calm the throbbing blood vessels beneath my skull. Snuggling under the thick comforter, I yawned then shivered. The room had a chill to it.

As I rolled over on the musky-scented pillow, my eyelids flew open. *Classical music? Since when did Dad play classical music?* I jolted upright, glancing around.

It wasn't my bedroom. A vase filled with lilies sat atop a large glass table gracing the far-right corner. Their sweet aroma wafted around as I took in a breath. An oversized red velvet chair sat in the far-left corner.

That wasn't good at all. I had to think. No, I had to stop falling the heck asleep.

The last time I passed out, I woke up in the stupid prison cell, and now, I was in some luxurious bedroom complete with flowers, decadent furniture, and expensive bedding. The headboard alone was impressive with its cherry frame, which rose to the ceiling. Inside the frame were cushiony black leather squares with a button set in the middle of each. They looked like small pillows. The cherry end tables on either side of the bed each had a lamp bolted to it, and a cherry wood dresser lined the right wall next to the flowers.

Salt air hung beneath the scent of musk.

I jumped out of bed, only to stumble as the room swayed. I quieted my rioting mind for just a second and heard the faint sound of water lapping against... a boat.

I ran three steps to the door then pulled on the doorknob, but it was locked.

I darted to the round window on the left wall

and peered out. Time stopped, my blood froze, and my brain fogged. In the distance, an orange glow painted the sky as the sun dipped close to the horizon. But that wasn't what had me in a tizzy. I was on a boat completely surrounded by water. While I loved the sun and the beach, I couldn't swim. I'd never learned how. *Don't panic. Think. Kate.* My heart rate increased. She couldn't have been with the Plutariums.

As my mind scrambled to make sense of anything, the doorknob wiggled. I tiptoed over to stand behind the door.

Keys jangled, and I grabbed the vase of lilies. I hated to ruin the lovely arrangement, but it was the only thing close to me. Heck, it was the only pseudo-weapon available. I thought at least it might startle the person.

Another jingle of keys, two clicks, then the doorknob twisted. My heart rate picked up, thundering in sync with the beat of the music overhead.

Slowly, the door opened inward, trapping me behind it.

With my hands tight around the vase, I lifted it level with my face. Then I took in a quiet breath and held it.

A tall figure slinked in with his back to me, and I swung the vase against his head.

The expensive piece shattered. Water sprayed everywhere, flowers flew across the room, and large chunks of ceramic sprayed down around the man.

Stunned, he listed to one side, creating an opening for me to run.

I grabbed the edge of the door then threw it back, ready to bolt out into the hall. But no sooner had I turned, than his large paw grabbed me by the arm.

"Not so fast, Princess," a very familiar voice said.

I turned and came face-to-face with Edmund Rain, head of the Plutariums.

"Edmund?"

"We meet again." His voice was like cut glass digging into my skin. "That wasn't very nice." He wiped the water from his face.

One thing was for sure. I wasn't dreaming, and Kate was a double-crossing bitch. Poor Webb. "Pissed off" wouldn't even begin to describe the indomitable vampire when he found out his sister was the enemy.

Someone came running down the hall, boots clamoring against the wooden floor. "Sir, is everything okay?" Jonah asked.

Gone was his signature blue bandana. In its place, he wore an army-green ball cap with the

Plutariums' insignia embroidered on the front. In thick black stitching, the capital letter P was superimposed on top of the letter L. In thick red stitching, a red diagonal ring circled the monogrammed black letters. The design immediately took me back to the first time I saw it on Neil Foster's neck at the funeral home. An icy chill pricked me.

"It's fine. Get out," Edmund commanded, waving his hand then closing the wooden door. He leaned against it as he crossed his arms over his chest, staring at me.

The asshole hadn't changed much. No longer did he sport a military crew cut—his black hair curled around his ears. His face was clean-shaven, and his eyes were golden brown. He was clad in black jeans and a light-blue cotton shirt that disappeared into the waist of his jeans. He motioned to the bed. "Sit."

I stood at the foot of the bed and didn't move. Instead, I crossed my arms over my chest and stared back.

He raised one eyebrow.

"Where am I?"

"You're home," he said in a clarion tone, pushing off the door.

Home, my butt. He was crazier than a mental patient. "What do you want with me? I don't have anything to give you. You took DNA from my twin brother. Besides, we're vampires now. You don't need me."

He walked over to the window and stared out, even though there was nothing out there except a vast body of water. "I just love the ocean. I always have. One of the reasons I joined the Navy. The sea is soothing and serene, especially during dusk and dawn."

"I don't give a shit about what you love. Are you going to answer me?" Anger rose, but I tamped it down. Expending my energy or allowing my telekinesis to take over my body would only have made me weak.

"I see you still haven't learned manners," he growled.

"Get over it. When it comes to you, manners are not the first thing on my mind."

"Then what is?" His tone softened.

I laughed. My enemy wanted to have a conversation about what I thought about him. I was convinced he should have been a mental patient. "Seriously?"

"We have a few minutes. Besides, your father is detained with other matters. My plan fell into place nicely. The valiant soldier, Webb"—he laughed, a heinous sound that made the hairs on the back of my neck stand at attention—"will be too preoccupied cleaning up the mess at the shipyard. They probably don't even know you're missing." He placed his hands into his jeans pockets, a smug look on his face.

My chest tightened. He was probably right about Webb, but he hadn't factored my brother into things. The noose around my neck loosened slightly. Sam had said he would come looking for me if I wasn't back from the ladies' room in five minutes. But as soon as a small bit of hope washed over me, dread set in. Sam wouldn't even know where to look for me. I was out in the middle of an ocean.

"It was you?" I pinched my eyebrows together. "You blew up the ship on base? And you had something to do with the Secretary of the Navy?"

I didn't know why I was surprised. Dad had said from the very beginning that Edmund was out for power and revenge, and he'd mentioned that the Plutariums might have been responsible for the first explosion. The Sentinels spotted Jonah outside of base, after all. One piece of the puzzle fell into place.

"Let's just say that the secretary had it coming," Edmund said. "He was worthless. Besides, if I want my plan to work, I... never mind. I shouldn't be having this conversation with a child. So, tell me, what don't you like about me?"

I shook my head. "You're evil. Need I say

more?" A hiss escaped me. I sounded like an angry cat just before it attacked its enemy.

"I like to look at it as defending myself. You know about defending yourself, don't you, Jo?" He grinned with glee.

"I don't know what you're talking about."

"You don't? Are you sure about that? That boy you killed today. Does that ring any bells?"

News traveled fast.

"Tell me how you did it."

"I didn't kill him." I sat on the bed before my legs failed me.

"Your powers are developing nicely. Over the years, your dad and I speculated about which of you twins would brandish more power. We even had a bet. You see, I bet on you. Although your brother will turn into a great fighter, no doubt, his powers will not match yours."

I met his gaze, tilting my head to one side. He was the second person that day to tell me Sam would make a great fighter. *Has Edmund been talking to Webb? No. Stupid thought.*

"Ah, you're confused." He bent down, removed his hands from his pockets, and picked a lily from the mess on the floor before sniffing its sweet scent. "Your father hasn't told you a thing, has he?"

He was right, to a degree. I *was* confused. Dad had only told me about a vampire's special abilities when I asked or when it was necessary. Otherwise, I was learning by trial and error or from books in the secret library room. No one had yet to sit down with me and explain everything in detail. In fact, Dad kept saying that school would teach Sam and me all that we needed to know. The way things were going, I was afraid I wouldn't be allowed back to school or even live long enough to find out if I would be. "What do you mean, Sam's powers won't match mine?"

Edmund smiled. His bronze eyes twinkled in the soft glow of the room as though he'd just won the grand prize.

Curiosity was a bitch.

"The question I've been waiting for." He let out a sigh, twirling the flower stem between his right forefinger and thumb. "I've had dreams about you. Dreams that tell me you will be very powerful one day. You'll have powers that the vampire world hasn't seen in all of their existence." He lifted the fragrant lily to his nose, and his nostrils flared.

I swallowed a gasp at his revelation.

Dad had mentioned that vampires' dreams could see into the future. But Edmund had to have been smoking some serious dope. *Me? Powerful? Absurd.* "What? Like I'll be the first female President of the United States?"

He laughed. "Much more powerful, *minha*

linda. So much so, in fact, that I can't have you walking around in this world, ruining my plans. You're a liability." His tone had turned cold-blooded all of a sudden.

"So kill me." The words rolled off my tongue as a shiver zinged through me.

He sauntered over to me and bent down. He snapped off a large part of the flower's stem before placing the lily behind my ear. "It's not on my agenda. Yet."

That three-letter word packed a punch that sent my pulse into overdrive. My body began shaking. The walls were closing in, and the boat started rocking as if the sea was getting angry.

I had to focus. I couldn't let my powers take over. If I destroyed the boat in the middle of nowhere, I would kill myself in the process. Then I wouldn't have to worry about Edmund killing me because I would drown first. I was on a death cruise. That was for sure.

"We have a few hours. I do want to play a little. I think Kate has a present for you." His right hand caressed my face, his lips curling at the edges.

I slapped his hand away. "Get your nasty claws off me."

"You look a little pale." He smiled a fake smile. "Let's see if we can put some color back into that gorgeous face of yours." He went to the door, opened it, then poked out his head. "Jonah."

Footsteps sounded in the hall. "Sir?"

"Get Kate. Tell her we're ready."

A sharp pain grabbed my temples. I sucked in a breath. Suddenly, a stir of excitement surged through me at the thought that Dad was nearby. I stilled, trying to quiet my mind. Dad was the only one who could make my head hurt without taking a baseball bat to it. Maybe if I drew images of him in my head and made the connection to him stronger, I could reach out to him telepathically.

I closed my eyes, placed my shaky hands under my legs, and pictured Dad and me sitting on the chaise lounge in the apartment. I remembered him explaining how a vampire's heart beats. It had been a quiet moment between father and daughter. My breathing evened out, my pulse slowed, and my mind cleared to only images of Sam and Dad—of family.

"Something wrong, Princess?" Edmund tapped me on the shoulder.

Dad and Sam quickly faded from my mind. As I opened my eyes and met his bloodthirsty gaze, my fangs dropped.

"I see you're hungry, like me," he said with a lopsided grin as if he was enjoying the scene more than a blood snack.

I wasn't hungry. The predator in me was emerging and aching to attack. However, I wanted to wait to see if Dad was nearby. I waited for another sign—I would even take the stabbing pain—to hit me.

Nothing.

"I hear Kate." Passion colored his voice as he scurried to the door.

I rose from the bed, nerves propelling me to do something other than sit and wait for death to come to me. Although Edmund said he wasn't going to kill me yet, I didn't trust Kate. I walked over to the window.

Her cinnamon scent wafted into the stateroom before she even entered.

"There you are, love," Edmund said, pulling her into his arms.

Their lips locked in a heated embrace. Kate and Edmund, swapping spit. My body went numb.

Suddenly, my heart ached for Webb. He was going to croak from this. His beloved twin sister had betrayed him with the leader of the Plutariums, his enemy.

They barely separated before Kate tipped her head to the side, sweeping a handful of her hair and twisting it upward. The smooth column of her neck was completely exposed. Then Edmund gradually and slowly trailed his tongue down her bulging jugular. As if in slow motion, he eased down, twin fangs extended, and bit.

I shrieked.

He looked up at me with dark-red eyes shooting sparks as he sucked the blood out of her.

Impulsively, I licked my own lips. The aroma of blood sent a fire blazing down the back of my throat. I tried to look away, but I was drawn to the act of an animal claiming prey, the raw need to survive.

Edmund continued to keep his eyes on me as his throat moved with each pull of blood.

I salivated for a taste. I balled my hands into fists, digging my nails into my palms. I had to feel pain to ground myself in reality. Otherwise, I was afraid I was about to lose all sense of who I was. *Damn him.*

He took one last gulp then licked her neck with his gross tongue. His eyes returned to golden brown at the same time as his fangs retreated.

Kate let her brown hair fall around her shoulders as Edmund kissed her on the lips.

"You're delicious, love."

Ew! Disgusting. I shook my head, trying to erase what I had just witnessed.

Kate turned. "Ah, she's awake. Nice." She giggled. "I can't wait for the fun to begin."

Her inhuman gaze swept me from head to toe

as she made her way over. Her navy-blue eyes shifted to black, a clear sign that the vampire within her wanted out.

I raised an eyebrow in challenge, a challenge I was delighted to entertain with the traitorous sister of the most gorgeous vampire in my world.

Her fangs slid out. I imagined she was dripping with the desire to kill me, but I had never given Kate London any reason to hate me.

We stood face to face as I searched my own mind for answers to one pinging question: *What happened that she would betray her brother, her family?*

Her voice pulled me from my thoughts. "I see the resemblance, but I don't see why my brother likes you. He's still in love with Nicki. You do look a little like her, though—the dark hair and the eye color. Only yours are more metallic silver, while hers are gray. It doesn't matter. Soon, you'll be a distant memory." She yanked the lily out of my hair, sniffing it as she stared at me.

Maybe Webb had kissed me because I reminded him of the woman he might still have been in love with. A sharp pain pierced my heart, and it hurt like hell, but I had to focus on the current situation. Thinking about Webb wasn't going to get me out of that mess.

"You're crazier than him." I nodded at Edmund.

"She's in a great mood for our little playtime. She looks hungry too. Probably very hungry now she witnessed you feeding on me. Doesn't she, darling?" She glanced over her shoulder.

"So, tell me, Kate," I said. "Why? Do you hate your brother that much?"

With no hesitation, she said, "My brother has rose-colored glasses on when it comes to what's right in this world. He believes that the military is the answer to the world's problems, and it's not."

"So you betray family because of Webb's beliefs?" I didn't buy it. There had to be something else.

"What goes on between me and my brother is none of your business."

While I wanted to explore the reasons, the situation didn't warrant an intervention. "You think your boyfriend, Edmund, is the answer?" I asked, flicking my head in his direction.

Her nostrils flared. "He's a better man than my brother and your father combined."

Edmund grinned.

Adrenaline zipped through me, and my insides came alive. I didn't know Kate's history or relationship with my father, but something was wrong there. Sure, Dad had his faults, but he was a far, far better man than Edmund Rain.

Without even a thought, I punched Kate in the mouth then grabbed the sides of her head before smashing it against my raised knee.

She fell backward for a moment then jumped at me.

As she lunged, Edmund grabbed her. "She'll get her due soon enough. We need to get this show started, love." He smoothed back her hair and wiped the blood from her mouth. "Jonah, bring in the boy." Gone was Edmund's lovey-dovey voice, and in its place was a ruthless, vengeful tone.

Silence filled the small room as Edmund escorted her to stand at the door. The air crackled with a surge of electricity. The three of us could have powered a small neighborhood.

I allowed my fangs to retract as I struggled to think of a way out. My options were extremely limited, though. My only escape route was through them and into a body of water that would swallow me in a nanosecond. "So where are we?" I stole a peek out the window.

Edmund's cell phone rang. "Tell her, love, while I answer this. What?" Edmund said into the phone, exiting the room. "We should be ready in fifteen minutes." His voice trailed off.

"You'll know soon enough," Kate said as she played with her own phone.

Jonah appeared in the doorway. "Ma'am. Here he is." He nodded to his right.

Kate held up her hand. "One moment."

A soft breeze blew in, carrying with it a burned-sugar scent. There was only one person I knew who had that enticing fragrance. I said a quick prayer in the hope that I was wrong. I had to have been wrong. But something told me I wasn't. Suddenly, my throat burned.

"Jo, are you ready? This is going to be so sweet." She smiled, venom dripping from her voice.

"And what a game it is," Edmund said, sauntering in before kissing Kate on the cheek. "Princess, we have something you want, and you have something we want." He was all business.

"You don't have anything I want," I snarled. *Please don't let it be him.*

"Oh, but we do." Edmund's voice exuded confidence.

Jonah pushed Ben into the room.

The universe came to a standstill. The waves lapping against the hull of the boat froze. Ben couldn't catch a break from those vampires.

He stumbled, falling onto the bed. His complexion was pale. His gray T-shirt hugged his muscular chest, and there were wet spots around the collar and underneath his arms. He righted himself then looked at me. His brandy-colored eyes were opaque. There was no sparkle or shine anymore. It was as though the Plutariums had taken his soul.

It took every ounce of energy I had to keep my fangs in place. Tears clouded my vision. *Please let him be okay.*

Kate and Edmund studied me as if watching a good movie, their vampire eyes flickering with pleasure. They seemed proud of their plan so far. If they were trying to get a tear out of me, then bravo, they succeeded.

I shook my head a few times, trying to get the fog to lift. I blinked, as well, just to make sure it wasn't a dream. Nope. I was still on a floating coffin in the middle of the ocean, in a bedroom with my enemy and Ben. To add to the pile of problems, my throat burned, and my gums ached. The predator within me was very hungry and eager for a taste. *Focus, damn it.*

"I still don't understand," I managed to say, thankful I had the willpower to keep my vampire sedated for the time being.

"We want Jewel. You know who she is. It's too bad she couldn't hold her own against you," Edmund said.

"Are you serious? You sent a human to kill a vampire?" I asked incredulously.

"No, I sent a vampire to kill you. It just so happens you killed him instead." Edmund stalked up to me.

"Blake Turner?" My voice definitely matched a high-pitched soprano.

"Blake was my first protégé. He was going to be a great vampire, but the first batch of the human-vampire serum, HVS-1, had some flaws."

My uncle Patrick had been close to a serum that would change ordinary humans into vampires. While more puzzle pieces fell into place, leaving more unanswered questions, the revelation was bad. Very bad.

Still, I couldn't understand why Edmund wanted Jewel, a human. Maybe he was going to transform her like he did Blake. "He wasn't a vampire. He was a demon." I peeked around Edmund.

Ben's complexion matched an albino's. My heart lurched. *Did they inject him with this concoction?*

"I'm so excited you said he was a demon," Edmund mused. "I trained him that way."

Sick and demented were two words that only scratched the surface of describing the lethal vampire. "If you already figured out your vampire potion, you don't need me for anything." I dropped my hands to my sides, allowing the blood to flow through my shock-infused limbs.

Edmund let out a guttural laugh that sent shivers skating across my frozen blood. "Oh, Princess, but I do. I told you, the serum hasn't been perfected yet. Blake was our first test subject, but he had a small glitch. One that wouldn't suit my needs of a vampire army. You see, he couldn't go out in the sun."

So that was why Blake's skin had blistered that day at school.

"I need an army that's going to be able to function twenty-four hours a day," Edmund said. "Your uncle is very close to perfecting a serum. He's also stubborn. Kind of runs in the Mason family, doesn't it? Which brings us full circle. I want Jewel unharmed. Your uncle Patrick can't seem to function without his daughter, and I need him to focus on the next batch of HVS-2. He's so close. Humans into vampires. It's exciting times." He grinned, showing off his pointy twin canines.

I didn't know whether to be relieved that the first batch had flaws or shocked that Jewel was kin to my uncle, which meant she was my cousin. Fear snaked through me as I leaned against the wall, hoping it would keep me upright. I gulped in air and kicked myself for not putting two and two together. "So you sent Blake, the test vampire, and my uncle Patrick's human daughter to kill me at school? Why the human?"

"For one, she believes in what her father is doing. And she was there to make sure Blake did his job," he explained. "She's a tough cookie among vampires."

"Obviously, neither of them did their jobs."

"You're right. What I didn't figure into the equation was your powers. I should have. After all, I dreamt that you would be a powerful force." Edmund sounded disappointed in himself.

"If you want to kill me, why the game?" The wall was doing its job of keeping me upright and stable for the time being.

Everyone around us was tuned in to Edmund and me.

"I love a good game. If you succeed, I'll let you live a little longer. If you fail, I'll make it my first order of business to kill your brother."

I narrowed my eyes, biting my tongue. Showing anger would only fuel his fire, and I sensed he was trying to get a reaction from me. I didn't want to play his game—I wanted to kill.

"I see I have your attention," he said.

I didn't say a word.

"Here's how it's going to work," he continued. "My team and I are late for an engagement that we can't miss. So you and your boyfriend will find your way back to port, grab Jewel, and bring her to me. Simple enough. Oh, and I do have one other demand. Your father's blood. Bring me all of it."

"Why couldn't your beloved there" —I nodded at Kate— "bring you Jewel and my father's blood? She has access to more places on that base than I do."

Kate laughed. "Smart girl. But I'm not stupid either. Getting past my brother would be a monumental task. Webb would never let me near Jewel. I'm not one of his Sentinels. My role was strictly intelligence.

"As for your father's blood, I was successful the first time, but it would be impossible to do it again with your father's senses on high alert. He's been keeping tabs on everyone since I got Edmund out of prison. And it didn't help that he had an alarm installed.

"So I tried to win your brother over after he came on to me in the stairwell where I dropped my phone that night. I figured I could use him in my plan. But Sam seems to have a unique ability to read emotions and people. I tried to turn on my feminine charm several times after our heated kiss, but he said no. He was paranoid whenever I came near him. After that, it was too risky. So I came up with a much better idea— you. We would kill two birds with one Jo Mason.

It's brilliant." Her voice rose in pitch as she bragged.

Inwardly, I rejoiced for a couple reasons. First, the mystery was slowly unraveling, though I wasn't sure how Kate got the combination to Dad's safe. Second, while a part of me hated the idea of Sam's tongue dancing with the bitch's, I was thrilled that he'd turned her down. If I got out of there alive, I would throw my brother a party. "So how did you get the combination to my father's safe?" I didn't think she would answer me, but I had to ask.

She flashed shiny white canines. "It's called a bug, Jo. In my line of work as an intelligence officer, gleaning information from people is my specialty."

I was surprised she answered. Maybe if I kept asking questions, she would tell me more about their plans. After all, she seemed excited to tell me the details. "And you think *I* can get into his safe?"

"You're his skanky daughter, aren't you?" Kate barked.

I ignored the "skanky" part. "You're not as smart as you claim. Sleeping with him" —I pointed to Edmund— "has fried those brain cells to a crisp. You should know that my father would never let me near the safe."

"Enough, both of you," Edmund said. "We're wasting time."

I glared at her. "And what do you suppose Webb's going to do when he finds out you're a traitor, Kate?"

She leapt like a tiger after its prey, flying through the air and into Edmund, who'd blocked her.

"Patience, love. I promise you'll have your chance."

"She's mine." Kate flashed bloodthirsty fangs.

"Looking forward to it, bitch," I countered.

"Edmund?" Ben's voice broke the tension in the room.

I'd almost forgotten Ben was in the room. Almost.

Edmund turned. "You don't get to speak."

Ben rose and matched Edmund in height.

"Stay out of this, Ben," I said, glaring at him. "Why is he even here?" I asked Edmund.

He rubbed his jaw. "We've trialed our first batch of serum on several teenagers. It seems your boyfriend here has a high resistance to our experiments. Nothing we've tried works on him. Your uncle wanted to keep him so he could keep testing his genetics, but Kate had a brilliant plan. You see, Jo, she's informed me you have a thing for this brute. Why?" He shook his head in disgust. "Anyway, since he's useless to me, we thought we'd have a bit of fun." He paused for a second. "Jonah," he called.

When Jonah appeared, Edmund nodded toward Ben.

As if Jonah knew what Edmund wanted, he pulled a pocketknife from his jeans and exposed the blade. Then he grabbed Ben's hand, angling the tip of the blade above his palm.

"What are you doing?" I snapped, taking a step toward Ben.

"No, no," Edmund said, holding up his hand, blocking me. "A human and a vampire stranded on a boat. Hungry, hungry, hungry. Can you stay afloat?" he singsonged.

"You're sick," I barked.

"You didn't think I would make this easy on you, did you? You're a brand-new vampire. Your bloodlust will kill him." He laughed, and so did Jonah and Kate. "I just love a good game."

My relief that Ben's system couldn't change into a vampire's quickly disappeared. The mere thought of Ben's blood had every taste bud in my mouth on high alert. My fangs pounded for freedom. It wasn't good.

Ben pinned me with an it-will-be-okay look.

Not a chance. Clearly, he didn't know the effect his blood had on me.

Edmund nodded once to Jonah.

I pushed off the wall and stiffened, holding my breath.

As if in slow motion, Jonah lowered the blade and cut into Ben's palm, dragging the knife down from the base of his middle finger to half an inch from his wrist.

Instantly, the aroma of Ben's blood punched me in the face. Darkness colored the edges of my vision. Then my fangs shot out of my gums, clicking in place. The predator in me was far from okay.

"Ooohh, it's working," Kate squealed.

I glanced at the three vampires, who had smirks plastered on their faces.

Asshats.

Ben stood still, an empty expression etched on his face as he stared at me.

Doesn't his hand hurt? Does it bother him to be standing in the middle of four vampires?

Jonah kept his hand locked around Ben's fingers, I imagined to prevent Ben from wiping away the blood.

"Let the games begin," Edmund said.

Jonah pushed Ben toward me with such force that Ben stumbled. He threw his hands out in front of him to balance himself. My brain told me to move, but my feet didn't listen. The scent of his blood had me frozen solid.

He fell into me. His bloody hand made contact with my left arm.

I growled, low and deep.

He quickly righted himself and jumped back.

Laughter erupted in the room. *Stupid vampires.*

"Jo," Edmund said, still laughing, "I almost forgot. One last thing."

Ben moved toward the bed.

Yeah. That wasn't far enough. Ben needed to get the heck out of the room.

"Bring her in," Edmund said.

Kate dragged Darcy in.

Ben and I gasped at the same time.

"Ow! Let go of my hair!" Darcy snapped, stomping on Kate's foot. "Fucking animals."

The Plutariums must've nabbed my friend after she left the base. Then another macabre thought skated across my mind: *Where is Mr. Jackson?*

"Just so you know I mean business. If you fail, then sweet-tasting Darcy Rose will die a slow death," Edmund said.

Darcy's eyes widened when she looked my way, clearly taking in my violet eyes and fangs.

Yeah. Your best friend is a vampire. Welcome to the new world.

"Ben? Are you with these animals too?" she asked.

In a step, Ben stood in front of Darcy with his bloody hand fisted. "Listen, I won't let them harm you."

"Are you helping them?" she shouted.

"I have to help Jo. If I don't, they'll kill you. You need to be strong, Darcy. I'll find you." He kissed her on the lips.

"That's enough, Slick," Kate said, pulling Darcy from Ben. "You're quite the Casanova, aren't you?"

I didn't know what to make of Ben and Darcy and the kiss he'd planted on her lips.

"I told you, Edmund, this is going to be fun," Kate said. "I do love drama."

"Ben, you can't help. That monster over there will kill you." My best friend pointed at me. Her eyes filled with fear as tears poured from them.

I bit back the hurt and the pain caused more by the truth she spoke than her harsh words. The possibility existed that I would kill Ben before the night was over.

Kate shoved Darcy out the door as she screamed.

My heart went out to her, but I couldn't dwell on her hysteria.

"You have until the stroke of midnight to meet me at the Second Street Marina," Edmund said. "Now, you two lovebirds, have fun. Jo, enjoy your snack." His lips tipped at the edges, curling into a murderous grin.

Then Edmund, Kate, and Jonah left.

Footsteps clattered above us. An engine roared to life.

"Jo."

Ben's voice fractured my trance. "What?" I snapped. I didn't mean to snap, but I had to keep my mind focused. If I let anger drive me, it might help us get out of the situation.

"Hey, don't get mad at me," he said.

"Get out of here! Find a sink and wash the blood off." I didn't move.

He walked out with no argument.

The engine noise faded. A sudden rush of fear blanketed me. *Is it just Ben and I stranded on a boat? If so, where are we? And where is the Second Street Marina?* I didn't know what frightened me more, potentially feeding on Ben or the large body of water.

Breathing slowly to get all the oxygen in the room into my lungs, I dropped to the floor. Within a minute, my fangs retracted. Tears cascaded down my cheeks as I covered my face with my hands.

"Jo." Ben came back into the room and sat on his haunches a few feet away. "We should try to get this boat moving."

I sniffed the air.

"The blood is gone," he whispered. "I washed it off. The bleeding stopped." He threw me a towel. "Wipe the blood from your arm."

"Are you worried about the blood or something else?" I swiped the wet towel over my arm.

"I'm worried about you."

How nice of him to be concerned about me. He really should have changed his tune about that, though, especially if I couldn't control myself.

Silence reigned between us.

"So. Why do you think the serum didn't work on you?" I asked.

"I don't know. What I do know is that it is working on the other boys Edmund kidnapped. Like Jack Powell and other high school boys."

"Do you know where Edmund's keeping them?"

"I only remember the inside of a room. It smelled musty like a basement. I was blindfolded when they took me there and when they brought me here. But I think the ocean wasn't far because I also got a whiff of the salt air." He stood. "Come on, Jo." He walked over to me and extended his hand.

Flaring my nostrils, I raked my gaze over him. A smidgeon of his scent lingered, but not as strong. Still, I swatted away his hand. I didn't trust the vampire within me. "None of this makes sense." I pushed to my feet.

"Yes, it does. Don't you get it? Edmund wants both of us dead. I heard him tell your uncle that I was no use to him since the serum wouldn't work on me. Edmund was going to kill me, but Kate stopped him. I didn't know why then, but I do now."

"He wants us to get Jewel."

"He wants *you* to get Jewel. He thinks your bloodlust is going to kill me."

"What did they do to you?" I asked as we climbed the stairs to the main cabin.

"It's nothing," he said. "Your uncle ran a series of tests on my blood and marrow. Then he hooked me up to several IV bags of his Frankenstein juice. I was supposed to go into all kinds of pain and then sleep. I don't know. All I know is that when it didn't work, it pissed him off. Then Edmund tore into him. I'm fine. I'm just glad that my system is immune to that shit. Fucking vampires."

His last two words rammed me like a Mack truck. That was what he thought of me. I suddenly realized I hadn't gotten all tingly when Ben walked into the room. Even standing next to him, I didn't feel anything except fear. I was afraid for him, terrified that he would get hurt by the Plutariums or me. But something else inched to the surface, weaving through the fear... anger.

Stopping mid-stride, I turned. "That's what you think of me? I'm just a fucking vampire?" I glared at him.

"Oh. No. I'm sorry. Not you." Lines formed on his forehead.

"Not me? Then who? Sam? Your best friend?" Rage drenched my insides. "What if I called you a fucking human? How does that sound to you?"

"Jo. I'm sorry. Truly. I am. I didn't mean to imply—" He reached out his hand.

"Don't." I backed away. "You don't get it, do you?"

Ben and I could never be more than friends, if even that was possible. But it wasn't the time to get into with him. It wasn't the time to be near the human, not with my hunger increasing by the minute.

I climbed the stairs into the main cabin then walked to the granite island that separated the galley from the living area. A small leather couch sat in front of a bank of windows that looked out into the open ocean. I took several breaths, trying to tamp down my anger and my hunger. A sense of doom dropped like a grieving widow's veil. The wind blew, creating whitecaps on the surface of the water. Dark clouds rolled in, contrasting the orange glow that colored the horizon. An ominous prickle skittered along the nape of my neck. Night-time was about to settle over the ocean, and my vampire intuition howled to proceed with caution, as I had control over Mother Nature.

I silently laughed. I didn't have control over anything. Nor did I understand Edmund's stupid game. Something Kate said kept nagging at me: *killing two birds with one Mason.* I had no idea what that meant or why they hadn't just kidnapped me and taken me somewhere close to the base. I didn't get the hoopla with the ocean, the yacht, and Ben. Well, the part about Ben made sense, at least, but nothing else was adding up. I wasn't going to figure out any of the answers in the next few minutes, so I parked the myriad of questions in a mental safe in the back of my mind.

Ben's scent grew stronger as he finally emerged from the lower cabins. Instantly, my throat caught fire. Darkness flashed, my eyes shifted, and my fangs descended.

"Jo?" Ben said, touching my shoulder. "Again, I'm sorry."

"Get away from me," I growled. I swallowed, trying to get the saliva to cool the burn in my throat.

"No," he spat. "I'm trying to apologize."

I looked up at him, but all I could see was his

throbbing carotid, pumping sweet nectar through his veins, calling to the vampire within me. "I'm trying not to kill you. I'm a new vampire, Ben. I don't have that much willpower. I would like to think that I do, just to prove my father wrong, but you're making this very difficult for me. It's not just your blood—the fact that I'm hungry isn't helping matters. Edmund may be evil, but he isn't dumb." The inner struggle to keep my hunger sedated was stronger than any other carnage I had faced.

"I just want to talk," he said.

"Now is definitely not the time. I get that you're sorry, okay? We need to get moving." I waved my hand around. "Do you know how to operate this thing?" I knew as much about boats as I did about driving a car—nothing.

"My dad and I go out with Chief Garrett on his boat. He's taught me a few things over the past few summers."

The boat rocked suddenly.

"What the heck was that?" I asked, glancing outside.

Ben ran to the door, and the boat swayed again.
Crack!

"When this is over, Jo, we need to talk," he said then opened the door.

A large gust of wind swept in, knocking an empty can off the kitchen counter.

I trailed behind him. "Holy shit! What the hell is happening?" I shouted above the howling wind. "Do storms pop up out of nowhere like this?"

"They can," Ben said loudly.

Waves sloshed against the boat, and ominous clouds rolled in. A chair on the deck slid into the side rail.

"I'll see if I can get someone on the radio. We need to beat this storm in. See if you can find some life jackets." He climbed the stairs to the top.

Fear suddenly replaced my anger. God, how I longed for my dad or Webb. They were both experienced Navy and would have known what to do.

The boat listed from side to side. Suddenly, my stomach lurched, and the hairs at the nape of my neck stood on end, warning me. The howling, whistling wind seemed to whisper the truth: if we capsized, I was a goner.

25

The sea only grew angrier over the next thirty minutes as we tried to get the boat going. The engine seemed to have a mind of its own and refused to cooperate. Ben was up on the bridge, trying to get someone on the radio with no luck. To make matters worse, there wasn't any safety gear on the stupid boat. I searched everywhere for life vests but found nothing, not even flares to signal for help.

Our time slowly dwindled toward the midnight deadline. I was worried about that, but the storm was more of an immediate concern. Waves pummeled the boat from all angles, making it sway from one side to the other. My stomach seemed to roll with it, but the bloodlust was stronger than the nausea, and I remained ravenous.

I stayed on deck, telling Ben that I didn't want to bother him, but it was more that I didn't want to be around him. Teasing my hunger any more than necessary would only stoke the predator lurking in the shadows, and he was stubborn about the word "no." I had come too close to sating my hunger with his blood, and he hadn't seemed to care. Maybe he was crazier than Edmund.

I held on to the railing, my knuckles white as the sea tossed us around like we were in a children's bounce house at McDonald's. Standing outside in the violent storm was better than sitting inside a closed cabin or sitting on the bridge topside with Ben. If I had been inside, I probably would have puked my guts out. If I sat next to Ben, he would more than likely be my dinner. I needed my wits about me, and the angry sea helped to stabilize my sanity.

I opened my senses to the world around me. Over wind and the crashing waves, the faint sound of a bell split the salt air. Listening, I concentrated, filtering out the raging sea. Suddenly, the sound of the engine turning over was music to my ears. Dropping my head, I bowed to the ocean god, Neptune, in thanks. As I did, a large wave crashed against the stern, spraying me.

Maybe that was his way of saying "you're welcome."

With step one finally completed, we needed to find our way through the massive body of water. Step two was going to be the ultimate challenge in more ways than one.

"Jo?" Ben shouted above the wind. "I need your help."

Staggering, I turned to glance up at him, my hands still tightly wrapped around the metal railing. I had no idea how I could possibly help him. My sole concerns were not to drown and not to kill him.

He waved his hand as his cinnamon hair whipped in all directions.

Nodding toward the irascible sea, I prayed one last time to Neptune then carefully walked to the base of the stairs. Bracing my hands against the sidewalls, I climbed each step with careful grace, but the wind had a different plan for me. I stumbled and fell backward. The water-slicked steps were more slippery than a sheet of ice.

Ben traversed the steps in two strides, holding out his hand. "You okay?"

I welcomed the human gesture as he pulled me upright.

"Come on. I need you to take the helm. I want

to look at the charts inside the cabin to see where we are. It's impossible to do it out here."

I had no clue how he would find out where we were. It wasn't as if the ocean had street signs. "No way, I can't drive this thing." I rubbed the back of my head.

"Jo, you have to. Look. Hold two hands on the wheel at ten and two. Just like a car."

"I don't know how to drive a car."

Ben looked at me with a pained expression. "Just do it. I'll be a minute. We need to keep moving. If not, these waves are going to push us even farther out to sea."

I guessed he was right. We did have a deadline. "What time is it?"

"Almost nine. I'll be right back." He rested his hand on my shoulder. "You'll be fine. You can see better than me with your eyesight, anyway." He disappeared with the rolled-up charts in his hand.

I scooted closer to the helm. A thick plexiglass windshield and side barriers kept the elements at bay.

Trying to keep the boat straight. I shifted the steering wheel slightly to the right then left. It was hard, considering that the waves grew larger with each passing second. It was as though Neptune was conducting a wave orchestra, leading the crescendo to a finale I was afraid I wasn't ready for.

Thank God it wasn't raining. I sniffed the air. It was coming, though.

As a human, I had always thought people who could smell a storm brewing were nutso, even though I'd learned in science class that before rain began, a sharp, distinct ozone smell permeated the air. As a vampire, with my heightened senses, I was one of those nutty people. I could definitely smell the sweet, pungent odor of ozone. But since it was dark, it was impossible to read the clouds above to determine when they would open up.

Brushing off the thought of rain, I stayed focused on the turbulent sea ahead. A light from the boat illuminated our close surroundings, guiding my way. I wanted to laugh. *What is the light going to show me? More water? More waves? What else could be out there?* Any boater in their right mind wouldn't have been out in that storm.

While I maneuvered the craft, I thought of Dad and Sam. God, I would have given my fangs in that moment to see them both, especially my brother.

"Sam? Dad?" I said into the raging wind. "I love you guys."

In my reverie, a bell dinged—no, wait, it was real. It was the same bell I'd heard earlier. I looked in all directions, trying to see if I could spot it. In my excitement, my hand slipped from the wheel, and the boat veered left. I panicked. Quickly trying to recover, I grabbed the wheel, turning it to the right. The bow hit a wave hard, jerking me sideways. I lost my balance. I twisted my body, trying to recover, but it was futile. The wooden floor on the bridge was just as slippery as the deck below. My feet flew out from under me. I extended my arms to break the fall, but my entire body skidded across the floor. My head hit a panel on the opposite side of the bridge. I quickly grabbed the bench next to me and pulled myself to a standing position.

Carefully, I made my way back to the out-of-control steering wheel, which seemed to have a mind of its own. The boat rocked and rolled before pitching forward. The bow hit a wave head-on, sending me backward. My butt hit the back of the leather captain's chair, then I bounced forward. Using the momentum, I was able to take hold of the wheel. I sucked in several breaths, spouting every bad word I'd ever learned. Finally, I managed to steady the course.

Biting back the pain from the bruises on my body, I let out all the air in my lungs.

Ben came running up the stairs. "What's going on?" He turned his head with mechanical precision.

"I heard this bell and lost control of the—"

"Bell? Like a ding? Deep sounding?" He moved me out of the way and took the helm.

Thank God. I had begun to think that jumping overboard would have been safer than me navigating that floating death trap.

Ding! Ding!

"There. Did you hear it?" I asked then choked on a gasp.

"What?" He peered at me from the corner of his eye.

"You're bleeding!" I yelled, covering my nose as my fangs shot out.

Blood dribbled down his temple, creeping toward his ear. I struggled against the urge to lick the sticky red liquid off him while my little devil friend blared in my head: *Do it! Do it!*

Ben pulled his attention away from the sea, glaring at me with wide eyes.

Please get rid of it. Please get rid of it.

"Oh, I'm sorry. I fell when the boat listed." He swiped his hand over his temple then rubbed the sticky mess onto his gray T-shirt. "Do you still hear the bell?" Excitement tinged his voice.

I stood frozen. *Does he not understand what is happening?*

"What's wrong? You look like a zombie," he said.

"You would, too, if you were a starving vampire. Don't tempt me with your blood if you want to live through the night."

"Get over it, Jo, and be useful. Listen for that bell," he commanded.

I so wanted to sink my fangs into him. "Why? What's with the freaking bell?"

"Hope." He steadied the wheel.

"I don't get it." I played with one of my canines.

"What you're hearing is a buoy bell. If we can get the boat close to one of the buoys, that means we can find out where we are. They're like markers in the ocean. They help boats and ships navigate. At least, that's what Chief Garrett taught me when I was on his boat."

The rain began falling, large drops pelting the windows.

Ben searched the dashboard then flipped a switch, and the windshield wipers came on. "Well, Jo, which way?" He kept swiping at his temple.

He was playing it cool, but I must've scared him. *Good.* He needed to have the fear of God instilled in him if he didn't want to die by the fangs of a vampire. The night was still young, after all. "It's coming from there." I pointed behind us.

"Hold on while I turn this thing around."

I grabbed a small table that was on the bridge as the boat listed to the left.

Ben downshifted, and the engine slowed. He

turned the wheel all the way to the right. Waves crashed. Saltwater sprayed over the deck below, and thunder rolled in the distance. It must have taken only a minute, but it seemed like hours before the bow of the boat finally pointed toward the buoy.

The rain was falling in sheets. Lightning split the dark sky in half. When a jagged bolt flashed above, hope flashed in front of us. The buoy lay right ahead. While I didn't get how Ben thought it was our lifeline, I silently rejoiced. Maybe Ben's fervor had rubbed off on me.

"It's red," he said, his hair blowing in all directions.

I assumed that was good. Red was my favorite color since I'd become a vampire. I mentally yelled at myself. It wasn't the time to be thinking of blood. The wind sure made my resolve that much harder to control. Not only was it whipping everything around, but it did a fantastic job of slapping me with Ben's human scent.

"There should be a number on it, but I can't see anything. Can you?" Ben shouted.

I dialed in my vampire night vision. "Ten."

The muscles in Ben's face relaxed.

"Are you going to tell me why you have relief written all over your face?" I asked.

"The numbers on the buoys indicate how far

from port we are. If you're leaving port, then the red ones are on the left and the green ones are on the right. If you're going into port, then the red buoys are on the right and so forth. And as you go into the harbor the numbers get smaller." Both his hands were tight around the steering wheel.

"So, are we going in the right direction?" *Please say yes.*

"I need to find the green one to get a baseline. Once we can see the green one then we can adjust our direction if we have to. Do you see it any-where?" He angled a spotlight, searching for hope.

All I saw were waves on top of waves.

I had a bigger problem. Hunger pangs wracked my body. My vision blurred. *How the heck do vamps like Webb and Dad control their bloodlust? How long will it take before I don't have to suffer?*

As if Ben knew my issue, he said, "Go down to the fridge. See if there's some blood. I'll keep looking."

Edmund fed on Kate, but they surely couldn't do it all the time, or they would be too drained. It was worth a look-see. I might get lucky.

I held on to the railing and was descending the few steps to the lower deck when the boat ca-reened forward. I lost my balance and fell flat on my face. I tried to stand, but the boat pitched again and rocked from side to side.

I grabbed a bench along the left side and managed to stand. The wind whipped hard in all directions, taking my hair with it and blinding me. When I finally turned into the wind and was able to see, a gasp caught in my throat.

Everything around the boat seemed to halt, including the blood flowing through my veins.

A large wall of water rose, gathering in height. *What kind of storm is this?* In slow motion, the crest of the wave broke. I didn't have time to react before the wall of water threw me against the cabin door.

Don't panic. Don't panic.

As I thrashed around, the boat swayed like a pendulum. I held my breath, and within minutes, the water ebbed, spilling over the railings. Well, that was one way to get rid of the bloodlust.

"Jo?" Ben called from above.

"I'm fine," I lied. Terror gripped me.

But there was worse to come. As I raked air into my lungs, I heard the engine choke, then sputter, then die.

"Try to see if you can find those life vests," Ben shouted.

"I already looked!" I yelled above the wind.

"Try again!"

Ass. I'd already opened every bench, closet, and cabinet on that stupid boat. I cursed Edmund and slipped into the cabin as a watery hell knocked hard on the windows, against the hull, and rattled the door.

Without forward motion, the boat listed strongly from side to side and practically dipped into the ocean. All the loose items in the cabin flew around. I latched on to the island, keeping my body anchored in place.

After several minutes, everything calmed. I braced myself for the next round, but it didn't come. It was as if the sea had relaxed. Maybe the storm was dying down.

Thinking it was safe, I made my way to the outer cabin door. When I opened it, I saw another massive wave about to barrel down again, bigger than before. In one breath, it crashed, throwing me back into the cabin and down the steps to the lower rooms.

I took in a gulp of air then held my breath as the water spilled in and threw me deeper into the bottom cabins. I bounced from one wall to the other in the narrow hallway, thrashing to get my head above water.

When my head finally bobbed to the surface, I was able to grab the edge of an open doorway that led to a stateroom. Panic and fear surged through me. Then I laughed. I'd thought I was immortal, but death by drowning was at my doorstep.

I gripped the doorjamb for dear life, tilting my

head back as the water continued to rise. The good news was that I had a small space of oxygen left. The really bad news was that it wouldn't last long.

With death imminent, I said my goodbyes. "Sam, I love you. Dad, I'm sorry for being a bad daughter. I really wish you were here right now so I could tell you all the things I've been holding back. If I make it out of this alive, I'll be good. I promise."

"Jo?"

"Ben?" I turned, taking in a mouthful of seawater.

He swam underwater toward me, and then his head surfaced.

"There you are," Ben said. "I thought I lost you. Are you all right?"

I nodded and gagged.

He grabbed my hand. "We don't have much time. The boat is going under. We can anchor ourselves to the buoy."

"I can't swim," I blurted out.

"I don't care. You're getting off this boat one way or another. Since the boat is sinking, there should be an emergency beacon that goes off automatically, alerting the Coast Guard. Hopefully, we won't be in the water too long."

"How do you know all this?"

"It doesn't matter. Okay, when I count to three,

I want you to take in as much air as you can. Then we're going under. I'll pull you as I swim. Stay to my side, so that I don't kick you as I'm propelling us to the surface. Hold on to me at all times. Do not let go. Ready? One, two, three."

We both took deep breaths before dipping under.

Reluctantly, I clutched Ben's hand firmly. I was afraid to open my eyes, but I did. I wanted to see where we were going.

We headed out into a world that was foreign to me, a body of water that could swallow me in one bite. To think I'd been worried about dying at the hand of my vampire enemy. I was nestled in the arms of a new adversary who held my immortal life in its grasp.

We swam past the lower staterooms, over the stairs to the main cabin, then through the door into the open ocean. The stern was completely submerged. Ben swam away from the boat with me in tow.

I looked over my shoulder and saw a light still illuminated on the boat, casting a glow around it as it slowly descended into the dark depths of the ocean.

Ben tugged my arm, and I turned around. We were being propelled to the surface. My lungs burned with the need to breathe. We both gasped for oxygen as our heads bobbed out of the water.

I coughed several times, taking in air. Ben did the same.

We both looked around. Waves churned violently. The wind roared, whistled, and hummed. The lightning show in the distance was in full force with thunder booming around us.

"Hold on to me, Jo. This is going to be rough."

"Rough" wasn't the word I would've used. More like "hell."

Holding hands, Ben and I rode each wave to its crest and down to its trough. As we did, I caught a glimpse of the tip of the bow of the boat before it disappeared and hoped that wouldn't be my fate. I closed my eyes, praying to the Virgin Mary, God, Mother Nature, and whomever else I could summon to protect me.

With my prayers said, I opened my eyes to find a large wave barreling down on us.

I had no chance. The wall of water pushed me, slapped me, and slammed me under. My hand slipped from Ben's. I fought hard, kicking and throwing out my arms and legs, but hysteria consumed me. I tried to catch my breath only to swallow a large gulp of water. My mind became fuzzy. A swirling sensation blanketed me. It was as if I was on an out-of-control Ferris wheel. My lungs burned. I wanted to cough, but if I did, I would only take in more water.

After several seconds of holding my breath, I relaxed. I tilted my head back and stretched out my arms. I acquiesced to fate, to the turbulent sea. The world spun as my consciousness slipped away. My eyelids became heavy. As I lowered them, something yanked at my arm, hauling me somewhere. Then a hand slapped my face.

"Jo!"

I gagged, coughed, and spat out water before taking in gulps of air. "Ben?"

"We're going to swim over to that buoy," he yelled over the wind, wrapping his arm around my waist.

The waves were too big for me to see anything, even if my vision hadn't still been cloudy.

Another wave crested then rolled over us. Ben held on to me as we submerged for a few moments before bobbing back to the surface.

He swam on, and we finally made it to what he had earlier called "hope," the red buoy.

"Grab it," he said.

I wrapped my fingers around a bar midway up. As soon as I did, another large wave crested, and Ben disappeared.

"Ben!" I shouted. "Ben!"

I saw movement in the distance as he waved

his hand. *How the heck had he gotten way over there?* He swam toward me, disappearing from sight as the waves rose, resurfacing when the waves fell.

As I released a sigh, waiting for him, I glanced out, watching Mother Nature conduct her best light show. Jagged bolts streaked across the darkened heavens above us—a range of long, thin streaks and shorter ones, zigzagging from one end of the sky to the other. When a bolt flashed, the bell on the buoy dinged.

Ben was a few feet from me when another large wave crested.

"Watch out!" I screamed.

Ben's eyes widened, and so did mine, but not from the huge wave that was about to consume us. My heart raced. I blinked a few times to make sure I wasn't delirious. I held his gaze as I sucked in air as a wall of water crashed down on us. The darkness captured me, and all I could see were Ben's eyes before we went under. There was no doubting it. They had flashed a bright red.

26

Pressure gripped my chest. I grabbed it as if I could stop the pain. I coughed a few times. Again, pain sat heavily on my chest, pressing down harder and harder.

I drew in air then jolted to an upright position, heaving the contents of my stomach.

"Miss. Miss," a male voice called. "She's awake."

"Get her blood pressure," another male voice commanded.

Disoriented, I glanced around. *Who are these men?* I took another breath and froze with the scent. Humans.

I bent forward, locking up the vampire within. I willed my fangs to retreat before I stole a peek at the human kneeling down next to me. He wore a dark-blue uniform with a Coast Guard patch on his sleeve.

Beacon. Rescue. That's right. Ben said the Coast Guard would find us.

My heart sped up. *Ben!* I tucked my legs under me, placed both hands on the wooden floor, then pushed up to stand. I swayed when the man in the blue uniform caught me.

"You need to stay still, miss. You're lucky to be alive."

"I need to find Ben. Where is he? Is he here?" *Where is here?*

My vision sharpened as oxygen filled my lungs. A burning sensation spread across my chest, but I didn't know if it stemmed from air-starved lungs or my dry, hungry throat.

Several humans stood in the distance, wearing the same uniform as the one holding me. My gaze darted in all directions. I cringed. I was on the deck of another ship. I promised myself that I would never set foot on another boat.

I searched every man standing before me. None of them was Ben.

"There's someone else?" the man asked.

Turning, I glimpsed the name that was scripted on his nametag, Hunter, before meeting his gaze. His eyes seemed to question my sanity.

"My friend, Ben. He was with me."

"Please, miss. Have a seat," he said, guiding me to a bench. "What's your name?"

I eased down with Hunter's hand around my arm.

Another man brought me a bottle of water then scurried away.

"Jo. My name is Jo Mason. I have to find him. Please help me." My voice cracked. My body shivered uncontrollably.

"Trace?" Hunter called. "Get me those blankets." He turned back to me. "Jo, we didn't find anyone else. We found you tied to a buoy with this." He handed me a gray piece of fabric.

Lifting it to my nose, I inhaled the faint scent of burned sugar. Tears stung the backs of my eyes. "Ben must have tied me on. This is part of his T-shirt." *But how?* The wave had swallowed him.

"Must have? You don't remember?" Hunter asked.

"No. The last thing I remember was a large wave crashing down, then another... then..." My airwaves constricted.

"Jo, I need you to breathe."

I buried my nose in Hunter's chest and sobbed.

His arms encircled me. "I'm sorry, Jo. I'm so sorry."

I cried as I pictured Ben, the waves, and his red

eyes. Maybe I had been seeing things, my hunger or the water I'd inhaled making me delirious. One of those things had to have been it. I shook off the thought. Only one thing mattered right this moment: *Where is Ben?*

I sobbed harder, soaking Hunter's uniform. I might not have wanted to be more than friends with Ben, but I didn't want him dead or even...

I eased away. "Did you check around the buoy for him?"

"When we got the boat's distress signal, the wind was blowing at fifty knots. The waves and swells reached at least fifteen feet. We were lucky to find you through the storm. When we did, we didn't see anyone else out here."

"No... he's got to be out here somewhere." My voice sounded hoarse.

"You should drink some water." Hunter lifted the water bottle.

I took one sip then pushed it away. The ocean had given me plenty.

Trace returned with two heavy blankets just as Hunter's name was broadcasted over a loudspeaker.

"I'll be right back, Jo," he said, standing. "Trace will stay with you."

Trace opened up the thick blankets. He placed one over my lap and wrapped the other around my back, securing it in the front. By the time he was done, I was strapped into warmth, though it did little to take the chill away from my wet clothes.

My teeth chattered as I thought of Ben. Fear gushed through me. Tears kept falling. He couldn't have been dead. Twisting the small piece of fabric in my hands, I tapped my foot erratically as I sat on the open deck, looking out.

The violent sea had calmed. The waves had diminished, the wind had died, and the bright rays from the moon above sprayed over the open ocean. In the distance, the lights of the city blinked and twinkled. We were close to home. My pulse sped.

Hunter returned and kneeled in front of me. "Jo, do you know a Lieutenant Webb London?"

My head shot up. *Oh, my God. Webb.*

"Yes. Where... is... he?" I hiccupped then swallowed.

Hunter placed his hand on my knee. "He just radioed. He's on his way. Do you know him?"

I met Hunter's blue eyes. "Yes. He's my father's second-in-command."

"Your father?"

I blew my nose on Ben's shirt. "Yeah. Steven Mason."

"Commander Steven Mason?" Hunter asked.

I gave two nods as Hunter and Trace exchanged looks. "Do you know my dad?"

"No, I know of him," Hunter said. "I've been trying to get into the SEALs to join his team forever. So has Trace."

My dad was a legend, and he probably didn't even know it. I didn't want to think of my dad. I would only start crying again. Two people I cared about had been taken away, one by the government and the other by the furious ocean. I shivered.

Looking at Trace, Hunter said, "Let's get Jo inside."

Then the ship's radios blared to life, including the one on Hunter's hip.

None of us moved.

"Captain Vic, come in."

"Go," the voice of the captain said.

"What's your position? We have a stranded swimmer," the other voice said.

The salty tears on my cheeks froze.

"Where?" the captain asked. "We're about eight nautical miles from the harbor."

Hunter didn't move as he listened.

"Point Judith," the radio guy blared back. "If need be, we can send *Bridle* in your place. She's a little farther than you are."

"We can respond," the captain radioed back.

"Hunter?" the captain called over the boat's speaker. "The SEAL boat is approaching, and we need to turn around. Get Ms. Mason ready."

"A stranded swimmer. Do you think it's Ben?" My voice hitched. I had no idea how far Point Judith was from us, but hope infused me for the second time that night.

"If it is, it'd be a miracle, Jo. People just don't survive in the ocean in that kind of storm," Hunter said in a temperate tone. "Your ride is here." He rose, slipping into his life vest.

"Is Point Judith the area where you found me?" I asked.

"No," Trace said.

Two other men approached and readied the ladder as Webb, Tripp, and Sloan came into view. They were in some inflatable boat with Tripp behind the wheel. They seemed to have gotten there pretty quickly.

"That looks like a fun raft," I murmured.

Hunter laughed. "That's one of the coolest boats the SEALs have. It's called a RIB, a rigid inflatable boat. That boat can do things you'd never imagine," he said, practically foaming at the mouth. "They're quiet and fast and can maneuver from water to beach without any trouble. Not to mention, that boat can handle waves as high as twelve, maybe even fifteen feet. They just don't sink." He sounded like a boy who had gotten his first Tonka truck.

Well, let's hope we don't have to test the RIB's sea-worthiness, I thought. I'd had my fill of water, wind, waves, and boats.

Our engine slowed, idling as they came closer. I could see them more clearly. Relief washed over Webb's face. Black overpowered the blue in his eyes.

Warmth settled over me as I met his gaze. I had never been happier to see him. But who I really wanted to see was Sam. Knowing my brother, he would've done everything in his power to make sure he was on the boat with Webb, but he wasn't there.

A sudden tickle brushed the back of my neck.

As if Webb could read my mind, his voice filled my head. *Sam is fine. Do you know how worried we've been?*

Where is he?

On base, helping out in the control room.

A small amount of tension seeped from my pores. *Thank goodness.* I couldn't take any more bad news.

Trace caught the rope that Sloan threw to him, wrapping it around the railing as Webb boarded the boat.

"Credentials, sir," Hunter commanded.

Webb pulled an ID card out of his cargo pants and gave it to Hunter, who read the front and back. Webb didn't take his eyes off me. They fluctuated from black to blue several times while Hunter inspected Webb's ID card.

"Thank you, sir." Hunter handed the card back to Webb.

Tears streamed down my face. The moment was surreal.

Webb extended his hand, keeping his eyes locked on me.

I stood, but my knees gave out. Hunter hurried to my side, grabbed my elbow, and guided me toward Webb.

My legs were weak. My heart thundered. A mix of emotions had my hormones fluctuating like a sine wave. Seeing Webb, Tripp, and Sloan certainly made my emotions crest. The fact that a stranded swimmer existed added to the peak of that curve. But my heart splintered when I thought how unlikely it was that Ben was alive. But I refused to believe he was dead.

Then I had another horrifying thought: *What about Darcy?*

I hadn't a clue what time it was, and worse, there was no way Webb was going to exchange the brunette for Darcy or any of the other students that Edmund harbored. At that point, I had to pray hard that a miracle would happen for all those involved.

Webb met me halfway, enfolding me into his warm, hard body. He hugged me so tightly that I thought my bones were going to break. I drank in his masculine scent, sobbing.

"It's okay. I'm here," he whispered, burying his face in my hair.

I didn't want to move. For the first time that night, some of the tension in me waned.

"Jo. Lieutenant." Hunter placed a hand on my back.

Webb growled before releasing me. "Let's go home."

"Take care of yourself, Jo. I'll come see you later. Will that be okay?" Hunter asked.

Grabbing Sloan's hand, I turned. "I'd like that."

Sloan guided me to a seat on the RIB before Hunter gave him a blanket. "She'll need this for the ride," he said.

He was sweet. I wrapped myself in it, waiting for Webb, who said his goodbyes, thanking the captain and his team. Then he eased into the boat and took a seat next to me.

Tripp gave the RIB power, and suddenly, we were moving.

"What happened?" Webb's voice cut through the wind.

Turning my head toward the open ocean, I shivered then tightened the blanket, but it didn't help. "What time is it?"

"One-thirty. Why?"

My heart stopped. I'd missed the deadline. Darcy was probably dead. "Edmund gave me a deadline of midnight to return the brunette you have. If I did, he would let Darcy live." Tears streamed down my face. *Was Edmund even serious about letting Darcy live?*

"What're you talking about?"

I turned to face him. I wanted to tell him everything, but I had to keep two things to myself. First, I couldn't tell him that I saw Ben's eyes turn red. Telling someone else would make it more real, and delirium was the only reason I was willing to believe. The second thing was even harder and more unbearable to say. I couldn't tell Webb about his traitorous twin sister, Kate.

I was frightened to tell him for many reasons, but mainly because it would break his heart and then break mine to see him devastated. Plus, it might not have been the smartest move, given where we were. I was afraid of his outrage. I knew Hunter had said the RIB couldn't sink, but a raging vampire was far worse than a raging human, especially with our super strength. I decided at that moment to wait at least until I had two feet planted on shore.

I told them how I'd woken up on Edmund's boat. I told him about Edmund's experiments, his sick game, his hope that I would kill Ben out of sheer hunger and find a way to get the brunette and a supply of my dad's blood to him by midnight in exchange for Darcy's life.

Webb angled his head. "If Edmund had Ben, why not experiment on him?"

"He did. According to Edmund, Ben was immune to Uncle Patrick's vampire serum. Even Ben said they loaded him with it, and it still didn't take. But Edmund has a few guys from Durfee who may not be so lucky."

As the boat sped through the water, I went on to tell Webb about the storm, the boat sinking, and how Ben saved me by tying me to a buoy.

He watched me closely as I spoke. "What's wrong, Jo? Is there something you're leaving out?"

He was good. "My mind is still foggy. I almost drowned out there, you know," I said quickly. "Anyway, I want to see my brother and my father. Is my father back yet?"

Webb raked his hands through his hair even though the wind was doing a fine job of keeping it out of his face.

"What's wrong?" I asked. "Did something happen?"

"Your father has been—"

An explosion rocked the shoreline. Then another.

Webb stood. "Fuck. Speed it up, Tripp."

"What was that?" I peered around Tripp.

Bright-orange flames soared high into the sky. Then several more explosions boomed, splitting the silent night air.

The boat sped through the harbor as fast as my heartbeat.

I followed the line of the flame to land. "Is that the base?" Trepidation soaked my voice.

"Yes," Sloan said.

I lost all air in my lungs. "Sam!" I exclaimed.

It couldn't have been happening. Ben was missing or dead. Dad... I didn't know where my father was. Darcy... was she still alive? And my brother could be in danger. My heart couldn't take one more second of any of that crap. I wanted to kill Edmund Rain, for sure.

"When we land, Sloan, you're with me. Tripp, secure Jo in the safe house. Do not let her out of your sight." Webb turned to me. "Jo, I need you to cooperate. I'll check on Sam. Go with Tripp. No antics. If you don't listen to Tripp, I'll make sure you don't see the light of day outside the base. Is that understood?" He raised one eyebrow, glaring at me.

Whoa! Where did the attitude come from? What is it with alpha males?

"Jo?" Webb asked.

"I'm not going anywhere with Tripp. While Sam is on that base, that's the only place I'm headed."

The fire raged in the distance as smoke billowed then disappeared into the night sky.

"You will obey me," Webb said calmly, but there was no mistaking the bite behind those words. "Do you hear me?"

His staunch power commanded compliance, which I was unwilling to give when my brother's life could be in jeopardy. I wasn't losing any more people close to me, not that night. "If I don't?" I challenged.

"I already told you the consequences. The more you fight me, the more I will make your life hell."

At Webb's last words, Tripp said, "Lieutenant" as if shocked.

I guessed he didn't get the text message that my life was already a living hell. A violent storm swirled inside me, and I couldn't contain it. "Well," I said, the words rolling off my tongue, "let me make *your* life hell right now, Lieutenant. None of this would've happened tonight, or maybe even ever, if your stupid sister wasn't sleeping with the enemy."

A loud, collective intake of breath came out of each of the hulking vampires, even over the wind.

I searched inwardly. *Did those words really just spill from my lips?*

Webb's fangs immediately shot out as he pulled me on to my feet. His grip was tight, his eyes pure rage as they swirled, shifting to onyx.

Immediately, I wanted to take it back. I'd seen him mad at Ben, but the power emanating from him was so strong that it felt like he was about to kill me.

"Sit her down, Webb. We're about to hit the beach," Tripp yelled.

Webb let go of my arm, pushing me into my seat. I threw out my hands, latched on to Tripp's chair, and braced for impact.

The RIB rode smoothly onto the sand about a mile from the base. Hunter was right. The RIB was slick.

Tripp cut the engine as Webb and Sloan jumped out.

I didn't move. My heart burst into infinite pieces and kept shattering the more Webb paced around on the sand.

"Sir," Sloan called. "We need to go."

"Get her to safe house four, Tripp. ASAP." Webb seethed. Then he and Sloan ran down the beach, toward the burning base.

I wanted to jump out and run with them to find Sam, but I was tired, and my chest hurt. There was something about my words and his reaction that rendered me immobile. My system was shutting down, and so was my life. Everyone around me that I cared about was vanishing. I wanted to run and hide. I had to get away from the turmoil and evil.

As if the gods above me shot me with a dose of adrenaline, I jumped out of the RIB and ran for the woods that lay beyond the sand.

"Jo, come back!" Tripp called. "Shit."

I didn't turn around. I didn't hesitate. I kept running, but hell if I knew where. I ran deeper into the canopy of trees as Tripp's voice faded behind me, with only the unknown lying ahead.

27

I'd been wandering in the woods for nearly an hour, or so I thought. I didn't really have any sense of time. All I knew was that I desperately needed to feed. Since being a vamp, I'd never been that long without blood. The trees swayed along with my body. The dense woods blurred even as I tried to sharpen my vision, blinking several times.

Not knowing where the safe house was or if I really wanted to go there, I figured the most sensible thing was to head to the base. We had landed the boat not far from it. I tried to follow the glow of the fire that raged, but the dense canopy above limited my ability to see clearly. Or maybe it was the lack of blood fuzzing my vision.

The forest floor had its own challenges, with

rocks and mounds of debris piled every few feet to try to trip me, as if someone had deliberately placed them in certain spots.

The crunch of dried leaves crackled somewhere behind me. I opened my senses and scanned the area but found nothing.

Then an enticing smell wafted in my direction. I turned and came face to face with a coyote. All sense of getting back to base vanished instantly. I didn't care about rules or laws and drinking Dad's blood. The only thing on my mind was to capture the animal and feast on him. Somewhere in the back of my mind, a voice screamed, *Gross!* I ignored it, licking my lips as we stared at each other for a split second, both deciding our next move. I knew mine, and I didn't even blink. I just lunged. The sucker was fast. Yeah, he should have been, considering I didn't feel like I had even an ounce of energy left. But hunger fueled me, powering my adrenaline, and I ran after the creature.

I dodged low-hanging branches and jumped over rocks, mounds, and a large tree stump. The coyote darted to the right, and I followed. He ran in and out of trees, leading me deeper into the woods. He sailed over a low rock wall. With no hesitation, I did the same. All I could think about was sinking my teeth into him, tasting his blood to ease the inferno in my throat. My heart raced with pure excitement. I was so close. Then he sailed into the air over a mound of debris. I lunged, holding out my arms, and I caught his back paw.

Then everything happened so fast.

He howled and fought me before I lost my grip. Unbalanced from the struggle, I fell to the ground but was suddenly jerked high up in the air. I shrieked and spun to find a rope tied around one ankle, suspending me like an upside-down music-box ballerina. Someone had put traps in the woods.

Great. I'm starving. My brother and best friends could be dead. Oh, and I'm hanging from a tree.

Don't panic.

I laughed at those two words, which I had been chanting every minute since my encounter with Blake Turner. The mantra wasn't helping me in the least. I had to find a new one.

I laughed even harder when I surveyed my situation. I was hanging high off the ground, with a noose tied around my right ankle. My free leg had a mind of its own. It flailed with gravity, flopping around as I continued to spin in circles. Laughter consumed me. My tear ducts were empty, my rage fizzled out, and my body was detached from my brain. I almost thanked the tree I was hanging from.

Now what?

It didn't matter that my brain and body were disconnected. I had two desperate missions—feed and get my butt back to base.

Okay. First, figure out how to get down.

I relaxed both arms. I crossed my free leg over my tethered one. I swung my arms behind me, trying to gain some momentum to swing my torso upward into a sit-up. I'd seen Sam do an upside-down sit-up in the training room on one of those pull-up bars. I sucked in a breath and reached in front of myself as my upper torso came forward. I let out all the air in my lungs as I grabbed the rope with both hands. I stilled for a moment. Then my gaze followed my hands upward as I scaled the rope, hand over hand just above my shackled foot. I slowly reached down with my left hand, keeping my right one tightly wound around the rope. I released my ankle then lowered my legs as I secured my left hand to the rope. Hanging, I closed my eyes and counted to three. Then I took in a breath and released my hands.

Within seconds, I hit the ground—or at least what I thought was the ground, until someone gasped at the impact and warm arms wrapped around me.

My eyelids flew open and met Webb's stark blue gaze, reviving my deadened heart for a moment. Then I remembered what he'd said to me. "Put me down," I snapped.

"Okay." He threw me to the ground.

"What the heck?" I lay flat on my back.

"You said to put you down. So I did."

"You're an ass." I stood then brushed the twigs, leaves, and dirt from my back.

"And you're a brat who doesn't listen." He glared at me with hardened eyes. Then he stalked up to me. "You are the biggest pain in the ass. I told you to go with Tripp. To obey my orders." His tone hardened, matching the madness in his vampire eyes.

Irritating vampire! "I'm not your soldier, and you're certainly not my father!" I yelled. "So don't order me around like I'm one of your robots."

"You test me, tempt me, and make me crazy." He walked away from me but was back in front of me in two strides. His darkened gaze fired red sparks at me.

My eyebrows furrowed in shock or maybe confusion. *Test him, tempt him, and make him crazy. Welcome to my wacky world!*

He growled, grunted, and swore under his breath as he searched every pore of my face.

"Mad, are you?" I struggled not to laugh. It was rather funny to witness the emotional rollercoaster he seemed to be on.

He growled again. "Tell me about Kate." His voice was even, barely. His hands shook as he cupped my face between his palms.

"Tell me about Sam." I mimicked his words almost to perfection.

He grunted this time. "Maddening, you are."

I laughed. I seemed to have developed a fit of the giggles since the tree snagged me. I shouldn't have been laughing at all. I should have been running, crying, and searching for the people I cared for.

"You find all this funny?" he asked.

"Please. Kate's alive. I don't even know if Sam's alive," I said in the softest tone possible.

He dropped his hands then began pacing and fiddling with his cell phone. Nervous energy surrounded him, pricking my skin every time he drew near. "Let's get something straight. You and Sam are adults now. And believe it or not, your brother can take care of himself." He slid his phone into the pouch on his belt before removing it again. He kept doing that. Maybe it was his way of keeping his rage and nerves inhibited. I couldn't blame him. If I'd learned that Sam batted for the enemy, I wouldn't have been as visibly placid as Webb was.

While sympathy skated across my brain, my mouth had a mind of its own. "Then start treating me like an adult," I added.

"Start acting like one," he quipped.

"Sam. Is he—"

"He's fine. He's still a little freaked that you were taken under our noses, as am I."

"Was anyone hurt in the explosions we saw from the boat?"

"No. The base is secure, which is why I came looking for you."

I let out a sigh, and he did the same.

Then his arms snaked out, and before I blinked, he had me in a tight hug, much like the one earlier on the boat. His heart thrummed against his sternum as he kissed me on top of the head.

Wow! Is he an emotional wreck or what? His emotions switched in a matter of seconds.

"You told him I was okay?" I craned my neck to look up at him.

"Why would I do that when I found you ran from Tripp?" A grin pulled his kissable lips upward.

"Webb?" It was my turn to growl.

"Yes. When I caught your scent a few minutes ago, I sent a text to him and Tripp."

"You know my scent?"

He laughed. "Yes. We're predators, Jo. We may meld into the human world well, but we're still high on the food chain."

Yeah, tell that to the coyote I couldn't catch.

He backed away slightly, his hand resting on my arm as if he didn't want to let me out of his reach. "Now, you told me that Edmund wanted the brunette and your father's blood, but you still haven't told me how Edmund kidnapped you. Or about Kate."

Discussing Edmund would only lead to telling him more about Kate—it was inevitable. A breeze blew, and branches rustled above us as we stood between two large tree trunks. "When I went to the bathroom, Jonah snagged me. Then Kate stuck me with a sedative. When I woke up, I was on that stupid boat."

"What did you mean by 'she's sleeping with the enemy'? Who? Jonah?" The harsh timbre of his voice stilled me while his jaw ticked furiously.

Oh God. I couldn't tell him it was Edmund. He would go mad. "Webb? I really need blood."

He inspected my eyes much like a doctor would have, turning my head from side to side. "When was the last time you fed?"

I had to think back. "When I was in Dad's office, right after the first explosion."

"Christ. And you didn't kill Ben?"

"If not for the storm, I probably would have," I whispered, dropping my gaze. "Webb, I'm hungry. Very hungry."

He looked at his wrist, rubbing it as though prepping his vein.

"Oh, no. I'm not... I can't... it's forbidden." I jumped back.

"You're right, unless it's an emergency. This constitutes one," he said.

Suddenly, images of Edmund feeding on Kate's neck tore through me. My stomach lurched. I couldn't bite into Webb, not after seeing the lust in Edmund's eyes as he'd fed on Kate. It was gross.

"You're pale. As I said, we're high on the food chain, Jo."

I got that part, but he had no idea, and I wasn't telling him about Edmund and Kate. No way. Not in this lifetime. "I don't want to. I want my father's blood. I have to drink his." Moreover, I remembered what happened when I'd bitten into Kraft's wrist and the eerie ride I'd had when I tasted his blood, complete with pictures of Kraft and another woman, who had seemed to be hurt and crying. I still didn't know what that was all about. I didn't want to taste Webb's blood and see something I wasn't prepared for or something he would have preferred to keep hidden.

"Jo. All your father's blood is gone. Sam ran to the apartment to get me a container for you, and he said every ounce of it had been taken, including the reserve that your father kept in his office safe."

"Where's my dad, then? When we were on the RIB, you were going to tell me something about him. Is he back yet? I can go to him."

"Unfortunately, he won't be back on base for another few hours. You can't wait that long. You won't make it. Now, come here." His tone was low, commanding.

Fear had me walking away. Fear of him, my control, and the unknown.

"This is not optional," he called from behind me.

"I'll find my way. I can wait for my father." I had to wait for Dad. There was no way I was sinking my fangs into Webb.

As I dodged a branch, my body swayed to one side before an audible click echoed in the forest, causing me to straighten my spine. Before I turned, Webb's scent hit me, tempting me, making my mouth water. My fangs shot out instantly.

I turned to find a blade in Webb's left hand and blood coagulating on his right wrist.

Smart vampire! Sneaky vampire!

I froze at the sudden change to my brain, body, and soul. I was so hungry that if I didn't feed, I was afraid I would kill someone. I had already restrained myself beyond the extent of my willpower.

He approached me, lashes lowered to half-mast, his deep-blue eyes holding secrets I was certain I wasn't ready for.

The world around me spun again. The sound of the forest faded. The creatures of the night held their breath with me, waiting to watch the scene unfold.

I lifted my heavy gaze, meeting Webb's. My brain became foggy, my knees went weak, and my heart raced. "Petrified" wouldn't even have begun to describe my emotions. Before my mind rioted with any other thoughts, he turned me so that he stood behind me, tucking me into him. He wrapped his left arm around my waist and placed his palm flat against my stomach. He threaded his right arm through the hollow between my shoulder and chin.

"Breathe," he whispered softly against my ear. "Take your time. Go slow."

I wanted to laugh. I think I'd forgotten how to take in oxygen. His scent, his blood molded me into a pile of mush. I swallowed. The act reverberated loudly.

"Calm down," he whispered as he tucked me tighter into him.

His hard body, his broad hands on my stomach, and his gentle voice were too much. At any second, I was either going to run for my life or pass out from the drug his presence infused me with.

His wrist touched my trembling lips. I inhaled and closed my eyes, and my fangs grazed his skin.

He let out a groan. He was enjoying the scene while I broke out in hives.

Don't think about him. Think about blood. The blood necessary to survive. It's just blood.

He pressed his wrist harder against my mouth.

His blood!

I bit, the last of my resolve snapping, shattering.

His blood spilled into my mouth, and I relaxed against him. I suckled, and my taste buds came alive from how his blood tasted. The need to sate my hunger was sweet, but the desire that slowly built was downright sinful. Heat rushed upward from my stomach and warmed my cheeks. An explosion of emotions hit me all at once as I continued to draw his life into me. On one level, I was a simple predator taking what I needed to survive. On many other levels, it seemed our souls were fusing together to become one, which frightened the holy crap out of me. Tears spilled down my face.

"Shhh," he said. "Take your time, beautiful." He rested his head against mine, his lips caressing my temple.

His energy and emotions poured into me. At that moment, I realized that in my heart, I had strong feelings for the vampire behind me, but I was torn between what my heart told me and what my brain was trying to say. A danger sign flashed before me, but I didn't know why. For the time being, I wanted him. I needed him and only him.

28

Webb and I emerged from the woods surrounding the base about an hour later. We'd barely talked. After drinking his blood, I got a little lightheaded, so he wanted me to rest before making the trek back to base.

Standing on a trail along the edge of the tree line, I let out a huge sigh for many reasons. I was close to home, which meant I would see Sam, and hopefully my dad, soon. I wasn't in the ocean, on a boat, or in the woods. I had Webb by my side. I just fed, and I didn't have any visions when I drank from him. Maybe it had been just a fluke with Kraft. Maybe his blood was somehow supernatural, sort of like Neil Foster's was for healing wounds. I shouldn't have been dwelling on it... unless it happened again.

While I was relieved to be going home, the events of the past several hours made my insides do a nervous dance. I was extremely worried about Darcy and kept wondering whether Edmund had kept his word to kill her if I didn't follow through with my end of the deal. Then there was Ben and the thought that maybe the Coast Guard had been successful in rescuing that swimmer—and maybe it was Ben.

The trail was narrow, so I had to walk in front of Webb. As we made our way toward base, he explained that the military had placed those traps for trespassers. In the past, humans had ventured onto the property for various reasons. Since the area was used for military training, it was dangerous for anyone or anything to wander through.

A bluish moon sat low in the sky, silhouetting the brick buildings in the distance. An orange glow peeked between two of the buildings to my right. Smoke still billowed as several firefighters tended to the dying flames. Apparently, the explosions had destroyed a new set of military barracks that was being built.

We rounded a slight curve on the trail, and the main structure on base came into view, the cold, sterile, brick building that was home to me now. It was the opposite of Ben's house overlooking Mount Hope Bay, rich and ornate with green grass, flowerbeds, and the cozy feeling I had always longed for, but the military compound was where Sam and Dad resided, and they were all that mattered to me.

"Webb? Is the brunette you were questioning still in custody?"

Given that Edmund wanted the brunette and my father's blood, and the latter was gone, I was ninety-nine percent sure I knew the answer. Still, I didn't want to assume.

"When Sloan and I reached the base earlier, she was gone. There was no trace of Kate or any Plutariums either. Sam said it was chaos when the explosions hit, and it still was when we got there. Before I left to find you, we did one more sweep of the building and base and found nothing."

A coyote, probably the same one that escaped me, howled his victory to his brethren.

A sudden thought flashed in my mind, and I stopped abruptly.

Webb plowed into me, grabbing me before I fell forward. "Hey, give me a warning next time," he said. "What's wrong?"

I turned, looking up at him. "Something the Plutariums said about killing two birds with one Mason." Absently, I placed a hand on his chest.

"Well?" he put his hand over mine.

"Bringing me out to a boat in the ocean, telling me about this game and how they wanted me to deliver the brunette by midnight... it was all a ruse. They knew I wouldn't get back in time. They knew you would come looking for me. They probably got on base the moment you left, created the explosions to clear the building, then took the brunette and my father's blood. But how did you know where to look for me?"

"We didn't. When we realized you were missing, we scoured the base then tuned into the police radios. Some anonymous caller told the police that a girl matching your description might be in trouble. They described Jonah with his blue bandana and you with your purple streaks."

I guess the purple streaks came in handy after all. "Where did the caller spot us?"

"Entering the state forest," he said, rubbing the back of my hand. "Do you remember being near the state forest?"

"No. I woke up on the boat. Perhaps that was part of Edmund's plan. Tell the police about a girl in trouble matching my description. He knew you'd probably be monitoring the radios. And he also knew you would come looking for me. So did you leave the base after that?"

"Olivia, Tripp, and I did, but then Sam called

us. He heard a description on the Coast Guard channel of a girl they rescued from the ocean. I called the Coast Guard, and they patched me through to the ship. They gave me your description. I turned around and headed back to the base. When I returned, Captain Vic called and told me your name. Then Sloan got the RIB ready, and you know the rest. We weren't far from the ship."

"Everything worked in their plan. But Darcy... and Ben might be—"

"Jo, one thing at a time."

"I can't help it, Webb. Everyone around me is disappearing."

Strong arms enveloped me. "We'll check with the Coast Guard on that stranded swimmer," he whispered.

"How do you know about the stranded swimmer?" I craned my neck, looking up. Webb hadn't been on the boat when Captain Vic got the distress call.

"I just told you. Coast Guard channel. Now, I know you don't want to talk about it, but I have to know. Kate was there, wasn't she? Did you talk with her at all?" Webb's voice had turned sullen.

There I was, worried about Ben and Darcy, when the vampire's sister had switched sides. His family had deserted him. He must have been in turmoil. I was such a freaking idiot. "I'm sorry,

Webb. I didn't mean to be so selfish about my friends when—"

He placed a finger on my lips. "Shhh. It's not your fault."

"I know Kate's actions aren't, but I shouldn't have blurted it out about her like I did. I'm so, so sorry. I was a brat. There's so much going on. Sometimes I don't even know how to breathe."

I gazed into his swirling blue eyes as my thoughts rewound to the moment I drank from him. How he'd held me made me smile. His blood had tasted so good that my throat ached for more. His lips caressing my temple had made my own lips tingle. Out of all that, what had my cheeks burning was the intimacy of the act of drinking from him. It wasn't predator taking from prey. No, it was far more than that.

His expression flickered with sadness, hurt, and confusion, but suddenly, his eyes flashed from blue to black, emblazoned with a hunger I had never seen. Maybe he'd read my thoughts.

My heart kicked into gear, and so did his.

Through hooded lashes, he leaned down, grabbing my face between his large hands. His lips were a hair's breadth away from mine. "I smell your desire, beautiful."

I had a lot to learn about vampires. Part of me was embarrassed. Another part of me, well... a rush of warmth spread throughout my body. My breathing became shallow as his tongue grazed my lower lip, then my top lip.

I was afraid. It was new to me. I still didn't know the first thing about kissing. While my brain was deliberating, my body leaned into him.

He nibbled on my lower lip, and the sensation sent a wave of heat sliding down my belly.

"Webb?"

Shaking his head back and forth, he placed a finger on my lips then began tracing them. "Do you trust me?" he asked in a hushed whisper.

I swallowed. I did trust him. It was *me* I didn't trust. A long blink of my eyes gave him the key to my heart.

He replaced his finger with his sensuous lips, drawing me closer. Tingles and butterfly wings tickled every nerve ending as his tongue probed my lips. Drunk on his heady scent, I could barely stand. I whimpered then acquiesced to the gorgeous creature, opening my mouth ever so slightly.

He placed one hand at the base of my spine and rested the other lightly against my cheek. I followed his lead as our tongues touched. Our lips sealed together, and a soft sound, one that was new for me, escaped me.

He changed the angle of his kiss as he pulled

me tighter, our bodies molding to each other. Then he slowed, sucking on my tongue.

Heat rushed through me like wildfire. I ran my fingers through his hair, the silky strands slipping between them.

He growled a husky growl.

I should have melted into him at the sound of his approval. Instead, I placed my palms on his chest and gently pushed. I didn't want him to stop, but confusion and raw fear made me act. Maybe it was my inexperience, or maybe it was his experience that made me do it. After all, he might have been in love with another woman, as Kate had mentioned, but I couldn't imagine him kissing me with that much intensity and emotion if he was. I had to know for sure.

He raised his head and locked eyes with me.

"Who's... Nicki?" I asked, the words barely audible.

"No one you should worry about." His hand got tangled in my salt-knotted hair.

"Are you still in love with her?"

When he managed to free his hand, he whispered, "I've never been in love with anyone." He dragged his fingers down my cheek.

How sad. "Do I look like her?"

"Jo." He dipped his head slowly, stopping when

his nose touched mine. "You don't look like anyone I've ever known. Now, why all the questions?"

I swallowed. "Kate said you liked me because I look like Nicki."

"Kate was only right about one thing. I like you." He brushed his lips against mine.

I had an inkling that there was more to that story. For the time being, though, my body couldn't resist his touch. I stood between his muscular arms, taking in his masculine scent. I wanted to stay like that forever, but life just didn't play fair.

His cell phone rang, shattering any lasting moments we had, and he pulled away.

"We're almost there," Webb said into his phone. "I'll call him back as soon as I can. Good. Sweep the entire base for bugs."

The last word triggered a memory of something Kate had said. As we began walking again, I organized my thoughts, filtering through my conversation with her.

The trail had widened as we drew closer to home, with a line of trees edging the path on my left.

As we walked side by side, I said, "Um... you asked me earlier if I talked to Kate, and I did. She didn't say a whole lot except something about a bug. She also confirmed that she was the one who'd helped the Plutariums break out and that she stole my father's blood out of his safe. What I don't understand is how she got the combination."

"We did find a tiny camera in the ceiling in your father's office. It was positioned so that if your father opened his safe, they would be able to get the combination. We think that's what happened. Afterward, your father changed the combination and had an alarm installed in his office."

"But what about tonight? How did she get into the safe if my dad changed the combination?" It seemed impossible to break into any safe, but I didn't know much. Regardless, I was living on a government compound, and Sam had said that the government could do anything.

"I'm not sure. The safe has an electronic keypad lock. So my guess is they got in by reading your father's fingerprints. It's a sophisticated process using ultraviolet light." Webb looked at me closely. "Anything else you want to tell me about Kate?"

Not really. But I heard the pain in his voice and knew there was no sense in delaying the inevitable. Taking a deep breath, I twined my fingers in his. "She's... um... with Edmund."

We came to an abrupt stop near a large oak tree.

Webb growled and squeezed my hand at the same time.

At the strength of his grip, pain shot up my arm. I held my breath and tamped it down. I didn't want him to go through this alone. I deserved some of the agony for the way I'd blurted out the whole secret in the first place.

The color drained from his face. He let go of my hand and began pacing in long, furious strides. After a few seconds, he froze. Before I knew what was happening, he rammed his fist into the trunk of the oak tree.

I ran toward him then decided to stop. He probably needed some space. I knew I would.

Sympathy and compassion made my chest ache for the gorgeous vampire. His anger and pain radiated off him in waves. His emotions ripped through me as though they were my own. If I could feel his emotions, I suddenly sympathized with my brother, the Empath. God, Sam had to have had a heart of steel to deal with others' emotions. No wonder Dad had said being an Empath was the worst of the special powers.

Webb growled low and loud.

Standing a few feet from him, I considered my options to calm the raging vampire. When I was sad or angry, Sam had never used words to settle me. He always hugged me. Maybe a simple hug would help. I guessed there was only one way to find out.

I blew out a breath, making my way over to him. I touched him lightly on his bicep. His arm vibrated, or maybe my hand was shaking. Without another thought, I wrapped my arms around his waist and pressed my head into his chest as he leaned against the tree.

His hands fisted in my hair as he rested his chin on my head.

We didn't move for the longest time. His heart slammed against his ribs. *Holy cow.* The reserved Webb London had emotions—intense ones. In a short time, he'd shown me anger, frustration, and passion. The world seesawed again.

After some time, his heart slowed. He leaned down and whispered, "Thank you." Then his hair fell forward, tickling my cheek. He placed a soft kiss on each of my eyelids then dragged his satiny lips down the left side of my face, over my scar, before settling them on mine.

I gently stroked his cheek. "I'm sorry, Webb."

"I know it was hard for you to tell me and that you didn't want to hurt me. It warms me to know that," he whispered against my lips.

I hated that he was hurting, and my heart actually ached for him.

"Come on." He pushed off the tree. "We need to get back."

Just like that, he seemed to be a lot calmer, at

least on the outside. Maybe hitting the tree had worked to release his anger.

We walked the rest of the way in silence. I imagined Webb was deep in thought over the news of Kate and Edmund. Before long, we were standing in front of the doors to the main building.

"Good evening, Lieutenant," the Sentinel on guard said.

Webb nodded. "I'll be in the control room, Jo. I'm sure Sam is dying to see you."

"Sam? Where is he?" I couldn't contain my excitement.

"Ms. Mason," the Sentinel said. "Over there." He pointed to my left.

I hesitated, looking at Webb.

"Go," he said.

Suddenly, I was torn. I didn't want to leave Webb's side. I wanted to make sure he was okay.

As if he knew my inner struggle, he leaned down and whispered, "I'll be fine as long as I know you're here for me."

I looked up at the gorgeous vampire. "I am."

"Thank you, beautiful." Then he walked into the building.

I stood immobilized for a few seconds, trying to shed the drunken Webb state I was in.

Sam sauntered up the sidewalk. When he saw

me, he stopped. I didn't hesitate but ran to my brother and jumped into his arms. He caught me and hugged me tightly before setting me down on two feet.

"Let me look at you." He took a step back. "Christ, you look pale. What happened? No, wait." He grabbed me, hugging me. "God, I thought I'd lost you, sis. I really thought I had. Don't do that to me again. I can't go through something like that, ever." His breath hitched.

"I love you, Sam. I'm sorry." I shuddered several breaths between sobs.

I made a mental note to get Dr. Vieira to examine my heart after things settled. It had been shattered, torn, and split into a zillion pieces. I doubted anything was even left in my chest, especially after my time in the woods with Webb.

"It's not your fault." He released a sigh. "Come on. Let's go to the control room. The Coast Guard is waiting for Webb's call. The captain wants to speak only with Webb. Let's see what they have to say. Maybe it's Ben."

I pulled away. "You know?"

"Sure. I've been glued to the radios since I found out you were missing. Webb asked me to stay and help the team. Since I know he cares for you, I trust him. Otherwise, nothing could've kept me here when I knew you were missing."

My mouth fell open as I tried to decide what to process first, the fact that Sam said Webb cared for me or that my brother trusted Webb. The universe tilted on its axis again. I decided I was more shocked that Sam trusted Webb. After the way he'd kissed me, I would have been crushed if Webb didn't care for me.

I slanted my head to one side. "Okay, but are you sure you're really my brother?"

"For eternity, Jo." He tapped his heart twice. "Let's see if we can get some good news from the Coast Guard."

Good news would have been fantastic. My theory of events happening in threes had been blown to pieces. Maybe that was just a human superstition. Maybe it worked differently for vampires. It seemed that bad things around me were happening in tens. If that were true, then maybe the good ones would happen in tens as well.

Pulling open the door to the main building, the Sentinel nodded and waved us in.

The lobby hadn't changed a bit—still cold as the North Pole in the dead of winter. My damp, salty clothes and hair only added to the shivers wracking my body.

I closed my eyes and inhaled the sterile air. Nothing but clean, fresh air had my nostrils flaring and my body relaxing. In all of my new eternal life, I never thought that I would have been ecstatic to be standing in that lobby. As cold as it was, warmth spread through me—I was home. I dropped to the floor and kissed the cold tile.

When I stood up, Dr. Vieira was leaning against the receptionist's desk. Ruth wasn't in yet, since it was the dead of night.

Dr. Vieira had his arms crossed over his chest, one ankle over the other and an I'm-going-to-kill-you look on his face. Before I moved, he smothered me with a hug. "Don't ever s-scare us like that again," he said. Yes, the doc actually stuttered.

He ran his hands down both my arms. He turned my face to the right and left, much like Webb had, then tapped my chin a couple of times. I guess that was his way of telling me to tilt back my head. Before I could protest, he had a penlight shining in my eyes.

"You need more blood," he said as he placed the instrument in the pocket of his lab coat.

"I feel fine. And by the way, it wasn't my fault I disappeared."

"You're going to give your father a heart attack."

"You sure you're not going to have one?" I held back a smile. I believed the doc had some feelings he was holding in.

He smiled, and my heart warmed. Maybe it was still in there, after all.

"And what blood do you propose I drink if my father's blood is gone?" I asked.

"Jo, your father is the most organized individual I've ever met. He always has an emergency backup plan." His eyebrows practically met in the middle, as if I should have known that important detail.

I cocked my head to one side. "Where is it?"

"The walls may still have ears. Until Webb has the place scrubbed for bugs, I can't say any more. But you do need to feed. Your skin is still very pale, and the whites of your eyes have black spider veins and specks. This is a sign of blood deprivation." He turned to go. "I'll meet you and Sam in the control room," he added.

"Wait. You said I needed *more blood,* as though you knew I already had some," I said.

"Jo, I may be an old vampire, but I'm not dead."

"Huh?"

"I smell him on you," Dr. Vieira said.

I had to get with the program. I knew I could smell Webb, Sam, and all the others. Everyone had their own distinct scent. However, I guessed I never thought about my scent and how others could rub off on me. God, he probably smelled the pheromones my body was emitting. *Yikes!* "It was an emergency," I blurted out. My cheeks warmed as I thought of Webb.

"I know," Dr. Vieira said.

I glanced at Sam, waiting for his reaction. "What? I knew too. But before the doc. When we found out Dad's blood was gone and Tripp called in to tell us you took off, Webb wanted to go find you. If you needed blood, he wanted to be the one to give it to you."

I didn't know what to make of that statement. Or maybe I did. Still, Sam was taking everything very well.

The three of us piled into the elevator. Sam punched two and four on the panel. I guessed Dad's blood was in the lab.

The elevator stopped on the second floor. Sam jumped out first. As I followed, Dr. Vieira took hold of my hand. "It's nice to have you home, Jo." He let go then jammed his finger on a button.

"It's nice to be home," I said as the elevator doors clanged together.

Sam smiled, grabbing my hand. An electrical charge zinged up my arm. One half of my life was solid. I just needed Dad to complete the other half. Only then would I be truly home.

Sam walked in as if he owned the place and had been working with the vamps forever.

"Mason, get your ass over here. I didn't say you could leave," a vamp shouted from a desk that had four computer screens on it.

"Cool your jets, Sawyer. I'll be there in a minute," Sam retorted. "Sis, Webb should be in that office over there." He pointed to a doorway right next to Sawyer. "Can you sit in there while I help the dude? You need to be with Webb or me from now on."

"What? You're babysitting me?" My tone had lost the nice-sister luster.

"Sorry. After what happened, we're not convinced this is over. Webb suspects someone else here was working with Kate."

I gasped. "You knew about Kate?"

"No. I didn't know until I ran back to the apartment to get blood for you and found that Kate had been in the apartment."

"How?"

"Her scent. When I mentioned it to Webb after the explosions, he wasn't surprised. That's when he told me what you'd said."

"You two have become awful chummy." My mouth was catching flies.

"Trauma can bring people together. Where you're involved, Webb and I are on the same page. Plus, we do have a lot in common."

I wasn't ready to touch the last statement. I had to process that he and Webb were even on the same page about anything, let alone me.

I breezed past Sam and made my way to the cubicle where Sam's new best friend, Sawyer, sat. Like the majority of the Sentinels who worked for my dad, Sawyer appeared to be tall, although it was hard to tell since he was sitting down. He was in great physical shape, and he had shoulder-length light-brown hair with blond streaks throughout. His fingers were flying across the computer keys, and the four screens shifted viewpoints several times before stopping on a dark, blurry satellite picture of something.

As I looked, Webb's voice filtered through my mind. *Come into the office and have a seat.*

I ignored him for the moment, enthralled as Sam asked Sawyer question after question about this and that on the screen. Curiosity and concern had Sam's eyebrows twisted in an odd fashion as his green eyes reflected the computer monitor. As Sawyer answered, his eyebrows loosened.

Jo, are you ignoring me?

I hadn't seen my brother for what seemed like an eternity, and Blue Eyes thought I was ignoring him. *Never.*

Leaving my brother for the moment, I turned and took three steps before leaning against the doorjamb. I was watching Webb listen to the caller on the end of the phone when a door in the control room behind me opened. Suddenly, the voices in the room ceased, as did the tapping on keyboards. Curious, I turned around and lost my breath.

All thought whooshed out of my head as I ran and jumped into Dad's waiting arms. He planted his feet and caught me.

"Oh my God! Dad?" I buried my head in the crook of his neck.

He ran his hand over my back. "I missed you, too, Pumpkin."

I began to cry.

"Hey, I'm okay. I'm right here."

Relief zipped through me. "I'm sorry, Dad. I'm so sorry."

"Shh. Please breathe. You're scaring me. Your heart is racing so fast."

I hiccupped. "I've missed you. I... love... you, Dad. I really do."

"God." He squeezed me tighter and whispered in my ear, "I know this life hasn't been good to you. For that, I'm sorry. I love you, too, more than you know. I haven't said it before because I thought it would've been too soon and you wouldn't have believed me. I couldn't have taken your rejection, even though I deserve it. Jo, I love you more than life itself." He let out a breath. "You're my little girl. You always have been since the day you were born."

I sobbed like a child. I didn't care that the entire control room was watching us. Thousands of emotions rolled over, under, and through me. My heart had stopped when he told me he loved me. His words weaved my shattered heart back together. My body, mind, and soul knitted into one as I relaxed against the most powerful vampire in the world. I was finally home.

"Carry on, folks," Dad commanded.

At his words, the noise resumed.

"Pops," Sam said behind me.

I raised my head, still wrapped in Dad's arms.

He extended his free arm, pulling Sam in for a hug. "I love you both. I don't ever want you to think otherwise. I know I have a funny way of showing it sometimes, but you're my family," he said, hugging both Sam and me.

"Pops? You're hurting me." Sam's voice was muffled.

"Sorry." He released Sam. "Jo, you okay?" He set me down and wiped the tears from my face. "Hey, I'm here. I'm not going anywhere."

Overcome with too much emotion, the only thing I could do was nod.

He wrapped an arm around me. "Let's go see Lieutenant London, so I can hear all about what happened."

Webb rose from the only chair in the small office when Dad walked in. "Commander, good to have you back," he said in his soldier's voice.

"Good to be back, although we have many issues to resolve not only with the Plutariums but with our own personnel, as I understand."

"Yes, sir." Webb circled around the desk. "We can't talk here, though. Our compound is compromised."

"I'm sure it is. Get Tripp, Sloan, Olivia, and Kodiak together. Meet me in the pyramid in an hour. Leave Fehherty and Sawyer in charge out there." Dad flicked his thumb toward the door. "I need to see Dr. Vieira first."

I hadn't heard Fehherty's name in a while. He was Olivia's partner. Each of the Sentinels teamed up in pairs. Tripp and Sloan were partners, but I had only recently met Kodiak Snow. I didn't know if he had a partner.

"Jo, get your brother. You two are coming with me," Dad said.

"Dr. V. said he would meet Sam and me here," I added.

"Dr. V.? Since when did you start calling him Dr. V.?" Dad raised an eyebrow.

"Sam called him that the other day. I guess it just stuck." Bracing for a reprimand, I steeled my shoulders.

None came. He just smiled. "I've already talked with him. He's waiting for us in the medical facility."

Okay, that was new. Dad had been so archaic about manners and all that, I thought he would've told me to stick with "Vieira." I pinched myself just to be sure I wasn't dreaming or walking in the afterlife. Before Dad could change his tune, I hugged him again.

"Sir, before you go, one thing." Webb's voice was low.

I trembled in Dad's arms. I hadn't forgotten that Webb had been on the phone with the Coast Guard. Dad had been a welcoming distraction, helping to calm my nerves while I waited for Webb. But from the somber look on Webb's face, I had doubts that it was good news.

"The Coast Guard rescued a person off Point Judith." Webb ran his hand over his day-old beard.

Staring at the tall, sexy vampire, I waited for his lips to move and for him to tell me that the swimmer they'd found was in fact, Ben. I clasped my hands together in front of my mouth, praying.

"Captain Vic was successful in rescuing the man, but he has only a weak pulse. The Coast Guard will be docking at the Naval Base in Newport. Once there, the medics from the base hospital will meet them at the pier." Webb's tone was even and steady.

"Well, is it Ben?" I blurted out. My insides were doing some type of twist-and-shout dance. Jeepers. It was like he didn't have a clue that I was dying to know.

"Captain Vic isn't sure," Webb said.

I eased out of Dad's embrace to lean against the wall and pull out the piece of gray T-shirt that Ben had used to tie me to the buoy.

"What is that?" Dad asked, concerned and puzzled, painting his chiseled features.

I rubbed the fabric between my fingers. "This is Ben's T-shirt. He used it to tie me to that buoy so I wouldn't drown."

"How come you didn't have a life vest, Jo?" Webb asked.

"We couldn't find any on the boat." I kept my eyes fixed on Ben's shirt. "When will they know if it's Ben?"

"Petty Officer Hunter is going to stay with him until they can identify the man," Webb said. "Captain Vic will call with any news."

"Lieutenant, we have much to discuss. An hour in the pyramid. Are we clear?" Dad barked.

Pyramid. There was that word again. I didn't know what it meant.

"Yes, sir." As usual, Webb didn't waste any time. He stalked out of the office with his cell phone to his ear.

"Let's go, Pumpkin. Grab your brother." Dad's tone changed instantly from commander in charge to loving father.

"Dad, not that I mind—I don't—but what's with the new pet name?" I hated when Edmund called me any of those Portuguese names or even "Princess," but Dad had always used "Sweetie" as his term of endearment before.

He wrapped his arm around me. "From the day you were born, I always called you Pumpkin. Your skin was orange when you came out of your mother, and it fit. I hesitated to use it when I first saw you again. Like I said, I was trying to ease into our relationship."

"Well, I love it."

"I'm glad."

"Sam," I called behind me. "We need to go."

Webb was talking with Sawyer as Sam listened, arms crossed over his chest. I was proud of my brother. He had changed so much since turning vampire. Sure, he still had anger issues, but they weren't as prevalent, and over the last two weeks, he had shown a side softer than I'd seen.

When I was finally able to steal Sam from Sawyer and Webb, we followed Dad out of the control room. Ben dominated my thoughts the entire way to Dr. Vieira's office. He'd said when all it was over, we needed to talk. He was right. I had a few things of my own to say to him, including thanking him for saving my life. I prayed that the man the Coast Guard had rescued was Ben.

WHILE DAD SPOKE with Dr. Vieira, Sam traipsed off to get me some clean clothes. Dr. Vieira allowed me to use his shower in the medical facility since Dad wanted me near him. I stripped off all my clothes and threw them in the trash. It would have taken a thousand washings to get the fishy smell out of them, and the truth was that I didn't want any reminders of that night.

I hesitated before stepping under the hot spray. After my ordeal in the ocean, I was still a little apprehensive about water, but I had to get the layers of salt off me and especially out of my hair. I took a deep breath, closed the door, and let the hot water rinse the sea from me. I scrubbed myself from head to toe. By the time I had toweled off, Sam had placed some clean clothes for me in the dressing room outside the bathroom.

"Jo," he called from the other side of the door.

"I'm almost done."

I raked Dr. Vieira's wide-toothed comb through my hair before stealing a glance in the mirror. My breath caught. Dark circles stained the area under my eyes. Upon closer inspection, I could see that Dr. Vieira was right. Black veins webbed the whites of my eyes, and an opaque gray replaced my normal metallic silver. My eyes changed instantly to violet, perhaps because the thought of blood sparked my vampire neurons.

"Jo." Sam banged on the door.

"Two seconds."

I slipped on my jeans, a simple T-shirt, and my boots before walking out.

Sam and I met Dad in Dr. Vieira's office. He was standing in the doorway, listening to the doc.

"We'll meet you over there," Dad said to Dr. Vieira. "Oh, and, Damon, can you bring three glasses?"

"Sure," Dr. Vieira replied.

"Pumpkin, you look... amazing," Dad lied as he leaned down and planted a kiss on my head. "I want you two with me. Jo, you're not to be away from Sam, Webb, or myself. Is that understood?"

"I—"

"No argument. Until we can get a handle on this entire mess, you're to stay within sight of one of the three of us. Clear?"

"Yes." Arguing would've been pointless. Besides, we were getting along better than ever, and I didn't want to disrupt the synergy we had. Suddenly, my stomach growled, and my throat burned. I needed blood.

"Dr. Vieira is getting you some of my blood," Dad said.

With Dad back, I had to curtail my thoughts so I wouldn't piss him off. Then my whole body froze as a thought punched me in the gut. If normal vampires could smell my arousal, that meant Dad would certainly have known. *Yikes!* I thought back to all those times I was around Webb and Dad. Embarrassment heated my cheeks. Oh well. I was a growing teenager with raging hormones, and Dad would just have to chill. As if that would happen.

Nevertheless, I released a huge sigh as I thought about the progress Dad and I had made in our relationship. Sam was right. Trauma had a way of bringing people closer together.

We stopped at the back entrance to the library. Dawn loomed on the horizon.

Dad held the door open as Sam and I entered the lobby. Straight ahead stood another door with a raised panel where a doorknob should have been. Dad secured the outer door before placing his hand on the panel. After a few seconds, the lock clicked, and the second door opened inward. A collage of scents bombarded me—pine, lemon, pineapple, wood, and musk all hung in the air. The mixture was odd, almost as though someone had brought the forest indoors and cleaned every tree. Maybe it was just the polish on the wooden steps I was standing on.

Dad secured the door, and Sam and I followed him up the stairs, where Dad again used his hand-print to unlock a third door.

"Isn't the library in this building?" I asked.

"Yes. The room we're about to enter sits above

the library. It was built for seclusion and secrecy. It's a place for us to plan missions and discuss top secret information."

"You don't suspect that this place has any bugs, Pops?" Sam asked.

"I don't. Only three people have access to this room—me, Webb, and Dr. Vieira. Plus, as you just saw, I had to use my handprint to unlock the door. Having said that, though, we always sweep it for bugs before we start any meeting."

I walked into the room, my eyes widening.

"Welcome to the pyramid," Dad said.

30

I gazed around in awe. It was literally a pyramid room. Each wall was an equilateral triangle and sloped to form a pyramid, rising to a point in the ceiling's center. Hanging down from the point was a large, ornate chandelier with several lights circling a planet of some kind. Scribed on one wall was the Jupiter Sentinel mantra:

Jupiter Sentinels
A SEAL Team Community
We protect the Superior World from all enemies,
human and non-human, and uphold the laws of our
existence. We strive to shield and protect the Inferior
World from those who seek harm upon them.

A map of the city dominated another wall, and a map of the United States was tacked to a third. Scattered around the room were groups of oversized chairs placed around small wooden tables. In the center of the room, two large couches were separated by a table that appeared to resemble a large block of ice. Between the maps, bookcases were lined with military books on weapons, strategy, tactics, and history.

Sam walked around, looking at the books, while I stood near the door, admiring the soothing blue, black, and purple splashed around the walls. I especially loved the way the top of the pyramid was painted to resemble the night sky with stars and planets peppered around, creating a mystical feel to the room.

"Jo," Dad called. "Have a seat."

Dad had Webb cornered in one sitting group, while Tripp, Sloan, Kodiak, and Olivia looked at the city map. Kodiak pointed to a square box in the bottom right.

Dad stood. "Let's gather around the couches. Tripp, pull some chairs over, please."

Tripp and Sloan dragged a couple of the oversized chairs to fill in the gaps between the couches.

Everyone gathered, taking a seat on a sofa or a chair. Sam chose a chair, so I joined him, sitting on the arm. The tight circle was too claustrophobic for me, but more importantly, I didn't want to sit near Webb in case my emotions decided to take over.

Dad stood behind a couch. Once everyone was settled, he cleared his throat. "First, I wanted to say thank you for doing your best to contain things while I was detained. We have work to do and a large mess to clean up. All of you are here because I trust each of you implicitly. And this room is a place where we can speak freely. However, in keeping with protocol, Webb, is the room secured?"

"Yes, sir," he said. "The room is free of any bugs."

"Very well. Let's start with what we know." He placed his left hand in his pants pocket. "One, Edmund is desperate to amass an army to take revenge against me, my family, and the U.S. government. Two, his idea to build an army is to use Patrick Mason's genetic expertise to engineer a serum that will change humans into vampires. What else do we know?" Dad asked.

"I think Jo has some more information," Webb said.

Everyone turned to look at me.

Christ! I was only there because I had to be in the presence of Sam, Webb, or Dad. I didn't know that I would be contributing to strategy.

I squirmed on the arm of the chair. "According to... Ben, Edmund has a few boys from Durfee. He thinks they're in a basement somewhere. The serum, which Edmund calls HVS-1, was their first batch, and it didn't work as well as he would've liked. Apparently, Blake Turner was his first test subject," I explained, looking at Dad.

Dad's eyes widened. "The boy you killed was Edmund's test vampire?"

Sam gasped.

"Yes. That's what Edmund told me. Blake wasn't up to Edmund's standard of a soldier because he couldn't go out in the sun. The serum had flaws. Although Ben said the second batch is working on the others, Patrick probably wants your blood—the most powerful blood there is—to perfect it."

"Commander, Ben was tested on, too, but is immune to the serum," Webb added.

"Maybe," I murmured. *Did I just say that out loud?*

"Explain." Dad glared at me with one eyebrow raised.

I glanced at Webb, who was sitting in the over-sized chair opposite Sam and me. He had an un-blinking expression as his cobalt eyes penetrated me. I immediately lowered my gaze.

First, you look absolutely stunning. Second, why didn't you tell me that part?

"Jo." Sam nudged me. "This is important."

I sighed. "Ben said that they gave him the serum several times, but nothing happened. Uncle Patrick was mad because Ben's system didn't react. He wanted to keep Ben longer for genetic testing, but Edmund had other sick plans to torment me with him. On the boat, Ben seemed fine. He smelled human. In fact, Edmund's game was to tempt me by cutting Ben's hand so I could smell his human blood." I fidgeted on the armrest.

Sam touched my arm. "I know this is hard for you, but you need to tell us everything, sis."

My superstitious mind believed that if I said what I was thinking out loud, it might come true.

Sam's right, beautiful. I'm sorry this is hard on you, but we need to know what we're up against. You want us to get Darcy, right?

Every time he called me "beautiful," my body tingled. I did want Darcy back. *She's probably dead by now, Webb.*

We don't know that for sure.

I kept my fingers crossed that she was alive. "After we reached the buoy, I latched on to it, but the waves were huge and came one after another. The last one swallowed him, but not before I met his gaze and his eyes turned bright red. Edmund's eyes are like that when he's in his vampire guise."

Sam squeezed my hand. "We should have news soon about the man the Coast Guard found."

"I know. I just hope it's Ben." I choked on the word *hope*. If not for Ben, I would have had no more hope.

Dad rubbed his jaw. "Let me get this straight. Blake Turner was Edmund's first test subject. Since then, they tested the serum on a few other humans and may have turned Ben into a vampire?"

I nodded.

"Do we know how many humans?" Sloan asked.

"No. Ben didn't say. But Mr. Jackson had said there were five boys missing from Durfee, and that included Ben," I replied.

"Lieutenant, did we ever figure out who the brunette was with the Turner boy?" Dad asked.

"Sorry, sir," Webb said.

"Jewel, the brunette, is your niece, Dad," I blurted out.

The vampires froze. No breathing, no blinking, no movement whatsoever.

"How come you didn't know that?" Sam asked Dad.

"Patrick and I were never close, son. Which begs the question—do we know if Patrick is a vampire too? If he was able to change another human, then—"

"I don't know, Commander," Webb said.

Patrick had still been human when I attacked him in the prison. I rummaged through the conversation I had with Ben, but Patrick hadn't come up. I didn't even think to ask but should have.

"The brunette was human, sir," Sloan said. "So she doesn't pose a threat."

"Yet her capture was the reason my daughter was taken out to sea to play some screwed-up game where she almost died." Dad glared at each Sentinel. "And Kate, Jo?"

I looked at Webb, who nodded his consent. So I told them all about Kate while keeping an eye on him.

Webb stood immediately and walked to the other side of the room. That was the part I'd dreaded. I didn't want to see him in pain. I grabbed Sam's hand, thankful my brother and I were extremely close. I wasn't sure what I would do if Sam ever betrayed me.

Pain seeped into my temples before Dad's voice did. *I don't want to see Webb in pain, either, but we need to talk about this.*

"There's nothing to discuss about Kate." Webb turned then walked to stand behind the chair. "We find Edmund and his team, and we deal with all of them in the best way we know how. We're Navy SEALs. We take out the enemy." His eyes had blackened. "I only ask that when the time is right, I'll be the one to deal with Kate. I don't want that hanging over anyone's head. Are we clear?"

I swallowed a gasp. I couldn't believe what I was hearing. Kate was his sister, his kin. I couldn't fathom him killing her.

"Are there any other facts that need to be put on the table?" Dad asked, claiming one of the arms of the couch adjacent to me.

"Edmund kidnapped my friend, Darcy. I was supposed to bring him your blood and the brunette by midnight in exchange for Darcy. If I didn't, he said he'd... kill her."

Dad patted my hand. "I'm sorry, Pumpkin."

"What about the Secretary of the Navy?" Kodiak asked. "Do they think you killed him, Commander?" He rested his elbows on his knees as his blond locks fell forward.

Dad let out a sigh. "The human government is going through their protocol of asking questions and gathering all the evidence. Right now, I'm a person of interest."

I'd left out one thing. "Um, Dad? Sorry, but I forgot. Edmund admitted to me that he killed the Secretary of the Navy. He said the secretary was worthless or something, and he didn't fit into his grand plan."

"I'm not surprised," Dad said, "but it will be hard for the government to prove Edmund did it. More than likely a grand jury will convene to decide how they want to deal with the investigation."

Webb's cell phone rang.

"Yes," he said into it. "Where? Coordinates? Text them to me." He pushed a button then looked up. "We have a location on Edmund."

Everyone looked at Webb.

"After Jo told me about her conversation with Ben," he said, tapping his phone, "I got a hunch. Ben told her that wherever he smelled musty and damp and he thought it was a basement. He also thought that he was somewhere near the ocean because of the salt air. So I checked with the Coast Guard on exactly where they found Jo. They picked her up off the coast of Portsmouth, Rhode Island. I sent out a team to scout Portsmouth and Newport. We got lucky. Fernando and Jonah were seen switching vehicles near an abandoned building on the outskirts of Portsmouth. They tailed them to a mansion on the coast in Newport."

Tripp handed Webb a pad and pen. He scribbled some notes then handed the pad back to Tripp.

"Okay. I laid out the facts," Dad said, shifting on the arm of the couch. "Let's talk about short-term strategy. First, we need to rescue those teenagers, including Darcy, if they're still alive." Dad looked at me when he said Darcy's name. "Second, we need to shut down Edmund's operation. While I want to destroy all the data associated with Patrick's genetic research on this topic, Dr. Vieira is going to need the research data, including the serum. This may potentially help Dr. Vieira to figure out how to help the teenagers. So once we're in, we need the hard drives and any files, et cetera. Third, we take out as many of Edmund's vamps as we can, including Edmund. Remember, we don't kill humans, so Patrick and the brunette will need to be taken into custody."

"Commander," Tripp said. "What about those teenagers who may be vampires now? Do we take them out too?"

"Great question. I would proceed with caution if we encounter them. If there is a way we can help them, then let's do our best to. Ideas on strategy?"

Olivia, who had been quiet until then, piped up. "I say we wait until this evening. Between now and then, we make sure we have eyes on them to ensure they'll be there when we attack. This way, Viking II will be back on base in time. We'll need them for this mission. Plus, the night gives us some cover, and there will be fewer humans around." Her voice was as soft as her brown eyes, but underneath her femininity, a predator lay ready. I would hate to fight her in a battle.

"I agree with Olivia," Tripp said.

"What about you two?" Dad pointed to Sloan and Kodiak.

They both nodded.

"She's right," Webb said. "We need to tie up some loose ends on base. The firefighters are still out working. We need to plan who will man the compound. I want everyone well rested and ready before the assault."

"We're going to need it," Sam agreed.

I pinched him. "Hey, you're not going."

"Sorry, sis. Not your decision," he said, looking at Dad.

Dad nodded.

I jumped up. "No. You can't let him go, Dad."

"He's ready. He's more than ready, in fact." Dad stood.

I stared into his emerald eyes. "Then I'm going too."

"No, you're not," Webb blurted out.

Everyone snapped their heads in Webb's direction, including me.

"Webb is right," Sam said, standing. "You're not going."

What is it with all these alpha vampires? "Not your decision, Sam." I glowered at him.

"Commander, if I may?" Olivia asked. She rose from her spot and stepped around the furniture. Her hair was French braided as usual, and her toned arms nicely filled out the black Henley she wore. "I've trained the twins. While Sam is a far better fighter and ready for combat, Jo has talents that we're not considering. For one, her telekinesis might come in handy. If she destroyed the Turner boy, she could be an asset. Kraft informed me that Turner was also beaten pretty badly. We still don't know what Jo did, but he had welts all over his face."

"Pumpkin, what did you do to him?" Dad had a baffled expression.

"I don't really know. It's patchy," I explained. "I think when I got angry, I managed to turn the water from the faucet into ice. Then I threw it at Blake. But I don't know how I did it." I shook my head. I sounded like a crazy woman. "I still don't know how I killed him either."

"Sis, you did what?" Sam's mouth hung open.

"It's one of the powers over the elements, son," Dad said. "I'm still hoping that you develop a few of those elemental powers. In fact, while all the Sentinels have the ability to manipulate water, Sloan is the expert in using it as a weapon."

Then something hit me like a bag of rocks. "Can Edmund manipulate water?" I asked, holding my breath.

"Sure," Webb said. "He was a Sentinel. It's one of our requirements. We want all our Sentinels to wield at least two of the elements. Your dad is the only vampire to manipulate all four. I have water, earth, and fire. Olivia and Sloan have water and earth. Tripp and Kodiak both have water and fire."

"Could he manipulate a storm in the ocean?" I was still holding my breath. That ability clearly defied all logic, more so than the existence of vampires.

"It's not impossible," Dad said, "but highly unlikely. First, Edmund's elemental powers would need to include the ability to manipulate air. And as far as I know, air isn't one of his abilities. Only water and earth. Still, if he did have the capability, it would take a tremendous amount of energy to conjure a storm of that magnitude. He'd be out cold for days, even weeks. Edmund doesn't have the strength to do that."

Tripp cleared his throat. "If Edmund did do it, it would only be confined to that area. Since we experienced the storm here at the base, Edmund couldn't have done it."

I released all the air in my lungs.

Sam sat on the arm of the chair, looking dejected.

"Son." Dad placed a hand on his back. "Don't worry about your powers. You've only been a vampire for two months. These powers don't show themselves for at least a year. It'll come. I'm confident."

"Then why can Jo do it?" he asked.

Tripp laughed. "Your sister is weird."

Wow! Tripp cracked a joke? I laughed, too, so that no one would take it the wrong way. If Tripp had the nerve to say that, I had to commend him for coming out of his soldier's shell to lighten the mood and make Sam feel better about things. "Yeah, Sam. Tripp is right. I am weird. You know that more than anyone."

"It still doesn't make me feel any better, you know." Sam bit his lip.

"Let's stay on point," Dad instructed. "Webb, let's map out the coordinates."

Webb and the rest of his team, including Sam, gathered in front of one of the maps. They quickly engaged in strategic conversation, and Webb barked orders to everyone.

"Jo," Dad said, "we need to discuss the Turner boy. We never finished our conversation. Let's sit in the corner." He pointed to a seating area on the opposite side of the room, away from Webb and the team.

I claimed one of the chairs, pulled my knees to my chest, and wrapped my arms around my legs.

Dad sat opposite me.

"I'm not sure what you want to hear about Blake. I just told you what I did with the water. Maybe he was just a time bomb from when Edmund changed him into a vampire." I smiled at the thought.

"That very well may be, but we still need to debrief the Council of Eternal Affairs. The school has called a hearing," Dad said. "It's standard procedure. Dr. Vieira is still working on the autopsy. We need to share the news with him about this vampire serum being used on Turner. And if we can capture the research data during our raid, then it may help support your innocence, Jo."

"*May help?*" I asked. I hated the ambiguity of those two words.

"One thing at a time, Pumpkin."

He sounded just like Webb.

The door opened, and Dr. Vieira walked in, carrying a tray of what looked like milkshakes. Well, three milkshakes and five large stainless-steel containers.

My nose tickled. Blood. "Dr. V., is that for us?" I licked my lips as my fangs slowly descended.

Dr. Vieira set the tray on the large ice-block table then picked up one of the tall glasses that had a straw in it.

He walked over and handed me a glass. "Yes."

"What is it?" I asked.

"A special bloodshake that has a complement of vitamins to replenish your system."

"Is Dad's blood in it?"

"Of course, in yours and Sam's," Dr. Vieira said as he gave one to Dad. "Steven? When you're ready, the Turner boy's body is prepared for you to view."

Ew! My face twisted in all directions. *Body to view?* I sipped the bloodshake as I thought about Blake, wondering why Dad would want to view the body.

"Damon, I was just informed Turner was one of Patrick's human-vampire test subjects." Dad didn't use a straw to drink his shake.

"I know. I'll show you the lab results. It's clear he was still part human for some reason, which is odd since he had fangs, but the results of the genetic tests will make it all clear to you."

I almost choked on the part where Dr. Vieira said Blake was still part-human. I suspected something different about him, but I couldn't grasp how that was possible—he had fangs.

"Jo, how does it taste?" Dr. Vieira asked as he withdrew his penlight from his lab coat.

I'd been thinking of Blake, so I really hadn't drunk much of the shake. I took a long sip, letting it sit on my tongue for just a second. "It's awesome. It's smooth, sweet, and milky. Can I have another?" I asked.

"No, dear. One is enough for a while. The vitamins in that shake will pack a punch for a few weeks. You'll still need to drink your father's blood, though. Now, turn your head to the right for me," Dr. Vieira instructed, turning on his penlight. After shining it in both my eyes, he said, "I know your curious mind, Jo. When all this mess is over with, you and I will spend some time in the lab. I'll take you through a few medical theories on vampires and what nutrients help us."

"Thank you. But why aren't the Sentinels drinking power shakes?"

"Their systems are older and don't require the nutrients like you and Sam. Your father needs this power shake, as you call it, to help build his system so he can keep producing healthy blood for you and Sam. Until you both are weaned off his blood, we'll keep you on a regimen of drinking one of these per month and his blood on a twice-daily basis."

The Sentinels and Sam had finished their

strategy session and were relaxing, drinking their elixir. Dr. Vieira engaged Dad in a private conversation for a few minutes while I finished my shake. My eyes were heavy, and my belly was full. In fact, I would have bet that Dr. Vieira slipped a sleeping pill into the shake.

Dad cleared his throat. "A couple of final items. Whatever the outcome of our raid on the Plutariums, we must make sure that the humans are not hurt. I've also decided that Olivia is right. Jo's powers may come in handy, so she'll accompany us but will stay close to Tripp and Sloan."

"Sir," Webb said quickly.

Dad held up his hand. "Lieutenant, I know what you're going to say. I would like her by your side or mine, too, but if Jo can manipulate water, then Sloan is her best coach and protector."

"Is the mansion near water?" I asked.

"It is, actually," Sloan said.

Sam muttered something under his breath before letting out a low growl.

I wasn't going to argue. While fighting didn't appeal to me like it did Sam, I needed to be there if Darcy was still alive.

"She'll be fine, son," Dad added. "We'll reconvene later this afternoon. Between now and this evening, get some rest. We'll meet back here at dusk.

Webb, I need an hour of your time. I'll meet you in the medical facility in thirty minutes. Sam and Jo, the apartment is safe to sleep in, but keep the conversation to a minimum until we can scrub it for bugs. Am I missing anything?" Dad looked at each Sentinel.

While he waited for a response, Webb's cell phone rang, breaking the silence. He walked away from the group to answer it.

"Get some rest. You're dismissed," Dad said to the remaining Sentinels.

Everyone filed out except Webb, Dad, Sam, and me.

"Petty Officer Hunter is on his way in. He just drove through the gate," Webb said, sliding his phone into his pocket.

"Is it Ben?" Sam asked.

"I don't know," Webb said. "Commander, I'll meet you as soon as I'm done with Hunter."

"Very well," Dad said to Webb before turning to Sam and me. "Why don't you two head to the apartment?"

"Hell no, Pops. I'm going with Webb," Sam said. "I need to know."

Dad looked at me.

"It's a no-brainer, Dad. Sorry," I added.

"Fine. Just make sure Jo gets back safely, you two. If she's taken from this base again, heads will roll." Dad's tone was as lethal as the look in his eyes.

"You don't have to worry about that, Pops. I won't make the same mistake again," Sam stated.

We all walked out of the pyramid room together.

Once outside, Dad went a separate way. Apparently, there were shortcuts to the medical facility. As we made our way to the main entrance, Sam and Webb talked about what buildings still needed to be swept for bugs. I tuned them out, thinking about Ben, praying Hunter had come bearing good news. I longed for Ben to be alive with his humanity intact. God help him if he wasn't.

THE THREE OF us arrived to find Hunter waiting outside the main entrance, on a bench under the small portico. Since it was still early morning, the building wasn't open to visitors yet. My heart raced as we approached. If it had been good news, I figured he would have called. In the movies, police officers only showed up at the door to give loved ones bad news.

Hunter stood. "Good morning, Lieutenant London." He wore the same blue uniform I'd seen him in on the ship. He pulled off his ball cap. "Jo. Wow. You look a lot better." His eyes glimmered in the morning light, but dark circles marred the area beneath them.

"Petty Officer Hunter, this is my brother, Sam," I said.

Hunter extended a hand to Sam. "Hi. Call me Hunt."

Sam shook his hand. "So, what's the verdict?"

Webb nodded to the Sentinel guarding the main entrance, who opened the door for us.

"We'll talk inside," Webb said.

He directed us to a meeting room in the back of the lobby, the same one that Sam, Tripp, and I had used before we talked with Darcy and Mr. Jackson.

Webb flipped on the lights. "Have a seat."

"No, thank you, sir. I prefer to stand." Hunter folded his ball cap and shoved it in his back pocket. He took a position near the table.

I stood by the door. Sam, on the other hand, walked over to the built-in credenza adjacent to the table and leaned against it.

"Very well, then." Webb made his way to stand opposite Hunter, on the other side of the table. "You came a long way from Newport to deliver the news. Why? You could've called,"

"You're right, sir. We can't identify the man.

He's still in a coma, so I took pictures. I know Jo was worried about her friend, and I wanted to see if she could help identify him by these." He set three pictures on the long conference table.

Sam sprang to stand beside Hunter.

I held my breath while Webb and Sam looked at the pictures. Dread kept my feet from moving, so I didn't even attempt to walk closer.

Webb examined each picture. "You could've emailed these to me." Again, Webb's suspicious nature took center stage as he looked pointedly at Hunter.

"Sure, sir. Truth be told, I wanted to see Jo. I wanted to make sure she was okay."

Sam's head snapped up before turning to study Hunter. After sizing up the human as though he was some freak of nature, Sam darted his gaze toward Webb.

"Petty Officer Hunter, I appreciate your dedication in making sure your rescue victims are doing well, but as you can see, she's fine. A simple phone call would've sufficed. As far as these pictures go, she doesn't need to see them. I can confirm it's Ben." Webb slid the photos back to Hunter.

I used the wall as my guide as I sat on my butt. Tears fell instantly. Ben was alive.

Sam threw down the picture he was holding, crossed the room, and sat next to me.

"What's his prognosis? Has the doctor said?" Webb asked.

"No, but all his vital signs have improved since we pulled him out of the water. I'm really surprised he didn't drown. He didn't even have any water in his lungs."

Sam placed his hand on my back. "He'll get through this, Jo." The solace in his voice helped to relieve the tension inside me.

I expelled a loud sigh. The questions were whether he would come out of the coma, and if he did, whether he would still be human.

Hunter touched my arm. "Jo, are you all right?"

"I will be. Thank you," I managed as tears slid down my face.

Sam stood. "We appreciate your help, Hunt."

"Petty Officer Hunter, if that is all, we thank you for taking the time to get to the bottom of this. Next time, please call before driving all this way. It's been quite a long night, and Jo needs to get some rest. As you know, she's been through a great deal." Webb's tone was resolute.

"I'll walk him out," Sam said, nodding at Webb as though they had communicated telepathically about their next move.

"I understand," Hunter said. "I'll check in with you later, if that's okay. I'm headed back to the base hospital in Newport. I'll phone if things change."

He collected the photos in the folder and walked to the door.

I stood.

"Things will work out," Hunter said.

Glancing at me, Sam tapped his heart twice. "I'll see you back at the apartment."

Hunter turned. "Jo, it was great to see you again. Lieutenant." He nodded at Webb. Then he and Sam were gone.

My body swayed. I placed my palm on the wall, taking in a deep breath.

"What's wrong?" Webb wrapped an arm around my waist.

"I don't know. Probably just lack of sleep." A bead of sweat slid down my temple. "I am tired."

Webb laid his hand on my forehead then my cheek. "God, Jo. You're burning up. Let's get you up to the medical facility." He lifted me, cradling me in his arms as he walked to the elevator.

I rested my head on his shoulder and nestled into him while we waited for the elevator doors to open. "Webb?"

"Yes, beautiful?"

"Do you think Ben will be okay? I mean, do you think he's turning into a vampire?"

"Don't worry about that," he whispered, dragging the backs of his fingers down the side of my face.

When we got in, and the elevator doors closed, so did my eyes. The rise and fall of Webb's chest, coupled with the sound of his breathing, lulled me toward sleep.

His cool lips touched my forehead. "Don't fall asleep until we know what's wrong, Jo." His voice was distant.

The dream world loomed. My body was in shutdown mode, probably from all the stress over the last twenty-four hours. "I'm... fine. I'm... tired... sleep. Take... me... to... bed," I slurred.

The last things I heard were his heartbeat speeding up then the sound of his breathing fading.

31

I slept for twelve hours. When I woke, I barely had time to change before the assault team was due to leave.

We exited the base as soon as the sun set. Sloan, Tripp, Webb, and I were in one SUV, Sam, Olivia, Kodiak, Kraft, and Dad were in the van up ahead of us, and four Sentinels from Viking II were behind us in a Hummer. Every one of the Sentinels wore their hair tied at the nape of their neck, black cargo uniforms, black fingerless gloves, stab-proof vests, ear communicators, and several weapons hidden on their bodies. The only weapons visible were their Sentinel swords and daggers strapped in sheaths to their legs. They reminded me of a badass SWAT team. Even Sam was clad in their uniform. I hated that he was so eager to fight, but it seemed to suit him. Maybe it was a way for him to quell his anger issues.

I was the odd one out. I didn't have my hair in a ponytail, and I wore blue jeans and a short-sleeved dark-blue cotton Henley. The only black things on my body other than my hair were my boots and the stab-proof vest Dad had strapped me into. I knew of bulletproof vests, but the Sentinels had special armored vests designed since they mostly used daggers and swords when fighting other vampires. Dad had explained that the vest was made out of strong synthetic fibers to prevent a blade from penetrating. I was given no such weapon, though. My only defenses were my physical ability and my special powers.

"How do you feel?" Webb asked, placing his hand on my knee.

I swung my gaze from the passing landscape to meet his. He sat in the back seat with me while Sloan drove and Tripp rode shotgun. It reminded me of the day I left Durfee with them. The day had changed my life forever. I just prayed it wasn't about to change again. "Fine."

What did he want me to say? *The butterflies are awake now that your hand is on my knee, and I'd rather have your lips on mine instead.*

He grinned as if reading my thoughts.

"Am I missing something?"

His grin morphed into a downright sexy-to-die-for smile as his eyes flashed vampire.

I guessed I was missing something. It couldn't have been that he was worried about me coming along, not with a look that spoke of sinful pleasures. "Care to share?" I asked.

"You had a slight fever when I brought you to Dr. Vieira this morning."

"I was just tired. Isn't that what Dr. Vieira said?" I tilted my head to one side.

He nodded. "Do you remember anything before you fell asleep in my arms?"

I thought for a second. I remembered him carrying me. I'd asked about Ben. Then I couldn't keep my eyes open. I didn't want to go see Dr. Vieira. I asked him to take me to... bed. My eyes widened. My cheeks flushed red. I didn't have to feel my face to know it was blazing hot.

He still had that sexy, impish grin on his face. *No need to blush, beautiful.*

I turned away from him.

Look at me.

No.

Jo, don't be embarrassed. I'm just playing with you.

He was seriously being playful. I had a ton to learn about Webb London.

While I was sleeping, the Sentinels firmed up

their plan to attack the Plutariums, and Webb filled me in as we rode along. Webb and Sam had argued with Dad for me not to accompany them on the raid, but Dad stuck to his guns.

I agreed. If I could survive the events of the past two days, then I could manage to help the Sentinels with the raid.

"Sloan, you're responsible for Jo. Don't let anything happen to her, or the commander will have our heads," Webb said. His playful tone melted away.

Thank you for changing the subject.

Anytime, beautiful.

"Good luck with that, buddy," Tripp muttered.

"Hey, I heard that!" I said.

"Sorry, Jo, but you did take off on me yesterday," Tripp reminded me.

"Jo, if you give Sloan a hint of trouble, I'll cut *your* head off," Webb said lightly.

I glanced at him, smirking. "Yeah. Okay." I would have liked to see him try.

"You don't believe me?" His tone hardened all of sudden.

"If you cut my head off, my father will kill you, so what's the point?"

"She's right, sir," Sloan said. "Don't worry. I got this. Jo and I will get along fine." He peeked in the rearview mirror. "If you try to hit me in the balls again, Webb won't have to cut your head off."

"Why are you guys ganging up on me?"

They laughed.

"In all seriousness, you need to listen to Sloan," Webb said. "Tripp will be there too. He's just as responsible. Once we get there, Kraft and your father will run point, meaning they will scope out the premises and report back. We have RIBs standing by down on the water. The property is surrounded by the ocean on two sides. Once your dad gives the signal, we'll go in. It's a large place, so we'll have some challenges." He didn't take his eyes off me as he spoke. He turned to Tripp. "Tripp, you have the blueprints?"

"Yes, sir. The mansion has four access points. There are the front and back entrances to the main level. Then the basement can be accessed from two areas on the outside of the house. It looks like one was the servants' entrance and the other was the owners'. Inside access to the basement is through the kitchen." He studied the document, using a penlight like the one Dr. Vieira had.

While they continued to go over their plan again, I gazed out the window, thinking of Darcy. Edmund had said if I didn't return her, he would kill Darcy. But if he'd had his own agenda to lure the Sentinels away from the base by stranding Ben and me in the middle of the ocean, I couldn't figure why he'd used Darcy as a pawn.

"Yes, Commander," Webb said suddenly, slanting his head to one side.

With my heightened hearing, I could usually decipher the voice on the other end of a cell phone, but I couldn't hear a damn thing with the earpieces the Sentinels used.

"Nothing we can do right now. Fehherty and Sawyer will handle it." Webb touched his right ear.

"We're there in five," Tripp called from the front seat.

"What's going on, Lieutenant?" Sloan asked.

"Mr. Jackson and a Mr. Rose are at the base gate, asking for the commander. They're quite upset. Jo, do you know Mr. Rose?" Webb asked.

"Darcy's dad? I've only met him a couple of times. He works in Boston. He's a big-time lawyer who defends criminals. That's all I know."

Webb growled for some reason.

The two times I had met Mr. Rose, he'd seemed preoccupied and not that friendly. Maybe he had to be that way to defend criminals.

We zipped through the streets of Newport, mostly hugging the coastline. The moon illuminated the ocean to my left, while the lights of large, gated mansions lit up the landscape to my right.

As the raid loomed, I kept thinking about what would happen, especially with Kate. I was worried about Webb. After I told him about his sister, he'd vented some of his anger. Since then, he'd seemed to be in pretty good spirits. But I didn't know how he would react if Kate was there. The question reminded me of something I had been itching to ask him, only I didn't want to ask out loud. I could have used telepathy, but I had a problem with that idea. I had never initiated a connection. Webb and Dad always had. It wouldn't hurt to try. Anything to do with vampires' powers seemed to begin with opening up the senses, at least for me. Okay, then.

I inhaled then released my breath, letting out all the tension in me. Once relaxed, I pinpointed Webb's scent and focused on his presence and his energy. His woodsy scent filled my nostrils before I silently asked, *Were you serious about killing Kate?*

A zap of electricity stung my ears, and then his voice filled my head. *Did you say something?*

I smiled as I turned to face him, elated that I'd done it.

Impressive.

I flashed him a wider grin.

Now, what were you asking?

This morning in the pyramid room, you led me to

believe that you would have no problem killing Kate if it came down to it. I raised my brows.

Jo, by nature as predators, vampires are very possessive and protective and trust their family and loved ones. I love my sister and have always trusted her. So I'm not sure if I even believe she's sided with Edmund. I'm not saying you were lying. Sometimes, seeing is believing, right? If it is true, the struggle for me would mean that Kate broke that trust bond between us. I don't know how I would react to that. What I do know is that breaking my trust doesn't mean I would kill my own sister. In fact, I don't want any Sentinel harming her. But... their job is to protect themselves, and Kate is a good fighter. Which is why I said what I said. I will do everything to capture my sister if she is here. That's all I can give you right now.

That was more than I expected. Then again, I didn't know what to expect. I did agree with him that seeing was believing. If I had been in his shoes, I wouldn't believe me either. I would definitely need proof.

Thank you.

I grabbed his hand and squeezed. I wanted him to know that I was there for him and that I empathized with him.

He smiled and winked as he rubbed a figure eight several times on the back of my hand.

Sloan followed Dad's van, twisting and turning

around the curves and switchbacks. I held my breath. One small error would have propelled us into the freaking ocean.

As we turned the last curve, the mansion came into view. Webb had been right—the house was half surrounded by the ocean. The van pulled into a small parking lot off to the right side of the road about a mile or so back. A yellow sign said Whale Watch Area.

We drove in, following the van into an opening in the rocky cliff that stood about ten feet high—a cave. The Viking II team parked alongside us.

The four of us got out of the SUV.

Dad opened the back door of the van, reached in, and pulled out a small box. Kodiak grabbed it from him and set it on the SUV.

"What is this place?" I asked, looking around. A musty scent hung in the air, making my nose itch.

"That's not important right now," Dad said.

Turning, I peeked into the van. The vehicle was equipped with monitors and computers like a surveillance van police would use for covert observation. Two of the computer nerds from the control room were inside, typing away on their keyboards.

Everyone huddled near the van.

Kodiak handed glasses to everyone except me.

"I don't get any glasses?" I asked.

"No, Jo," Dad said. "We want you to concentrate on your powers. Glasses like these can be a distraction. Besides, you'll be with Sloan and Tripp. They will be your eyes on this mission."

I wasn't going to argue. Dad was the military soldier, and I trusted him.

"As you guys know, these are the high-end glasses that we've been waiting for," said Olivia, holding up a pair. "They're new tech, so not something Edmund is aware of from his days as a Sentinel. They have a few components that will come in handy tonight. All the glasses have a transmission signal built in that talks to our satellites."

"First, the camera," Olivia continued. "In the upper right corner of the lens, there is a screen that will engage once you twist the dial on the side of the frame. The first click clockwise is the team view. This will allow you to see everything the team leader is seeing. For example, when the commander's glasses are recording, we'll be able to see what he's seeing if we're on channel one. Second click, channel two, is the recording mode itself." She turned the knob. "You won't be able to see anything on the screen, but a signal will be sent back to the guys here in the van to show them what you're looking at. That way, they can clue everyone in on comms. Questions?" she asked.

She waited for a few seconds. "Okay. We'll keep it on channel one until we're all in position. Once we disperse, switch to channel two until told otherwise," Olivia instructed. "Next, the small red button on the left side of the frame." She flipped the glasses, pointing to it. "Like the camera, when this button is active, a small screen will emerge in the upper left corner of your glasses. This is a temperature view and will distinguish between human and vampire. Since our core temperatures run about ten degrees cooler than a human, the screen will show a human as bright white and a vamp as dark gray. Clear?" she asked.

Everyone fiddled with their glasses before putting them on.

"Remember," Webb said, "do what you need to do to stay alive. If Kate is here, I want her captured alive if at all possible. I'll deal with her. Agreed?"

If Edmund was there, Kate was here. I was confident about that.

They all said yes, dropping their heads. I wouldn't have wanted to be in their shoes in that moment. They all knew Kate well. Heck, some of the Sentinels, like Tripp and Sloan, probably had a soft spot for their boss's sister. Now, they were faced with her as one of their enemies.

Dad adjusted his vest. "Kraft and I will head out. We'll give you the heads-up when we're ready.

As Olivia stated, you'll have my eyes until we go in. Kodiak and Sam, remember to grab any files or hard drives that you can. The Viking II crew will back you up. Kraft and I will take the second floor. Olivia and Webb, you got the first level. Sloan, Jo, and Tripp, backyard, servants' entrance.

"Make sure Viking II has the RIBs ready. We'll need to get any victims out as fast as we can, and that includes any humans and humans-turned-vamp. We have four RIBs waiting half a mile out.

"Get in. Get out. This is a rescue mission. We're not here for revenge. If assaulted, defend yourself, but no humans are to be harmed. If Kate is there, remember she's one of us, folks, so heed the Lieutenant's words as best you can."

I wanted to argue that point. She certainly wasn't one of us anymore.

"Any questions?" Dad asked, meeting each gaze in turn. "Very well. Be safe. Be fast. And stay alive." Dad walked up to me. "Listen to Sloan. I love you." He kissed me on the head then turned to Sam. "Son, you're new at this, follow orders, and I love you too." Then he and Kraft were gone.

Between Olivia's speech on the new glasses and Dad's orders, I was a little dizzy. Sam seemed to be wide-eyed and ready to head into battle.

"So do the computer vamps stay here alone?" I asked.

The nerdy vamps didn't look like they could defend themselves, but what did I know?

"One of the Sentinels from Viking II will stay behind to guard the opening," Webb said.

"Lieutenant," one of the nerdy vamps called. "Commander is live."

"Make sure your glasses are engaged to team view, channel one," Olivia said.

Since I didn't have a view of what they were looking at, I jumped into the van to check the monitor. Four guards patrolled the front of the house with two more on the outer perimeter near the cliff. Kraft ran toward the two and pushed. Their bodies disappeared into the night air.

"Move now," Dad's voice said through the computer.

"Everyone knows their job," Webb said. "Sloan and Tripp, cut through the brush on the side of the house then make your way around back. The rest, follow me. We'll meet the commander at the front. Be safe. Be fast. And stay alive," Webb said, repeating Dad's words.

"Let's go, Jo," Sloan called.

"Sis," Sam called. He tapped his heart twice and mouthed, *I love you.*

"I love you, too, Sam." I repeated the gesture.

A fuzzy tingle hit the base of my neck, then

Webb's voice filled my head. *Listen to Sloan and Tripp. I want you back in one piece, beautiful.*

Nerves made me laugh as I followed Sloan while Tripp ran behind me. We made it around the property line, dodging rocks and tall weeds. We stopped at the edge of the weeds.

"We're in place, Lieutenant," Sloan said, tapping his earpiece. "I got three vamps in the back. One is on the top deck. Two are down near the dock."

The yard gradually sloped down to the water in the back. A large yacht sat moored to a dock. A light glowed from inside, then someone stepped out of the cabin.

I tapped Sloan on the shoulder and pointed toward the yacht.

"We need to do this fast if we're to get into the basement," Tripp said.

"Jo, we need to take out the vamp on the yacht and those two standing near it. Tripp, you take the one on the deck," Sloan said.

"How are we going to take those three out?" I asked.

"Do you remember what you did with the water when you formed it into ice?" he asked.

"No. I was kind of in a trance. I think that's the only way I can use my powers," I said.

"No matter," he said. "Okay, I'm going to stir up

the water around the yacht. Jo, when I do, I want you to concentrate. Feed off my energy. As the water rises, we're going to change it into an ice block covering the three vamps down there." He flicked a finger.

"I'm sorry. Feed what?"

"You'll feel the energy from Sloan," Tripp added. "Trust me. If you can do anything with water, Sloan's energy will make your ability stronger."

"I want you to concentrate, relax, and follow my lead," Sloan instructed. "We're about to absorb the natural energy of the elements and use it to our advantage. Believe and clear your mind."

Tripp stood on one side of me, Sloan on the other.

I closed my eyes and inhaled. I had to help in some way. I really didn't remember how I'd done what I did in the girls' bathroom at school, but that didn't change the fact that I'd done it. The problem was that I wasn't angry. Anytime I had used my powers before, it had always been during a fit of anger or rage.

Sloan hummed in a low and steady rhythm, as though practicing yoga. I joined in with him. The vibrations rumbled through my body. The longer we chanted, the more energy jumped from him to me and back, as if we were trying to spark a fire.

I opened my eyes and saw Sloan with his arms

out in front of him, his palms up. I did the same. With his palms still facing up, he slid his arms out in an arc, bent his wrists inward, and then snapped them forward. His palms faced each other, fingertips pointed at the water.

"When I clap my hands, Jo, the water is going to rise. I want you to drop your arms to your side with your hands on your legs. When I clap my hands a second time, I want you to raise your arms out in front of you, keep your palms facing each other, then slowly bring the tips of your middle fingers together. Then I'll clap a third time. That's when I want you to raise your arms over your head. Once they're over your head, stop and don't move until I clap a fourth time. This will go really fast. Ready?"

I nodded.

"Hurry, you two," Tripp whispered.

Sloan clapped his hands once, and the water around the dock rose quickly in a thick wall. I did as he instructed. He clapped again, and I went through the next step. He clapped a third time. Again, I followed orders, waiting for him to clap a final time. When he did, the wall of water froze around the three vamps and the boat.

"Let's move. The ice block isn't going to last long," Sloan said.

I stood with my mouth gaping, disbelieving my eyes.

Sloan pulled me as the vamp on the top deck jumped down, spotting what had happened at the dock. Tripp's Sentinel sword engaged, and it was no match for the vamp who only had two daggers. Tripp's sword penetrated his chest.

Sloan whipped out his sword as we made our way to an open door. Grunts and noises filtered up through the basement.

"Stay close," Sloan whispered.

We traversed the steps in three strides, with me on Sloan's tail. The smells of dirt, urine, death, and blood all mixed together, causing my stomach to churn slightly. A bright light shone through the crack in the door at the bottom of the stairs.

Suddenly, all the noise stopped.

Sloan tapped his ear. "Call in the RIBs. Call in the RIBs."

"Why are you calling in the boats?" I asked.

"Webb is in my head. He's down."

"What does that mean, *down*?" I whispered.

Sloan raised a finger to his lips.

Footsteps sounded behind us.

Sloan and I both turned.

"Ice block is melting. The other vamp is dead. What are you waiting for?" Tripp asked in a hushed whisper.

"Princess? Please join us." Edmund's voice boomed from behind the door. "Your scent is intoxicating. I'm sure your brother here would love to see you before he dies."

Tripp and Sloan exchanged surprised looks.

I pushed Sloan out of the way, but he stopped me.

"No. Let me by," I said, not caring about my voice since Edmund already knew I was standing there.

"It's a setup, Jo," Tripp whispered.

"So? I'm going in there. If he does have Sam, I'm not letting him die."

Tripp and Sloan both shook their heads in disbelief or defeat. It didn't matter. I would fight these two Sentinels if I had to. Nothing was going to stop me from going through that door.

Sloan grunted. "Then let us clear the path." He made eye contact with Tripp. "Two bogies. One here." Sloan pointed to the left of the door. "And one here," he said, gesturing to the right.

Tripp stepped in front of me. Sloan held up a fist before raising a forefinger. He waited one second then raised his middle finger.

They moved on three, storming through the door. The fluorescent light blinded me as it beamed into the dark stairwell. Tripp banked left, and Sloan's elbow flew upward as he darted right.

Bones cracked, swords clanged, and daggers flew —along with a metal star. I leaned to my left, stealing a peek at the vamp Sloan seemed to be dueling, Fernando. He ducked as Sloan's sword swept over his head, but as Fernando bobbed up, Sloan angled his sword upward, and before I even blinked, the blade of Sloan's sword sliced through Fernando's neck. His head dropped to the floor before his body fell. I covered my mouth, stifling a shriek. It wasn't that I had any remorse for the vamp who had tried to kill me in the basement of Highland Memorial Hospital. I'd just never seen anyone's head being chopped off like that.

"Princess," Edmund called again. "Oh, Princess."

His voice grated on me.

Sloan shook his head, telling me not to enter.

As if I was going to listen. Before I moved, Tripp soared through the air, hitting the back wall. His body slumped as he hit the floor with a splat. *Oh God! Please be okay.*

I placed a palm on the wooden door and pushed slowly. Sloan sent me another warning look. Ignoring him, I walked into the dirt-covered room and sidestepped a vamp who was out cold on the floor. It must've been the one Tripp was fighting. So how did Tripp...

Turning my head left, my brain froze, and all the air in my lungs caught.

Sam stood bare-chested with his ankles and wrists shackled, a brown-haired vamp standing behind him. The tip of a very large blade protruded from Sam's bare chest, and blood trickled down his abs. The good news was that the blade wasn't near his heart. The bad news was that another sword was poised at his back, with a vamp I hadn't seen before at the handle, ready to push it through to his heart.

To add to my horror, Webb stood next to Sam, in the same position but with one key difference: the vamp waiting to push the sword into Webb was none other than his bitch of sister, Kate.

I couldn't be sure what had me more shocked, that my brother was about to die or that Kate London stood ready to kill her own brother. Anger, fury, and rage were weak words to describe my emotions.

Next to Webb and Kate stood Edmund Rain, holding a very large sword and wearing a malevolent grin on his face.

Instinct drove me forward. Jumping through the air, I had one thought on my mind—*kill Edmund Rain*. The hairs on my skin stood up as I got closer to him. Before I knew what was happening, a large jolt of electricity zapped me, and instantly, I was flying backward. I landed on top of a pile of trash that smelled like death.

What the heck just happened? I pushed to my feet, stumbling in the process.

Sloan ran over to me.

"What... in... the world was that?" I asked as I took hold of his hand.

"An invisible wall?"

My brain tried to make sense of what Sloan had just said.

"Elemental magic," he said. "It seems Edmund can manipulate air and somehow energize it."

There wasn't any time to understand that mumbo jumbo. Tripp was still out, but I could hear his heart beating, so I knew he wasn't dead. The impact must've knocked the wind out of him.

"Tripp will be fine," Sloan said. "Here's what we're going to do..."

Edmund laughed.

My head shot up.

Edmund paced in front of Webb and Sam as though protecting his prisoners. "You do have yourself in a bit of a quandary. Here's how this is going to work, Jo. I'll give you one life. I'll even let you choose who lives, Sam or Webb? In return, I want you. Simple, isn't it? I get you, and one of them gets to breathe for a while longer on this Earth."

"How about you stick that sword where the sun doesn't shine." I hated that vamp.

Webb raised an eyebrow. Sam wore a blank expression.

"So, you want to play it that way. Well, let's see if I can persuade you." Edmund turned and scored the blade of his sword across Sam's stomach.

"No!" I shouted as I ran at Edmund, forgetting that the invisible wall was even there.

I hit it hard, sailing backward as the electricity coursed through me. I landed at Sloan's feet, muttering all kinds of swear words.

Edmund chuckled. "Keep doing that. It's so much fun to watch you get zapped."

I snarled as I stood, clutching my fists at my sides.

Sam winked at me while blood spilled from his abdomen.

I didn't have time to analyze why my brother had just winked at me.

A violent rage erupted, making my skin prickle with power that built within me as though I'd started a car engine. The tighter I clenched my fists, the more my body started to shake. My vision blurred then cleared. Suddenly, I had hawk-like vision, so sharp it practically blinded me. My ears popped, and my hearing became crystal clear. The heartbeats of everyone in the room sounded like a rock band playing a heavy bass line. It was as though my vampire senses were on crack.

I drew a breath. *Keep it together. We need to get Sam and Webb out of here,* my inner voice warned. *But how?* I didn't have any weapons. I would have loved a sword to cut Edmund's head off.

The glass cabinets along the right wall rattled, as did the small brown boxes inside.

I took one step when Webb's voice entered my head. *Calm down, Jo. Use your powers in a controlled fashion. Your telekinesis is taking over, and you need to use your elemental powers.*

I pinched my eyebrows, wondering what the heck he was saying. I could only manipulate water, and there wasn't even a faucet in that dungy basement.

Jo, look down.

The dirt from the floor was swirling around my ankles. What in the world...

You're making the dirt rise. Earth. Elemental. Now, picture yourself walking over to me. Allow the energy in you to spill forth so that it can cut through the invisible wall.

I wanted to laugh so hard at what Webb was telling me, but I couldn't. I had to get him and Sam out of there. Sucking in a breath, I pictured myself walking into Webb's strong arms. As I moved,

Sloan grabbed me. "What are you doing?" he asked.

"I have to get through that wall."

"The only one who can counteract that invisible wall of air is your dad. None of the Sentinels have any magical powers," Sloan explained in a low whisper.

Just great. Where is my father?

He's battling the other Plutariums. Webb answered.

I hadn't realized the connection between Webb and me was still open. *How many of them are there?*

Focus, Jo. Don't worry about the others. You can do this.

"I love to see you keep trying, Princess. But there's nothing you can do," Edmund said. "Unless you give yourself to me."

"Sis, don't do it," Sam said.

Edmund's head snapped toward my brother. "Do you have a death wish?"

"Fuck you, asshole," Sam barked.

Edmund nodded at the brown-haired vamp.

"Wait!" I yelled.

Edmund held up a hand. The vamp behind Sam dropped both of his from the pommel.

"On one condition," I countered.

"You're not in any position to barter, Jo."

Sweat trickled down my temple. "How wrong

you are. You need me. You said yourself that I would have powers this world hasn't seen. So that alone is worth more than one life. Release my brother, Webb, and Darcy." I had to get her out if she was still alive.

Edmund let out an evil laugh. "You're a smart one, Princess. I'll tell you what. If you can figure out how to get through my wall without my help, I'll let Frick and Frack go, but not your friend. I promised her to a very dear colleague of mine. Her father hasn't repaid a debt that he owes. Now, if you *can't* get through the wall on your own, then I'll choose which one of these two bozos die." He tapped the sword against Webb's bare stomach then Sam's.

How is Darcy's father involved with vampires? I shook off the thought, relieved that she was alive.

He's not going to let any of us go. So you have to get through the wall. Tripp is on his feet now. So he and Sloan will take care of the rest, Webb said.

I cast a look over my shoulder, and Tripp was standing next to Sloan.

"Those two behind you can't help you. Now, time is wasting," Edmund said.

I turned back.

Edmund's red eyes bored into me as though he was preparing my soul for death.

I was about to move when pain grabbed my

temples. Dad's voice slowly filled my head. *I'm up-stairs. We've found Darcy. Where are you?*

In the basement. We're in a serious bind down here.

How many down there?

Three, including Edmund and Kate. The vamp I'd stepped over earlier was still down. I didn't know if he was dead or not.

I'm on my way. Olivia and the Viking II Sentinels will get Darcy to the van and bring the vehicles back. The Sentinels on the RIBS have taken out the three you and Sloan froze at the dock. There are only two humans lying on tables in the lab. If there were more, they're not here. Kodiak has my brother and his daughter detained in the lab until Kraft can get there.

I couldn't wait for Dad. I had to act now.

Instead of envisioning Webb, I pictured myself killing Edmund Rain. As I did, the power in me rose. My adrenaline kicked into gear. I took two steps then shot out my hand. When I did, a blue light radiated outward. Suddenly, chaos ensued. Tripp and Sloan flew past me as Edmund turned and drove the sword into Webb.

A scream caught in my throat as I vaulted into the air and landed on Edmund's back. Burying my fangs into his neck, I bit into his jugular. He head-butted me, but I clamped down harder, tearing off a layer of skin before spitting it out. He grabbed my head in his hands and flipped me over him. I landed hard against the cement floor, my back taking the brunt of it.

Using my upper torso to propel me forward, I jumped up.

In the far corner, Tripp was battling the vamp who stood behind Sam. Sloan was removing the swords from my brother.

Edmund let out an evil laugh as he stood before me. "Webb will die before you take another swing at me," he growled.

Rage overpowered all thought in my head. Drawing on all the strength within me, I let out a breath and unleashed my power. Dirt swirled around like little funnel clouds. The glass doors of the cabinets shattered as the pressure in the room dropped. I swung out an arm, and the brown boxes that sat inside exploded. Hundreds of nails shot out.

"Kate, kill him," Edmund barked. "Now!"

On his command, everything around me froze. The nails hung in the air, my blood gelled, and my breathing halted in my lungs.

She wouldn't. I slowly turned toward her. When I did, the nails fell to the floor, and so did my heart. She jammed the sword into Webb's back, causing the tip of the blade to protrude several inches through his front.

My body tensed as she twisted the sword to the right and left. Darkness lurked in her eyes, as though Edmund had burned her soul.

Webb tilted his head to the side as his eyes latched on to mine. Pain, sorrow, and sadness flashed across his face. Blood seeped out of his mouth, streaming down the corner. His eyes wavered from black to blue then black again before his eyelids closed.

An explosion rocked the ground. White chunks of the ceiling rained down, mixing with the brown dust still floating in the air from the funnel clouds.

Edmund lunged for me, but I charged Kate, who still had her hand on the pommel of the sword. My body impacted hers from the side. We both hit the far wall, knocking Sloan down in the process, as though Kate and I were the bowling ball, and he was the spare pin. She bunched her knees, planting her feet on my stomach, and pushed. I hit the opposite wall. Dizziness clouded my vision for a brief second. I shook it off.

As Kate stalked toward me, Edmund snagged her.

Another explosion rocked the mansion. The room filled with a dense white cloud. I gagged, squinting. The visibility was worse than staring through a thick layer of fog.

"Jo!" Dad's voice boomed nearby.

"Over here," I called.

I still couldn't see two inches in front of me. I needed to find Webb and Sam. I dropped to my knees and began crawling with my hands out in front of me, feeling for bodies. As I crawled, glass and other objects embedded in my legs and palms. I moved a little farther before my hand touched a body. The cloud of dust dissipated slowly. I rubbed my eyes to clear my vision. When I blinked, I saw Webb lying motionless on his side. Kate had driven the sword completely through his chest, leaving only the hilt visible at his back and several inches of the blade jutting out of his chest. The other sword that Edmund had used was buried in his abdomen.

Panic set in. "Webb! Webb!" My fingers nervously tried to locate a pulse. Tears poured down as my hands shook. I wiped the dust off his face. Blood covered his mouth. I tapped his cheek a few times. "Webb! Wake up. Please, wake up."

Suddenly, the ceiling caved in. I covered Webb's body with my own as chunks of sheetrock rained down. I craned my neck to glimpse what was happening as debris settled on my face, in my mouth, my nose, and my eyes. I spat, trying to get rid of the detritus. Then I blinked a few times before my vision cleared. When it did, I saw Jonah standing over me with a malicious grin stretching from ear to ear. He saluted me then disappeared.

Ass!

"Jo!"

Sam's voice filled my ears.

He emerged through the white cloud that still hung in the air, though it wasn't as thick. Sloan and Tripp were right behind him. "You all right?" Sam asked.

"Help Webb! He's not breathing. I can't feel a pulse."

Both Tripp and Sloan gasped, pushing Sam out of the way.

Tripp bent down. "Oh Christ!" He placed his fingers on Webb's neck. "Pulse is there, barely."

"It is?" I asked. Maybe my hands had been shaking too badly to feel it before.

The air around us cleared.

"We need to get him back to Dr. Vieira," Tripp said.

"Jo? Sam?" Dad called.

"Dad!" I shouted.

Suddenly, hands grabbed me.

"Help Webb!" I pleaded.

Dad knelt down. "Is he breathing?" Dad looked at Tripp.

"He has a very weak pulse, sir," Tripp replied.

"You and Sloan, get Webb back to base. Take

the SUV. Once you get him in the vehicle, force some blood down his throat. It should help his injuries."

"Sam, are you okay?" Dad asked.

"I am now," Sam said.

I surveyed my brother as he stood. The swords were gone, the shackles were off, and his chest wounds had a small amount of coagulated blood around the openings, but there was no sign that the swords had done any real damage. Even the large cut Edmund had made on his stomach had healed.

"Close your mouth, sis. I'm good. Sloan gave me some blood."

"Sam, get in the lab and help Kodiak. We need to get out of here," Dad instructed.

Sam disappeared.

"Sloan, when I lift him, pull this sword out," Tripp said, pointing to the pommel sticking out of Webb's back.

Tripp eased his fingers under Webb's shoulder. Then he raised Webb to a sitting position. His body remained lifeless as Tripp held him and Sloan removed the sword. Blood oozed out at a steady rate. Then Sloan pulled out the sword stuck in Webb's stomach.

Tears streamed down my face as my heart shattered into a million tiny pieces.

"Get me his shirt," Tripp said, nodding to it on the floor.

Sloan threw the dusty piece of fabric to Tripp.

"We'll slow the bleeding when we get in the van, but this will have to do for now," Tripp said. Then he lifted Webb in his arms and disappeared out the basement door.

Dad touched my shoulder. "We need to go, Jo."

"Where's Edmund?" I asked, wiping the tears with the back of my hand.

"Edmund, Kate, and Jonah are gone. The earlier explosions were their diversion for an escape."

"Commander, the place is ready to blow in five minutes," Sloan said.

"Blow?" I asked.

"Now we need to blow the rest of the place. We can't have evidence hanging around for the humans," Dad said. He looked at Sloan. "Everyone else out?"

"Affirmative, Commander," Sloan said before he slipped through the door.

Kodiak and Sam returned. "We got all we could, Commander," Kodiak said.

Dad grabbed my hand. We followed Kodiak and Sam through the servants' entrance.

On my way to the door, I spotted a headless Fernando and the other vamp that Tripp had knocked out. Next to both of them was the vamp who had stood behind Sam.

The salt air accosted me when we emerged out of the dust-filled basement, a welcome change from the death and blood that clung to me.

We ran to the front of the mansion, where the van and one vehicle remained. The SUV was already gone. I prayed like hell that Tripp and Sloan would get Webb back to Dr. Vieira in time. Tears spilled like a waterfall as I continued running toward the van parked near the road.

"Kraft, send the RIBs home," Dad directed. "Olivia and Kodiak, take the van. Get our guests to the medical facility. Kraft and Sam, you're with me in the Hummer."

"What about the Viking II crew?" Sam asked.

"They're heading back on the RIBs with the other members of their team," Kraft replied.

"Dad, where's Darcy?" I asked.

"She's in the van. You'll see her soon enough. Now get in the car." Dad's tone was even but stern.

The van took off first. I jumped into the back seat of the Hummer with Dad. Sam sat shotgun, and Kraft drove.

We had just negotiated a curve about two miles down the road when a boom blasted behind us. I glanced over my shoulder to see a large plume of fire lighting up the area and the ocean beyond.

Turning back, I looked at Dad. "You said Kodiak had Patrick and his daughter."

"Patrick got away, but his daughter wasn't so lucky."

"Really? Jewel is dead?"

Dad nodded.

I didn't know what to make of that, but something told me her death would only compound our war against the Plutariums, especially since Uncle Patrick couldn't seem to function without her. "What about the two humans in the lab?" I asked.

"Kraft was able to get them into the van. They're heading back to base, where Dr. Vieira will examine them." Dad turned to Sam. "Son, were you able to get anything from the lab?"

"Only a thumb drive that we found on the floor, Pops. I'm not sure it's any good."

Dad chewed the inside of his left cheek as he stared out the window. He didn't move, speak, or flinch.

Silence filled the space around us as we drove home. Sadness, shock, and anger kept my adrenaline in high gear. I wanted to get out of the car and run. We couldn't get back to base quickly enough. My thoughts were completely focused on

Webb. My heart ached so badly that it felt as though Kate had stabbed *me* in the heart. Nothing but Webb mattered to me. I hated vampire life, I hated Edmund, and more than anything, I hated Kate London. When I had the chance, retribution was going to be far, far worse for her than for anyone else on this planet.

32

Thirty minutes later, the Hummer entered the base through a back gate. The guard waved us through after he verified who we were. I tapped my foot until Kraft threw the vehicle into park behind the main building.

I'd opened my door, ready to jump out, when Dad grabbed me. "Pumpkin, wait."

I turned. "No. I want to see Webb."

"Sam, Kraft, leave us, please," Dad ordered.

Kraft hightailed it out of the vehicle in a blur. Sam, on the other hand, turned and gave me an apologetic look before he jumped out.

"Close the door," Dad said.

Against everything I wanted to do, I did.

"I know you like Webb." Dad's voice was low.

My heart dropped to my feet. *You do?*

"I do. I've known for a while."

"You have?" I snapped my head toward Dad, my heart pounding. *Oh no. Did he sense my...*

"Pumpkin, between your thoughts and the way you look at him, it's not hard to figure."

I shouldn't have been surprised that Dad knew how I felt about Webb. I knew it was inevitable. Even so, a part of me was shocked. I guess hearing Dad say it out loud made it more real.

"I want to prepare you for something." Dad took my hand. "If Webb makes it through, he's going to be in a bad place. Kate tried to kill him. Webb loves his sister more than anything. She's his only family left. This is going to be extremely hard on him. You need to be aware that he may not be well up here." He touched his temple.

"You sound like you say that from experience," I whispered.

"As a vampire, trust is the soul of our existence. We trust our family and loved ones, explicitly. When that bond is broken, you lose a part of your soul. I love Webb as a son, and I hurt for him, as I know you do. But tread lightly with him if he comes out of this. I've seen him in a bad place once before. And no, I won't discuss that with you, so don't even ask."

I dropped my gaze, staring at nothing. I heard him, but I wasn't ready to process what it all meant. My mind was in a daze. I was still visualizing Kate driving a sword through Webb. Edmund had done the same. Those images alone were going to haunt my dreams for eternity. I tapped my foot on the floorboard of the car. "Can I go now?"

"Jo."

I lifted my gaze. Emerald-green eyes met mine. "I'm here for you. I know I'm an old man up here" —he tapped on his head— "but I'm a wise old man. I know I haven't given you any reason to confide in me. And sure, there are some things that will make me upset. But please don't be afraid to talk to me." His tone was tender, matching the softness in his eyes. "You ready?"

Suddenly, I wasn't sure. When we'd first arrived, my adrenaline had driven me to jump out of the car without thinking. But Dad's words started to sink in. He knew I liked Webb, but I didn't know if it was okay with him. All of a sudden, part of me cared what he thought. Maybe it was his honesty and the gentle way he spoke. He was treating me like an individual and not like one of his soldiers. I looked away. "Dad, are you okay with the fact that I like Webb?"

He laughed. "I'm not sure that I'm okay with

you liking any male. But... you're growing up. You're turning into a beautiful woman. I can't stop your feelings or change them." He guided my face so we were looking at each other again. "I told you. I'm here for you."

"What kind of answer is that?"

"It means I love you. Now, let's go see how Webb is doing." He opened his door.

He didn't answer the question, but that was okay for the time being. I wanted to see Webb. We had been sitting in the car for far too long.

I jumped out and ran to the door. "Come on, Dad. Hurry," I called.

Once Dad joined me, he pushed a button on a panel and spoke into the speaker box. "Control room?"

"Commander. Password," a voice instructed.

"Juno," Dad said into the speaker.

I raised an eyebrow. "My middle name?"

He shrugged one shoulder.

The door clicked then opened.

I ran up the stairs to the fourth floor, but another locked door stopped me from going in.

Dad pushed a series of numbers on a panel and bowed down so his retinas could be scanned. The door opened into the back of the medical facility. "This way, Jo."

"Where is he?" I glanced around the main room of the lab.

Sam poked out his head and waved a hand. "Over here."

I ran around lab benches, desks, chairs, and tables. There were too many flippin' objects in my way. I leapt over a small table, but the floor rose too quickly. Before I could hit it, Dad caught me in his arms.

"Slow down. He's not going anywhere," he said.

I righted myself then ran into the room. I stopped short. Standing in a patient room in the medical facility was getting to be a familiar thing for me, with Ben, Sam, and now Webb. Suddenly, I couldn't help but think of Ben and how he was doing, but I was even more worried about the gorgeous vampire in front of me, whose eyes were closed. His chest rose and fell with every sound of the machine that appeared to be helping him breathe. Sam and Dr. Vieira were the only other people in the room.

"How... is... he?" I asked, holding back tears, which was hard as hell.

"One of the swords punctured the sac surrounding his heart. An eighth of an inch to the left, and..." Dr. Vieira didn't need to finish that sentence for me. He, too, seemed a little choked up, which just opened my dam of my emotions.

Tears streamed as I inched closer to the bed. My hand shook as I touched Webb's.

Sam wrapped an arm around my shoulder. "I'm sorry, sis."

Dad walked in. "How is he, Damon?"

"I gave him blood, and his open wounds have healed. Now, it's up to him. His pulse is very weak. He needs rest."

"Is he going to make it?" My voice cracked.

"Time will tell," Dr. V. said.

I didn't take my eyes off the beautiful creature. His hair had dried blood caked in it. His complexion was gray and pasty. None of that mattered. He still was as handsome as the day I met him. "Why is his skin ashy looking?"

"Cobalt will do that. When the metal gets in your bloodstream, it breaks down the blood platelets. It can give your skin a grayish color," Dr. Vieira explained.

"Was that how I looked when I had all those swords in me?"

Dr. Vieira scrutinized me. "Jo, you looked much worse."

"How come I was able to heal in a few hours from my ordeal, but Webb hasn't? Even Sam healed right away."

Dr. V. sighed. "The sac I just mentioned is a double-layered membrane. It's filled with what is called pericardium fluid, which is designed to protect the heart from any kind of shock. As vamps, we can endure quite a lot, but not when it comes to the heart. It's just going to take longer for him to heal."

"Where are the two humans we brought in, Doc?" Sam asked.

"In the operating room. They're off-limits right now," Dr. Vieira replied.

"When are you going to start your examination of them?" Dad asked.

"They're stable, so as soon as I can get a handle on Webb and make sure Patrick didn't do anything to Jo's friend, Darcy."

My head popped up.

"She's in the last room down the hall. Olivia is with her." Dr. Vieira fiddled with one of the machines. "Now, Webb needs to rest. You can come back later, Jo."

"I want to stay." My tone sounded like it belonged to a six-year-old child.

"Jo, you heard Dr. Vieira. Webb needs rest." Dad lightly touched my arm.

"Sis, he'll still be here later." Sam took my hand.

"But we never found out who was helping

Kate. What if that person is still among us? What if—"

"Jo. No one is going to come in this room with Dr. Vieira here. Besides, I have guards posted outside in the hall, and no one unauthorized can get through the door without setting off an alarm," Dad said.

"But if they're one of us, they can get through." I didn't trust a soul anymore. I would probably have a hard time trusting anyone again, except for Dad and Sam... and Webb, if he survived.

"I understand your worry. We're doing everything we can to sniff out the other mole. For now, we're fine. We're doing a final bug sweep of all the rooms and buildings. Now that we know about Kate, the other person is not going to do anything to show themselves." Dad sounded confident.

"Come on, sis. Darcy awaits." Sam tugged on my hand.

Satisfied with Dad's logic, I gave in to Sam's pull. "Is she still... human?" I asked.

"Yes," Dr. Vieira said before adjusting another monitor that had beeped.

Sam let go of me and left the room when Dad wrapped his arms around me and squeezed. "He should be okay," Dad whispered.

Those four simple words packed a punch that opened my tear ducts again. I sobbed in Dad's arms as relief that Webb had a pulse flooded through me. Still, I had to keep myself guarded until Webb's eyes were open and I was looking into those deep ocean-blue orbs that grabbed my heart every time.

Dad escorted me out. "Why don't you go see Darcy? I want to talk with Dr. Vieira. I'll meet you down there."

I managed to get my legs to move from one room, where my heart broke, to the other, where I had no idea what I was in for. I steeled my shoulders, wiped my eyes, and removed the heavy vest I had on.

Immediately upon entering, Darcy's cotton candy scent tickled my nose. She was sitting up in bed, clad in jeans with a hospital gown covering her upper half. Her blond hair was disheveled, and her chocolate eyes were red where the white should be. Her skin appeared much paler since I'd last seen her on the boat.

There were two chairs just inside the door to my left. Olivia sat in one, and Sam took the other.

Darcy smiled weakly when I walked in. "Hey, Jo." Her voice was hoarse as if she'd been screaming.

"Hey, yourself." I didn't move from the doorway.

Olivia inclined her head slightly, as though

trying to tell me it was okay for me to enter. I wanted to wait for a minute or two. I was still trying to get my body to calm after seeing Webb. Moreover, I just didn't know what to say to Darcy. Since she'd called me an "effin' animal" on the boat, I would have been surprised if she wanted anything to do with me. Her words had hurt, but I couldn't blame her.

"So how long have you two been vampires?" she asked, breaking the silence.

"A couple of months," Sam said. He was relaxing in his usual position with his legs extended and ankles crossed, slumping in the chair.

Hearing Sam's answer made me shake my head. It seemed as if we'd been vampires for a thousand years.

"Is Ben okay?" she asked.

"We don't know if he's out of the coma yet," Sam said. "We're waiting to hear from the hospital."

A tear escaped from Darcy's left eye. "Is he… human?" she asked.

I prayed he was, but… "Yes," I lied. I didn't want her to think anything else.

More tears fell down her cheeks.

I started to cry too.

"Darcy, do you know anything about your father's latest case or any of his recent cases?" Sam asked before reaching out a hand to pull me into the room.

I had forgotten about Edmund saying her father owed a debt.

Darcy wiped away tears with her fingers. "I don't understand. Why would that matter?"

"When you were at the mansion, did Edmund share anything with you about why he kidnapped you?" I asked, wiping away my own tears.

"No. Once we left the boat, he took me to the mansion and locked me in a room on the second floor. The only per—I mean, the vampire who came into my room was that tall guy, Jonah. He brought me food. I didn't eat it. Then your dad showed up. Why are you asking if I know anything about my father's cases?"

"It seems you were kidnapped because your father owes a debt to someone that Edmund knows," Sam said.

"I don't know anything about my dad's business," she said.

I sat on the arm of Sam's chair as Dad ambled in. He glanced at me before sitting on the edge of the bed.

Darcy jumped into his arms.

Olivia, Sam, and I exchanged looks. I couldn't

speak for them, but I was completely astounded by Dad hugging her, trying to comfort her. It was as if they were father and daughter. She was terrified, and after seeing Edmund in action on the boat, not to mention me, I couldn't blame her for seeking shelter and comfort in the arms of the vampire who had rescued her.

She began to sob.

"Shhh," Dad said. "It'll be all right. We won't let them harm you."

Her grief seemed to pull me to her. I wanted nothing more than to help her. So I rose to sit on the other side of the bed. Pulling away from Dad, Darcy looked at me.

"I'm sorry this has happened to you," I said. "I know all this is too much to handle. Believe me, I had a hard time with it, myself. Even now that I'm a vampire, I'm still struggling with it," I explained, stealing a look at Dad before swinging my gaze back to Darcy. "We're here for you. All of us."

I was about to stand when she threw her arms around me. I froze for two reasons. One, I didn't think she would ever talk to me again. Two, and more importantly, her scent made my fangs descend. Seeking help from Dad, I raised my eyebrows, keeping my lips glued together.

You can do it, he mouthed.

I wasn't so sure. Her smell burned my nostrils

and my throat. Taking in a deep breath, I tamped down the urge to sink my fangs into my best friend. The last thing I wanted to do was frighten her. "Darcy... um... can you let go?"

"Oh, I'm sorry," she said, wiping tears from her eyes again.

When she did, my fangs retracted. How my fangs went back in was beyond me because the sweet cotton candy scent still called to me. "No worries. It's just hard for me. I'm not as strong as my dad yet. You smell amazing, and I'm trying really hard not to let the vampire come out." I stood.

"That's why you haven't called, isn't it? Because I'm human." She crossed her legs underneath her, picking at the blanket.

"Yeah."

Dr. Vieira came in. "How are you feeling, Darcy?"

She kept her tearful gaze on Dad. "Okay. I want to go home."

"We'll contact your parents. Your father was here earlier, and I owe him a phone call. For now, you need to get some rest. Trauma has a way of doing damage to the body," Dad said, rising.

"I'm going to give you something to help you sleep for a while." Dr. Vieira plucked a syringe from his lab coat.

"No, I don't want anything," she muttered.

"Hey." Dad rubbed her arm. "It will help. I promise there's nothing in the sedative that will harm you. You can trust me." He nodded at the doc.

Dr. Vieira lifted Darcy's sleeve near her right shoulder then eased the needle into her arm before pushing down the plunger.

She relaxed against the bed. "Will you be here, Mr. Mason, when I wake up?"

"Someone will be. Now sleep," Dad said. "Sam, Jo, let's take a walk. Olivia, you may leave. Dr. Vieira will be here to monitor her."

"Yes, sir," Olivia said then left the room.

"Jo, will you come back?" Darcy asked.

"I sure will. My dad's right. You need some rest now, but I'll definitely be back. Maybe we can go see Ben together when we get word from the hospital."

"I would... like... that." Her voice trailed off as her eyes closed.

With Webb still out and Darcy asleep, Dad, Sam, and I exited the building. Since the Sentinels were still sweeping for bugs, Dad thought it best to talk outside the base. I didn't blame him. I was still worried about someone getting in to harm Webb, and Darcy was still in danger too. Edmund had kidnapped her for something her father had done, so the threat wasn't over for her yet.

The three of us walked down the beach, not far from where Tripp had landed the RIB the night before. Clouds dotted the sky, occasionally blocking the moon's bright rays as they skated by. The low tide gave way to several holes in the sand. As the water receded, a crab popped out of one of them then scurried down the beach with its black eyes glinting in the moonlight.

We stopped not too far from the base.

Sam picked a few rocks and tossed them into the bay. Dad leaned against a large flat rock near the edge of the woods, chewing on his cheek. I sidled up to him, and he put his arm around me. "It's been one hell of a night," he said.

I rested my head on his shoulder. "I wouldn't say that. The past two days were horrific."

"I'm sorry you went through hell on that ocean, Jo." He squeezed me. "I'm really sorry for everything that has happened to you and Sam in your lives. I have many regrets that I can't change. I've made mistakes. Please know that while the future will not be easy, I will always be here for you and Sam."

I didn't doubt his words. His tone rang with honesty and love. Nonetheless, the part about the future scared the crap out of me.

Sam walked up, looking worried over something.

I straightened. "What's wrong with you?"

A soft breeze ruffled his hair. "You scared me in that basement."

"*I* did? You're the one who made my heart stop. You seemed calm and in no pain. What's up with that?"

"Once the swords were in me, I didn't feel a thing. I blocked all the pain, even when Edmund sliced through my stomach. Then when Sloan removed the swords, it hurt like a mother—well... it hurt." He let out a deep breath.

"So how did you and Webb get captured?" I hadn't thought about that yet.

Sam combed his fingers through his hair.

"Yes, son. How did you?" Dad had a confused expression on his face.

"When Kodiak, Olivia, Webb, and I walked into the mansion, we immediately engaged in battle. The vamps were coming out of nowhere. We fought until all seven were dead. Olivia and Webb disappeared down a hallway, and Kodiak and I were headed to the basement. But then I heard Kate's voice behind me. So I stopped and backtracked. When I did, I walked right into her and a Taser, and I went down. It hurt like hell. I didn't know they made Tasers to incapacitate a vamp," Sam said.

I did. I'd seen Sloan use one on Jonah the day Webb picked me up from school.

"Then," Sam continued, "the vamp with her shackled me with those cobalt restraints."

"And Webb?" I asked.

"He must've heard Kate's voice too. No sooner than I was down, he ran into the room. He stopped cold when he saw Kate with the Taser in her hands. He asked her what she was doing, and she told him that she was living her life. They argued. He tried to reason with her, but Edmund came out of nowhere. Webb wasn't prepared for him. He tried to fight Edmund, but Kate used the Taser on him too. They dragged us down to the basement. By the time we got down there, the effects of the Taser had worn off, but the shackles kept us immobile. So we couldn't do much. Then Edmund got word that you, sis, were on your way into the basement. That's when he set up the scene that you walked into. He thought it would be great for you to see us die."

My blood boiled as I listened to him. I hated Kate and Edmund. I abandoned my spot near dad and went to hug Sam.

"I'm okay, sis."

"I know. I just want to hug you. Is that all right?"

I took his silence as a yes.

Suddenly, Dad joined the hug fest. "I love you both of you," he said, his voice cracking.

After another second, the three of us broke apart.

"So, Pops?" Sam said. "Given what we know about Kate, do you think she had anything to do with tainted boxed blood?"

"It's possible," Dad said, resuming his position on the rock.

The subject of Kate reminded me of something she'd said. "Sam, Kate told me you came on to her that night she lost her cell phone. Is that true?"

Dad growled.

"What else did she tell you?" Sam's voice was low.

"That after that night, you didn't want anything to do with her."

"Son?"

Sam dropped his head back to look up at the night sky. "I did kiss her in that stairwell. She came running in." He lowered his head. "When she saw me at the door, she froze. I sensed something from her. I couldn't tell what it was. I didn't know I was an Empath then. She gave off this strong vibe. I asked her why she was in such a hurry and what she was doing in the prison building. Before I knew it, she had me up against the wall under the stairwell, and we were kissing. After that night, she tried to continue where we left off on several occasions, but her emotions seemed fake. While I didn't know at the time what it meant, I still wanted to steer clear. Besides, I couldn't really get into Kate when I had a hard time with Webb near you." He glanced at me.

"Admirable, son. But why didn't you tell me she was in the prison building?" Dad asked in a calm tone.

"Kate is one of you. She works for you. Why would I question that?"

"She's not a Sentinel. She did a lot of intelligence work for us, but she's far from a Sentinel," Dad said. "It doesn't matter. She's made her position known. Now we have to decide how we're going to handle her and the Plutariums. She's going to be more of a problem for us than Edmund. She knows all our secrets. This war is going to get much, much worse."

Just what I wanted to hear.

"On another note, I wanted to share some news with you and clear up a few things before anything else happens," Dad said.

Sam sidled up to Dad, and I parked my butt on the sand. The adrenaline that had kept me going was slowly draining from my system.

"Let's start with school. Jo, as I mentioned in the pyramid room, the school and the Council of

Eternal Affairs will be conducting a hearing about the Turner boy. You and I will be present for the hearing in two weeks. Until then, you're not allowed back."

Oh joy!

If he read my mind, he ignored me. "Sam, you'll return to school when classes resume next week. In the meantime, I need you here to help clean up some of this mess."

"Anything, Pops."

I raised an eyebrow at Sam. He hated school, or at least his uniform.

He grinned at me.

He was probably doing a silent jig in his head.

"As for my situation with the murder investigation of the Secretary of the Navy, I'm not sure what's going to happen." He let out a sigh then continued, "We have a lot to do to get our lives back in order. I'll need both of you to contribute where you can. Sam, I want you to continue training with Tripp on the weapons."

"Jo should learn too," Sam added.

My head shot up, eyes wide.

Sam glared at me. "You should learn how to handle at least one."

"It's a good idea, Pumpkin," Dad said. "Also, I do want both of you to continue your physical training with Olivia. She's done a great job with both of you. Are we clear?"

"Yes," Sam and I said in unison.

I didn't want to argue the point of learning how to use a weapon. After that night, I was warming to the idea.

"Now about your friend, Darcy. Her—"

Dad's phone rang. He removed it from his belt. "Yes. When? We'll be right there." He tapped the screen before slipping it into its case. "Webb is awake."

"What? Already?" I sprang up.

"Not so fast." Dad wrapped a hand around my arm. "Remember what we talked about, Jo," he said, searching my eyes.

"I know. I want to see him."

Dad had said a lot, and none of it mattered just then. All that was important was getting my tail into the medical facility, and I couldn't unless Dad unlocked those freaking doors.

The three of us made our way back. I cleared my head as much as I could. I didn't know what to expect when I laid eyes on Webb. On one hand, Dad had said he would be in a bad place, but I took comfort in knowing that Webb was awake. On the other, uneasiness grabbed me. My pulse raced as I considered whether Webb would still be the same blue-eyed vampire I had come to care so much about.

VOICES TRICKLED out of Webb's room. Tripp and Sloan were laughing. Olivia made a snide remark to one of them. Dad and Sam barged in, but I hung out in the hall. I was thankful that the closed blinds on the room's window shielded my view. So close to Webb, I wasn't sure what to do. The first thing that came to mind was to run in and jump on his bed, but that wouldn't have been proper. With everyone in the room, I had to be a grown-up.

I leaned against one of the lab benches for a minute, trying to calm my quivering stomach.

"She's outside," Dad said. "She's fine. She'll be in shortly."

Sam stuck out his head.

I shook mine.

As if he knew what I was trying to say, he ducked back into the room.

Then Webb's voice was in my head. *Why don't you come in, beautiful?*

Oh God. My cheeks burned. I couldn't. They would read me like a book. Plus, Dad would read my mind if he wasn't already. *Give me a minute.*

There are too many people in there. I'm claustrophobic. It wasn't a lie, just not the whole truth.

Within a few seconds, Tripp, Sloan, and Olivia walked out. "Hey, Jo," Tripp said. "You okay?"

I looked into his bronze eyes. "Yeah. I'm tired, that's all."

"Why don't you go in? I'm sure Webb would love to see you." He met Olivia and Sloan at the double doors. "See you soon."

The three of them walked out.

I took a deep breath and braved my way in.

Biting my bottom lip, I met Webb's soul-stealing blue eyes but immediately dropped my gaze. Sam and Dad were still in the room. Sam couldn't read my emotions. At least, that was what he had told me in Ms. Lawrence's office the other day. We hadn't had a chance to discuss the topic to find out why. Maybe because he was still a new vampire. On the other hand, Dad...

"Son, why don't we get down to the control room? Maybe you can call the hospital and check on Ben," Dad suggested.

My head snapped up. I knew I should go with Sam to find out if Ben was okay. After all, I owed him big time. But while I wanted more than anything for Ben to come out of his coma, every fiber of my being kept my feet glued to the floor, as though a metaphysical source held me there.

"Sure. Webb, good to have you back, man," Sam said.

"I should go with you, Sam," I said, not looking at Webb. I knew if I did, I would break down.

"Sis, I can handle it. There's not much you can do for Ben right now." Then he whispered in my ear at a very low tone. "Webb needs you. He needs comfort. I can feel it. By the way, I can also feel your emotions now. I sense you're struggling with this, and you're scared. Don't be. I'll let you know about Ben. Now, go to Webb."

My brother continued to surprise the heck out of me, and not so much because he could feel my emotions. Nope, that wasn't it. "Webb needs you" rendered me speechless.

"Jo, don't stay too long. Webb needs to get some rest. I need him healthy." Dad kissed me on the head.

With everyone gone, the tension suddenly skyrocketed. My feet were still glued to the floor. My hands shook, and a bead of sweat dripped down my back. I kept my gaze down. My breathing became shallow. Webb was awake. He was alive. And I was a basket of nerves.

"Jo, are you okay?" His voice was low. "Would you sit with me?"

I peered at him through lowered lashes.

"Hey, are you afraid of me?"

God, I wasn't afraid of him. It was me I worried about. My body was about to shatter for some reason. I blew out a breath and slowly ambled toward his bed.

"Sit here." He patted the small space next to him as he scooted over.

Easing up on the bed, I placed my hands in my lap. They didn't stay there long. He grabbed one of them. His touch was cool, not warm like it usually was. He probably still needed more blood, but I noticed his skin had lost the grayish pallor.

"Are... you... going to be..." *Where is my voice?*

"I just need to rest, and Dr. Vieira is making one of those bloodshakes you like. He says it should help energize me and heal my system a little faster."

"Minus my dad's blood, I hope."

"I'm sure he'll add the right blood." Bringing my hand to his mouth, he kissed it. "Look at me."

Tears escaped all of sudden. Between his voice, his lips on my hand, and the fact I was sitting close to him, I lost it.

"Hey, beautiful. Please don't cry." He wrapped me in his arms. "I'm going to be fine. Why don't you put your legs up on the bed? You'll be more comfortable."

I stopped breathing.

As if he sensed the change in me, he said, "Relax. It's okay."

I adjusted my body so I was curled up next to him, with my head on his chest and his right arm over mine.

"Now, close your eyes. I'm not going anywhere," he whispered.

I released a sigh as my head rose and fell with every breath he took. "Webb, I'm sorry. I tried to stop them."

"Shhh. Is that what has you so upset? You blame yourself? None of this is your fault. Don't ever think that. Let's rest," he said in a silky tone, kissing my temple.

"I should go. My dad will lose a fang. He told me not to stay long." Images of Dad yelling and growling flooded my mind, although he had said he knew I liked Webb, and he had left us alone. Still, relaxing against the gorgeous vampire might be quite difficult. Not only because of Dad, but...

"Don't worry about your father."

Okay, that statement got my attention. "What does that mean?" I tried to sit up.

He wouldn't let me.

"It means I know your father. He knows I'd never do anything to hurt you. Let's just lie here."

I guess it wouldn't hurt to rest for a while.

Closing my eyes, I snuggled deeper, adjusting my right arm so it wrapped around his stomach.

"That's better," he whispered.

His voice, his breathing, his touch all lulled me into a world that I could get lost in forever. As sleep tugged at me, my mind cleared, and my body relaxed. The earth tilted on its axis for the tenth time in a matter of days, but my intuition told me that it wouldn't stay like that for long.

33

Someone was playing with my hair while the light in the room burned my eyelids. I squinted then rubbed my eyes with my right hand. I had no feeling in my left arm. Then it dawned on me. I couldn't have slept the entire time in Webb's arms.

I blinked several times to clear my vision, but I didn't have to. Webb's body against my face and his hands in my hair told me I was still lying next to him in his hospital bed. *Oh God. How long was I asleep?* Dad was going to stake me.

"Hey, there," Webb whispered. "Feel better?"

I didn't know how to answer that. I didn't feel better. I'd fallen asleep with the gorgeous vampire.

"Your heart is beating hard. Don't panic. Your father came in a couple of times."

It was a good thing he couldn't see the horror on my face. "Dad came in... here?" My tongue could barely move.

"He did. We talked about several things while you slept."

"And?" Oh, I had to hear that part.

"And nothing. I told him you were fine. Not to move you."

I swallowed so hard it echoed in the room. Or maybe I choked. If I could've jumped off the bed, I would have, but my legs were asleep. I must've stayed in the same position for hours. "What time is it?" I asked.

"About ten in the morning. By the way, Sam spoke with Petty Officer Hunter. Ben woke up a few hours ago. We're having him transported back here. Dr. Vieira needs to run a series of tests on Ben, given Edmund's experiments on him."

I raised my upper body, but the strong vampire wouldn't let me up yet.

"Not so fast, beautiful."

"Why?" I loved that he didn't want me to move.

"I like you next to me." He stroked my arm. "And we need to talk."

My heart rolled off the bed. He sounded as if

he was about to deliver bad news. "We need to talk" was never good.

"A lot has happened in the past couple of days."

Boy, that was the understatement of the century.

"And I'm sorry that you've had a rough go of it as a vampire. Some of it, of course, was your own stubbornness."

"Hey, are you trying to get to a point about something?" I asked. "Remember, my limbs are going to fall off if I don't move soon."

"I am. I'm also sorry that Kate used you in her quest to support Edmund. What she's done devastates me beyond belief. I don't know how I'm going to process all of it. I know right this moment, I'm numb. I'm telling you all this because I know you're worried about me, and I don't want you to be. I don't want you to bear this burden. It's mine to bear and mine alone. Okay?"

"My dad told you that I was worried, didn't he?"

"He did, but he also didn't have to. I sensed it when you walked into the room."

I was about to climbed off the bed. "I need to stand, Webb. My left arm lost circulation hours ago."

"One minute. I'm not quite finished." He let out a breath, and his heart rate picked up.

What is he so nervous about?

"After we settle things with Ben and Darcy, we all need some quiet time." He cupped my face, peering down through mile-long lashes that framed those amazing eyes of his. "I would like to show you a special place of mine this afternoon," he said, his gaze sweeping over me.

My heart either stopped beating or beat so fast it seemed that way. Webb London, gorgeous vampire, was asking me out.

"You can close your mouth. Don't be so shocked. Since the day I laid eyes on you in Mr. Jackson's office, I haven't been able to get you out of my head. And I think those few times we've been alone recently are proof of that."

Silence grew like a thick fog on a humid night.

"I have to ask my dad," I said, cutting through the soupy silence.

"Is that a yes?"

"It depends on my dad," I lied.

Dad could try to barricade me in one of his prison cells, but there was no way I was turning Webb down. Not in a zillion years.

Webb grinned. "Your father will agree."

"You're sure?" I knitted my brows together.

He smiled. "I already asked him."

"You did?" My voice hitched. "Doesn't matter. I still need to ask him."

"Jo, your father is a very old-fashioned vampire. He believes a man should ask permission to court his daughter. I acknowledge that. And he is my boss, so I need to respect him as such."

"Still, I need to have my own conversation with him. But the answer is yes."

He bowed his head, his lips brushing mine. A bag of feathers exploded in my stomach, raining down, tickling the lining.

"Thank you. Now you can get up."

I eased out of bed and walked around, trying to get the blood circulating. "Are you feeling well enough to move around?" I asked as my limbs came alive.

"I'm fine. Dr. Vieira gave me one of those shakes while you were sleeping. It seemed to do the trick."

Yeah, Dr. Vieira and I had to talk. I wanted to know all the ingredients in those shakes. "Are they bringing Ben here now?"

"I don't know. Sam has the information. Come here, Jo."

I didn't hesitate. I walked over to the bed.

We stared at each other as he searched my face. "You never answered my question. Are you feeling okay this morning?" he said, his tone husky.

My heart was beating too quickly as I continued to get lost in his blue depths. I wasn't sure I could speak, so I nodded.

Before I knew what was happening, he reached up to frame my face with his hands, and his lips caressed mine softly, and it made me shudder.

"I'll see you this afternoon," he said against my lips. Then he sat back against the bed.

Wow! What a way to get the blood flowing, but I wasn't sure I could move. The only thing that made me head for the door, although on shaky legs, was the thought of a desperately needed shower.

Halfway out of the room, I turned. "Webb, what if I'd said no?"

"I wouldn't have let you off this bed." A playful grin tugged at the edges of his luscious lips.

I smiled then walked out. I didn't even want to think how that would've worked. In the meantime, I needed to get as far away from his room as possible before I decided to jump back in bed with the vampire who was stealing my heart more and more every day.

34

After I left Webb's room, I ran to the apartment. Halfway there, I remembered that Darcy had been in one of the rooms next to Webb. I almost backtracked to see her, but a shower topped my list, and I was hungry.

Once in the apartment, I snagged a container of blood from the fridge then went to my room and flopped on the bed. My mind raced with all kinds of questions. *Is Ben still human? Will he be okay? Where are the Plutariums now? What's next on their agenda?* Then school loomed in the distance. I had the hearing to attend regarding the death of Blake Turner and could be facing a murder sentence. Then there was Dad's plight over the death of the Secretary of the Navy. The future was stacking up to be quite a blowout.

I must've dozed off because the next thing I knew, Sam's voice penetrated my hazy brain. "Jo, wake up."

I raised my head to find my brother standing over me.

"Hey," he said. "I just spoke to Webb. He told me that he's taking you off base today."

"Yeah." I rubbed my eyes.

"Like a date?"

"I guess." I sat up.

He scrunched his eyebrows together. "Where is he taking you?"

"A special place of his."

"Mmm."

I waited for him to say more or complain or even tell me I couldn't go. But he just stood there with his arms crossed over his chest and a blank expression on his face.

"No words of wisdom?" I asked.

He smiled. "I hope you have a good time."

Ooookay. Is this my brother? The one who tried to beat the crap out of Webb? The one who pulled a gun on Webb?

"You aren't going to stop me?"

The mattress dipped as he sat. "No. I told you

that he cares for you. I feel his emotions, Jo. Besides, he knows that I'll kill him if he hurts you."

I didn't want to think about that last statement, so I changed the subject. "When does Ben arrive?"

"He's been here for a couple of hours already."

"Really?" I looked at the clock. "It's one in the afternoon?" I guess I did more than just doze off.

He shrugged. "Everyone is waiting for you. Dad and Darcy are talking with Ben right now."

"Where's Webb?"

"I don't know. I haven't seen him for a couple of hours. Come on, sis." He stood.

"I have to take a shower."

"Then get moving." Sam ambled to the door. "I'll wait for you in the family room." Then he was gone.

The shower felt good as I scrubbed the crud off me. I washed my hair three times just to get all the dust and debris out of it.

As I toweled off, a ball of knots took root in my stomach. I was about to see Ben, and I had no idea what I was going to say. And I had a date with a handsome vampire. Anxiety and excitement waged a serious war in me.

I combed through my wet hair and took one last look in the mirror before getting dressed.

I settled for a pair of jeans, a light-pink blouse with a wide band underneath my breasts that tied in the back, a pair of flats, and a light sweater. The weather was warm, but I didn't know how long Webb and I would be gone. When the sun set, it still got cool in the evenings.

Satisfied, I joined Sam at the front door.

He sized me up. "Nice, sis."

My brother had changed from his jeans into a black cargo uniform, as though he was going on another mission.

"Why are you wearing that?" I asked.

"I'm off to train with Tripp out in the woods this afternoon."

"Train?"

"We're going to be crawling around, shooting, sword fighting—all the things the Sentinels train for," he said as we walked to the medical facility.

He was taking all the training seriously. "Do we know if Ben is..."

"Human?" Sam finished my sentence.

I nodded.

"Dr. V. didn't say."

I really wished I knew before I walked in to see him. I guess it didn't matter. In the end, I had to thank him for saving my life.

We made it to the medical facility and stopped at the double doors. Dad had given Sam access to a few of the security locks and retina displays. I didn't have access yet, but that was the last thing on my mind. Besides, the codes changed frequently, especially since Kate made herself known as a traitor.

"You ready?" Sam held open the door.

I shrugged. "As I'll ever be." I didn't know what I was walking into, but mere minutes would reveal the answer.

A mixture of scents lingered in the lab, cotton candy dominating over the alcohol. As I drew closer to Ben's room, I sniffed, trying to capture that burned-sugar fragrance of his, but Darcy's scent overpowered everything.

Sam stalked in before me with confidence, as though he owned the place. He sure was morphing into a different person. I didn't know if I was happy or scared. The past two months had whizzed by like a bullet train. Day by day, Sam and I both seemed to be growing and changing constantly, not only in our physical appearance, but in the way we thought, acted, and lived. Maybe because we were vampires. Maybe because we had our father back. Or maybe because we were getting older. Whatever the case, the future made me nervous as hell.

Ben was sitting up in bed with Darcy standing on one side and Sam on the other. My brother had engaged Ben and Darcy in conversation by the time I walked in. They jerked their heads in my direction as I sidled up to Dad, who was standing near the door. I smiled and waved to them.

Darcy looked ten times better than she had the day before. The rest she'd gotten from the sedative worked wonders. It looked as though she had taken a shower. Her silky blond hair spilled over her shoulders, and her skin had a soft glow to it.

"Come here, Jo." She waved.

"Just a minute." I looked at Ben.

His eyes met mine, and he smiled.

I couldn't help but return the gesture. I was a sucker for his dimples.

He blinked, motioning with his head for me to join them. He seemed to be ignoring whatever Sam was saying.

I nodded, keeping my eyes locked on his as I subtly inhaled, trying to scent if he was still human.

Dad's voice resonated in my head. For some reason, I didn't feel the pain associated with his telepathic connection that I usually did. *He's human. Dr. Vieira had a complete DNA and blood screening workup when Ben came out of the coma. The results just came in.*

You're sure?

Dad nodded.

So, do we know why he was immune to the serum? I asked.

That will take more time. Ben's father is on his way, and so is Mr. Rose. I talked to them both this morning. This doesn't look good for us. Mr. Jackson has friends in high places, and he has made a lot of waves over this, which I was afraid would happen.

What about Mr. Rose? Edmund kidnapped Darcy because of a debt he owes.

That, Pumpkin, is a topic I'm not sure we're going to get to the bottom of anytime soon.

So... we trust Ben not to tell his dad about vampires, but what about Darcy? I looked up at him.

Wait, I've never trusted the boy. On the other hand, I'm not too worried about Darcy. If her father owes a debt to a friend of Edmund's, I can promise you that Mr. Rose is very well aware of vampires. And after speaking with Webb, it turns out Mr. Rose has defended a few vampires over the years. His eyebrows were pinched together.

Okay, I wasn't touching any of that, though it did confirm why Webb had growled when I said Mr. Rose defended criminals.

The gorgeous vampire sauntered in. His hair was pulled back in a low ponytail. He wore a pair of jeans that hung low on his hips and a T-shirt that showed off his toned biceps and broad chest. I took in a heartening breath at the sight of him. It was the first time I had seen Webb in blue jeans. I swept my gaze over him, trying not to make my racing heart known. It was useless.

He flashed me a grin as he moved next to Dad. Heat built inside me, causing the butterflies to go wild. I swallowed hard as I read the words stamped on the front of his T-shirt: *SEALs Rule.*

Boy, wasn't that the truth. That vampire without a doubt ruled my heart and quite possibly my soul. I realized in that moment that it was the first time I had paid more attention to him than Ben when they were in the same room. In the past, I'd always given Ben my full attention, but not anymore. Everything had turned a hundred and eighty degrees, as had the temperature of my skin.

"Jo, I want to speak to you outside."

Dad's voice pulled me from my drunken stupor over Webb. It took every ounce of energy to knit the molecules back together in my brain so that my feet would move. If Dad had read any of my thoughts, I didn't care, not in the least.

When we were in the hall, Dad rubbed his jaw. "You—"

"I know, Dad. Webb asked you if he could take me out. I was going to ask you if I could go, but I haven't had the chance."

"You have my permission. I know he'll be a gentleman, but that's not why we're out here. You and Sam need to wrap this up with Ben and Darcy.

I don't want you around when Mr. Jackson arrives."

"Why?" I scrunched my nose.

"Fewer questions. Fewer emotional outbursts. Sam is headed out to train with Tripp. Say your goodbyes. Webb is ready to go. He needs some time off, anyway. Sloan is standing in to help for the day." Dad kissed me on the forehead then went back into the room.

It was one time I wasn't going to argue with him. After seeing the drool-worthy vampire in jeans and a T-shirt, not to mention the smile that sizzled my insides, I didn't know if I could even speak to anyone. Still, I had a few things to clear up with Ben. It should have been easy, but my stomach suddenly hurt.

Buck up. Talk to Ben, my inner voice said.

Yeah. So, were you not there when Ben said, "When this is over, Jo, we need to talk." I screamed back.

I straightened my posture, took a deep breath, then walked in, stopping near the door.

Sam and Darcy were still chatting with Ben. Webb and Dad were whispering about something near the far window.

My pulse began to race. There were too many people in the room. If I was going to talk with Ben, I couldn't do it in front of everyone. I'd already been through that once, and it had been painful, especially with Webb and Dad in the room.

I kept my focus on Ben. I needed to get my head in the game if I wanted to get it over with. Looking at Webb would only make me more nervous.

"Sam, it's time. You need to go," Dad said.

No doubt he had read my mind.

"Hey, buddy, you get better. You're in good hands with Dr. Vieira," Sam said.

He and Ben exchanged some weird handshake before Sam stopped next to me. "Have a great time today, sis," he whispered in my ear. "Love you." Then he was gone.

"Darcy, can you please go with Webb? Dr. Vieira wants to check you one more time before your father arrives," Dad said. "Lieutenant, Dr. Vieira is in his office."

Darcy said her goodbyes to Ben then walked over to me. "Jo, can I give you a hug?" she asked.

I looked to Dad for permission. I didn't have to, but he seemed to be directing traffic.

He nodded.

"Sure," I replied.

We hugged each other. As soon as I wrapped my arms around her, my eyes watered. I did miss her. She could be annoying at times, but she had a heart of gold. She was the only person at Durfee

High School who'd come to my rescue that day in gym class when Blake Turner tripped me, and I fell face-first into the mud. I hated that she was caught up in all this.

"I'm sorry about everything, Darcy. I've really missed you. Maybe we can hang out sometime." I had no clue if we could or how that would work. We needed time to settle things. If her dad was mixed up with vampires, maybe our paths would cross again soon.

"I would love that. I have one stipulation, though. No biting. If you bite me, I'll have to bite back."

I laughed.

"Darcy," Webb said, touching her shoulder.

"He's hot, by the way," she whispered in my ear.

Same old Darcy I loved. Always checking out the opposite sex.

No doubt Webb heard what she said.

"Don't give him a big head," I whispered back, grinning at the vampire standing behind her.

She let go and disappeared with Webb.

I let out a deep breath, trying to calm my racing heart. It was crazy. Somehow, it was easier to talk to Ben in a fit of rage and panic and hunger on a sinking boat than it was in the quiet of the room. All that aside, I did owe him an apology, for two reasons. I wanted to explain why I couldn't go to the dance with him. We hadn't closed the book on that one. Plus, I'd been a jerk to him on the boat when he was trying to tell me he was sorry. But more importantly, I owed him a huge thank you for saving my life.

You can do this. You have to do this.

"Jo, I'll be right outside," Dad said. "Make it quick, though."

Ha. Quick? We'll see.

I waited for Dad to leave before I made my way over to the bed.

Ben studied me for a long second. "It's really good to see you," he said. "You look fantastic, by the way."

"You too." Tears pooled in my eyes.

"I'm so glad you're alive, Jo." He reached out and took my hand. "I can't believe we're both here."

"I know. I thought you were dead. When I saw that wave swallow you... anyway." I gulped in air. "Thank you for tying me to that buoy and saving my life. If not for you, I wouldn't be here."

"You don't have to thank me. I'd do anything to save you, Jo." His voice was soft.

"I still don't know how we survived all that."

He tugged me lightly, motioning for me to sit

down, so I did. Then he brushed away a tear that fell with his fingertips.

"How did you tie me to that buoy? You went under with the large wave." I sat facing him with one knee bent.

He placed his hand on my leg. "After the wave washed over me, I was able to swim to the surface. When I did, you were floating toward me, unconscious. I tried to get you to wake up, but I think you swallowed too much water. I managed to get both of us to the buoy. The waves were still out of control. We were thrashing around pretty good. My arms were weak, and I was getting tired. I couldn't hold you and hold on myself. So I ripped off my shirt and tied you to the buoy. I had just finished when a wave swallowed us, and I went under. That was the last thing I remember."

"Thank you again," I whispered. "Ben, I'm also sorry—"

"Don't, Jo. I'm the one that should be apologizing. I'm sorry about what I said about vampires. I don't think of you like you're a 'fucking vampire.' I just don't see you as a vampire, *period*."

"What?" I asked. I couldn't believe what I was hearing.

I was about to stand when he said, "Please, let me explain."

I straightened my posture, pulling back

slightly. "I could've killed you on that boat," I reminded him.

"I don't believe that you would have, Jo."

"Did you lose brain cells in the ocean?" He was stubborn or insane.

"Remember that night in the women's barracks, after you got the news that you would have to turn vampire to save Sam?" he asked.

I nodded. I did remember that night. We'd talked, and something had sparked between us, but I was human then.

"I've always liked you, Jo. But that night, I realized how much I like you. I told you that night I didn't want to lose you. I still don't. I don't care that you're a vampire. To me, you're still the same person I knew as a human. I care about you, Jo."

I sprung off the bed and backed away. "Ben, I'm not the same person. I'm not even the same species as you."

"I get that," he said. "We could try to make us work."

"What about Darcy? You kissed her on the boat." I ran my fingers through my hair and let out a deep breath.

"We're just friends," he said.

"What? Friends don't kiss like that."

"She was frightened. I thought it would help to

calm her," he replied. "Jo, we could start slow, you and me."

"Ben, you're not listening. There is no you and me."

"I saw how you struggled when I was sitting in your father's office. I saw the look in your eyes," he said in an unwavering tone.

"You're right. When you saw me in my father's office, I was struggling. Not for the reasons you think, though. It took every ounce of energy I had not to sink my fangs into you. That's what I feel. Do you get it?"

A muscle in his jaw ticked, his lips tightening.

A long few seconds of silence settled in the room.

His nostrils flared. "I don't give a shit," he said, raising his voice.

"I'm a vampire, Ben. I'm not human. When will you get that through your head? I spoke in a calm tone, holding back my anger.

All that serum that had been injected into him had to have been messing with his brain.

"Look." I moved closer to the bed. "I'm ecstatic that you're alive. I'm overjoyed that you saved my life. I care what happens to you. I consider you a good friend."

His eyes bored into me like he was trying to change me back to a human.

"Pumpkin, is everything okay in here?" Dad asked. I looked to see him leaning in the doorway.

The door to the room was never closed. I imagined Dad had been listening the entire time.

"Yes." Then I turned my attention back to Ben. "Just so we're clear. I care what happens to you. I would like to be friends. However, if being friends is not possible, I understand." My tone rose with every sentence. I wanted to wrap my hands around his throat and shake some sense into him.

"Are you leaving with Webb?" Ben asked angrily.

"Son, that is none of your business," Dad cut in.

I jerked my head toward Dad. His eyes silvered.

Power charged the room. Ben was about to piss off the most powerful vampire. *Christ! Didn't he learn his lesson with Webb?* He had no idea what he was getting himself into. "Dad, stay out of this," I pleaded. I needed to leave. Ben's anger was climbing quickly, but I had to make sure he understood. "Ben..."

Before I could finish the sentence, Ben reached out and yanked my wrist, pulling me onto the bed. God, he was strong. I landed in his lap.

In a blur, Dad had his hand around Ben's arm. "What do you think you're doing? Remove your hands from my daughter," Dad said through gritted teeth.

"What's going on?" Webb had returned. His eyes narrowed, and he stilled.

"Get her out of here, Lieutenant," Dad growled.

Ben stared at me like I was the spawn of the devil before his gaze darted to Webb.

"Ben, let her go," Webb said calmly.

"Listen to him, son," Dad added.

After several long quiet seconds that felt like hours, Ben released me.

I stood. "Why are you acting this way?"

Ben jerked his head toward me. "I told you I wasn't giving up. I'm not, Jo." His voice was shaky.

"Humans and vamps just won't work, Ben. Why can't you get that?" I asked.

"Because I don't agree," Ben snapped.

"Lieutenant, now." Dad's deep voice indicated he was on the verge of exploding.

Webb took my hand. "Jo, let's go."

I stared at Ben as Webb tugged me to the door. Anger painted Ben's face red.

"I'm sorry, Ben," I said before I lost eye contact with him and the door to his room closed.

Why didn't he understand? Why would he lash out in front of my father?

Webb and I made it into the elevator, and he

pushed the button for the lobby. Once the doors closed, he pulled me to him. "Are you okay?"

I nodded once. "I don't get it. Why would he act like that?" I asked, more rhetorically than anything.

"I don't know. But let's get out of here." He leaned down and placed a light kiss on my lips when the elevator doors opened.

My heart skipped like a schoolgirl playing hopscotch from his gentle kiss, but I was still baffled and angry with Ben. *Damn it! This is supposed to be a good day. No, a great day. I have a date with a sexy-as-hell vampire. My first date, no less.*

When we walked out into the warm sunshine, I froze.

"What's wrong, beautiful?"

"Is that for us?" My mouth hung open.

He held out his hand. "Yes. Now, come on."

I walked toward a tall man in a black suit who held a door to a limo open, and tears came to my eyes. A limo!

All thoughts vanished. Nothing mattered in that moment except one vampire.

WE HAD BEEN on the road for over an hour. The car was still dead silent for some reason. Maybe it was my nerves keeping my brain from functioning. I'd never been in a limo before, and I had no idea where we were going.

Suddenly, anxiety took hold of me. My hands became clammy, my throat became dry, and the inside of the car became too small. I started tapping my foot.

"You don't have to be nervous," Webb said, placing his hand on my knee. "There's nothing scary about this. We're safe."

My brain screamed in laughter. *Nervous. Safe. Yikes.* I wasn't worried about my safety. I was afraid, but not for the reasons he might have thought. He probably assumed I'd been out on dates before. He probably had no clue that I had never been kissed until his lips grazed across mine in the prison cell. I turned. "I know we're safe." I actually got out those words.

"Then why are you afraid?" he asked softly.

"Where are we going?" I asked as the city disappeared behind us, ignoring his question.

"We're going up the coast to Maine."

"What's in Maine?"

"You'll see. Now, I asked you a question, beautiful."

He really didn't play fair. Him calling me beautiful made my brain shut down. I darted my gaze between Webb and the driver.

As if he understood my silent gesture, Webb said, "It's okay. You don't have to answer me right now."

I could have talked to him telepathically, but I wasn't ready to bear my secrets just yet.

We rode in silence once more. My body relaxed as Webb traced figure eights on my leg.

"Mr. London, another fifteen minutes," the driver finally said.

"He called you Mr. London." Surprise tinged my voice.

"You have a problem with that?" Webb grinned.

"No. I guess I'm just used to people calling you Lieutenant."

"I'm not working. And George is a... family friend."

"So why would he call you by your last name if he's a family friend?"

"Well, let me rephrase. George works for my family," he said.

A crease formed between my brows. "I thought it was just you and..." I stopped short. I didn't want to ruin the day by bringing up his sister.

"There's a lot you don't know about me. In time, you will, though." His silky tone promised a future of guilty pleasures.

The limo pulled into a long driveway that led to a cottage-style home.

"Where are we?"

"This is my hideaway."

"You own this house?" I sat up straighter in the seat.

He nodded. "I come here when I have time off, which isn't often."

"Miss," George said, extending his hand to me through my open door.

When did he stop the car and open my door? Hesitating, I swallowed.

"Jo, please don't be afraid." Webb slid out on his side.

I placed my shaky hand on top of George's palm. Thank God he had a hold of it. My body trembled. Webb came around and replaced George's hand with his own. "Come on," Webb said excitedly.

The place was breathtaking. The two-story, shingle-sided home had four dormers on the front and a large porch that wrapped around three sides, disappearing into the back as though it was a path to the pristine ocean behind it. Rocking chairs adorned the front porch, and plants and flowers decorated the steps and the ground below it. Rose bushes climbed a trellis on the right side. A fountain took center stage in the front yard, surrounded by the greenest carpet of grass. In the distance, waves crashed against the shore.

He leaned down, his breath tickling my ear. "Do you like it?"

"It's amazing." I closed my eyes and inhaled. The salt air drifted up, mixing with his clean, soapy scent.

"I'm glad you do." He threaded his fingers through mine. "Let me show you the inside."

As I climbed the steps, a sudden thought flashed in my mind. *Does Kate own this house too?*

Webb opened the door and waved me in first.

Thoughts of his sister went out the window when I entered. My mouth fell open.

The entire first floor was completely open. Thick, exposed beams traveled across the high ceiling, giving the home an expansive feel. A fireplace, a large leather couch, two oversized chairs, and a couple of tables took up the majority of the left half. To the right, a bar separated a small kitchen from the rest of the room. All of that paled in comparison to the awesome view in the distance. The sun glinted off the Atlantic Ocean, throwing bright light through the floor-to-ceiling swivel doors that sat slightly ajar. A breeze trickled in, carrying with it the salt air.

I made my way to the back and stood admiring

the view. The waves roared, repeating their pull and push routine against the shore.

"What do you think?" Webb asked, encircling me from behind.

"It's... beautiful," I whispered, my voice escaping me.

"Just like you," he whispered back, nuzzling his nose behind my ear.

I leaned back into him. I was standing with Webb London in his house overlooking a breathtaking scene. I was surprised I could even speak.

"Come." He guided me to the pillows on the floor in front of the window.

I lowered myself between his raised knees with my back to his front. He snaked his arms around me and rested his head against mine.

I sank into his arms, his touch, his strength. He held me tighter as the quietness between us grew. The lack of words didn't bother me. In fact, nothing bothered me in that moment.

We sat, taking in the view, the hum of the ocean, and the serenity surrounding us. Then he turned me slightly. His gaze dropped to my lips, and my heart tripped. His palm caressed my cheek as he lowered his lips ever so slowly.

A warm, soft breeze blew through the doors, causing goose bumps to pebble my skin—or maybe those were in anticipation of his kiss. His ocean-blue eyes met mine before our lips touched. My heart pounded in my ears while his pounded against me. He hesitated, his gaze never wavering.

His blue eyes bled to black before he pulled away a fraction. "Your beauty grabs my soul." His voice was silky. "I want to kiss you, but I'm afraid when I do, I won't be able to stop."

"Webb?"

He threaded his fingers through my hair. "What is it?"

Instead of answering, I rose up. My lips parted when his touched them. He explored, and I followed his lead. It was still quite new for me, but every sensation, every touch, even his taste made my muscles weak. He was gentle as his hands roamed through my hair.

My heart was doing a gymnastic routine on the uneven bars, and my stomach was performing a floor routine that would have made Olympic judges proud. Heat, lots of heat, infused my cheeks. The large ocean outside suddenly became a backyard pool, small and tiny.

Abandoning my lips, he trailed kisses along my cheek, making his way to my ear.

I swallowed, trying to catch my breath.

"Now are you ever going to tell me why you were petrified in the car?"

I thought he'd forgotten about that.

He looked down, raising one eyebrow.

"You promise you won't laugh?"

"I promise."

"This is my first date... ever," I said in a low tone.

He touched my cheek, causing me to fall into those otherworldly eyes.

The sexy vampire had an impish smile plastered on his face.

"You promised you wouldn't laugh," I said, trying to break away from his stronghold. The heat in my cheeks spread.

"I'm smiling, not laughing."

"Why?"

"Because you're even prettier when you're embarrassed."

I slapped him on the arm. It was like hitting a rock.

He grabbed my hand. "And this is just the beginning for us. You and me," he said, kissing each finger.

Warmth spread through me at his declaration. "Do you think life will always be this crazy?"

His lips glided over mine. "We have a lot ahead of us, but whatever happens, I want you with me. I will protect you, beautiful. Always."

I believed him, though a sense of foreboding

said something different. But for the time being, I was right where I wanted to be.

Webb and Jo's story continue in On the Edge of Destiny. Available now in Ebook and paperback formats.
Turn the page to read a sample

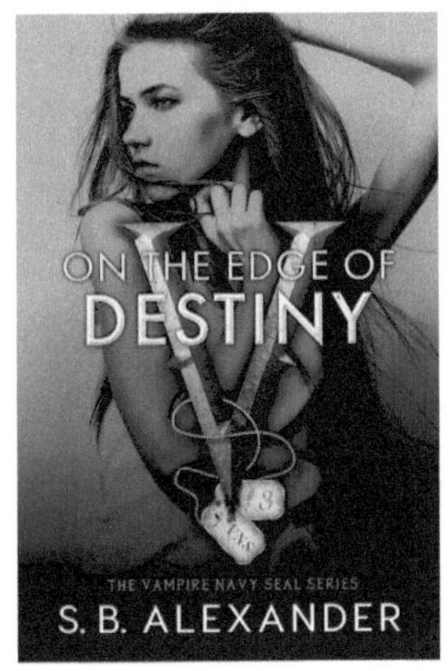

I should be terrified.

I'm days away from standing trial for the death of my nemesis. My next home could be a cold dark cell in a vampire prison, and my DNA is the secret ingredient my enemy needs to build an army of vampires.

But nothing can faze me.

I have an expert lawyer on my case. The facts are indisputable. My powers are lethal and stronger to combat my enemy, and my relationship with the smoking hot Vampire Navy SEAL, Webb London, is thriving.

Until... the nightmares begin.

Haunting visions of Webb's demise play on a loop every time I close my eyes. With his next mission looming, I want to believe that he'll be okay.

Yet I can't shake the feeling that darkness is coming for him, and there's nothing I can do to stop it.

Chapter 1

If today were my last day, then there was no place I'd rather be than nestled in the arms of the most gorgeous vampire, Webb London. I'd never imagined a world where my heart—and, quite possibly, my soul—connected to another so strongly as it did to him. I was drunk from his touch, his kiss, his presence, and I didn't want our date to end.

But reality trumped the world I lived in, and life knocked on the door. It was time to leave.

Reluctantly, I slid back into the limo. I had three hours before I lost my glass slipper. Midnight loomed, and Dad was expecting me.

Threading his fingers through my hair, Webb kissed my temple. "I had a great time today, Jo," he whispered. "Did you?"

"I did." I sneaked my hand under his shirt, tracing circles around his navel.

Any chance he gave me I explored his body, learning every curve, dip, and valley above the waist. I had an inkling my bloodlust was going to take a back seat to my craving for the sexy vampire.

As the limo rolled down the coastal highway, I reminisced about the magnificent day that Webb and I spent together at his secluded house on the coast in Maine. It was my first date ever, and I'd had no idea what to expect. Most of the girls in school went out on dates to movies or out to eat. My best friend, Darcy Rose, had shared her experience with me. Her first date had been with a boy who had taken her to see one of the Harry Potter movies. At first she'd been nervous. They hardly talked on the way to the theater, but after the movie ended they went for pizza and discussed what they liked and disliked about it. According to her, the movie was a great icebreaker.

I couldn't think of an icebreaker that released some of the nervous tension I had except maybe time. As the day progressed, I became more comfortable with Webb. We took advantage of the sun and sand as we walked along the beach, dipping our toes in the surf. Maybe the soothing sounds of the waves helped to relax me. When we weren't outside, we snuggled in front of the windowed doors, which overlooked the Atlantic Ocean. I'd learned Webb had built the house four years ago as a place to relax and find peace.

The moon lit the way as we continued our trek home, towards what I'd hoped were better days. A light tickle at the base of my spine, however, warned me to be cautious. Why? I didn't know. I was still growing into my vampire body. Yet my sixth sense grew stronger and more acute every day.

George, a family friend of Webb's, was driving. He'd picked up Webb and me from the military base earlier that afternoon. The little amount of time I had to chat with him, I'd found he loved the game of basketball. I wasn't surprised, given that he was tall and lanky.

The soothing hum of the tires caused my eyelids to droop. I tried desperately to stay awake. I wanted to spend every last minute with Webb.

"I don't want to go back," I mumbled as my fingers roamed north over his toned abs.

Sure, I wanted to see Dad and my brother, Sam, but I didn't want to deal with whatever lay ahead. We had actually gotten through a day without any craziness—no phone calls, no explosions, no fires to put out, and no one kidnapping me or trying to kill me.

He groaned, gently pulling back my hair. We locked gazes for a second before his lips devoured mine, far from gentle as our tongues collided. He broke away, breathing heavily.

"What you do to me," he whispered.

I blushed as I kept my eyes locked on his.

"You have no idea how much you affect me, do you?"

I kind of did. We'd been inseparable the entire day. Still, I wanted to hear his words, so I gave a slight shake of my head, my stomach fluttering in anticipation.

Suddenly he lifted his head, his eyes widening. "George? What's wrong?"

What could possibly have Webb spooked? I sat up.

To my horror, the limo was barreling down a steep incline.

"Sir," George said. "The brakes..."

The headlights illuminated a warning sign. *Slow down. Ten miles per hour.* I glanced at the speedometer, and my body turned to ice.

We were traveling at sixty miles per hour, and the needle was ticking higher.

"Emergency brake," Webb called.

I checked my seat belt. It was already fastened.

To the left, the ocean whizzed by, as did the high mountain range outside my window on the right.

"It's on, sir," George said frantically.

"There should be a runaway for truckers before you reach the curve," Webb said without a hint of fear or panic in his voice.

How the heck were we going to survive? This was a limo, not a NASCAR vehicle.

His hand grabbed mine. I leaned back and closed my eyes.

What a freaking way to end a date.

My eyelids flew open as the car banked around the curve. George's hands clutched the wheel so hard, his knuckles glowed white.

"Now, George!" Webb shouted.

George turned the wheel hard, and the limo barreled up the hill where it stopped for a brief second before rolling backward.

"Straighten out. We'll go up the embankment behind us and slow some more. Then we can get out," Webb said, still without any trace of panic.

George did as Webb instructed. The car rolled down before creeping a bit up the hill behind us.

I gripped the seat belt, ready to free myself and jump out, when I spotted a glow in the distance. I dialed my vampire vision, zeroing in on several pairs of eyes gleaming in the night. I couldn't tell if they were animals or...

I didn't get a chance to figure it out before a rumbling noise pierced my ears.

"Jo. George," Webb said calmly. "Get out and run up the hill behind us. Whatever you do, don't look back."

A large boulder up the mountain crunched over the gravel, making a beeline straight for us.

"Out. Now!" Webb growled.

I punched the release on my seat belt, but either my hands shook too much or the flippin' belt was stuck. I tried again. Nothing. Panic grabbed me.

Halfway out of the car, Webb turned, glancing between the seat belt and me. The rock clipped the front corner of the limo. My head bounced off the leather seat. Webb fell from the car out of sight.

The boulder rolled down onto the pavement, breaking through the concrete barrier between the road and the ocean, and disappeared into the night.

Time stood still. I dared a peek out the window. The vehicle sat at a slight angle, facing the road.

Holy hell! Much more movement forward, and the limo would likely plummet into the Atlantic.

Webb suddenly appeared and grabbed the door, nudging the car forward.

"Rip off the belt and jump. Now!" His inky black eyes were wide with fear. "I'm not losing you tonight."

And I wasn't dying tonight, especially not in that ocean. I'd recently had a close call when the boat Ben Jackson and I were on sank during a freak storm.

Tearing the belt from me, I opened the door. I took in a breath, ready to leap, when the limo started sliding down the gravel incline, fast approaching the road.

Jump, tuck, and roll had been what the gym teacher had taught me in gymnastics class. So this should be easy. Not.

"Jo. What are you waiting for? Get out!" Webb barked from somewhere, panic in his voice.

I tucked my chin, covered my head with my arms, closed my eyes, and jumped. My hands hit gravel before my entire body slammed against the ground. I rolled as though I were a snowball, barreling down the hill and gaining momentum. Pebbles embedded in my skin. Larger rocks jabbed me in the legs, back, and stomach.

I opened my eyes. The gaping hole in the concrete barrier grew closer, and at the rate I was going, I'd probably plow right through and into the Atlantic Ocean. I had to find something to stop me.

"Jo, grab onto the pole," Webb shouted.

Pole? What was he talking about? I didn't see anything except death.

As I hit smooth pavement, a bright light lit up the roadway. Didn't people see a bright light just before their life ended?

I rolled once then twice before I relaxed my

body, prayed, and braced for whatever fate had in store for me.

The light grew brighter before the sound of an engine roared in my ears. I was either going to roll through the broken barrier behind the limo and into the dark depths of the ocean below, or the car speeding toward me would claim my life.

Out of nowhere, a strong wind hit me, followed by a whooshing sound. All the air left my lungs.

"Stay still," Webb whispered.

How could I move? His weight kept me pinned to the ground. While I loved the vampire's arms on me, even his body on top of me, which was a new position for him, I couldn't freakin' breathe.

"Um...can't...breathe," I managed to squeak out.

A loud crash echoed. A bright orange light graced the sky followed by pillows of smoke. Was it the limo or the other car that fell to its death?

Webb eased up slightly. "Are you okay?" he asked, sweeping his gaze over my face, his hands furiously searching my body. His heart was beating uncontrollably.

"I will...be...when I can breathe...better."

"Oh. Sorry." He lifted up slightly.

I gulped in large amounts of oxygen, and the tightness in my chest slowly dwindled.

His hands were still checking every inch of me.

"I tried to roll over so you wouldn't take the impact. I'm sorry. I didn't have a good hold on you. You sure you're okay?"

"I will...be." I sucked in more oxygen.

"Stay here. I need to check on George." He jogged down to the road.

I sat up as George met Webb.

"Are you two all right?" George's brown eyes were wide with fear.

Webb opened his mouth to respond but quickly shut it when a woman appeared behind George.

"I'm so sorry. I narrowly missed you and that car." She stabbed her thumb toward the ocean.

"Can you give us a ride into town?" Webb asked.

"Sure. But I need some help. My car stalled for some reason after I skidded to a stop. It's a ways down the hill." Her brown hair glinted in the moonlight as she flicked her head to her left.

I stood up, brushing the dirt and rocks from me.

"George. Help the lady, please."

"Yes, sir. Hang tight."

George and the brunette made small talk as they both disappeared.

Webb walked back to me, pain painting his handsome features. "Are you sure you're okay?"

"I'm breathing." I looked into his molten onyx eyes.

Webb's eyes shifted between the most amazing cobalt blue and black when his emotions changed.

"Why aren't we going?" I asked.

"She's human, and I want to make sure your thirst is okay before we get into the car." His heart beat wildly.

"Hey." I reached up and touched his face. "What's wrong?"

He cocooned me in his arms. "You scared me. I don't know what I would've done if I'd lost you." He again ran his hands over my entire body before easing back and sweeping his gaze over me for the tenth time.

"I'm fine, Webb."

His forehead kissed mine. "You would tell me if you weren't?" Apprehension threaded through his words.

My throat closed with emotion. So, I gave a slight nod and blinked my answer.

He sighed heavily, and his heartbeat began to slow. Mine followed suit. It seemed our hearts were in sync.

"What happened?" I asked.

"I don't know." He pushed his strong hand through his shoulder-length brown hair.

A crescent moon dotted the sky, and smoke lingered in the air. I imagined the crashing waves put out the flames from the burning limo.

"Do you think someone messed with the brakes?" Given the way my life was going, I had to be suspicious of everything.

"The thought has crossed my mind."

George was a longtime family friend, so I couldn't imagine it would be him. However, stranger things had happened. Like how Webb's sister, Kate, had switched sides and was now sleeping with our archenemy, Edmund Rain. Plus only a day had passed since Kate staked her brother with a cobalt sword, missing his heart by only an eighth of an inch.

As if he knew what I was thinking, he said, "It's not George."

"How do you know?"

"I just do." He scanned the area.

"Not good enough. If someone is trying to kill us, we need to look at everyone. Even you know this."

I didn't want to play the Kate card, but if I had to I would.

He grasped my shoulders, hard. "George...has

been loyal to me for many years." Anger supplanted the worry on his face. "Besides, why would he tamper with the brakes then get in the car with us?"

He had a point, I guess.

"Webb, you're hurting me." I didn't know if he realized his grip was like a vise.

His left hand slid down to the small of my back while his right hand cupped my cheek. "I'm sorry," he said. "I didn't mean to."

I leaned into his palm. "It's okay."

I wanted to shoulder some of his pain. I didn't want to see him hurt any more than he wanted to see me hurt, whether physically or mentally.

He peppered kisses down my neck, his fangs grazing the skin.

I shuddered at the sensation. When I did, an image materialized of me sucking on his wrist the night in the woods. My body quaked at the remembrance of how his blood tasted, sweet and sinful. How he reacted, melting into me, moaning in pleasure as I sated my hunger.

I mewled as I tilted my head to give him better access.

He growled.

My fangs dropped. I desperately wanted to taste his blood again. As I licked my lips, I stilled.

What was I doing? What was he doing? Our laws dictated new vampires could only drink from another vampire if it were an emergency, meaning if I were hurt or needed blood. Neither was the case at the moment. But was he hungry? Was it legal for him to drink from me?

"Webb?" I breathed.

"Yes, angel," he said in a husky voice.

"Are you hungry?"

I didn't want to get in trouble with the Council of Eternal Affairs. They were the vampires who governed the laws in my world. Regardless, I would do anything for Webb, even though my head was on the chopping block for the death of my nemesis, Blake Turner. He'd been a product of Edmund Rain's sick plan of converting ordinary humans into vampires.

"I'm not." He jerked up his head as if I had thrown ice-cold water on him.

"If you are, I don't mind."

His expression flickered with confusion or something I couldn't figure out. Did he think he would hurt me if he bit into me? He smiled as though he had found the answer to whatever was plaguing him.

"Why are you smiling? Seriously, if you're hungry—"

His finger grazed my lip. "I'm fine. It's..." His gaze penetrated me as if he were searching my soul.

Now I was confused. "What? I know it's not legal for new vampires like me, but can you drink from another vampire?"

"I'm not bound by the law like you are. Soon enough, you will not be, either." His eyelids dropped to half-mast. "My struggle right now...is my desire...to taste your blood. And, beautiful, it has nothing to do with my blood thirst." His seductive voice caressed every inch of my body, inside and out.

My lips formed a silent O. I'd remembered how sensual it felt when I drank his blood.

"Exactly," he said in response to my facial expression.

Heat stung my cheeks while a butterfly winged through my abdomen.

"Don't be embarrassed. It's life and part of being a vampire."

I thought back to when I witnessed Edmund sinking his fangs into Kate. I felt as if I'd interrupted some private make-out session.

"Webb?" George called from the road.

"We'll talk more later. We need to go."

Oh, my was all my brain kept repeating.

He took hold of my hand, and we walked to the

car. Well, Webb walked, and he pulled me. I was still in zombie mode, trying to get my brain unstuck. How would it feel if he drank from me? My cheeks were going to be red and hot the rest of the night.

When we were strapped into the back seat of the car, the fragrant strawberry scent inside snapped my brain back to the present, reminding me the woman driving was human.

Webb threaded his fingers through mine as the lady turned the wheel and gave the car a little bit of gas, then we were moving. I let out a sigh, grateful we were alive. After the boating accident and fighting Edmund and his gang, I was beginning to think I had nine lives.

"What was wrong with the car, George?" Webb asked.

"Not completely sure, but the engine seemed to be flooded. It took a few tweaks, and then it started."

"Thank you, George, for your help," the lady said. "And again. I'm so sorry about what happened." Her voice was soft but shaky.

She looked to be in her thirties. A studded clip secured her brown hair into a chignon. She had pale skin, which I imagined might be from her almost killing me or herself.

"By the way, I'm Lauren. I've met George here."

She flicked her head toward George, who was sitting in the front. "And you are?" She checked in the rearview mirror.

I slid a sideways glance at Webb. "I'm Webb, and this is Jo," he said.

"So what happened?" she asked. "One minute you were in the road, and the next you were gone. Like in a flash."

"We're not sure," Webb replied. "We lost the brakes on our car."

I didn't think that was what she was asking. Webb had swooped me up at vampire speed.

"You don't even have a scratch on you." She looked at me in the rearview mirror with a suspecting look.

"What were you doing up here?" Webb asked. *Way to change the subject.*

"My dad owns one of the homes up on the hill," she said. "Webb, you must be the gentleman who owns the magnificent house not far from his? I have to say. You look awful young to own that home."

There were two other homes that sat along the coast about ten miles from Webb's home.

Webb and I exchanged glances. I was surprised she directed the checking question to Webb and not George. Sure, her father probably told her. But

Webb didn't spend a lot of time at his house. He lived on the naval base ninety-nine percent of the time. Plus he'd told me it had been awhile since he had been up here. To me that meant Webb had little interaction with her father.

"Actually, I own the house," George answered.

She eyed him briefly. "Oh," she said in a surprised tone.

She seemed to know George was lying.

"Well, my dad is getting old," she offered.

"Who is your father?" George asked her.

She's fishing for something. Webb's voice sounded loud and clear in my head.

"Robert Pride." Her eyes stayed on the road ahead.

"Both of those properties are vacant right now. Their owners aren't here yet for the summer," George said.

"My father will be up in a couple of weeks. "I came up to unwind. It's quiet up here."

Silence ruled.

The lights of the town came into view as Lauren maneuvered the last curve on the winding road.

"There's a diner up ahead on the left. Do you mind dropping us there?" Webb asked.

"No, not at all. I'll stop a minute with you before I make my way back to Boston," Lauren answered.

We rolled into the diner, and a neon light flashed Open in the window. All of us exited the vehicle.

"You should be okay to make it back to Boston," George said. "But now that we have more light, let me take one last look at the engine."

"That would be wonderful," Lauren said. "I need to use the facilities." She snatched her purse and headed inside.

"George." Webb followed him to the front of the vehicle. "Did she say anything to you when you were helping her?"

George popped the hood of the Lexus and buried his head underneath, fiddling with a few things.

"Just small talk. She's a bit shaken up," he replied. "I'm not sure she is who she says she is. A Robert Pride does own one of those homes, but I wasn't aware he had a daughter."

"Is he a vampire?" I asked.

"No. He's not." He stopped what he was doing. "And he doesn't know most of this town is made up of vampires. The folks who own those two homes up on the coast are only here a few times a year."

"When you left the house earlier, where did you go?" Webb asked him.

"I came down and sat with Trina for a bit and had some pie. Then I got gas and a few things at the store. Afterwards, I worked in the yard. The only time the limo was out of my sight was when I was in the diner and in the store."

"Mmm. When you finish, can you round up Stan from the sheriff's office and alert him to what happened tonight? I need to call in." Webb reached into his pocket for his phone.

"No problem, sir." George bent forward and resumed tinkering with the engine.

Switching my attention to Webb, I followed him across the parking lot to the edge of the diner. "Are you calling my father?"

"If we want to get back tonight, I think it's wise. He is expecting us."

I'd overheard Webb telling him before we left we'd return by midnight, and we were at least three hours away.

Webb talked on the phone as I leaned against the building. The area outside was quiet. A gas station sat across the street. A trucker was filling up. Two blocks down, a marquee for Tam's country store lit up the darkness.

My mouth was parched, and water sounded

good, although George had mentioned pie. For some reason, the thought of something sweet tickled my taste buds. Food had not been appealing to me since I became a vampire. Dad had said we needed to eat human food, protein mostly, and although I did consume a few of my favorite meals like hamburgers and pizza, they didn't have the same lure to me anymore.

I pushed off the building only to be stopped by Webb. I swatted away his hand as he continued to listen to my dad.

"Um. I need some water." I glared at him.

"Hold on, Commander." He pressed the phone to his chest, covering the speaker. "Wait until that woman comes out. I don't trust her." He planted a soft kiss on my nose then resumed his conversation with my dad.

How could I refuse? *Smart vampire.*

He draped an arm over me, and I snuggled into him. My senses tuned in to Dad's voice.

"Lieutenant, do you think it was on purpose?" Dad asked.

"Not sure. I can't check it out, either, since the limo is in the ocean. My instincts tell me this wasn't an accident."

I jerked up my head as Webb pulled me tighter. He must've known how I was going to react.

"Well, stay put for the night," Dad said.

I stiffened in his arms. Stay overnight with Webb? Alone?

My heart sprinted.

Webb rubbed a hand down my back, as though he were telling me we'd be fine, just the two of us.

Silence reigned over the line.

I envisioned Dad biting the inside of his cheek. I glanced up. Webb's eyes waffled from blue to black then blue again. I flushed, remembering our recent conversation about how he wanted to taste my blood.

"Commander?" Webb probed.

"Sorry. Tripp walked in," Dad said. "Mr. Jackson is here. We'll talk tomorrow. By the way, how much blood did you take for Jo?"

"I brought a few extra containers in case of an emergency. If it's not enough, I'll check with Dr. Vieira. He'll advise if she'll be okay with what we drink."

"Can I talk to my daughter?" Dad sounded bothered by something.

Webb handed me the phone.

"Hey, Dad."

"Pumpkin. Are you okay?"

"It was a little scary, but I'm fine."

"Will you be okay for a couple of days?"

"Wait. You're asking *me*? I should be asking you that." I wanted to laugh and run at the same time. I was nervously excited at the idea I'd be spending time alone with Webb. Nevertheless, I couldn't believe my father, the old-fashioned vampire, was allowing me the freedom.

Dad laughed into the phone. I couldn't tell whether or not he was nervous. "First, Jo, I can't keep you chained, although part of me would like to." He laughed again. "Second, you're growing into an adult, and I need to let you make decisions. Finally, Webb knows I'd cut his head off if he did anything."

I didn't want to know what he meant by "anything." Dad must've put the fear of God into Webb before we even left the base today.

"What's going on with Mr. Jackson?" I moved on to something less awkward.

"I'm not sure," Dad replied.

Mr. Jackson was becoming more curious about Sam and me. I couldn't blame him. One minute we were living with him, and the next we had all but vanished. Lately though, his concerns were more about his son, Ben, Sam's best friend, who always seemed to end up in our medical facility. He'd had a few encounters with Edmund Rain and the team.

"Don't worry about Mr. Jackson. Before I forget, the council pushed out the hearing another few weeks, so I'm working on getting you a tutor for the summer," he said.

"Why are they postponing it?" Not that I wanted to go back to school right now. The whole incident with Blake Turner was still raw, and I didn't want any reminders.

"Something came up on their end. No need to be concerned about it," he said. "Look, pumpkin, put Webb back on. Be careful, and I love you."

I smiled. Mountains had moved, it seemed, for me to hear those three words from Dad. We had just shared our feelings about our father and daughter relationship a few days ago.

"I love you, Dad." I handed the phone back to Webb.

"Yes, Commander."

Lauren walked out of the diner and over to George.

Webb said, "Yes. Don't worry. She's safe," then he pocketed his phone. "Everything okay?" Webb asked Lauren as we met her at her car.

"Fine. Why?" She dropped her phone into her purse.

She seemed to take forever in the ladies' room.

"I want to make sure you're okay to drive back."

"Thanks for your concern," she said, eyeing Webb.

What the heck? She was checking him out. I didn't blame her for looking. Still, a tinge of jealousy zinged through me. I almost growled but caught it in my throat. I didn't want to call attention to us, given that Webb was suspicious of her.

George closed the hood. "Everything pans out. It was probably a fluke." He wiped his hands on a towel.

"I should be fine. Boston isn't far anyway." She got into her car, started the engine, and rolled down the window. "Mr. London, here's my card. If you ever need anything, please don't hesitate to call me."

Webb didn't flinch when she said his last name. I didn't remember him telling it to her. He just took the card and quickly read it before glancing up at her.

"I don't think we'll be needing a lawyer, Ms. Dryer," he said with no inflection.

"If you ever do, you have my number." Then her gaze flicked to George. "Thanks for all your help. I'll tell my dad to look you up when he's here."

George nodded. "Be careful driving."

With the good-byes out of the way, she drove off.

"How did she—?"

"Don't know, Jo."

I racked my brain, trying to figure out how Lauren knew Webb's full name. We'd only told her our first names.

Her last name was Dryer, not Pride like her father.

I shrugged it off. The difference in her last name could be from adoption, marriage, or even divorce.

"I didn't say anything," George added before we even looked his way.

"Well, let's not worry about Lauren right now. Did you happen to get ahold of Stan?" Webb asked George.

"I did. He should be here shortly. He was out at the Millers' farm. They had some cattle killed recently."

"Let's go see Trina." Webb slipped Lauren's card in his jeans.

The bell dinged when we entered the diner. A couple stood at the register. Webb nodded at the pair as though he knew them. Then a short stocky man rose from his seat, taking money out of his wallet. Webb guided me to a stool at the counter, and the three of us settled in as the patrons paid their bill. No sooner had the couple and the short man left than did the waitress turn the Open sign to Closed and glided over to us.

"Webb, darling," she cooed, throwing her arms around him. "I haven't seen you in ages. Where have you been?"

Webb stood and embraced the petite blonde. "Trina. Nice to see you." He kissed her on the cheek.

She had a perfect white smile and deep green eyes. Her short hair was pulled back with a wide headband, exposing her smooth, high forehead.

"Trina. I would like you to meet a friend of mine. Jo, this is my dear old friend, Trina."

She rested her fists on her hips and looked me over, her eyes growing wide. "She's lovely, Webb. Wherever did you find her?" She ran her fingers through the ends of my hair.

Why did people do that when they met me? My headmistress, Ms. Lawrence, did the same thing when she first laid eyes on me.

Webb glanced around before saying, "Jo, Trina is a vamp."

I rolled my eyes. Well, I'd known that, since her green eyes had flickered toward black when she first spotted Webb. Plus she certainly didn't have the delicious, sweet scent of a human.

"So, Trina..." Webb kept looking around.

"No worries, young man. Aside from the love of my life in the back, no one else is here."

I guess I didn't have to be jealous of the woman.

"Did you see the brown-haired lady who was in here earlier?" Webb resumed his position on the stool next to me.

"The human? Yes. She was arguing with someone on the phone in the ladies' room. I couldn't make out the whole conversation, but she repeated your name a few times." She wiped the countertop. "Do you know her?"

"No" was all Webb said.

"So, she didn't ask you about Webb?" George asked.

"George, old man, you know better than that. She didn't, but if she did, I wouldn't share any information about any of my friends."

"I had to ask," George said.

The concern in his voice led me to believe he wouldn't betray Webb.

"What happened, anyway?" Trina propped her elbows on the counter. "Someone said they saw an orange glow up on the coast."

Webb explained what happened while Trina served apple pie à la mode to George and me. I found it curious that she didn't give Webb a piece.

"Have you seen that woman in here before tonight?" Webb asked.

"No." She filled a cup with coffee and placed it in front of George.

The bell dinged, and in walked a tall, dark-haired man with a badge and a smirk.

"Gee, London. How many times do I have to tell you this is a quiet town? We try to keep a low..." He let out a whistle as his brown eyes swept over me. "Who's the beauty at your side?"

Webb growled, jumping to his feet.

"Easy, London. I know she's off limits." The man with the badge held up his hands.

I swiveled on the stool toward him while Webb decided to lean against his stool with his back to Trina. He and the sheriff exchanged handshakes.

Then the sheriff offered me his hand. "Hi. I'm Stan, the local sheriff around here."

"I'm Jo." We shook.

"Pleased to meet you, Jo," Stan said. "Be careful. He's one of the most possessive vampires I know."

I'd thought Webb was being protective. Yet the more I said the word *possessive* in my head, the more it started to make some sense.

Then again, what alpha male wasn't? Heck, my father exemplified the word and seemed to be proud of it. "You haven't met my dad."

Stan laughed, letting go of my hand. "If he gets too smothering, you let me know."

"Stan," Webb barked.

"Cool your jets, London." He rolled his eyes.

"You're a vampire too?" I knew the answer. I was just trying to break the tension between the two.

Stan nodded. "Now. What happened?" he asked, shifting to an all-business demeanor.

Webb explained to Stan that he'd been on the beach most of the day with me, and George added in where he saw fit. While the men chatted, I bit into a piece of the apple pie and lost all sense I was a vampire. My human memories flooded back. None of our foster parents had been big on giving Sam and me sugar, especially before bed. But that hadn't mattered to us. We would still sneak into the kitchen late at night and steal dessert.

As I closed my mouth around the next spoonful, I wondered... Who was Lauren Dryer? How did the brakes fail? Was someone trying to kill us? How did she know Webb's last name? Did she know vampires existed? As the delectable treat melted on my tongue, the questions likewise vanished.

By the time I scarfed up the last of the pie, Stan and Webb had finished their conversation. I suddenly became queasy. I guessed my vampire system wasn't used to sweets. Placing a hand on my abdomen, I stood.

"What's wrong?" Webb asked.

"Not feeling good." I blew out a breath.

He looked at the plate then at Trina before his eyes landed on me.

"Are you going to throw up?" Stan covered his mouth as though he were, too.

Acid rose in my throat. "Bathroom." My body became warm, and the room began spinning.

"This way," Webb said in a strained voice.

I followed him around the counter and down a small hall into the ladies' room. I threw open the stall door before dropping to my knees.

"I shouldn't—" I lost every bit of apple pie.

"You're right," Webb whispered as he held my hair behind my head.

How sweet was he to help me when I was puking?

After I heaved the contents from my stomach, Stan drove us back to Webb's place. I relaxed against Webb as the police cruiser rolled up the coast. Dizziness still lingered, so I closed my eyes. In the front, George repeated his day's routine to Stan. Both speculated about what could've happened to the brakes.

Webb didn't contribute to the conversation. Not that I wanted to read minds like my father, but right then I would have loved to be in Webb's head. His heartbeat was rapid. I couldn't imagine he was nervous. Was he thinking about the sleeping arrangements, like me? He only had two bedrooms. One was his, and the other belonged to George, since he stayed at the house most of the time, helping Webb with the upkeep of the property.

Stan pulled into the long driveway and let the engine idle. "George, buddy, why don't you crash at my place? I'll let you borrow one of my trucks in the morning."

"Not a bad idea," George said, turning and looking at Webb. "My car is in Boston. Is that okay with you?"

"Sure," Webb responded. "Jo and I will be staying for a few days. I want to check out the accident site tomorrow. Maybe we can fish the car out of the ocean."

"There are a lot of rocky areas off the side of the cliff," Stan said. "More than likely, it's sitting on the rocks. However, I doubt you'll be able to find much, especially if it went up in flames. But I agree. We'll take a look tomorrow."

We said our good-byes and slid out of the cruiser. We waved as the headlights faded from the driveway. When darkness replaced the light, my heart jumped into gear. Now what?

"No need to be nervous," Webb said as he unlocked the front door. "I'm not going to bite."

I laughed nervously. Maybe I wanted him to.

Once inside, an awkward silence stretched between us. Webb sauntered into the kitchen. I didn't move from the small foyer. It was as if someone had injected lead into my feet. Or maybe it was the ten thousand needles pricking my stomach. After all, a sexy-as-hell vampire and me alone all night spelled all kinds of heart-racing, mind-twisting thoughts.

He said something, but the buzzing in my head drowned out his voice. I closed my eyes, trying to calm my nerves, and his hand touched my cheek. "Hey?"

The closeness of our bodies only served to increase the jittery little beasts poking sharp pins into my tummy. My lids slid open, and his eyes latched on to mine.

"I told you I don't bite." He traced my bottom lip with the pad of his thumb. "But I do kiss." A smirk tugged at the corners of his mouth.

My heart did several jumping jacks. Nope, I wasn't going to make it through the night.

"You take my bed, and I'll sleep on the couch." He must have sensed my trepidation.

"I...can...sleep on the couch." I swallowed. "Or I could sleep in George's room tonight."

I couldn't take Webb's bed. This was his home.

His thumb moved to my cheek. "No way. George's room isn't clean. No arguments on this." He placed a soft kiss on my nose before taking my hand. "Come on. Let's get you tucked in."

I released a long, pent-up breath, and the pricking sensation in my stomach slowed. "Webb, I can stay on the couch." I didn't move.

I'd slept in worse conditions in foster care. I even slept on the floor once. It had only been temporary, since one of the other foster kids was scheduled to leave the home the next day.

"I insist. And if I have to carry you up to my room, I will. Your choice." He raised one eyebrow.

I stared at him. I could protest, but his don't-argue-with-me look told me I wouldn't win, and I just wanted to get through this freaking awkward moment.

"Would you stay with me?" my mouth said ahead of my brain.

My blood stopped flowing.

His eyes darkened to vampire black.

I lost my vision for a split second before my own eyes shifted while my heart fell to the floor. I mentally whacked myself a few times. What was I thinking? I wasn't ready for this. Sure, I'd slept next to him in his hospital bed, but that was a place where Dr. Vieira came in to check on him, and even my dad sat in the room, talking to him while I slept.

This was different, very different. It was him and me. Alone.

On the Edge of Destiny is available in Ebook and paperback formats.

GLOSSARY OF TERMS

Natural-born vampire: A human born with the vampire gene that, when activated, will turn them into a vampire.

Activation process: Those who carry the vampire gene can only turn by drinking the blood of their vampire father at the age of sixteen years or older.

Council of Elders – A group of five vampires who set the laws.

Genetic engineering: Turning humans into vampires through a process of restructuring their DNA.

Cobalt – A vampire's kryptonite. The metal will kill a vampire if staked through the heart. It will also burn a vampire's skin if they come in contact with it.

Reproduction: A natural-born vampire is born by a male vampire and a human female with a rare blood type of Vel negative.

Council of Eternal Affairs: The legal department of the vampire government.

Vampire characteristics: Sunlight doesn't burn them. Their hearts beat at <5 bpm. Skin temperature is ten degrees cooler than a human. Eye color changes to black except for a few chosen ones.

Steven Mason: Vampire and father to twins Jo and Sam Mason. He's dubbed the most powerful of all vampires because of his many powers, including his mind-reading abilities. He can only read minds when touching someone except when it comes to his children. His normal eye color is green. His vampire eye color is silver.

Jo Mason: Turned at sixteen. Powers include seeing the future through her dreams, mind-reading without touching a person, telekinesis, and she's an elemental with the ability to manipulate water, air, earth, and fire. Her normal eye color is silver. Her vampire eye color is violet.

Sam Mason: Turned at sixteen. Powers include feeling what others feel (Empath), telekinesis, and he can compel a person using a series of numbers woven into a magical spell. He's also an elemental with the ability to manipulate water, air, earth, and fire. His normal eye color is green. His vampire eye color is silver.

Jupiter Sentinels: A secret and elite Navy SEAL Team within the military. Their role is to help the human military and guard the supernatural world.

Plutariums: A rogue team of vampires who want power and to engineer an army that would change humans into vampires.

Guardians: Vampires who are equivalent to the human police.

ABOUT THE AUTHOR

Bestselling author **S.B. Alexander** is an independent author with over 20 titles to date. She writes paranormal, new adult, and sweet romances that feature hot heroes stealing hearts.

S.B. or Susan as she likes to be called is a navy veteran, former high school teacher, and former corporate sales executive. She's a lover of sports, especially baseball, although nowadays you can find her glued to the TV during football season.

When she's not writing, she's a full-time caregiver to her soul mate of twenty-two years who got a bad deal in life when he was diagnosed with ALS. Her motto: "Life is too short to waste. So live every moment like it's your last."

You can connect with S.B. Alexander in the following ways:

Reader Group: https://
sbalexander.com/beastsandbitches
Author Website: https://sbalexander.com
Newsletter: https://sbalexander.com/newsletter
Email: susan@sbalexander.com

NEVER MISS A NEW RELEASE:
Sign up for her Author App
iTunes: https://bit.ly/sbalexanderitunes
Android: https://bit.ly/sbalexanderandroid

facebook.com/sbalexander.authorpage

twitter.com/sbalex_author

instagram.com/sbalexanderauthor

amazon.com/author/sbalexander

bookbub.com/authors/s-b-alexander

goodreads.com/sbalexander

On the Edge of Humanity

On the Edge of Eternity

On the Edge of Destiny

On the Edge of Misery

On the Edge of Infinity

STAND-ALONES

New Adult Contemporary Romance

Crazy For You

Unforgettable

Holding Onto Forever

Breaking Rules

Rescuing Riley

THE HART SERIES

New Adult Contemporary Romance

Hart of Darkness

Hart of Vengeance

Visit https://sbalexander.com/all-books/ to learn more about S.B. Alexander books and future releases. Please note release dates are subject to change based on reader demand and the author's schedule. Subscribing to the author's newsletter or following her on Facebook is the best way to stay updated with planned new releases.

9 781954 888166